# THE EDGE OF THE CRAZIES

# THE
# EDGE
# OF
# THE
# CRAZIES

## JAMIE HARRISON

M HARRISO
HARRISO
1995

 HYPERION

NEW YORK

The author gratefully acknowledges permission to quote from the following:

*Making Game* by Guy de la Valdène, copyright 1985, Clark City Press. Reprinted by permission of Clark City Press.
*Selected Poems* by Federico García Lorca, copyright 1955 by New Directions Pub. Corp. Reprinted by permission of New Directions.
*A Season in Hell* by Arthur Rimbaud, copyright 1961 by New Directions Pub. Corp. Reprinted by permission of New Directions.
*The Big Rock Candy Mountain* by Wallace Stegner, copyright 1938, 1940, 1942, 1943 by Wallace Stegner. Used by permission of Doubleday, a division of Bantam Doubleday Dell Publishing Group, Inc.
*The Poems of W.B. Yeats: A New Edition*, edited by Richard J. Finneran, copyright 1934 by Macmillan Publishing Company, renewed 1962 by Bertha Georgie Yeats. Reprinted with permission of Simon & Schuster.

Library of Congress Cataloging-In-Publication Data

Harrison, Jamie.
The edge of the crazies / Jamie Harrison. — 1st ed.
p.   cm.
ISBN 0-7868-6085-5
I. Title.
PS3558.A6712E3    1995
813'.54—dc20          94-29374
CIP

Designed by *Claudyne Bianco*

FIRST EDITION

10   9   8   7   6   5   4   3   2   1

FOR STEVE

# ACKNOWLEDGMENTS

With special thanks to Leslie Wells, Bob Dattila, and Ray Yardley; to friends who were bullied into constructive criticism; and to my family for their endless patience and inspiring turns of phrase.

There had been a wind during the night, and all the loneliness of the world had swept up out of the southwest.

—WALLACE STEGNER, *THE BIG ROCK CANDY MOUNTAIN*

The urge to mate takes its toll on every species.

—GUY DE LA VALDENE, *MAKING GAME*

# THE EDGE OF THE CRAZIES

CHAPTER 1

**GEORGE** Blackwater made slight puffing sounds as he wandered down Fiske Avenue. No one paid attention to him; no one else was visible. It was eight A.M. on the first Sunday in May, and Blue Deer had too many bars for anyone to be up at this hour. George had returned from his mother's funeral in Portland a month earlier, but he'd saved the wake—a solo celebration—for the previous night.

There's nothing lonelier than a shabby, empty sidewalk on the Sunday morning after a Saturday night drunk. It could have been a sidewalk anywhere—New York, Peoria, Seattle— if you didn't notice the black-and-white magpies looking for garbage on the curb, or hear the whistle and chug of the train a block away, or raise your head to see the mountains that ringed the town and shrunk it to proper size. Almost everyone who actually lived in Blue Deer had forgotten to look up.

George veered around some vomit on the sidewalk and methodically checked the pockets of his overalls, then his shirt and jacket, for his office keys. At the doorway of number 58 he checked again, now a little frantic, and finally located them in the bib. He continued to puff as he unlocked the door and pulled his body up two dozen warehouse steps. He stopped at the top and let the darkness and quiet soothe him, then made his way down the long hall to the largest room.

George's office was airy and serene, with massive windows of old, wavy glass framed in fir. With a deep sigh, he lowered himself onto an ancient couch and briefly contemplated the neatly packaged bowling ball he carried at his waist. He was otherwise lanky, but today his center felt heavier than usual, and his bright yellow shirt made him slightly dizzy. The light was strange, and in the mirror facing the couch George's relatively handsome face looked blue-white and beaky, like an elongated seagull's, his dark brown hair metallic. Everything in the silent office looked foreign to him this morning, though it would have looked strange to anyone else at the best of times: Dust dimmed the spots and the glass eyes of the two-headed calf hanging over the door, and added varnish to an ancient girlie calendar, several photos and movie posters, an immense assortment of suspended bird feathers, and row upon row of books and screenplays on warped, off-kilter shelves. The only clean objects in the room were the telephone, the flashing answering machine, the computer, the stack of papers he'd left for Edie, his assistant, and a half-dozen oil paintings of various sizes, all showing fields of grass or the sea, all blue and green and gray.

George sighed again at the sight of the answering machine, and shambled back down the hall to make coffee. When he returned he still ignored the flashing light, and sat down at the computer. His balance was off, and he brought the coffee down a little too hard; he hissed with annoyance at the effort as he wiped it up with a dirty paper towel. He flicked the switch and waited patiently as the machine booted up, then squinted at the screen, which read *message pending*. He ignored this and opened a new file, *Great*. At the top of the screen he typed, somewhat laboriously, *Ideas for next script*. He hit return twice, paused, and bore down on the keyboard:

> *Crazy writer, victim of tragic error of youth, is dispossessed by soulless brother and bitch mother, embittered by fat wife.*
>
> *Suffers as situation worsens. Finally realizes redemption can only come with a clean slate.*
>
> *Redeems life and ability to love through fiendishly clever & violent revenge.*

George paused again, and the moment dragged on. He had no further thoughts. He moaned in annoyance and took a swig of coffee. The message light in the corner of the screen was boring a hole through his pupils. He punched two buttons and sat back, wondering what could possibly have happened in L.A. in the last few hours to warrant such an intrusion. The image blurred and shivered and finally came into focus, and George gave a little shriek as he shot backward in his rolling chair and came to his feet. The screen showed an etching of the tip of a shotgun firing a blast toward a goggle-eyed dandy, with these words centered beneath it:

> *George, you stupid shit.*
> *I told you this would happen some day.*
> *Sometimes sorry's not enough.*

The screen vanished, and it took George a moment to understand that it had truly vanished, that he was looking into the smoking interior of his monitor. A roar filled the room, and

George straightened and turned to watch as the old glass of the windows descended to the floor in a wave. He looked back at the machine, reached out to touch it, and a hole bloomed on the back of his hand. As the second report reached his ears, his shoulder went numb, blood spattered the shell of the monitor, and the hole in his hand turned red and liquid. Pain kicked in, and fear, and George fell to his knees and crawled with remarkable speed toward the hallway, screaming again and again for Edie. He'd forgotten that it was Sunday. There was no one else in the building.

FIVE minutes earlier and four blocks down Fiske, Peter Johansen and Alice Wahlgren walked silently, hunkered down against the wind. Peter was tall, with dark gold hair and a loping walk; Alice was much shorter, with straight brown hair and a habit of pushing her glasses up her nose. She had to scurry from time to time to keep up with him. They both looked a little surly, self-absorbed, and pale. They'd been out the night before, too, and were now retrieving the vehicle that hadn't made it home from the Blue Bat. Peter wanted to go fishing, but all his gear was locked in the back of the abandoned truck with the dead battery. Alice had wanted to sleep in and had pointed out that half the sky was blue-black with storm clouds, but it took two to push-start an ancient Mazda, and thus the day had gotten off to a rocky start.

They moved along, each nurturing a solid sense of injustice, dodging the same vomit George Blackwater had dodged earlier. Alice blew little clouds of steam into the cold morning air, and this was slowly driving Peter insane. As they approached an alley he turned to ask her to stop, and walked right into Mona Blackwater, George's wife. Mona had been running, not a characteristic pace—her hair shot out in strange directions, and her shoulders heaved—and she

bounced back a step, looked them over coldly, flung a cigarette butt at Alice's feet, and ran past them down the sidewalk.

Alice and Peter looked at each other, and at Mona's
bulky form as it receded. The truck was in sight now, two
blocks down Fiske.

"Maybe I'll just go with you," Alice said. "I think I'd like
to get out of town."

When they reached the yellow Mazda it came to life
with a feeble *putput* and a growl. Alice was behind the wheel,
wrestling with the manual choke; Peter trotted behind, still
pushing, his face deep pink and covered with sweat. Halfway
to B Street they hit a slight slope, and Alice picked up speed.
Peter ran alongside and jumped in the passenger door. Alice
ran the stop sign at B and Main, and they smiled at each
other in glee before they heard three huge blasts, one after
another, and glass smashed to the ground on their left. Alice
gunned the engine to thirty, almost the Mazda's top speed,
and ran the next stop sign while Peter craned his neck, trying
to make sense of the noise, wondering if they'd somehow lost
the last three years and were back on the Lower East Side of
New York. They made it to their house on Fifth Street before
they realized the glass had come from George's office.

CHAPTER 2

**JULES** Clement lay in his bed, dreaming that he was a small boy in a large boat on the ocean, watching birds wheel overhead as the boat swayed in large charcoal waves. He looked into the water and made out shapes, then leaned over the side and waited. One shape surfaced, a bright blue fish, flat and oval and inspecting him with one tiny yellow eye. When he saw a face reflected, not his, the gulls overhead began to shriek, and the fish sank away into the gray.

The phone rang three more times as he stared up at his ceiling, wondering if, perhaps, this day would be different from the others. It seemed unlikely that deliverance, romantic or otherwise, would strike at 8:30 on a Sunday morning, but Jules had faith in the strange. So he cleared his throat, sat up, and picked up the phone.

"Jules."

"Peter." His friend's voice was quavery; the night before it had been a bullhorn. "What's up?"

"Something's happening downtown. I think someone just shot out George Blackwater's windows."

Jules wiggled his toes and eyed the clean laundry in the corner of the room, past the dog bed. "You just had a hunch, huh?"

"Screw you. We were down there getting the truck. We heard some shots and saw a whole lot of glass."

"Okay. I'll go check it out." Jules hung up, stood up, and slid on a pile of magazines and newspapers on his way across the room. The phone rang again and he backtracked carefully.

"Yo," said Jules.

It was Harvey Moyers, one of his deputies. "I've got a report of a shooting downtown and I'm heading there. I thought you'd like to know."

"I heard already. I'm on my way. Blackwater's offices, right?"

Harvey was quiet for a second. "Right."


JULES pulled up to the Fiske Avenue offices with his eyes trained on the blown-out windows, and stopped just short of Bean and Al, the paramedics, as they wrestled a gurney from Absaroka County's only ambulance. Jules had assumed that the windows were the sole victims of some early A.M. crazies, and regarded the ambulance leerily. He didn't like blood, and didn't have to see much of it in Blue Deer. It made his skin crawl when it wasn't in the classic context of a bar fight or part of the inevitable sadness of countless alcohol-soaked car wrecks. He followed the paramedics slowly up the stairs, combing his hair with his fingers, glad he hadn't paused for a shower but wishing he'd put on his uniform. George

Blackwater was flat on his back on the landing, insisting in a high, shaky tone that Al and Bean take care of the hole in his hand, apparently ignorant of the fact that they'd needed to work first on the larger hole near his collarbone. The red hand waved in the air, and Jules edged past it down the hall, hugging the left-hand wall to avoid the bloody trail on the carpeting. Harvey's wiry frame was silhouetted in the doorway of George's office, and Jules walked past him and over to the empty windows, crunching glass, to gulp in the cold spring air.

"Shit," said Harvey. "Someone really doesn't like this guy. I thought I kept him out of trouble by driving him home last night."

Jules stared at him. "He fell down in the Blue Bat near closing time," Harvey explained. "Delly said he was talking about his mom and drinking straight vodka. They called me when he started his car and rammed the alley wall."

"Maybe you should have just brought him in, Harvey."

"I was trying to give him a break. I know the guy."

"You know everyone. Do me a favor and stop giving the town a break, okay?"

Harvey rolled his eyes and smiled at the ceiling.

Jules's circulation was working again. He looked at the computer and the tipped-over chair, the spray of blood, and the large pock in the plaster midway up the wall. He stuck his head out the window and eyed the ancient brick building across the avenue, two-storied like the one he stood in. All of the facing windows were open and he could see ladders and paint cans inside. "Have you checked it out over there yet?"

"It's just you and me here. I was holding down the fort."

Harvey weighed about one-fifty at the heaviest of times, and Jules pictured him on the roof, keeping a cap on things, the pale skin beneath his thin blond hair burning in the sunlight, light blue eyes flicking over the pavement below like a hungry sparrow hawk's.

"Keep holding it down. I'll be right back."

This time Jules went around the glass and made himself take in the quantity of blood on his way down the hall. George had quieted down, not necessarily a good sign; Bean and Al had him on the gurney and were strapping him down. Jules knelt beside George and wiped a smear of blood off his forehead, fighting down the urge to retch.

"Got any ideas, Mr. Blackwater?"

"Crazy fucks," muttered George. "No one loves me."

Al gave Jules an amused look and fastened the last strap. "He's in shock. It's a flesh wound. He'll be fine."

The door across Fiske was unlocked, and this time Jules ran up the stairs. He headed left at the top and peered into a suite of rooms covered with dropcloths. There was primer on the walls, and the floors not covered by canvas were polished wood. A taped sign on the open door said "Biddle & Rake, Attorneys at Law." Blue Deer's most prominent lawyers apparently planned to replace their old offices, across from the courthouse, with spacious new quarters. A wooden ladder lay open on its side in front of the far right window, and Jules crossed carefully over to it, eyeing the shine of metal. The three cartridges on the floor were .30-30s, and the paint on the sill, still rubbery and fresh, was scratched. The office across the street was empty now, with the door shut, and Jules could make out the two-headed calf and the empty computer monitor. He found some newspaper and a roll of duct tape in the corner, carefully wrapped the shells and stowed them in his jacket. He taped the office door shut, pulled out a red pen, and wrote "Room sealed, order of Absaroka County Police" over "Biddle & Rake." He wondered if the lawyers' children had ever thought of changing their names. Maybe it was all a question of context.

IT'S HARD to be a small-town sheriff if you're not a natural gossip, if you have no memory for the vagaries of your neighbors, their love affairs and petty scams and filthy or virtuous habits. It was Jules's major disadvantage as Absaroka County's head law-enforcement officer. He was a local boy, what passed for a born and bred Montanan in a state only one hundred years old, but he'd been away from Blue Deer for almost half his life, and knowledge of a larger world got you nowhere if you felt an essential distaste for the seedier points of a small town's history. He had a fabulous memory for some details—he always won *Jeopardy* when he made it to the bar by 4:30 to watch; he could give rainfall and river-depth statistics for the last forty years, and tell you exactly which birds were sitting in your yard and why they were there. He could even tell you part of why New York was New York, and Montana Montana, or what you might see out the window if you flew across the Russian steppes. But no one thought to ask him these questions, and he was often incapable of retaining information on the grimy past of Blue Deer's inhabitants, even though he'd lived his last two years and his first seventeen with them. He chose to forget most bad details, unless they struck him as humorous or unless they encompassed an actual crime. It was to his credit that he usually thought the best of people, and was otherwise philosophical about their failings, though it made the Absaroka County Attorney, Axel Scotti, grit his teeth on a weekly basis.

So Jules was one of the few people in town who might expect a sunny welcome when he drove up to George and Mona Blackwater's house on Marmot Drive, even though George's former employee, Alice Wahlgren, had often talked, or rather complained, about the couple since Jules had been back in town. He'd met George a few times, knew he was a screenwriter, and vaguely remembered his reputation as a rich summer boy when Jules was just a tot. He had the general impression, probably from the *Blue Deer Bulletin*, that Mona was one of Blue Deer's monied matrons, a supporter of the arts and sundry community works. He also had the niggling sense, probably from Peter and Alice, that she was capable of outstanding misbehavior. Such activity didn't particularly stand out in libertarian Blue Deer, and therefore Jules's sole critical thought, as he parked in the Blackwaters' driveway, was to note the soullessness of the house and the absence of any birdfeeders or suet for the sparrows and finches that dotted the scraggly Russian olives. He knocked politely on the door and rubbed his sharp jawline while he waited. He knocked again, just as gently, and smiled through the screen door at the boy and girl, about eight and ten, who materialized.

"Hello. I'm Jules Clement, county sheriff. Is your mother in?" His voice was soft and clipped.

"She's in a bad mood," said the girl.

Jules thought this over. "Why?"

The girl shrugged. She was very pretty and self-possessed, with wise owl eyes. "She pitched Charlie's Nintendo."

Jules heard a crash of crockery from within the house, and some distant growls. He began to imagine Mrs. Blackwater as a very large bear. Charlie had the same eyes as the girl, but his whole body shuddered in rage.

"It's very important," said Jules, resorting to the same stage whisper the girl had been using.

She shrugged again, obviously considering his persistence foolish, and bellowed, "Mom, someone's here!" Both children disappeared.

Jules began to fidget, hoping that George Blackwater's office had been locked and that Harvey had followed the ambulance to the hospital as requested. The screen door swung out abruptly, clearing his nose by an inch, but the woman inside smiled sweetly. She was fortyish, tall and heavyset in a puffy pink robe, but handsome in a looming, dark sort of way. Her hair was wet from a shower, and she had the slightly shiny look of someone who normally wears a good layer of cosmetics.

"Mrs. Blackwater?"

"Mona."

"I'm Jules Clement, county sheriff."

"Where's your gun?" she said coquettishly, her eyes curious but a little off-kilter.

Jules raised an eyebrow. "I've come about your husband, George."

"Isn't it a little early, or late, to be pulling drunks out of their cars?" Mona's smile was locked in place. She hadn't invited him in. This rarely happened in Blue Deer, with the occasional exception of minor drug busts, when people weren't socially inclined.

"Actually, ma'am, he's had an accident and been taken to the hospital."

"Poor boy."

Jules kept an eye on the screen door, which she swung back and forth as if airing out the house. "I think you should go to the hospital. He was shot at his office, shot twice."

"Finally," said Mona. "You're a good Christian soldier to tell me."

Jules realized his mouth was open, but he could think of nothing to say.

"Is he going to make it?" Mona twirled a hank of damp, dye-black hair and kept swinging the door.

"I really don't know." Jules's sense of humor had begun to kick in. "I'd be happy to drive you over."

They considered each other for a moment. Jules noted that Mona's upper lip looked as if she'd used peroxide on a mustache. Mona saw a tall, lean man in his thirties, with a deadpan, crooked face, pale skin and straight chocolate-colored hair that shot out in different directions.

"Thanks, but I'll get there in my own car. Tell George to leave the nurses alone."

She let the screen door swing shut, and Jules headed for his squad car, trying to summon up a sense of offense but feeling immeasurable relief.

Jules found Harvey reading *People* in the hospital cafeteria and reminded him to dust the Biddle & Rake offices. Harvey mentioned that his shift was over at noon, and the Cubs/Braves game started at one; surely the fingerprinting could wait for regular Monday hours. Jules said no, pointing out that Harvey would only miss the opening innings, and surely knew the national anthem by now. Harvey, showing rare irony, sang a bar or two on his way out the door.

George Blackwater was in surgery for the next two hours, but his wife never arrived. The waiting room receptionist gradually went batty fielding phone calls under Jules's fixed, expressionless gaze. He thought her eyes were much nicer than Mona's, but she lacked the certain charm a nurse's uniform might have lent to her figure, or to his imagination. He wondered idly about her life, but eventually decided that she was too easily flustered to be particularly interesting. After he'd given up on the receptionist and read all the *National Geographic*s, he took up position in the hallway near the two ICU rooms.

When Horace Bolan, the doctor who'd operated on George, swung wide out of one of the rooms—his belly was large and always seemed to carry him a step or two outside of an intended curve—Jules followed him to the nurses' station.

"Can I have a word or two with George?"

"Are you kidding?" Horace looked owly; emergency surgery was not his usual Sunday morning pastime.

"What time do you think he'll be up for it?"

"You can try this evening. I'll tell them to let you in if he's awake. I have to get out of here."

Horace scurried away, probably late for a golf game, and Jules eyed the nurse on duty, harassed but apparently friendly. "Just out of curiosity, if Mr. Blackwater's wife visits, will you let her in?"

"We have to."

"I wouldn't let her talk much. She might upset him."

ONE DAY in August when Jules was thirteen he'd lain on the shoddy front-porch couch reading *Goldfinger*. The phone began to ring and continued ringing as he read, oblivious. His sister Louise was off riding, and their mother, Olive, had to yell to him from the garden before he finally shuffled inside. It was Ed Winton, his father's young deputy; he was weeping and asked for Olive. Jules walked back out to the front porch while his mother talked to Ed and tried to start reading again, as if he didn't know better, but the page blurred and the mundane sound of a neighbor's lawn mower rose to an insectlike whine.

When Olive slammed through the front door and headed toward the hospital, two blocks distant, at a dead run, Jules followed, his gawky legs gliding over the pavement. Olive made for the emergency entrance and stopped running only when she reached a gurney in the center of the room and pulled back the sheet that covered it. Ansel Clement lay looking up at the ceiling. His face was still his face, though white and diminished, but Jules peered into the center of his father's chest at the large ragged hole, a washed-out red and white, lined with bands of torn blue muscle, that reminded him of the sheen of a skinned antelope.

JULES had never, in his youth, wanted to be a policeman. His father had been sheriff, a mildly crooked cop but a popular man, a Swede with a sense of humor, until his run-in with a crazed trucker, unwilling to be ticketed for speeding, on I-90. Jules waded through the social traumas of high school, graduated early, and left for the relatively bohemian settlement of Ann Arbor, where by the grace of high SAT scores and proven need he attended the University of Michigan on a full scholarship. When he left Michigan he headed for Columbia and a masters in archaeology, the least useful persuasion any of his friends could imagine. And when he finished Columbia he veered even further toward the exotic by taking a freighter across the Atlantic, and earned a doctorate by spending most of the next decade digging up remote medieval villages in northern Italy, Yugoslavia, and Turkey, filling up any lulls with trips to North Africa and the Caucasus.

Then one day he wanted to go home. He'd found one of the regions in the Atlas Mountains he'd always read about, a place where the snow of the mountains reached to a valley floor of blossoming orange groves. It wasn't something you'd find in Montana, which had been the point of coming, but it gave him the same vertigo he'd felt in the Crazy Mountains as a child, and a vast, sudden longing to see the prairie again. He canceled the next project, gathered his books and possessions in Paris, and lugged them to a ship in Havre. Two weeks later he was driving across North Dakota in a U-Haul truck. He knocked on his mother's door without warning at four one morning in April, but she took his reappearance in stride.

Jules slept for most of the next month, and when he truly woke up it occurred to him that his options were limited. He took another month to drive around the county, then the state, discovering in the process that most of his old friends and girlfriends were married, often to each other, or gone. Then one night in June he sat on Peter and Alice's porch after dinner, examining their clematis vine, while Peter, then a deputy county attorney and now a reporter for the *Bulletin*, talked about the craven dipshits in the sheriff's office and how difficult it was to get them to come clean about anything of moment in Blue Deer. Jules had a revelation—he would be a better version of his father; he would be able to do well by people on this small scale, one that surely would never spin out of control as in New York.

Peter and Alice thought he was joking, and when Jules told Olive she stared at him and suggested very nicely that he move out so that she wouldn't have to wait for him to not come home one night. Jules felt badly for his mother but could not believe that being a policeman in Absaroka County was an inherently dangerous career. More archaeologists were killed by beestings each year than the number of cops shot in the line of duty in the state of Montana. He moved his stuff into a small white frame house on F Street and left for training in Billings—a hideous town the local news station referred to as the "Magic City"—on July 1, his thirty-second birthday. He spent a year as a patrolman, scudding happily along high plains roads, before he decided to run for sheriff and surprised everyone (except Alice, who managed what passed for a campaign) by winning.

Jules knew he'd won because his father had been sheriff and because the other candidates had been known quantities and outrageously incompetent, but he was happy anyway. A month later, after a cheery local drunk tried to hang himself in one of Blue Deer's three cells, Jules felt a quaver of doubt, and wondered if the desire to be sheriff had come upon him during a prolonged bout of insanity. The president of a company might be blamed for a loss of money, but a head cop would eventually be blamed for a life. Jules kept an eye on his inmates and decided to live with the job.


LATE Sunday afternoon, Jules retrieved Blackwater's office key from Harvey and parked on Fiske again. Someone had attempted to clean the bloodstains on the carpet, and Jules followed the foamy track down the gloomy hall to George's office. Someone had also retrieved the pages of manuscript from the shards of glass and stacked them neatly on the table near the empty monitor, weighing down the paper with a chunk of illegal Yellowstone obsidian. The feather collection on the wall ruffled in the moist wind from the blasted-out window, fingerprint powder puffed free from the sills. Jules wondered if Harvey had dusted both offices or simply the wrong one, but lacked the energy to cross the street to check immediately.

He studied a half-dozen small landscapes, jewel-like oils of fields and one pearly sketch of the ocean, wondered about their proximity to several B-movie posters, and moved on to the framed black-and-white photos that dotted the wall. Most showed stiff ancestors posed by various posh houses, carriages, and cars, but three were views of the Blackwater ranch, George's hideout ten miles south of Blue Deer on a spring creek. Jules wandered around, eyeing the two-headed calf and the yellowed *Playboy* calendar, circa 1976 and terribly polite. Miss May, an airbrushed redhead, showed signs of having been the one to face the world for the last seventeen years, and Jules wondered if she had some special significance for George. She didn't look a bit like Mona. He moved on and found the happy couple posed, improbably, in what appeared to be a high school or college shot—George twenty or so, goofy and tuxedoed with sideburns, Mona virtually unrecognizable, oddly petite and very lovely. How many people who'd gone on to conquer the wide world kept a prom photo on their wall? He leaned forward, squinting, wondering how a woman could change so much, and nearly screamed when something touched his shoulder.

"Do you call this work?"

It was Edie Linders, George's assistant. Her black T-shirt was smeared with dust, and some pinkish soap had dried on her pale arms and in her curly brown hair.

"Not compared to what you've been doing," said Jules. "Do you usually work weekends?"

"George called me," said Edie. She carried an aluminum ladder and looked slightly harassed. "He wanted me to get the window fixed in case it rained, but no one would work on a Sunday, so I thought I'd clear the walls."

"George could talk?" Jules had checked the hospital a half hour earlier, and the author had been out cold. Now he considered the idea that George, even confined to a hospital bed, would be capable of giving him the runaround. It fit with what little he remembered hearing about the man.

Edie shrugged. "I had to move stuff around anyway to make room for the crap from the ranch." She flipped open the ladder and carried it to the wall, dismissing him. She was Alice's successor as George's aide-de-camp, and not inconsequentially the only woman in Blue Deer who seemed more than remotely worthy of interest, but Alice had explained to Jules months before that he'd shot this chance when he'd become a cop, that Edie thought him on the wrong side of the law, a hobbyist in pigdom. He'd gotten the point, and had backed off from the diffident circling of last summer. Edie wasn't truly pretty, but she had a wonderful openness and vitality, or at least he'd noticed the openness with others. Now he watched in silence as she positioned the ladder, started to climb, and retreated swearing when the second step swung loose.

"Goddammit," said Edie. She shoved the ladder aside.

"What are you trying to reach?" asked Jules.

"The paintings," she said, as if he were dense.

"I'll get them." He stepped forward and reached around her, over her head. Edie was at best five-two, and he had at least a foot on her. He handed her the first, carefully avoiding the gilt on the inner edge of the frame, and reached for another. "So, Edie, who wants to kill your boss?"

"Ask him."

"I will. I'm asking you."

"Most people like George."

"Alice doesn't."

"She used to. I just avoid the arguments. He means well."

"What about the people George works for? Anybody he screwed over in L.A.?"

"The screwing mostly goes the other way."

"Mostly?"

"Alice knows more. You should ask her."

Jules pointed to an Inuit-style mask. Edie nodded and accepted it without a thank-you, blew dust from the brow, and carried it into the inner office where she had deposited the paintings. Jules watched her retreat, hoping she wouldn't want to bother with the wall-eyed calves, and quickly took the last three paintings from the wall. In theory, he liked the idea of women and men who did not burble on needlessly, but in practice he was finding it daunting. He knew Edie could talk—he'd watched her at it countless times with Alice, slightly stunned by how quickly Edie could revert to a New Jerseyite from a large family.

"I will ask Alice," he said, knowing he sounded like a broken record. "The truck's parked at the Blue Bat. We can find her together now that we have these down."

"I have too much to do," said Edie.

Jules gave her an offended look and walked to the window. "Bullshit," he said. "Is that Mrs. Blackwater now?"

She joined him at the window. "Yep," she said. "Who's the guy?"

"I don't know," said Jules. "I only met the marvelous Mona this morning."

A very small smile flitted over Edie's face. "And what did you think?"

"A prime suspect," said Jules. "Memorable." Edie was

grinning now, and he gave up any semblance of a professional attitude. "A wide and very scary load."

She hooted, good nature restored, and they leaned a little farther out the window. The man and Mona were talking animatedly, so much so that she walked into a parked car as they crossed the street, but the actual words were lost in gusts of dusty wind. The man was in his mid-forties or so, city pale with plummy red hair; from twenty feet above Jules could tell the suit he wore was worth more than most of the cars the couple passed.

"I think they're coming up here," he said.

Mona and the man were directly below now, apparently arguing. Intriguing phrases like "deserved it" and "little bitch divorcee he hired" floated out of Mona's mouth and up to them.

"Could that be you?" asked Jules.

"She never comes up here," whispered Edie. "She hates me. She hated Alice. She hates George. Did you lock the door behind you?"

"I don't remember, and I don't think it matters," said Jules, craning to see the man place his hand on the latch of the office door as Mona handed over a key.

"Oh fuck. Fuck." said Edie. "Sorry. Damn it." They pulled back from the window and heard the door open and slam shut, then slow, heavy footsteps on the long stairs. "What on earth could she want?" asked Edie.

"Which way?" said the man, his voice echoing from the head of the stairs.

"Shit," hissed Edie. "It's Ray Blackwater."

Jules stared at her.

"I've never met him, but I recognize his voice."

"A brother?"

"*The* brother. The asshole who's kicking him off the ranch."

"What do you mean?" asked Jules.

"I told you," whispered Edie. "Never mind."

"Oh God," said Mona from the hall. "Look at the carpet, Ray. This is disgusting."

"You didn't tell me he nearly died," said the man, his voice calm.

Jules tiptoed toward the center of the room and peered down the hall. The man had knelt down by George's unfortunate track while Mona stood next to him, tapping her foot, fondling some pottery on the wall bookcase. "All I needed," said Mona, "was another reason for George to feel sorry for himself." She dropped a small vase in her big blue Naugahyde purse.

"You're being a tad hard on the boy." Ray Blackwater straightened and they moved down the hall again toward where Jules stood, watching them. Ray looked up from the blood and met Jules's eyes but didn't break stride. "This is a little extreme, even for George."

Mona, almost at the doorway, stopped at a figurine and again opened her purse. "One of his girls probably took a pot-shot at him. I'm filing before they miss him and get me."

It would have been amusing if it hadn't been a crime scene. "Hello, Mrs. Blackwater," said Jules, still enjoying invisibility. It took a moment for Mona's eyes to leave yet another knickknack and focus on him. "Can I help you with anything? Were you picking something up for George?"

"Oh," said Mona in a very high, small voice. "Oh. Who gave you a key?" She retreated behind Ray Blackwater, who lunged forward with exaggerated grace, hand outstretched. "Ray Blackwater, George's brother."

Jules shook the proffered hand, taking in the gold watch, the flash of cufflinks, the crispest, whitest shirt he'd seen in years. "Jules Clement, county sheriff."

"I seem to remember your name from an AP story a couple of months ago," said Ray Blackwater, pumping Jules's arm a few more times. "Something about a poor farmer having been devoured by his cows."

"Swine, actually," said Jules, freeing himself and edging away from Ray's cloud of expensive after-shave.

"Excuse me?"

"Pigs. Cattle aren't omnivorous." He kept an eye on Edie, who was circling Mona as a mongoose might circle a cobra. "This is Edie Linders, George's assistant."

"We've spoken on the phone," said Ray. "A pleasure. Have you met Mrs. Blackwater, Sheriff Clement?"

"Yes," said Jules, smiling. "Yes, I have."

A thick silence settled on the room, broken by the moan of the old couch as Mona plopped down, sending up a puff of dust and glass shards. She gave Edie an evil look, lit a cigarette, and struggled with her tight flowered skirt before she managed to cross white-stockinged legs.

"I don't think you should be here when George isn't around," said Mona. "You might take something."

"George is never here," said Edie.

Mona swung her crossed leg in annoyance while she pulled on the cigarette. Her shoes were large and white, too, and Jules smiled as some of his mother's ancient advice to his sister floated through his mind: Never wear white stockings if you're heavy (his sister wasn't); never wear white shoes before Memorial Day. In high school the term for legs like Mona's had been "thunder thighs."

Ray walked around the room, examining the walls, sticking his finger in the largest of the holes left from the rifle blast. He had George's bleak face and melancholy eyes, but everything about him—hair, build, expression—was somehow tidier.

"Is it possible that your father was a policeman, also?" he asked. "I seem to remember an Ansel Clement from my troubled youth. Or should I say my troublesome youth."

"Yes, he was," said Jules, pulling his eyes away from

Mona's physique. "And where do you live now? You made it out quickly after George's accident."

"Here," said Ray. "I moved into the family ranch a couple of weeks ago, after our mother's funeral, from New York. I'm writing now, not editing any more, you know—" he looked pointedly at Jules, who had no idea of what he was talking about or why Ray thought he would care "—so I'm not tied to the city, though I'll keep my house, probably visit often, when things get too quiet out here."

Ray, wealthy Manhattanite, would not of course need to bother with subletting his apartment. Jules, one of the little people, had never been lucky enough to have a lease during his years in the city. Now he knew he was dealing with something he'd hoped to leave behind, a paradigm of a New York prick.

"I heard something about the ranch," said Jules. He couldn't tell if this comment amused or annoyed Ray. Edie seemed to wake up and marched into the next office. Mona started to laugh. "Something very vague," said Jules.

"Our mother left me the ranch," said Ray.

"That sure pissed George off." Mona lit her second cigarette. "I thought he was going to pop you after the service." The notion seemed to make her happy. Jules thought that she was probably the sort of woman who would prefer to have men fight over her, and failing that—he couldn't imagine the idiot who would fight over Mona—any fight would do.

"I don't remember noticing." Ray looked at his sister-in-law with what might have been loathing. "At any rate, Mona called me to tell me about George's accident, so I drove into town. She wanted to see the scene of the crime."

"I'm sure George was happy to see you at the hospital," said Jules. Edie slammed some drawers in the next room.

Mona snorted on the couch and stubbed out her cigarette. "I'd like to have a drink soon," she said.

Ah, thought Jules. A common denominator.

"We haven't made it to the hospital yet," said Ray. "Didn't want to rush things. I called before I left and a nurse told me George was resting. Maybe we should check again, now."

"Maybe you should," said Jules. "I may call you tomorrow if I have some questions."

Mona extricated herself from the couch, little slivers of glass glimmering on her fanny. Ray shook Jules's hand again and waved to Edie, who ignored him, then paused by the door. "Look, dear," he said, pointing to the prom photo and touching Mona on the shoulder. "His heart's still on the wall."

She said something unintelligible and surged down the hall. Ray smiled at Jules and pointed to the calendar. "George's first actress. See you soon."

Silence ensued. Edie stared into space. Jules walked to the window and watched Ray and Mona make a beeline for the Blue Bat without a shred of indecision.

"Does Mona ever go hunting?" Jules asked.

Edie wrestled the computer's hard drive and printer into the next room, leaving the the shell of the monitor to the elements. "Did she look like a rifle type to you, the kind of woman who likes to crawl around in camo and blaze orange?" She shoveled two scripts into her purse, her normally happy, mobile face stiff with anger.

"Well," said Jules. "Maybe you'd like that drink, after all." Edie flicked off the light switch and hurried down the hall. He gestured to the sudsy blood stains. "Are you sure you don't want some help with this?"

"I'll do it in the morning."

The wind gusted down the street, and the clouds were black. The silence still not companionable. Jules gave way to irritation. "Just out of curiosity, how did you know it was a rifle?"

Edie smiled at him. "A handgun from across the street?

The whole wall would have been smithereens if it had been a shotgun, and so would George. How stupid do you think I am?"

"I don't think you're stupid at all." He swung the door of the Blue Bat open with unnecessary force, and watched her glide into the murk.

CHAPTER 3

STRANGE things happen on the plains, stranger things than in the mountains, the vertigo of emptiness as opposed to the edge. Finally most dreams consist of the less dramatic, more insidious sort of terror or happiness, but in either geography, in either sort of dream, you see a little too much.

The center of Jules Clement's fiefdom—Blue Deer, Montana, pop. 3,872, alt. 4500 feet—lay on the cusp, on the edge of the Rockies, beneath the 10,000-foot range of the Absarokas. To the west and south the world was bumpy and alpine and photogenic; to the east and north, with the exception of the fortresslike Crazy Mountains rising from the plains like a mirage and a stray cottonwood in a draw every half a mile or so, the land was open and ravined and lonesome. Absaroka County was ninety miles north to south and forty miles wide, half the size of Connecticut with only 12,000 people, perhaps because temperatures varied from forty below, Fahrenheit, to one hundred degrees in any given year. Blue Deer, the county seat, lay in the center, but it felt like a border town, the border of the divide, the border of trees and miles of dun-colored grass, of shelter and high, domed, windswept emptiness. It was rumored to be the second windiest place in the continental United States—no one knew who won the prize—and undercapitalized entrepreneurs tested and lost wind generators on the high bench land above the Yellowstone River, which ran north out of Yellowstone Park for sixty miles before it wrapped around Blue Deer. The town possessed nine bars, seven churches, the hospital, a Carnegie library, three schools, some massive and mostly empty machine shops owned by the nearly defunct railroad, a grand and also empty depot, various social service and government buildings, a lumbermill, a small theater, one supermarket, three banks, and the usual run of small plains businesses—feed stores, diners, five & dimes, car dealerships. Blue Deer was laid out on the railroad's 1890 grid, and the lots tended to be quite small; half the houses had been mail-ordered from Sears, Roebuck in the teens and twenties. There were six bona fide mansions, left behind by bank presidents, mine and mill owners, and quirky, health-seeking Easterners. Most of the newer dwellings were suburban pancakes and double-wide trailers.

Crimewise, things were slow. Jules's most newsworthy cases thus far, during his first six months as sheriff, had been the theft of a series of reapers and tractors from the local John Deere dealership (his first coup: He and Harvey had caught the thieves during a January blizzard, and most of the missing equipment had been intercepted on its way to Canada); the disclosure of a shed stuffed with marijuana in the valley, raided with regret; and the discovery of a gnawed-upon elderly body, a farmer who'd had a heart attack and provided a final meal for his swine. There was the other usual human stuff, none of it happy—speeders, fires, accidents, domestic horror—but George Blackwater's misadventure was truly big news in Blue Deer, a town that thrived on each Monday's weekly sheriff's report in the *Bulletin*.

Jules could easily tell himself that the best place to pick up the local word was in one of the local bars, and that entering the Blue Bat had nothing to do with escorting Edie there, or wanting a drink, or even being curious about Ray and Mona, jabbering at each other in a dark booth near the back wall. Almost everyone in the Blue Bat would have an opinion, because some had worked for George, and everyone who drank had had a drink with him. But Jules ordered very quickly, a whiskey ditch (the local term for whiskey and water, perhaps also referring to the driver's final destination), and chose the stool next to Edie rather than the free one next to Alice Wahlgren and Peter Johansen. Alice found most things amusing, and this maneuver especially so; she rolled her eyes when Jules insisted on paying for Edie's beer. They'd known each other for too long and were too alike for Alice to have any difficulty pulling apart his mixed, baroque motives. But today she seemed a little edgy, and her joke was forced.

"You're giving Edie the third degree, huh?"

"I helped her save George's belongings from the elements."

Alice had the occasional capacity for kindness, and Jules was thankful that she didn't snort. Instead she and Peter looked at him expectantly. "So?" asked Alice. "What happened up there?"

"We moved a few paintings," Jules said.

"You know what I mean."

"Someone shot George. He'll be fine."

Alice looked annoyed. "Happens all the time around here," said Peter. "I can understand that you'd be bored by it."

Edie squeezed a lime wedge into her beer bottle and craned her head to Alice. "Jules wants to know who'd want to kill George. I said that you'd have a better idea than I would."

"Pick a number, any number," laughed Alice. Peter snapped her on the knee. Alice had done her time in George's employ—more than two years in the Fiske Avenue office—before she bullied Edie into taking over. She was no longer a fan.

"People do seem to be volunteering at a fantastic rate." Jules took a long sip and stared glumly at the greasy liquid that Delly Bane, the bartender, left behind as he swabbed the counter.

"The tirebiter probably did it." Alice grinned, wickedly, and took a dainty bite from the olive in her martini.

"Which tirebiter?" asked Delly.

Jules's angular face, usually unreadable, took on a slightly confused air. "A tirebiter is a large, usually unfriendly female," explained Peter. "I believe Alice is referring to Mrs. Blackwater."

"So who the hell are you talking about, Delly?" Jules drained his glass and pushed it forward. A quick glance in Edie's direction told him that she'd had less than an inch of her beer, but he found himself willing to go only so far to impress her.

"Do you mean the tirebiter he's married to or the tirebiters he still has fun with?" asked Delly.

"George likes them big and troublesome, most of the time," said Peter. "I think he even still enjoys Mona when she gets truly pissed off."

"She came looking for him again last night," said Delly. "He didn't follow her out, though. You heard Harvey took him home, right?"

Jules nodded wearily and watched Delly carry drinks to Ray and Mona, far out of earshot.

"She was up bright and early this morning," said Peter, nodding in Mona's direction. "She came chugging out of an alley downtown a few minutes before we heard the shots."

Peter sipped his drink. Jules slowly turned on his stool, fighting back irritation. "What was she doing?" he asked calmly.

"Running," said Alice.

"Running?"

"Yes," said Peter.

"Is it possible that she was running in the general direction of Biddle & Rake's new offices?"

Peter and Alice looked at each other.

"Yes," said Alice.

"No," said Peter.

"She wasn't heading for the front door," said Alice, looking smug. "But there's a back door, off the alley."

"How do you know that?" asked Peter.

"Our head doctor had offices there, remember?"

Peter blushed slightly. Edie had been twirling from left to right on her stool but stopped abruptly when her knee ran into Jules's. Their eyes met for a moment. Jules looked into his ice cubes and fought away the image of the sports bra necessary for Mona to run without pain. The whole topic of other, fonder tirebiters had been lost in the shuffle, though he doubted one of George's sweethearts was murderous or smart enough to sight her lover in on a rifle from the Biddle & Rake offices.

"Tell me more, Delly."

"Jesus, Jules, ask Peter. His boss used George so hard the poor boy had a little heart attack a couple of years ago. Even though she's a tiny thing."

Jules regarded Peter, who in turn regarded the assortment of bottles on the back bar with a slightly angst-ridden expression. "Ada?" Ada Santoz owned the *Blue Deer Bulletin*. She was a small, blond widow, patrician and energetic.

"Where the fuck have you been?" asked Peter. "Of course, Ada. We've been together in this same bar when they were pasted together, Velcro wads of love. Are you blind?"

"It's a new one on me," said Jules.

"Only because you had your own pursuits."

None of Jules's pursuits had been memorable, but the comment was vaguely flattering. "Are they still seeing each other?"

"I don't think so," said Peter. "They've been bad-mouthing each other for the last couple of months."

"What have they been saying?"

"They spent Horace's birthday party trading insults," said Alice. "George was talking to Scotti and compared her to a cold mud pie."

"I don't get it."

"Like rolling in one."

Jules shuddered as they all watched him, amused. "Ada was sitting across the table," said Edie.

"He said that in front of her?" It made Jules's head spin. He'd always simply done the silent run himself, sometimes of necessity changing apartments, jobs, cities, whole countries. "What did she do?"

"She gave a lengthy speech on penis size," said Alice. "I was ready to call in your troops if it escalated."

Peter looked for Delly, but he was busy taking two more drinks to Ray and Mona. Ray was waving his arms in the air and Mona was chortling. Jules wondered if they were discussing the same topic. "Tell me something else interesting."

"You're the cop," said Peter. "You're supposed to be the fountain of information. I'm disappointed in you."

"You're the reporter. You pay attention to these people. Plus that, you owe me. You wouldn't be a local without me."

Peter flicked a finger in his direction. Jules smiled and swiveled on his stool, and Peter ordered another drink. They'd been roommates in Ann Arbor, and had both wound up in New York, where Peter toiled for *Newsday* and Jules studied for his masters at Columbia. Jules, still an anarchist, had spent most of his spare time in Manhattan working for minimum wage, first at a gourmet grocery called Dean & DeLuca, where he'd met Alice, and later as a social worker in the area known as Alphabet City. Peter's salary had been hefty in comparison, and the game of interview had gone on for years—Peter had written off dozens of restaurant and bar bills and found Alice while theoretically quizzing Jules on such topics as foie gras and persimmons and the early stages of the AIDS and crack epidemics. Jules in fact had never learned the difference between proscuitto and *bundnerfleisch*, and loathed social statistics, but Peter could rely on his unlimited capacity for bullshit and the intelligent phrase. Alice had managed to remain fond of Jules despite the boozy get-togethers, one of which culminated in Jules vomiting on her best friend and her newest ancient couch.

When Jules took off for Europe, after spending the intervening year trying desperately and unnecessarily to make up for the couch, he left both of them with a persistent urge to go sight unseen to Blue Deer, Montana. Peter spent the next three years in law school, having decided that the law was a trade he could travel with, and when Alice quit yet another kitchen job, Peter packed her into his Ford Escort and they headed west. They'd been in town for a year before Jules turned up again, only mildly surprised to find they'd stuck it out through a Montana winter. By then Alice and Peter had almost settled into the way Blue Deer thought—they'd shot the worthless Escort, for instance, one night when they were mildly bombed and feeling flush, and had learned to hibernate from November through February. Alice, having quickly discovered that no one in the county paid more than ten dollars for a meal, had given up catering in favor of working for George Blackwater.

Jules now took the attitude that Peter, the former New

York hotshot reporter, should provide him with the leads his staff was too unimaginative to muster; he played the naif well, an attitude that was more than a little misleading. Jules loved to minimize his vocabulary, to argue about politics from the point of view of an aw shucks bachelor in the Rockies, to be disingenuous about a decade of higher education and a passport that would have been indecipherable to most people from his birthplace.

Peter gave in. "All I know beyond the thing with Ada is that Ray has the ranch house now. Their mother cut George out of her will."

"I heard something about that," said Jules softly.

"You're way past your usual speed then," said Peter.

"So why did she do it?"

"She was crazy," said Alice. "Nuts. I got the impression from George that she'd been institutionalized for at least the last decade."

"That's it?"

"She sent him really nasty letters, mean stuff. Ray was her good baby. She put George through hell."

"Jeez, Alice," said Jules. "You almost sound sympathetic."

She wrinkled her nose and Jules sipped and watched her in the bar mirror for a moment before he spoke again. "Maybe Ray shot his brother."

"Why?" Alice's stony look seemed to imply that Jules's opinion was beyond stupidity. "It's much more likely that George would shoot Ray, given the ranch."

"I hope you're not saying that because Ray hired you for a party," said Peter.

"Ha," said Alice. "Can you work it, Edie? A Saturday, the fifteenth?"

"A dinner?"

"Yeah. About a dozen, four courses."

"I probably have Little League. Can you get someone

else?" Edie had three sons, and her husband had decamped the year before. She was always exhausted, always spread too thin, though she rarely admitted it.

Alice drained her martini. "I'll call Rita."

Jules struggled to get the conversation back on track. "Mona, then."

"Too stupid. Too lazy." Alice let a fragment of a smile ooze out.

"Ada."

"She'd poison him instead."

Peter drummed his fingers on the bar. Edie mooned out the one uncurtained window of the Blue Bat, and Jules imagined her waiting for summer or an easy day in her life. Ray and Mona rose and left through the back door, Mona a tad unsteady. It was all so strange, thought Jules, and he wondered what on earth they had in common, beyond an apparent and mutual dislike for poor George.

The evening droned on with largely harmless stories about George and Ray and horrific fairy tales about Mona. Jules began to feel sick to his stomach, whether from lost morale or lack of food, and pushed off his stool and faded into the night. But outside the rain had come and gone. The streets were wet and clean, and the wind had momentarily disappeared. He felt better. The door of his bedraggled Chevy truck creaked in pain, and he wondered, for the fiftieth time, why he was incapable of remembering to buy a can of WD40. He picked up a chicken sandwich at Morton's Diner and passed Ray's Mercedes, parked at Blue Deer's only tony restaurant, in the Baird Hotel.

Jules putted down the valley in the dusk, wishing that he'd stuck with his patrol car and could go ninety with the lights on, just for the hell of it. The highway lay at about 4,700 feet, slightly higher to the south toward Yellowstone National Park. To the west, long serpentine ridges ran toward Bozeman, about thirty miles distant as the crow flies. To the east, the mountains were alpine and sharp, eight to eleven thousand feet, softened on the lower slopes by lodgepole pine, and higher by scrubby alpine fir, with long gray alleys cut through the patterns of green by occasional landslides. In May the mountains were still white—early August was usually the only time of the year when it was hard to see snow in the crevices near the peaks, and at any point in the summer a rain in the valley might crystallize above six thousand feet. These mountains, the Absarokas, marked one side of a huge triangle of virtual emptiness that ran east to the Beartooths and south to the park. They were possibly not as showy as the Tetons, one hundred and fifty miles to the south, but looked less like an isolated facade and were in fact much wilder, with fairly stable populations of mountain goats, mountain lions, and grizzlies. Beneath the mountains proper the foothills sloped down to the river in smooth planes, dotted by small, illogical badlands humps like Indian Hill and divided by dozens of drainages, most of which dried up in the summer during irrigation: Mill Creek, Elbow Creek, Deep Creek, Six Mile Creek.

When you entered the valley from the north you could see thirty miles to the canyon lands that marked the final approach to the park. When you entered the valley from the canyons, heading north, most days you could see to the Crazies, perched like a fortress thirty miles northwest of Blue Deer, some seventy miles in all. The Yellowstone flowed along the full course of the valley, its banks lush with cottonwoods compared to the rest of the grassland landscape; as in much of the rest of the Great Plains, deciduous trees marked water, and survived only where it ran. Big stands of willows lined the irrigation ditches of older ranches. The owners of most of the newer ranchettes and luxury homes wanted the view, and wanted to be seen, and as a result their houses looked angular, ugly, and nonsensical, susceptible to the massive winds that swept up the valley from the south.

From the Blackwater ranch, really just the house and eighty acres, you could see only the top half of the mountains, and none of the dreck on the lower slopes. The house, surrounded by groves of aspen that fanned across the lush bottomland to a spring creek, was a hundred years old, as old as anything in the valley, though its real oddity was not age but stone construction in a land of stucco and frame. Jules had never understood why, with so much rosy insulating rock available, so few settlers had bothered with it. He supposed it had to do with haste, just like most of the bad ideas in Montana or anywhere else. Stucco and wood beat aluminum siding and brick any day, but this house grew right out of the ground and still managed grace. It had a classic ranch layout—a sprawling, thick-walled lower story with a centered porch and a smaller upstairs with dormered windows covered by a softly sloping roof with wide eaves to keep the sun back. It also had—or had had—gardens and trees that were almost English in size and variety, possibly because its first owners had been lesser peers from Devon intent on a sheep ranching get-rich-quick scheme that never quite panned out. That had been in 1889, the year Blue Deer was founded; by 1910 they'd graduated to saddlehorse breeding, providing stables much nicer than most of the homes in the nearby town. The Blackwater clan picked up the place in 1951, and turned the stables into guesthouses for people who rarely visited. They'd given up on the gardens almost immediately, with fitful attempts at control every decade. Peter and Alice had rented the house for a year when they first moved out, before George told them he couldn't do without a refuge, and Alice had spent all her free time digging and pruning and salvaging the walls of honeysuckle and lilac and mock orange, the beds of peonies and iris and campanula and malva. She'd never really recovered from leaving.

Jules knew the house well—he'd worked on shoring up the foundation as a teenager and had wanted it even then. A place like that was enough to keep you working, to make you put aside your socialist leanings, and he could understand why George would want to be able to run to it while working on Hollywood prose, why he'd want to keep it as an antidote to the house he shared with Mona. Maybe Ray loved it, too; maybe this was the one sign of integrity in each brother's character. Jules felt he was dropping into the middle of a French movie every time he drove up. The feeling was stronger today than usual, possibly because he'd begun daydreaming and nearly missed the turnoff. The truck wallowed to a stop in an empty driveway, sending gravel into a weedy flower bed.

Most of the lights were on inside. Jules marched up to the house and banged on the door. He counted to twenty and watched a flock of magpies search the grass for the last of autumn's fermented crab apples. At twenty-one he shook the door handle and found it locked. Jules stepped four feet to the right, climbed up on the still-solid foundation, slid open the window, and swung a long leg inside, into and over some dirty dishes resting in the kitchen sink.

There was a vase of long-defunct tulips on the kitchen table, surrounded by precarious heaps of pots and pans, dirty wine glasses, and crusty utensils. A bottle of Maker's Mark sat on the counter next to an open bag of tortilla chips, and Jules fought the urge to take a sip. In the next room, the dining room, the table was stacked with books; decidedly urban photographs; framed newspaper clippings, most showing Ray's smug face; and framed covers of the magazines Ray had run back in New York, most featuring equally smug actresses and actors. The living room was empty of anything but dusty furniture, and the bathroom held the usual after-shave and toothpaste and toilet paper, plus Ray's prescriptions for Seconal and blood-pressure medication and a stack of mundane, ancient pornography that Jules guessed had probably belonged to George. A lipstick and a woman's hairband had been relegated to the corner with a can of Comet.

He hurried upstairs, beginning to feel edgy and, quite rightly, illegal. Three closed doors faced him on the landing. The first held a stripped bed, more dead flowers in a vase, a mountain of boxes, all marked "George" in emphatic ink, and a couple of lovely landscapes. Some sheer black stockings, still showing the slender outlines of legs, and a gray slip had been tossed unceremoniously on top of the pile. Jules, curious, reached for the slip and held it up, noticing first that Mona would never have fit into it, and second that it was very fine real lace and smoky silk, not Blue Deer's sort of lingerie.

The second bedroom was mounded with kids' toys and more girlie mags, an unnerving mix that didn't have the look of Ray. Jules found his den in the third room: dusted and clean, with neatly folded clothes stacked on the bed quilt and a pile of galleys, manuscripts, and untouched Forest Service maps on the floor near the bed. A rifle was propped in the corner of the room, but it was a Holland & Holland, a big game gun worth thousands. It would have blown an elephant's skull off, and George to infinity. A laptop computer sat on a card table under the window, bordered by a pile of envelopes, a stack of manuscripts, and a Rolodex. Jules stopped short of examining the addresses or the printout but sorted quickly through the bills and letters and found, at the bottom, a color print of Mona's pretty, youthful face, the same photo that had hung in George's office. He leaned closer, just catching the zig of scissor marks where George, happy and tuxedo-clad, had been pruned away. Perhaps he'd underestimated her, or overestimated Ray. Jules replaced the photo gently with a sigh of disgust, and headed downstairs for the window and his truck.

# CHAPTER 4

## BLUE DEER BULLETIN
### *SHERIFF'S REPORT, WEEK OF APRIL 26–MAY 2*

April 26—A report was received of an injured deer south of Lewis Creek. An officer gave the property owner permission to dispose of the deer.

A report was received of an apparently unconscious man in the alley behind the Big Steer. An officer responded and the man said he was taking a nap.

A report was received of possible domestic abuse. Officers responded and took a suspect into custody.

April 27—A report was received of a possible reckless driver. The driver was reading out of a book on the seat of his car and was cautioned.

April 28—An individual requested a welfare check on a family member who couldn't be located. The individual was located.

A report was received from Madcap of an overdue motorist. An officer located the individual just south, and heading into, that fair city.

April 29—A report was received of a skunk in a garbage can. An officer responded. He left the skunk in the can and the lid on the can. A note was left for the garbage men to be aware of the situation.

April 30—A report was received of a breaking and entering. Officers are investigating.

A report was received of a large truck tire on the Interstate.

May 1—An individual reported three suspicious boys lying on the sidewalk smoking. The boys left, then returned. An officer was advised.

A report was received of a recalcitrant individual at the Blue Bat. Officers responded and discovered that the individual was difficult. The individual was escorted home.

May 2—A shooting was reported in a downtown building. Officers responded and took a wounded individual to Blue Deer Memorial Hospital. The incident is under investigation.


ADA SANTOZ'S *Bulletin* was a daily, Monday through Friday, but it provided the juicy stuff only once a week. Some of the quirky nature of the sheriff's report could be blamed on Grace Marble, the police clerk—Jules was unsure how much of her work could be put down to a literal mind and how much to a slightly warped sense of humor. The column didn't, of course, offer the totality of local crime. The "News of Record" for the same week listed three accidents (two under "Fire"), four arrests (two DUIs and two domestic abuse incidents), one dissolution, one marriage, thirteen citations for "exceeding the fuel conservation speed limit" (a five-dollar fine on the freeway, if the driver was clocked below one hundred), six other vehicle citations, and one stolen Angus calf.

By nine o'clock on Monday morning, after an hour at the station, Jules's list of facts on the latest crime was still meager. George Blackwater was alive, and so, undoubtedly, was the person who'd taken a shot at him; George Blackwater's wife was very scary, didn't seem fond of her unfaithful husband, and had been seen jogging at an unholy hour; George and his brother Ray, recently arrived, suffered from a lack of filial affection; Biddle & Rake (Diddle & Take, in the local parlance), contacted at home as they dressed for work, claimed no knowledge of why someone would use a rifle in their prospective offices; and no one, including George, claimed any real knowledge of why anyone sane would want to off a largely harmless writer. Punch him, maybe; shoot him, no.

On the other hand, Blue Deer had always boasted a high ratio of insanity, something Jules was reminded of as Grace warbled a forties song in the next room and the phone rang off the hook. They took turns: Grace got two calls from wackos belonging to the local new age church, claiming problems with a neighboring rancher; Jules took complaints about a barking dog and a vandalized Airstream. Grace was chatting with one of her daughters, who was at least ten months pregnant by now, when the ringing began again and Jules fought the urge to smack the phone with his baton.

"Absaroka County Sheriff's Department."

"Hey Jules, it's John Dribnitz. What are you doing answering the phone?"

"I always answer the phone." Dribnitz was the high school principal, had been for twenty-five years, and the potential reasons for the call were therefore endless. "What are the pipsqueaks up to now?"

"Nothing yet, but I wanted to warn you the board decided to go ahead with senior skip day after all. Wednesday. Make it your day off."

Jules's elbow hit the desk and his head hit the palm of his hand. Skip day was the senior class's officially sanctioned disappearing act, one that always became highly visible by nightfall. "You know this is a bad idea. I told you about that lawsuit in Georgia."

"That was Georgia. This is harmless fun."

"It sure as hell wasn't harmless when I was a senior."

Dribnitz giggled. "Not everyone drops two hits of acid and floats the river during high water. These kids are clean-cut."

"The hell they are." It made Jules feel weak just remembering. "There's already a Trout Unlimited banquet that night. Are you telling me we'll have drunken fishermen and feral little hormone-crazed assholes in the same twenty-four hours? Why Wednesday?"

Dribnitz was only slightly taken aback. "So we can count them the next day. Weekends the month before graduation are bad enough."

"Where are they going?"

"You and I will be the last to know." Dribnitz started giggling again, a little hysterically. "If the weather's bad they'll probably trash a motel in Gardiner. If it's good there's no telling."

"Jesus." They could flood Jacuzzis, fall off mountains, drown, rape each other, suffocate in their own vomit. They would most certainly drink and drive and impregnate, causing subsequent gunfire among the parents. "How many in this year's class?"

"Forty-eight, but a few juniors will probably tag along. Don't take the Lord's name in vain and don't worry. No one's died for a couple of decades."

"What the hell happened a couple of decades ago?"

"Never mind," said Dribnitz.

Jules spent another half hour at his desk, swilling coffee as the station filled up, a relative term in that only one other officer, Ed Winton, was on day duty Monday, plus Grace, who acted as dispatcher, and Archie Uhland, downstairs tending his scant daytime flock of prisoners. Jules scribbled a preliminary report on the shooting, left a message for Axel Scotti, the county attorney, and read over the half-dozen weekend reports. Most were open and shut, including one bad but nonfatal car accident, two violent drunks, and the sighting of an armed (definitely) and unstable (maybe) suicide candidate feeding ducks in the park. Bart Polgrave, the weekend jailer cum dispatcher, had taken the call, and he specialized in ifs and maybes. Harvey had dusted the Biddle & Rake offices for prints, but the matching process had yet to begin.

Grace started in on another ditty, reminding Jules that he had a slight hangover, but the Blue Bat hadn't been a complete loss. He'd learned several things about the Blackwater brothers, for instance.

George Blackwater was considerably more successful than most of his fellow citizens realized. Before Hollywood called, he'd written detective novels, at once fantastical, schlocky, and hard-boiled, not so much noir as purple. He'd started in his late twenties, after giving up his father's Portland paper business and decamping to Blue Deer to win over the mountain west. Ten books followed in the next fifteen years. He married Mona after number three, when he no longer had a problem getting published, and stretched his money thin on her version of a dream house (Mona thought the ranch house was shabby, old-fashioned, and too isolated) and the office he soon considered necessary for privacy. He dedicated book number four, *A Dead Blue Rose*, to her, and thanked her somewhat ambiguously on the copyright page of book number five, ignored her in six, then killed her off in books seven, eight, and nine. After ten, *Jungle Juice*, in which a thinly disguised Mona, "baying all the while," was macheted to death by a crazed parrot-keeping Nazi in Paraguay, George went Hollywood full-time, and his wife's doomed character was reborn in the bodies of various bumptious starlets, all of whom George used as thoroughly as possible. Mona always thought she was the heroine, either a steadfast girl Friday or a dazzling sexpot, and no one had the guts to disabuse her of the notion.

Now George specialized in big-budget action scripts, and

in the last five years he'd made a fortune on them, about $750,000 a picture. He'd done movies for Universal and Warners and Columbia and Paramount; for Eastwood and Schwarzenegger and Willis and Stallone. Each of them had earned out, and two had grossed more than $100 million, but none of the participants were eager to sign up for a second script. George blamed Roger Schotz, his producer, for this, and Roger blamed George, but the argument was moot—after each shoot, hardened, venal studio executives and actors could hardly bear the idea of facing the duo again, no matter the money they brought in. To this degree, George and Roger were true rarities in Hollywood. And while Roger could always find a new writer, and thus lure a studio into a potentially gentler situation, George would never be able to find a new producer. He was too much of a pain in the ass, and writers were at the bottom of the totem pole.

But they always found new money men, and George somehow came out of every disaster with the reputation of an artist, mostly due to the small Waters/Romero style flourishes that made it into every script or novel—a woman inhaling nitrous, blowing out a candle, and exploding; a man impaled from below on his toilet; a murderess who smothered male victims with size 50E breasts and amazon thighs; a man who hauled in a fat body instead of a halibut on a dream vacation; a psycho gardener who came up with a corpse for fertilizer before planting each precious shrub; a painter who used his sister's gold bridge work for gold leaf . . . It looked silly on paper, but it sold, and it was hard work, dreaming this stuff up year after year.

The actresses found his open-minded randiness, general goofiness, and obvious devotion worthy of attention. George was very convincing—he believed everything he said, when he said it—and he managed to combine an absolute lack of social grace with an easy, disingenuous charm. In the months before each production every player thought him an amusing overgrown boy with a slightly bizarre take on life. When the shit finally hit the fan—after George turned snitty over script changes, delayed revisions with an insistence on driving versus flying between Montana and Los Angeles, and dogged his persecutors loudly across town, threatening innumerable lawsuits—they came to see him as the ultimate flake, a sulky, paranoid, turgid egomaniac who could no more accept blame than he could remember to wipe his mouth during a meal.

There was a better side to George. He loved his children, for instance, and they were the only conceivable reason he stayed with Mona. He loved his friends and was good to them until he embarrassed himself in front of them, at which point he generally avoided them or blamed them for the misbehavior. Guilt did not bring out the best in him. He usually meant well, at least before he thought things over. He loved to work, and rarely complained about overwork, except to Mona. And he had an artist's ability to recognize lovely things and humor, though not a writer's ability to translate them, or the strength of mind necessary to bring that grace into his life.

George painted to relax, and when his life became unbearable he retreated to the ranch house and spent hour after hour filling in small canvases with scenes of water or grass. No rivers, or streams, or lakes, or any horizon—certainly no trees, or mountains, or cows, or fences. Just the ocean and soft fields, in blues and greens and grays and white, water and meadow, over and over again, but all different. He gave most of them away or destroyed them; no one really knew what to think, but no one cared, because they were lovely. Peter and Alice had one from the days when they'd all been friends, and even though Alice could no longer bear to read the man's novels or see his movies, she looked at the oil every morning when she had coffee and felt quiet.

But Ray Blackwater had made it into a higher league,

and this galled George horribly. He'd headed to New York after college, and spent most of the seventies and eighties editing two national magazines, *Downtown* and *Real Life*, to a fair degree of acclaim. George spent those decades calling his brother a working stiff, when he mentioned him at all, but five years earlier Ray had shocked everyone by churning out the first of three wildly best-selling high-society thrillers. Ray didn't have to write screenplays for a living—his film rights alone went for one, one and a half, and two million for each successive book, not counting hardcover deals and paperback rights. He made sure his younger brother got the point. And as was George's habit with Mona, Ray gave his sibling dubious and recognizable minor casting in each manuscript— George as the pickled scion of a good family, rolling damsels off train platforms with aplomb; George as an unsavory biographer killed by a green mamba hidden in a soup tureen; George as a foul director, blown away by a prop harpoon. Things never ended happily for this fictional George.

Ray's favorite sport on his rare visits to Montana was to outline new plots featuring George, and when he did this in his brother's presence (usually at dinner parties) George, not usually a stoic personality, would simply leave the room. Ray had had one short marriage, with no children, and though he also had a reputation as a lady's man, he and his brother had thus far avoided doubling up on the same love object, with the possible exception of the ranch house.

When Jules had drained the station's supply of coffee he headed to the hospital. The mere mention of the word "ranch" turned George's twitchy face beige, with little red spots on each cheek and his chin. He didn't say a thing but tried to shrug his good shoulder. Jules put aside his agenda temporarily for the sake of curiosity.

"Have you talked to Ray much since he got out here?"

"No."

"Why don't you two share? You're both smart enough to

be reasonable. I can't see him spending all his time here."

George blinked and averted his head. "We don't share. It's his. It's in our mother's will."

So buy another house, thought Jules, thinking of the Blue Bat estimate of George's bank account. "You've got another place."

"Do you think I want to spend time there? Have you met my wife?"

George's huge gray eyes fixed on Jules's face, then began to dance again around the hospital room, desperately and rather furtively. It made Jules nervous—in New York, as a social worker, he'd always felt like the DTs were catching.

"Yes, actually, I have. I wanted to ask you about that."

"Fire away." George eyeballed Jules and tried to smile, but his mouth quivered. "Can you see if there's anything left under that shopping bag, the one in the locker? Fucking nurses are always hiding things on me while I sleep."

Jules sighed. "I'll fix you up." He located an almost empty Absolut bottle and added some ice from George's water pitcher, though George obviously couldn't give a shit about the temperature of what he drank. Jules didn't want one himself, but he noticed that George didn't show a sign of offering. The Blackwaters all needed to go to charm school. George drained his first glass in two long pulls, and Jules went to the locker again without a word, this time shutting the room's door with a little wave to a not particularly toothsome nurse.

Jules scooted his chair closer and crunched a knee against the steel bedstead. "So, George."

"Thanks for the drink."

"No problem. I need to ask if this annoyance your wife seems to feel toward you is a recent thing."

"Why would you assume that she was better once?" George's cheeks were pink and he had a sudden, deceptive look of health.

Jules stared at him. "Because you married her."

George rolled his eyes. "Let's say it's been about ten years of hell, out of fifteen or so of marriage. Would you call that recent?"

"With that in mind, is it possible that Mona could have taken a shot at you?"

"She might have liked to, but I know she can't tell a gun from her asshole." George smiled cheerily.

Wonderful, thought Jules, fighting the urge to get up and wash his face. "Do you own a .30-30?"

"Is that what did this?"

Jules nodded.

"No."

"Could she have asked someone to do it for her?"

"I can't think of anyone who'd want to do her a favor."

"There's always money."

"Nah," said George. He waved his bandaged hand as if to dismiss this line of questioning.

Jules pressed on. "She was seen downtown at the time of the incident."

"She was probably on her way to church with the kids." George hissed out "church."

Peter had mentioned that Mona had found religion; he said she liked to talk about it at dinner parties in the virtuous, shrill tones of the fake born-again, usually before her fourth drink. Jules hadn't seen the halo of the devout around her permed head, and wasn't buying it. "She was running, and she didn't have any kids with her."

The bandaged hand flopped through the air again. George lifted his glass, sipping now. "Have you asked her?"

"No. I found this out last night. Has she come to see you?"

"I pretended to be asleep. I think Ray knew I was faking, but he kept his mouth shut." He smiled at his cleverness. "The nanny's bringing the kids by after school."

"Your wife and Ray came up to your office yesterday."

"Edie told me."

"I gathered a visit was out of the ordinary."

"She was probably looking for cash or my little black book." George smiled a little weakly. "Or Ray was digging up trouble. He gets bored."

"What kind of trouble?"

"The little black book."

"I tried reaching Mona an hour ago and she didn't answer. Any idea of where she might be?"

"At large," giggled George, red-faced from the pain it caused his shoulder. "She's always at large. I keep hoping that someday one of those dopes from back East will mistake her for a fat elk and put me out of my misery." He wheezed again; sweat started at his temples and he drained his glass. "They took me off that little morphine buzzer this morning. I can't believe they'd be so cruel."

Jules drummed his fingers on the arm of the chair and examined the goose bumps moving up his arm. He had a low tolerance for hatred, and he reached for the ice water, chugging a glass before beginning again.

"What about Ray?"

"He didn't have any reason to. He's always found a cleaner way to make me suffer." George looked away.

Jules would have given a lot for what was being left out. "Did you inherit anything from your mother?"

"A bunch of money. I don't need it now. I needed it ten years ago so I could leave that bitch. Not giving me the ranch was my mother's last shot at giving me a spanking."

"Ada Santoz?"

"We're still fond of each other." He peered into his empty glass and gave Jules a sidelong, hopeful glance that he ignored. "We ran into a little problem, and now we're in a bit of a lull."

Outside the window the sun was shining and the hospital lawn had taken on a vaguely green tint. Jules wondered how many lies had already multiplied in the air. "Anybody else want to kill you?"

"Not here, and no one who cares enough to come all the way up from L.A."

"Anybody at Biddle & Rake?"

"Those guys brought me this bottle. They said they felt bad that they hadn't locked the new offices."

"The lady who left her slip behind in your bedroom?"

"I wouldn't even know who to return it to."

That didn't exactly answer the question. Jules stood up. "Ex-employees?"

George giggled. "Only Alice, but she doesn't even want to *think* of me anymore. I've always been a good boss. Really. Ask around." George spread his arms wide. "Make sure everyone knows who's in charge, give bonuses, buy drinks from time to time, and you can't make an enemy. You should try it with your deputies."

Jules nodded. He left with a distaste for all things Blackwater, but on his way back to the station he bought two dozen donuts—enough for everyone, including the prisoners.


**ALICE** Wahlgren stood in front of the refrigerator of the small stucco house on Fifth Street she shared with Peter, drumming her fingers on the open door for a full minute before she remembered she was looking for shallots. She found only three in the lower drawer, sprouting and rotten, and slammed the door hard enough to rattle the pile of china platters on top. She sat down in front of the list on the table, scribbled for a moment, then stared out the window at the garden, still bare soil with some specks of green on marked-out rows, the budding trees, the other houses on the block and the mountains behind them, lost again to the chore at hand until the stockpot foamed over and drowned the gas flame. She swore, relit it, and started another clean list:

*Trout Unlimited Banquet, May 5, Final Menu*

Alice brought her head down onto the paper, picking up a little of the fresh ink on her nose. Trout Unlimited was a worthy, earnest organization, devoted to protecting local waters and pure strains of trout in the hope that its members could fly-fish for eternity. The members were wealthy on average, but cheap compared to the less WASPy, more bloodthirsty members of Ducks Unlimited, and there was no earthly way to make money off the debacle. Ada, who'd never fished a day in her life but was banquet chair, would continue to quibble over the use of items as expensive as cream for the game-hen sauce, chanterelles for the trout, shallots for the steak pies. So Alice would pay for the difference, because she couldn't bear to not use them. Game hens and farm-raised trout were boring and expensive enough, but Ada liked tidy little packages, and said that whole hams or roast beef or sides of salmon sounded messy and smelly. Alice liked messy and smelly.

It always came down to the same problem, at least according to Peter: Alice didn't like working for other people, couldn't work obediently for people. To put it politely, she didn't take direction well. She always thought she was right, and couldn't fathom people who wouldn't spend money for food; she classed them with people who would rather simply shoot a wounded dog than take it to a veterinarian, or people who wouldn't buy their children books, or people who believed right-wing, obese television commentators.

When she'd first moved to Blue Deer she'd been hired for a series of gallery caterings, and mistaken the budget for the whole series—$150—as a cheapish budget for the first event. The ladies couldn't believe their luck at the initial party, but were stuck with potato chips thereafter, while

Alice was stuck working for George. Admittedly, in Blue Deer, she had yet to meet people like the Upper East Side couple who'd thrown a party for their son's second birthday. White walls, not an onion to be found in the kitchen, red leather furniture, and an anorexic mother, also dressed in red leather, who ate only whipped cream. Half a dozen toddlers and a dozen parents lounged about, sullen despite the hundred-a-head spread. The birthday boy himself was miserable and vicious and spent most of his time ramming the other tykes with his new Swedish tricycle, ignoring a spare bedroom stacked eight feet high with FAO Schwartz boxes. Alice, a little detached from a long shift on cocaine, thought the saddest note was that Mom and Dad hadn't wrapped a single present themselves.

She had always worked hard, if grouchily, and it helped that she was now at least nominally self-employed again after serving under a succession of assholes for the last decade. Any desire to turn down a job when she disagreed with a client, even those who requested pigs in blankets, was deeply self-destructive—they needed the money, badly. Peter did all right at the *Bulletin*, and had begun writing book reviews for two magazines on top of his newspaper duties when Alice quit George and left them in the lurch. Alice tried to drum up cooking magazine and editing work by half-heartedly calling old bicoastal cronies, but it was apparently difficult for friends in Los Angeles or New York to believe that anything resembling thought or cuisine could take place in the state of Montana. Surely Alice would prefer to open a dude ranch or a B&B or a restaurant, maybe even a plant nursery, or move east or west, where her friends would be happy to pony up a hefty salary to revamp tired kitchens. Alice, though, took independence only so far—she'd rather be shot than open her own business and give up her life. She liked time off. So she'd gritted her teeth and buried herself in the Blue Deer social circuit, and had been hired for three jobs immediately, T.U. being the third.

She steeled herself and dialed the newspaper.

"Problems?" asked Ada.

"No," said Alice, already pissed off. "Questions and options."

"With two days to go? I gave you the budget. Go wild."

Jesus, thought Alice. Spare me. "If we cut the Jell-O you requested, we could serve another appetizer."

"These people expect Jell-O. Call it aspic."

"Never mind," said Alice. Both she and Ada were using their best midwestern metallic twangs now. "You'll have tomato aspic. I got your message on the answering machine."

"Good," said Ada.

"I've told you several times that service isn't included in the plate bid. It's spelled out in the agreement."

"That just isn't how it's done here."

Alice felt a nightmare settle down over her head. Ada was rivaling the worst Fifth Avenue dragon lady, outdoing theater prima donnas, interior decorators, and Fortune 500 WASPs who'd never peeled their own shrimp. Alice would have enjoyed serving the aspic in the form of a death mask, if only Ada would have sat still for the fitting.

"I know quite well you haven't been here all your life. I put it in writing, you signed it, and it's absurd to think it would be otherwise. Headcount times eight dollars—that's a joke, anyway—including everything but booze, linens, settings, and waiters. It *does* include my labor, and anyone I'll need to hire to help with actual cooking. You'll have to pay the servers directly at the end of the night, and they'll expect a tip."

Ada was silent. Alice imagined her next comment and pushed on, even angrier. "So is the head count still a hundred ten?"

"More like one twenty-five. Up to one fifty."

"If you want game hens—" she wanted to say little itty bitty tasteless birds "—and other neat packages you have to give me an accurate count. I'll do five extra, no more."

"I can see why Peter starts a day looking exhausted," said Ada.

Now I know why he comes home looking like he's been kicked in the head, thought Alice. "What's the count?"

"I've got to go," said Ada. "Someone's waiting to see me. Someone important."

"Ada, I have to add to the order. What's the count?"

"I'll give it to you when I give you the seating chart."

"You're doing a chart for a hundred and fifty people at eight dollars a head?" Alice was screaming into the void, because Ada had hung up.


**MONDAY** was one of only two full days Peter Johansen usually spent at the *Blue Deer Bulletin*. It always seemed like a waste of time. He wanted to work out of his own house—he inevitably got more done there—but Ada Santoz had insisted, and Ada almost always got her way. Five years ago, she'd wanted a divorce, and her husband had quite conveniently chosen to die; she'd wanted her own newspaper, and the inheritance was handy. Now she wanted to keep tabs on Peter, watch him earn his money, and she perhaps enjoyed encouraging the resentment of the rest of the paper's staff, people who slogged through forty hours for the same pay she forked over to Peter, the hotshot from *Newsday*, for exactly sixteen spent on the premises and a total of three pieces a week. This didn't mean Peter made a lot—Ada paid the rest of her staff about $4.50 an hour, with a maximum of $6.00 dished out to her long-suffering managing editor. It was criminal and profitable, but the *Bulletin* had a monopoly, and a few disgruntled workers weren't going to shake sales.

Now he was slogging through past clippings on the last few timber sales on local drainages, most of them sold by the Forest Service for a loss. Despite the braying of the state's conservatives, Montana was simply too dry on the eastern foothills of the Continental Divide for most stands of spruce and pine to earn out, and it took eighty to one hundred years for any tree to reach an appreciable size. But the sales continued on public lands, and Blue Deer was dotted with neon green and pink signs proclaiming, "This Family Supported by Timber Dollars." Since Blue Deer also lacked much in the way of social strata, the local eco-faction—the tree huggers—usually tried to keep a companionable silence with their drinking buddies and pool partners, who more often than not stripped bark or stacked studs at the local mill. Everyone knew where everyone else stood, but they tended to save the firepower for rancorous county meetings and letters to the editor.

Peter didn't particularly want to write this story, at least not now. It had been written by better writers than him, quite often. But he'd pitched Ada on a series about the gradual trashing of the area, and she wanted the timber sales to come before the questions of subdivision—the breaking up of larger ranches into twenty-acre ranchettes—or zoning, or the sump of oils and solvents the railroad company had left behind when they closed down Blue Deer's machine shops, or the current, albeit minor, population explosion, of which Peter and Alice were admittedly a part.

Ada wanted to start out with a bang, and Peter knew she also wanted the first salvo aimed directly at her most recent former lover, the manager of the mill. George Blackwater, another former lover, would get his comeuppance in the population piece, for the town tended to either blame or thank George for luring various writers, directors, artists, and actors into their midst, a cache of wealthy fun-seekers who rarely stuck it out for the winter and who therefore managed to avoid the state's income tax. No matter that most of the people moving in, like Peter and Alice, were a tad humbler than the matinee idols with four sections of land in the valley—everyone new seemed to come from New York or California, and that was that. When Peter first arrived he'd often tried to point out that no one in their right mind wanted to stay in either of those states, and that Montana had a long way to go before it reached the status of Queens or Anaheim. But after three winters he felt proprietary, local, and the sight of yet another former bonds specialist, discussing renovation while dining *en famille* with color-coded kids and wife at the Baird Hotel, made him queasy.

So did Blue Deer's bloodless, craven realtors, good ol' boys from the class of 1970, who were the human equivalent of dirty April snow, replete with melting dogshit. A tree was there to cut down or piss on, and a cow, translated into as many steaks as possible, was the popular equivalent to a painting of a weeping Jesus on the parlor wall. The Yellowstone River, the longest undammed watercourse left in the lower forty-eight states, had banks simply so houses could be built on them, and water so the lawns would look nifty and the aforementioned cattle could pack on some extra weight. The state's politicos and captains of industry had dreamed up the tag line, "Land of Many Uses," without considering that at least some of the population would simply add an "Ab" before the last word.

Peter selected eight clips and carried them back to the desk Ada had provided for him. It faced a window—another point of envy—and he looked up to see Alice chug by in the Mazda pickup. He waved but she was oblivious; even though the window was closed he could tell she had the manual choke open too far, and he cringed. Bringing it up later wouldn't get them anywhere, and he decided, as usual, to let it drop. Alice was proud of the fact that she could even start the thing, and it had only cost $700. In Blue Deer, and in most of Montana, this was a perfectly reasonable price for a car that worked. No rust, no salt, a scarcity of other bumpers to knock against. Houses were cheap, too—theirs had cost $30,000, about two years' worth of New York rent. Not that they'd have come up with the money for a down payment without his parents' help.

Peter started in on the clips, then gave up and looked out the window again. After a moment he noticed that his co-workers had begun to snicker quietly, a sound just barely discernible over the hum of computers. Peter craned his head, thinking that they'd been watching him stare out the window. Instead he saw Ada through the glass wall of her office, gesturing violently and noiselessly at Jules Clement, who nodded as if he was being laced with a series of sharp punches. This went on for several minutes before Ada seemed to ask Jules a direct question, and Jules shrugged. Ada touched her finger to the glass, and pointed directly at Peter, who was gawking at them. Jules scratched his head and peered at Peter under his hand, with the squinty look of a five-year-old who realizes his fib isn't floating. The glass door slammed open, nearly taking out the AP editor, and Ada hissed across the room.

"Please come into my office, Mr. Johansen."

Peter smiled innocently at the fascinated staff and tried not to shamble on his way into the office. The door crashed closed behind him, and Ada put herself six inches in front of his chin. Jules stuck to the other side of the room and busied himself with the tie of his uniform. Peter hoped it was too tight.

"Why would you be interested in spreading gossip about my love life?"

Peter considered her double meaning. He hoped she wouldn't be that nasty. "I was answering a question about George Blackwater's love life. I didn't think you'd want me to lie."

"You did lie. I've never told you of any such liaison, because I never had such a liaison." Ada's Shaker Heights shellac was in danger of cracking. Her normally porcelain skin was pink, and her Chanel-style suit no longer fit her expression, the sort you might see on a female mud wrestler. Peter dug in for the battle.

"George told me. Anyway, it was common knowledge— you two were always out together. Jules didn't just get it from me."

"George Blackwater would say he slept with the Lakers cheerleading squad."

"George probably has slept with the Lakers cheerleading squad."

"As if you should talk."

"Ada . . ."

She blew. "Don't fucking 'Ada' me."

Jules, looking deeply confused, caught Peter's eye, and Peter stared out the window over Ada's blond head. He wished fervently, not for the first time, that he hadn't gone to bed with her. Only once, but once looked like it would be enough for revenge.

"Did you tell him who else I slept with?" she demanded.

"I don't know who else you've slept with. Why don't you stick to the point and answer his questions?"

Jules noticed the vein beating at Peter's temple and decided to step in. "Mrs. Santoz, why don't you just tell me when you and George started up, and broke things off, and give me a rundown on the present nature of your relationship. These are routine questions. You're not the only one I have to see on this matter."

"I'm sure," said Ada, backing off with a final filthy look in Peter's direction. "Please have a seat." She shut her eyes for a moment, trying to get the blond angel look back in place as she headed for her chair.

"Would you like Mr. Johansen to leave?" Jules's voice

was very soft, but a smile tugged on one half of his crooked face. Peter wondered if he'd ever started laughing in the middle of an interview.

"I don't mind him staying." Ada smiled back. "He might be able to help me remember some details. How is George, anyway? Any lasting damage?"

"No, not really. He'll go home in a couple of days."

Ada twitched slightly at the word "home." Peter watched Jules watch her, and tried to read his mind.

"Good," said Ada. "Well now, George and I saw each other off and on from about two years ago till February or so. I'm sorry I misled you, Sheriff Clement—"

"Call me Jules."

Peter thought of Jules's current unhappy monasticism and hoped he wouldn't have to beat some sense into him.

"Well, though my husband is deceased, George is married, and I'd hate to cause problems for him. He has plenty already."

"Are you referring to his marriage?" Jules looked demure.

"His marriage, his mother, work, all sorts of little knots. George is always in a state of crisis. He's always in a snit about something," Ada was enjoying the explanation. "If he doesn't have a worry, he'll create one. He *wants* people to feel sorry for him. He makes the most of being miserable."

"He didn't shoot himself, ma'am."

"I wouldn't put it past him. Though I want to make it clear that we parted with few hard feelings."

"George suggested there were none. He was fond of you but circumstances changed."

"Circumstances." She snorted, an inelegant touch. "Not to make myself a suspect, but no apology could cover the things George did to me."

"Another woman?"

"So I gathered."

"Who?"

"Ask George. He's an arrogant prick. He'd love to tell you. He's never kept a thought to himself in his life."

Jules doubted this. "Do you know his brother Ray?"

"I've met him, but that was back when Paul was alive. He happened to call last night, a pleasant surprise. He's a charming man."

"There's a little misunderstanding about the ranch house."

"I heard about that." Ada smiled, a real, heartfelt grin. "Where on earth will George take his ladies now?"

"I don't know if he loved the place just for convenience." Jules liked tangents too much to be a good questioner, but tangents, in his limited experience, paid off.

"Let me tell you something," said Ada, leaning toward the sheriff. "If George has a soul, I never found it. He used that house as his soul. He'd say, look at this beautiful place I love. Ergo, I must be lovable. How will he pretend to have a soul if he's stuck in that cardboard shitpile with Mona all the time?"

My, my, thought Jules. The things I miss in this town. He didn't bother with her rhetorical question and gave them all a moment of silence. It seemed to make Ada nervous, and she doodled on some printouts while he studied her. Peter had told him that she'd received an M.A. in psychology in her youth, that she'd ditched her true calling for the greater desire to bully a staff, and Jules found the story believable. She was pretty, in a wiry, inbred sort of way. George was obviously capable of veering away from large models on occasion.

He sighed and went back to the basics. "Could you tell me where you were on Sunday morning, at about eight?"

"Entertaining a guest in my home." Ada looked directly at Peter this time, and Jules shifted nervously. "No, Lonnie Biddle is the man you need to talk to, but please have some discretion." She shuffled some papers on her desk and gave Jules a little wave. "Good luck with your investigation."

Peter followed Jules outside to his car, and noted that he was parked by a fire hydrant.

"Rather than suggesting you see a shrink, I'll just ask one question," said Jules, drumming his fingers on the hood and looking vaguely in the direction of the Crazies. "Is everyone in this town bumping uglies on a nightly basis?"

Peter rubbed his forehead. "I think you've just located a few hot spots."

"I see," said Jules. "Anything to add?"

"I thought Biddle was Mona Blackwater's main flame."

"Jesus Christ." Jules climbed in, waved through the bug-splattered windshield, and peeled away from the curb. Peter walked back inside very slowly.


**JULES** knocked, once again, on Mona Blackwater's front door. The inside door opened, but she left the screen in place. She was packed, sausage-style, into striped stretch pants and a short T-shirt. The inch-wide gap at her waist was not flattering.

"You're a persistent boy, aren't you?"

Jules would turn thirty-four on his next birthday, and wasn't feeling particularly boyish this afternoon.

"Mrs. Blackwater, as I've explained before, I have some questions, and I must insist that you attempt to answer them."

"Try me. You've got five minutes."

"Would you prefer to go down to the station?"

"No. Ten minutes, then." She tried to smile, too late. Jules stood stonily in the doorway, loathing her. He focused on her upper lip, then veered away from her frosty lipstick. He loathed frosty lipstick, too.

Mona took a step backward. "Okay, come in then. Can I get you a drink?"

"No thanks." Jules followed her and found himself in a huge room that was beige in every sense of the word. Ada's description came to mind—the house was an expensive pre-fab monstrosity, utterly characterless, the living room lacking a single piece of art, a book, anything. Mona gestured to a colorless couch and swung through a doorway, reappearing with a diet soda.

"I'd like you to tell me what you were doing downtown on Sunday morning, at about eight-thirty."

"I wasn't downtown. I was here, getting ready for church."

"Mrs. Blackwater, let's not be silly about this. People saw you downtown."

"They're lying. George has turned so many people in this town against me." She smiled and adjusted the waistband of her pants. Jules could almost hear it squeak against her skin. He smelled bad wine, but maybe she wore it for perfume. "Ask my children. I never leave them home alone. Ask my pastor. We go to Saint James Episcopal Church, the ten o'clock service."

"I stopped by at nine forty-five to tell you your husband had been shot, and you weren't exactly dressed for church." He said it calmly, flatly, with a slightly vicious emphasis on the last phrase.

"I was running late. I *was* late, thanks to you."

"Is it possible you were visiting a friend earlier? Mr. Biddle, for instance?"

"I don't have any legal work at present. Maybe soon, if George keeps his crap up." She lit a cigarette blithely and took a series of long puffs.

"What crap? Getting shot?"

She ignored his stab at humor. "Same old stuff, and fucking around."

"Anyone in particular?"

"No. Not since he gave up Mrs. Santoz. Though how would I know?"

How indeed, thought Jules. "Are you a good friend of Mr. Biddle?"

"No." She located an overflowing ashtray and stubbed out the cigarette.

"Do you get along well with your brother-in-law?"

"Seems like it, doesn't it? Believe me, I know I married the wrong brother."

Jules wondered if she ever let down her ferocious, paranoiac guard. Maybe George, so apparently relaxed, made all his women this way. "Perhaps Ray agrees with you."

She looked surprised. "What do you mean?"

"He has a photo of you, down at the ranch."

The blush of pleasure that traveled over her face was honest, and almost made him sad. It also confused him. "Oh," she said. "I didn't know that."

"So there's no reason that Ray would have a grudge, want to shoot George?"

"Nothing current," said Mona, smiling sweetly, back on track. "They may not like each other, but they still spend time together. They usually get drunk together two or three times each visit."

"Does your husband have any rifles?"

"How the fuck would I know what he has?"

For a churchgoer, she sure had a potty mouth. "I would like to take a look, ma'am."

"Suit yourself. He keeps his toys in the basement."

"Would you mind if I walk through the rest of the house as well?"

She took a chug of soda and moved in the direction of the kitchen. "You can stick your funny nose wherever you want to."

So he did, and found nothing but dusty fly rods and a

disassembled shotgun. They apparently used a double bed, a simply amazing concept. Such bullshit reminded him that life was speeding by. When he finished the house seemed emptier than usual, and he looked out the kitchen window to see Mona sunning herself in a lawn chair next to a dry, leaf-strewn swimming pool. It was, all and all, a good thing that the Blackwater children were school-aged.

CHAPTER 5

BLUE DEER had been so named by the Crow tribe, not for
a romantic dream of indigo antelope, but because the railroad
workers stationed there had turned to whitetail and mule
deer for sport after the bison disappeared, and shot so many
that carcasses dotted the plains for miles along the tracks, the
bellies ruptured and blue in the hot light of the summer
prairie.

Jules used this story once during his most persistent
argument with Peter, one that had changed little over the
years since they'd started it in Ann Arbor. Peter claimed that
human nature was sweeter in the small towns of rural
America than in urban ghettos, that crime in a place like Blue
Deer shocked only by virtue of its rarity. He said that it just
stood out more, but Jules disagreed. It was the same old shit,

made crueler by a pastoral setting, by the violent who were oblivious to beauty, with less excuse than those who lived on Morningside Heights. The vertigo of the open struck constantly—half of the people who came to Blue Deer thinking to build a life had rooted themselves in the wind and absorbed the loveliness around them, and the other half had spun off into error and plain, stupid badness. It was possible that, proportionately, as many lives were ruined by whiskey and by pickup trucks and furniture sets bought on credit as were ruined by crack or the current drug of choice in the cities. Jules had grown up in Blue Deer—if he was capable of forgetting sordid details about its citizens, it was because he wanted to forget. Peter had been raised in a small town, too—Patagonia, Arizona—but he'd left, and he'd never come home to the ugliness his old friends might have been capable of. Blue Deer was new to him, and he could pretend to be innocent. Peter had, after all, given up the law after a tentative year of practicing in Montana, largely to maintain this innocence, after umpteen custody cases, protective orders, and broken paroles; two-year-olds with vaginal abrasions, five-year-olds who wept constantly and shat their pants, parents who drank antifreeze. Montana was second in the nation in child and spousal abuse. In his first few months on the job, Jules had seen children with cigarette burns running up their spines, and a woman with bitten-off ear lobe and brain contusions that made her as punch-drunk as a hardened boxer. The first autopsy he'd witnessed had been on a sixty-year-old beaten to death, finally, by her husband of forty years. The only real surprise had been the kitchen utensils they'd found in her vagina.

This being the nature of things, it was hard to give a shit about the healing holes in George Blackwater, or to want to know who had put them there. Axel Scotti showed token curiosity, and the county commissioners muttered to Jules about violence in their fair city, but George, mending away and flirting with nurses, didn't seem to care who'd done it, and no one who should have cared for him was interested in being helpful. Lonnie Biddle, when finally tracked down, gave neither of his love interests, or George's, an alibi—he said he hadn't met Ada or Mona that morning, at his new office or at his home; that neither of them had a key, and that, in fact, he'd never known either woman in the biblical sense. This was plainly bullshit, but Jules put Biddle aside for a rainy day. Privately, he would have staked his house deed on Ray Blackwater, who never seemed to be at his prize ranch, as the man behind the gun, but he let other things trouble his sleep.

So he spent most of Tuesday finishing the paperwork for April and training a new officer, an acne-mottled young pup named Jonathan Auber whose very walk, not to mention driving ability, filled Jules with pity and mild despair. On Wednesday morning he swung by the high school and drank a pot of coffee with John Dribnitz as the principal took him through the senior class list, both of them morose because the weather was gorgeous, sunny and seventy before noon, and this somehow heightened the trouble index. About half of the class Dribnitz described had the potential for damage to self and others, which left Jules with twenty-four loose cannons and as many places for them to comfortably commit suicide. He'd asked Jonathan and Harvey to quiz any likely underclassmen and parents for possible locations, but this had been predictably unsuccessful. The junior class, half of which would undoubtedly join the seniors by nighttime, treated the party site as the darkest, most sacred secret imaginable, understandable as most had no grasp on birth, death, marriage, or divorce despite unhappy firsthand experience. But there were three people on the senior list whose families owned sizable ranches, and three of those were especially promising; if Jules banked on things never really changing, he could look at these three ranches first, with the idea that a really good orgy, a true wallow, required space, a varied landscape, and private property. In each case the parents claimed to know nothing, but also confirmed that there were older, distant houses and other crannies on their property.

Jules sent Jonathan, who was only twenty-two but hadn't, unfortunately, attended high school in Absaroka County, out to the least promising ranch, a bit of beautiful grass near some old hot springs east of town. He found nothing, the weather evidently too fine for heated water to be an attraction. Ed Winton checked out an old log bunkhouse in the foothills of the Crazies, an easy walk from Horse Glacier and a small lake; he'd volunteered for this duty because he said he liked to walk and, as the oldest man on the force, needed the exercise. So Ed, who had a substantial stomach and crippled knees, got to spend three hours in the spring sunshine, romping and daydreaming in sylvan glades, without ever seeing another human. Jules kicked himself and headed out to the Boskirk ranch, fifteen miles south of town in the valley, after an afternoon spent doling out traffic tickets and discussing budgetary concepts with the mayor.

Somewhat to his regret, he found what he'd been looking for. The advantage, at least, was that he could park on the other side of the river and see them without ever being noticed. He didn't want to stop them, but he wanted to know where to find them when they stopped on their own accord. The cars—an incredibly varied assortment—were parked on the bluff above the river, near a lone patch of cottonwoods and a sheep barn, and the seniors were a swarm on the beach and islands below, a stream of humanity running in and out of tents and the wide-mouthed cave halfway up the hundred-foot bank. Jules lay high on the opposite bank in the sun with binoculars, partially screened by a wild rose bush. Things were so sedate it was hard to pick out the half who'd be trouble, except for usual clues like the surly, stoned, weight-back walk of some of the boys, and the fact that he'd personally hauled a half-dozen of them down to the station at some point in the past. All but the shyest, the least adept at that cruel world, wore skimpy bathing suits, and a few of the bravest girls went topless on a spit a quarter of a mile downstream from the others. They tended toward rubbery blandness, with no interesting hollows or adult refinements, and Jules's attention quickly strayed to the river itself. He left when he knew he'd fall asleep if he stayed. The real mayhem wouldn't begin for hours.

After the Boskirk ranch sunshine he made a last, resentful attempt to clear up the case before finishing his report. The hospital told him George had been released that morning; the Blackwater's housekeeper/nanny, who proved to be Mrs. Ball, Jules's third-grade teacher, said that Mona was off having a haircut in Bozeman, and that George had been home for approximately five minutes before leaving again, but, yes, the couple planned to go to the Trout Unlimited Banquet that night. Ray's answering machine now carried a polite announcement that the author was en route to New York. And Peter said that Ada was already at the Elks Lodge, supervising the preparations for the banquet. Alice was surely thrilled.

Jules's Wednesday was complicated because he was in fact a member of Trout Unlimited. Sooner or later he'd need to become an Elk or a Moose or a Mason, or at least join Rotary, to be in keeping with his position as a pillar of the community. However, most of those clubs espoused vastly different philosophical views from his own, and also required nasty initiation ceremonies. T.U. was easy—he loved to fish, and could get away with hitting up friends for raffle tickets and attending three or four meetings a year. A good chunk of the town, at least that part of the town with disposable income, belonged, including Peter and Ed Winton and George Blackwater.

The logistics of handling such a night with a staff of four

were tedious. Jules had come on duty at eight in the morning and would go off at six for the banquet, though everyone knew he'd be back by nine or so to track down stray postpubescents. He didn't mind the idea of leaving the banquet, though he could have imagined far, far better reasons. Harvey had Little League that evening and was saved for after midnight, when Jules would double up with him if things were especially bad. Ed and Jonathan had each put in four hours during the day and planned on at least four that night.

At six they headed south to check out the Boskirk shindig for a last time in daylight and reported that the party had grown only mildly rambunctious; i.e., no one was swinging from a rope, vomiting, or rafting naked, though a sweet-smelling waft of air reached them on the far bank. Jonathan, who hadn't recognized the scent (this worried Jules) and was assigned to the twerps for the night, began to twitch expectantly when Ed brought it up, and Jules explained, in a roundabout fashion, that the sheriff's department had no interest in ruining the senior class's collective life for the sake of a few joints. Jonathan was to watch and listen from downstream and try to ensure that no one came to harm. Jonathan looked crushed until Jules pointed out that the night would also be rife with drunk drivers and Jonathan was welcome, indeed encouraged, to help himself to them. He could not lie in wait near the Elks or in any bar alleys, but he could cruise the main drags all he wanted.


THE ELKS basement, covered entirely by linoleum and acoustic tiles, smelled mostly of cigarettes and cheap perfume. Jules and Edie and Peter threaded through the room with their drinks, amusing themselves by bidding on stray silent auction items—fly lines and reels and bad art—and wondering over Ada's seating arrangement. She'd placed herself across from George and Mona, and next to Biddle. They were happy to have a separate table.

George himself was the ghost of Sunday past, gray and ghastly. He didn't seem to be drinking that much, but whatever he'd had was mixing badly with painkillers, and Jules wondered if the shoulder would open up if he keeled over. Mona, a bit larvalike in a cantilevered green silk thing, avoided her husband and acted frolicsome with other members of the male hoi polloi. Jules caught Biddle's eye when Ada, grim and pinched in putty-colored linen, put a death grip on the lawyer's arm and whispered in his ear. She headed to the kitchen several times and almost always came out again looking annoyed; once Alice came to the doorway and watched her go, looking smug and just a little vicious in her apron. Ada twice scanned the crowd and made for Peter; each time, Peter saw her coming and wove his way toward the bar or the men's room. Mona once seemed to track Ada, but hustled back to her table when the food arrived and people found their seats. Jules knew this good timing on Alice's part was completely inadvertent—the cook would love to see the matrons duke it out, though she'd probably prefer that it happen after the meal. And the food was quite good, considering. Alice had somehow managed to make little water-injected game hens taste like plump, buttery capons, and bland trout (he helped himself from Edie's plate, and she let him) taste wild and redolent of chives. Peter's steak and turnip pie tasted nothing like Dinty Moore.

The mood in the room seemed to go up a notch after dinner. The auction began and Jules watched the tables, bored by the dry-fly talk. He was relatively pragmatic about such snobbery, having grown up fly-fishing; so was Peter, who'd spent a small fortune on equipment before realizing the trout didn't necessarily care how much his rod had cost. Alice joined them, fairly happy, and Jules saw a small blush of pride cross her face when George came by to congratulate her on the meal and ask her opinion on an etching. He bid too much money for it, flicking away his wife's increasingly urgent hisses, waxing merry with Horace Bolan and two real-estate agents.

George won. Jules stopped paying attention and started arguing with Peter about one of the fishing guides in attendance, and whether he was or wasn't an asshole, until a hand on his shoulder brought him up short. Mona, quite drunk now, was using him for balance as she bent to speak to Edie. It was a little like discovering a large scorpion on your collarbone. Jules's forehead turned clammy.

"A little art for his little darling," whispered Mona.

No one moved.

"I'm talking to you," said Mona, tapping a finger on Edie's arm and digging her other hand into Jules's muscles for balance. "He told me it was a thank-you present for someone, and I said thank you for what."

Edie's face was pale and wary. Jules peered past Mona's meaty forearm at George, who rose and started to totter toward them.

"I said thanks for what, dear? A blow job in the hospital? A little roll in the alley? Maybe a boff on the car hood."

"Mona," said Alice, "it may surprise you, but most sane people don't have any interest in seeing George naked."

"Hah," said Mona. "Where's your tray? Maybe he just unzipped his fly for you."

Peter covered his eyes with his hands and Alice twitched. "I used to be a curious girl, but I was never that curious."

Jules pried away Mona's hand. "Go sit down." George was behind them now.

"Don't fucking tell me what to do, hotshot." She bent until her nose was two inches from his face, displaying endless, rough-textured cleavage, but George reached her before she spoke, and jerked her back a step with surprising strength.

"Mona," said George. "Come with me. The print was for you."

His wife expanded like a het-up Siamese. "Boy, buster, do I have the goods on you. I know what you're up to. If you don't want to talk about these cows why don't we just talk about Ada, or Bobbi, or that drip Sally, or your waitress, or maybe we should talk about poor Jane, you dumb prick."

George turned a shade greener, and Jules was up, piloting the unwieldy Mona back toward her seat next to Horace Bolan, who watched, appropriately full of dread. In the background the emcee was trying, somewhat haltingly, to start bidding on a fly rod.

"I get to offer you a ride again," said Jules softly. "Behave or we're leaving."

"Screw you."

He nudged her in the direction of the door, keeping up a fast tango, and saw one of the waiters collar Ed, who headed to the phone. "Let's go then," said Jules. "Come sit in my nice cold squad car and we'll get to know each other."

She stiffened and brought them both to an abrupt halt. "Skip it. Get your hands off me. I'll mind my manners."

"Congratulations," said Jules, slapping her large white back. Ed was waving to him now. Jules wanted a drink, and sensed he wouldn't be having another for quite a while. Ed looked unhappy and handed him the phone.

"What's up?"

"Well," said Jonathan, sounding fuzzy and far away. "I dunno but I heard someone puke and one girl started singing, not in a normal way, and now they're fucking with these chains up on the cliff by the cars, so I guess I'd say things are kinda heating up."

"Chains," said Jules.

"Yep," said Jonathan, happy that the word was impressive. "They were tying one to an old truck when I left to call you."

"Ah, crap," said Jules. The supermarket owner's wife, waiting for the phone, frowned at him. He scowled at her and she retreated. "I'll be there in ten minutes."

Which meant that he hit one hundred, no sirens but lights, when the highway straightened out, and ran very fast when he pulled up next to Jonathan's car, parked on the party side of the river near a sheep shed. The moon was full, but he still stumbled over tussocks of grass before he groped for the flashlight on the police belt he'd strapped over his khakis, all the while heading toward the shrill sound of Jonathan's raised voice. Jonathan sounded terrified, and this terrified Jules, especially as he gradually made out other voices, some weeping. He came over a rise and saw a crowd standing in headlights by the edge of the cliff, Jonathan on his hands and knees, peering over. Two chains were looped around the cottonwoods, one snapped, the other taut and squeaking on the rocks at the edge of the cliff. In another ten seconds he was next to him, trying to make out the shapes below.

"Ah fuck, I saw it, but I was too late." said Jonathan. "Two of them jumped out of the truck, but she couldn't get out of the Volkswagen in time."

"When?" Jules could just make out the lump of a dark, battered Volkswagen thirty feet below, hanging from the taut chain, the groaning cottonwood.

"Now, just now. I think she's still in the car."

"We were seeing if we could pull the trees out," said a peevish, quavery voice behind them. "We brought the cars down specially for it."

Jules told Jonathan to call for an ambulance, collared two large, glandular types, told the others to stay put, and scrambled down the cliff path. Chicken, the time-worn suicide game, had never made his roster of potential nightmares, especially chicken played with trees and chains. The truck lay on its nose in the gravel at the bottom of the bluff; the

Volkswagen dangled eight feet from the ground, the girl flopped over the open door, hair swinging gently.

"It's Maribeth Arnhold," said one of the football players. "She's pretty heavy."

She was heavy, thought Jules. He wanted to beat their heads in on the ruined truck, but would have to use them first. He climbed up on the largest idiot's shoulders and had the other hold his flashlight. He touched the girl gingerly, trying not to think of the links of creaking, rusted chain, and found a pulse. Jonathan joined them, panting, and after he'd climbed onto the other boy they lifted the limp girl off the door, retreated, and lowered her to the ground with difficulty.

After the ambulance came, and they struggled back up the cliff with the stretcher, they took names, determined who could drive, and pocketed the rest of the keys. Jonathan climbed down to the beach, shouted an all clear, and Jules shot the chain on the tree, standing well away as it sang past him, enjoying the solid crunch of the Volkswagen smashing to the gravel. They made a last search for stragglers and found two juniors in the sheep shed, not just out cold but comatose. Jules threw the boys into the back of his car, left Jonathan to do a final inventory of license plates, and was actually relieved when both idiots started to vomit halfway to Blue Deer.

JULES was standing in the hospital hallway, just where he'd been standing for George only three days earlier, when Ed came down the hall and handed him a T-shirt.

"Time to get out of here," said Ed. "They said she'd be fine. Go wash up and I'll buy you a drink."

Jules allowed himself to be piloted into the bathroom. He stripped off his now rust-colored white shirt and tossed it in the garbage can, then stared at the dark blots on his blazer and tossed it as well. He wiped his face and scrubbed his arms, put on the T-shirt, and wandered out into the hospital parking lot where Ed waited with the engine running. The air was crisp, and it cleared his head.

"Why didn't you ever take this job?" asked Jules.

"Need you ask?" Ed rolled down his window and lit half a gnawed cigar. It smelled delicious. "Don't kick yourself. Blame it on the full moon."

"How'd the banquet finish up?"

"Don't ask."

"Just tell me. Then maybe I can sleep."

"Mrs. Blackwater is still at the station, unless someone claimed her. She cooled out for about a half hour, then kicked into gear again, threw a chair at Mrs. Santoz. The woman needs to dry out."

"Did the chair hit Mrs. Santoz?"

"Nah, hit the wall. She wanted to press charges but I told her to shut up. They did this once before."

Jules eyed him blearily. "They did?"

"Yep. Depot ball a few years back. They were partners in some gallery and stopped getting along. They beat each other silly, got blood on their nice dresses. That time they spent the night together with Archie in the basement."

Ed hummed, cruising slowly down the streets with his cigar arm out the window. Jules watched the small houses slide past them in the dark. Very few people still had their lights on.

"Just like the last mudbath," said Ed, pulling up a block from the Blue Bat. "This is my déjà vu night."

"Like Mona?" Jules felt for his wallet and was relieved to find it in his pants. The bank clock said 1:10, temperature 48°F, May 6. It was someone's birthday, and it troubled him that he couldn't remember whose.

"No, Mona was like Mona. I hope someone else gets her next time." Ed hauled his bulk from the car. "This is like the girl who died my first year on the force. She fell at one of these parties, too."

It was stretching things to say that Maribeth Arnhold had fallen. "Who?"

"Girl named Jane Semple. You know Nick? His big sister."

Jules could barely remember his own name. "What happened?"

"She went off a cliff in the dark, broke her neck, broke her skull like an eggshell. I had to help carry her out. No blood, but her head was all soft with sharp edges inside. Your dad gave me a week off, but I never got over it."

"Why didn't you tell me?"

"I thought you might remember, and if you didn't remember I didn't see a point in bringing it up. Same place, same time of year. I couldn't believe it would happen again."

They walked past the bowling alley and the air filled with dull thuds and yells. The moon was so bright that Jules could see colors, the spring green of the post office lawn.

"So this isn't so bad," said Ed. "Everyone said she'd be fine."

Jules thought of the still, blood-speckled, chubby face. He kicked an empty quart of engine oil, then stooped to retrieve it, looking for a trash can as they reached Fiske.

"Let's have two nightcaps," Ed said. "We'll bully Harvey into driving us home so we don't break the goddamn law."

Jules nodded and watched a woman walk out of the door of the Blue Bat and away from them after the briefest of glances. She was tall with long hair that glowed under the street lamp, and she moved with so much grace, on such slim legs and with such a fine pivot, that he wanted to scream wait for me and take me home and roll on me and remind me what it was I liked about life. He stopped on the sidewalk, staring after her, and Ed, who probably understood, had to push him into the bar.

## CHAPTER 6

**JULES** was up again at eight with an excess of adrenaline and a pinched feeling in his temples. At the station, things seemed strangely muted. Maribeth Arnhold was better, skull pressure abated, blood pressure up; the vodka and barbiturate princes who'd ruined his backseat were pumped even cleaner and sleeping quietly. Harvey, looking frail at the end of a long shift, told him Lonnie Biddle had bailed Mona out at three, and two drunken anglers, unfortunate enough to run into Jonathan after his skip-day trauma, had left by seven.

The day washed by with phone calls to the hospital and the school board and parents and the head Elk, who wanted to lodge a complaint about the hole Mona had left in his cheap plaster wall. Jules gave Peter an interview, suggesting that skip day, no longer good clean fun (he felt only vaguely sarcastic in saying this), be abolished in favor of a well monitored, educational trip elsewhere, maybe Idaho, maybe a week roughing it in Yellowstone. Anywhere would do—send the scholars to Guatemala, as long as it was out of his jurisdiction. Ed showed up looking gray and jowly, and Jules sent him home again; Jonathan bounced in, and Jules praised him and told him to nap up for the evening shift and night call. Jules went back to the hospital at the end of the day, watched the girl with the shaved skull sleep, scorched the boys with a lecture on stupidity and early death, and headed home, wanting a huge joint, a veritable spliff, for the first time in at least a year. It was bad form for a sheriff to buy dope, so he settled for a big shot of tequila and his down comforter.

Jules slept from eight o'clock on Thursday until ten on Friday morning, dealt with some mundane chores at the station, rented a bad comedy, and was back asleep by ten. But that night he had a dream, predictable in its horror. It began with a hailstorm. The balls of ice were blue and ripped holes through houses, but left everything else untouched, kissed trees gently, and fell softly to the ground at their bases. When the hail stopped the sun came out, and he had to leave his shredded house and drive to the river, where he slid down the bluff on small marbles of ice. At the bottom, standing unsteadily on a blue pile, he looked up to see a dark-haired girl hanging from a tree, glittering with melting hail. When he jumped to pull her off, he sank down and realized there was something rotten, something really blue beneath his feet, and the clean, new air gave way to a wall of smell, of death.

He woke, his head screaming with the pain of a migraine, and lay in the dark listening to the wind. His ceiling was in one piece—he could trace the usual cracks of the plaster in the dark—but the stink and the vision stayed with him.

Jules dreamt constantly, in Technicolor, and such nights

usually filled him with dread. He wanted to blame his migraines on hallucinogens in high school and college, but the feeling was older than that: He remembered dozing on the grass as a child, watching clouds and magpies, feeling his heart thump in a cave or near a tree or even in his cellar. His only accurate dreams were about the weather, and even these he tried to play down or turn into a joke, though he sometimes couldn't resist mouthing off at the bar. He hadn't had a glimmer of misgiving for the pig farmer, or George, or any number of unfortunates. The truly tragic incidents of his life, the death of his father and the death of a lover, had come upon him entirely without warning. The girlfriend had been loony and happy; they were driving, drunk, through mountains in eastern Austria one summer when they hit a freak blizzard. She screamed "snow!"—actually *"neige!"*—and started laughing so hard that she plowed into the back of a Mercedes semi and took off her head. Jules spent the next two months lying silent in a Viennese hospital bed with two shattered legs and a perfectly intact skull, wondering when and if his mind would ever make sense to him.

Lately, the feeling that he was coming apart at the seams had infected his waking hours. It was as if his eyes had little faulty sensors of doom, which switched on without warning. He was afraid that his mother would die soon, and the idea that she was healthy gave him no solace. He was afraid that his sister, happy in her San Francisco townhouse, would die in an earthquake. Sometimes when he saw a child he was terrified it would meet with an accident; sometimes when he drove across a bridge he was convinced it would collapse underneath the next driver. He'd even given up reading good fiction because he'd started believing everything he read, and couldn't bear to encounter pain or death in whatever world he'd immersed himself in. Mystery novels were okay—you went into them knowing that someone would die, and rarely found yourself caring. Jules knew he had to put a halt to such bullshit, probably by falling in love or going fishing on a daily basis, but he'd forgotten how to do the first, and didn't have time for the second.

ON SATURDAY night, Peter and Alice had a huge fight, a true ugly-award-winner. It began with Peter's critique of her behavior at the T.U. banquet, which had netted her all of $150, and moved on to her utter inability to like anyone she worked for. Alice suggested Peter had liked his current employer entirely too much, and they were off and running. The next morning when he woke she was gone, possibly venting her rage at a garden center. This didn't particularly bother him; he may have started the argument, but she'd upped the ante. This was how it usually went—he would say something mild, go on the defensive and add something stupid, and they would wrestle over the wrongness of what he'd said for some time. By the time he gave up apologizing and added to his crime, and Alice lost control and said something truly horrible—something lasting and crippling—Peter would have drunk enough to forget what she'd actually said and only remember the flavor of it. This was, in a way, a blessing. It allowed them to continue on, with apologies, for a solid week or month or two months of being careful with one another. But he knew it added up, and the funk of wondering when and if things might break compounded a hangover that resembled the beginning of stomach flu.

So Peter called Jules and browbeat him into going floating. He left Alice a note with a fairly enigmatic apology and the promise of a four-course dinner. The Mother's Day caddis hatch was due to start, and if the day stayed warm they might hit the beginning of it. Some friends had sent proscuitto and cheese from New York, and he packed the cooler with ice and beer and sodas. He drove down the valley to meet Jules with a quart bottle of Coca-Cola locked between his slightly numb thighs, the battered, hundred-dollar drift boat banging and creaking behind the Mazda.

The mountains looked surreal that day, a function, he was sure, of the light rather than damaged brain cells. For one or two months of the year this pocket of Montana achieved a true, vibrant green, usually beginning in late April or May, and it was always shocking. The Rockies are never quite as drab as the Midwest or the East in winter—the hayfields turn gold rather than olive, and dogwood and willow and aspen look garnet and yellow and silver when dormant, rather than the charcoal gray of a hardwood tree. But spring was still visceral in comparison, and the smell of water and wet dirt and cottonwood fluff was cool and sweet. Peter began to wake up, and yodeled along with a Grateful Dead song on the radio until the ridge to the west cut off reception from Bozeman. Fifteen miles south of Blue Deer he cut down a sharply graded dirt road and found Jules leaning against his truck, sectioning horse grass. They drove in companionable silence another ten miles upstream to the launch near the tiny settlement of Emigrant, where they unloaded the boat and bickered a little about who would row first, and which flies to use, and whether Peter was competent to make decisions.

Jules started out, his narrow face melancholy and his long arms slapping the oars in the water. He usually avoided every obstacle with enviable grace. Peter watched him flail for a while, and, when Jules nearly took the boat out on two successive logs, asked him what was wrong.

"Everything."

"Like what?"

"I had a dream about hail and dead bodies. We've locked up two wife-thumpers in the last two days and investigated one case of possible arson. And I shouldn't give a shit about who shot George, but if I'm already in a bad mood, I do."

Peter went back to casting. After a minute he squinted

up at the perfectly clear sky despite himself, wondering about the hail.

Jules rowed on, scraping the boat over some rocks. "My flying Volkswagen passenger, the salutatorian, is having trouble remembering her ABCs. I still hear my dead dog moaning at night, and no one loves me."

"You should throw out the dog bed." Marv, a sixteen-year-old Airedale, had died in January. "Alice thinks your clinging to his pillow is a sure marker of clinical depression."

"I want to get another dog when things quiet down."

"Get the new dog a new bed. I made some sandwiches. Maybe you're suffering the early stages of low blood sugar."

"Some days you have no soul."

"Maybe if you acknowledged that it's hard finding someone dangling from a cliff, just gave yourself a break, and watched where you were rowing, you could enjoy life. The little shit is overwhelming you."

"You're right," said Jules. "No death, no limb loss, just your average, unpredictable closed-head injury."

"You missed all the fun after you left the banquet," said Peter. He already wanted a beer, and it was only eleven. "Seeing that might have helped your sense of humor."

"Ed told me. What got Mona ticking?"

"She started in on Edie again, and Alice told her to shut up, to sit on it and spin, and for some reason Ada weighed in on Alice's side, told Mona that as hostess she'd have her ejected. That's when Mona threw the chair. So Ed stood up and asked Mona to calm down and she punched him in the face and he put her in a headlock and hauled her out."

"What did George do?"

"He watched. He mostly seemed drugged up, maybe a little offended because Alice had to repeat the line about no one wanting to see him naked."

Jules concentrated on rowing and began to enjoy it, the

tight muscles in his back and neck and arms unfurling with each stroke.

"I spent some time in the station yesterday."

"You need a vacation," said Peter. "You need a real life."

"Like yours?"

Peter blushed.

"Sorry, said Jules. "I matched some fingerprints, the sets we found in Biddle's new office."

"Who did they belong to?" asked Peter, missing a fish.

"Mona. Mostly on the floor, though. None on the windowsill." Jules smiled.

"Oh boy," said Peter. "Can I use it?"

"Use what?" asked Jules. "How on earth are you going to print that Mrs. George Blackwater, admittedly not a missionary's wife, left her fingerprints, her *palm* prints, on the hardwood floor of the office of the attorney she was regularly fucking, and was seen near the scene *before* two rifle shots struck her husband but somehow, rather artfully, failed to kill him?"

Peter's mouth clamped down and Jules pulled the boat into a pool under a high bank. Swallows flushed out of holes banding the top of the ridge and swirled angrily over their heads.

"How'd you get Mona's prints?"

Jules rested the oars across his legs and tilted his head back to watch the swallows. "Ed took them after the T.U. mess, and anyway he'd taken them once before, a few years ago, after another fight." He swung the right oar gently and motioned for Peter to cast, but Peter only looked at him, waiting. "That fight was with Ada, a real doozy according to Ed, and her prints were on file, too. Both of them were charged with drunk and disorderly, and Mona was also cited for assaulting an officer, that asshole Bunny McElwaine."

"So?" said Peter, ready to throttle Jules for more information.

"So Ada's prints match up with the last unclaimed set from Biddle's office. We found them all over the place, next to Biddle's. And some of them were on top of Mona's."

Jules pointed to a rising fish; Peter still ignored him. "Therefore you could also print that the attorney with whom Mrs. Blackwater has cavorted has been given an alibi by another woman, Mrs. Blackwater's husband's former mistress, who also left her prints on the aforementioned hardwood floor. Though the attorney denies being with either woman. The fun theory is that Ada and Mona were meeting each other."

Peter finally cast to and missed a rainbow, wondering if perhaps Ada, as the possible shooter, would want to move on to offing other former lovers. The palm print detail had brought back unfortunate memories. Jules met his eyes and started cackling as they rounded a bend. The river opened out and split, moving through flat plains; Jules moved the boat steadily and smoothly along the deeper channel, with Peter still casting along a riffle. Cows watched them from the muddy bank, and Jules lowed, causing the calves to skitter and eye him nervously. He dropped the oars and stood up and gave a perfect wolf howl, and the calves stampeded, farting, back over an irrigation ditch. The boat rocked and Peter gave Jules a nasty look. He was having no luck, and his head was beginning to hurt. The river shimmered, and he'd forgotten his sunglasses. His voice cracked when he spoke.

"Let's pull over and eat."

Jules rowed along the west side, looking for a break in the cottonwoods; he pointed and Peter saw three dogs circle a brushpile downstream. Jules howled again and they spooked, baying at the boat and circling, not wanting to give ground.

"I'll head past them. They've probably found something stinky."

"This is fine. Just pull in."

"I don't like those dogs, and I'm sick of spending time on Mr. Boskirk's property."

Peter looked downstream and saw the bluff in the distance. "Just pull in." He was suddenly desperate for food. Jules gave him a hurt look before grounding the boat on a sandbank fifty yards down, and Peter jumped out, not quite clearing the water, to drag the boat.

"Goddammit."

Jules swung onto the sand, keeping his feet dry. "Your depth perception is sadly lacking."

"Screw you."

The sandwiches resembled warped doughballs; Jules, who was skinny but tall enough at six three to weigh 180, had sat on them. He tried to point out that this would not affect the flavor. The potato chips had been pulverized. Peter opened a beer and swatted at an early mosquito, wondering why biting insects always preferred him, and how Jules could have missed the crunching sound of the chips dying.

"Those bugs like all the sugar that comes out of your skin after a big drinking night." Jules was drinking a beer, too, watching a heron slip up the river toward them, moving ten feet over the surface of the water. "Can I ask you a question?"

"It beats you reading my mind."

"Why do you hate George Blackwater?"

"I don't. I just got sick of him, got sick of Alice complaining about him, talking about him."

"Did they sleep together?"

"Jesus, Jules." Peter pulled some mashed bread off his proscuitto and swatted a mosquito on the side of his head. Jules had already finished his sandwich and was watching him carefully, his large brown eyes rust-colored in the sun. "No, that's not it. I just didn't like the way she'd work for him, take his advice, even though she said she despised him."

"He helped you both out a lot, right? When you first moved here?"

"Still does," said Peter. "He's fixed her up with half of her caterings. Not T.U. but one next weekend for Ray, and a big wedding this summer for some old friends."

"What does she think of Ray?"

"She thinks he and George deserve each other. Ray was always a real shit to deal with on the phone back when she worked with George, always telling everyone George owed him. She says between the two of them they've put most dysfunctional families to shame."

Peter started sorting through his flies. Jules tried to banish thoughts of the Blackwaters by lying down on the bank, in the sun, and instead thought of a girl he'd gone out with in Ann Arbor, right before he moved to New York. Her name was India, and this word seemed so dark and exotic that he managed to not fully take in the fact that she was a public-policy major. Her hair was long and straight and blond, and Jules could see the blue veins through her skin, all over her body. She thought her professors were all wonderful, and that the government was sane and competent and needed to be tough in the right places, and this point of view was so strange that Jules was charmed.

They were going to move to the city together, and headed to South Carolina first to pick up some furniture and meet her folks. After twenty-four hours in the Parrish family house, a dry-rot manse decked out with wisteria and dark portraits of men and women who all seemed to be in terrible pain, the exotic had become pale and claustrophobic and terrifying. India's mother corrected Jules's table manners and told him little people like his dead father were important to the state of the union; her girdle cut into her back and thighs under a flowing, flowered, nightmarish rayon dress. India's father, a crinkled-up, silvery ferret who hinted at a CIA career and listed innumerable dead Confederate ancestors with morose pride, doused him with whiskey and opined that starvation was a necessary cleansing mechanism for the third world. Jules began to remember his own mother's sole romantic advice: check out the parents to see what your beloved might become.

Three days into the stay Jules fell deeply in love with Lajean, the obviously mistreated maid; he felt honor bound to save her from her terrible fate. Two days after that Millie Parrish opened the summerhouse door to discover Jules driving himself into Lajean on the floor, his skinny, pale ass waving to her between long dark legs. Lajean smiled over his shoulder at Mrs. Parrish, and an hour later she and Jules were on their way to New York in his turquoise blue Chevy, a Montana heirloom. They lasted a year together, and the whole thing had made Jules very happy, almost as happy as the girl who died in the snowstorm had made him feel.

He felt a cloud pass over the sun and sat up; the hail would be right on schedule. He picked up his rod, tied on a caddis fly, and joined Peter down the bank. "Any luck?"

"Hell no. I don't know why I thought of doing this today. Those dogs are bumming me out. They probably have a calf."

Jules decided not to remind Peter that he hadn't been too hot on the dogs either. He put his rod down and walked upstream toward the dogs, feral and emaciated, whining with impatience and snapping at each other as they dug and circled. Only Harvey was on duty that day, so Jules, on call, was wearing his revolver; at twenty yards he pulled out the gun and fired into the air. The dogs backed away and began baying again. Peter joined him and Jules walked closer, plopping another bullet into the sand at the dogs' feet. They scattered into the trees and the river was quiet again. The pile of brush and rocks the dogs had staked out was surrounded by a clean area, and when Peter and Jules got closer they saw it had been carefully raked before the sand was trampled by dog prints.

"Maybe someone's trying to make a nice little beach area," said Jules.

"Boskirk buries his old cars in the river bank. He isn't into appearances. It's probably a calf."

"He throws them in the river. We're always citing him."

A puff of wind came up the Yellowstone and Jules shuddered. "I'm not looking in there. Something's going bad." His heart thumped and his nose was cold; he wanted to get back in the boat.

"Maybe I'll cover it up better." Peter walked closer, edging to the water side of the pile. He peered for a minute, then screamed and jumped backward into the water. Jules stayed where he was.

"Jesus, go look!"

"No."

"You're the fucking sheriff. Go look. There's a foot sticking out." Peter's arms windmilled around his body. "It's your job!"

Jules walked slowly up to the pile and looked down on the white and red and gray foot the dogs had pulled loose from the rocks. He pulled back a large branch and carefully moved some rocks to the side. He started to move another branch, really a small tree, but it wouldn't budge without disrupting more rocks. He looked at Peter, who still stood in the water. It started to rain.

"Come and help me. Go up there and lift it with me."

Peter went to the top of the pile and they carefully lifted the aspen to one side, then stood in silence. The wind gusted and some leaves blew off the body. Jules bent down and carefully removed the last few rocks. She was on her back—they saw thick, bruised legs and a muddy torso, with a canvas coat still on the arms and wrapped over the head. Her shirt and skirt had each hiked up, and her panties, ripped and too small, were askew. Ants hurried out of the woman's navel and pubic hair, making for the rocks below. Jules walked toward Peter, bent again, and very gently unwrapped the coat from the head. Her eyes and her mouth were open and dry; her neck was black, swollen, and indented.

"It's Mona," said Peter. He moved back a step and gagged.

"Yes," said Jules. He tried to make himself concentrate, look for something that meant something, but the sand was still raked and trampled, and he could only tell the obvious, that the woman had been strangled and stank and dogs had eaten part of her foot. He heard a growl over Peter's retching and looked into the cottonwoods, where they still sat and watched. The cows on the other side of the river watched too, and the magpies overhead looked down patiently. Jules brought out his gun and shot two of the dogs quickly and the third as it started to run. He'd only wounded it and had to climb the bank to shoot it in the head. He went back to the body to cover the face from the rain.

Peter crossed the irrigation ditch and started walking through the pasture to the road to flag someone down, and Jules started to search the beach, the rain dripping off his flattened hair and down his face.

CHAPTER 7

JULES saw what remained of his quiet existence hit the fan. He spent five hours in the rain by the river with Mona's body, two before Peter reappeared with Harvey and Horace Bolan, the only doctor they could find. By the next day his calm, clipped tones became squeaky and hoarse, making him feel like a nitwit when the state police called and he assured them the situation was under control.

It wasn't. George Blackwater's nanny said he was in Los Angeles, but no one could reach him at his usual hotel. Irv Ruddle, the county's medical examiner, was a very dim bulb after a stroke, and Horace said he wouldn't have any information on time of death for at least twenty-four hours. Jules couldn't quite understand this last, but didn't trust his own forensic training. He hated bodies, hated the morgue, and didn't push the issue. He'd taken two showers at the police station in the first hours after returning with Mona, trying to wash the smell off his body, before realizing that it was lodged in his brain, back there with his last fun dream. Horace had muttered something about looking for fly larvae on the body, checking out its age and type, but Jules had seen that article in the *New York Times*, not the cut-up AP version the *Blue Deer Bulletin* carried, and anyway it was too cold for common flies to be out yet. Surely caddis flies would hatch on something other than bodies.

Jules had a small block-printed sign on the bulletin board above his desk at the cop shop. It read, "Treadmill to Oblivion," a memento from college. A girlfriend who was a film nut saw it and told him it was a line from an old comedian named Fred Allen, and made him watch one of Allen's movies. Jules managed to not let this experience ruin his fondness for the sign. He'd never particularly liked working, though he'd worked all his life. He'd mowed lawns and sold lemonade as a kid, bussed dishes and worked on construction sites in high school; while in Ann Arbor he'd worked full-time at an Italian deli. During graduate school he'd put in weekends at Dean & DeLuca, hand-slicing salmon for beminked matrons, before he started his stint as a social worker.

Working was finally more interesting than taking classes, and he would never have run for France if the ramifications of this last job hadn't hit him full force during one muggy summer spent trying to seduce a woman who taught classes at the Marxist School, and whose sexuality was deeply ambiguous. One August night at two, following their prolonged and final wrestling match, he walked home to find his favorite client, a mildly psychotic father of five, waiting on his stoop. The man said, "I wanted you to be the one to mop me up. I like you." Jules stared, uncomprehending and a little drunk, as the man pulled out a kitchen knife and cut his own throat. Jules got on the boat two weeks later.

This is what he'd known but failed to consider when he ran for sheriff after a year spent daydreaming as he patrolled the long county highways: that in a town as small as Blue Deer, there may be less total violence, but the ratio remains the same, and knowing the stories behind the problems makes them sadder, less apparently soluble. That he had gone to school with half the dreck he would pick up for DUIs and domestic abuse and methamphetamine sales; that greedy realtors, petty commissioners and mail-correspondence lawyers would all pat him on the back and remind him of what a great guy his father had been, or what great teammates they'd been in the junior-varsity basketball game of February 1973, or how important their plentiful dollars were to the limping local economy. That some of the dumpy, bitter women he hauled in for bad check charges had been beautiful and sweet in the first-grade sandbox; that charging one person for anything would offend five friends, plus family; that becoming a cop meant that he would always be on the side of the prosecution, rather than the defense, and that if he softened his stance, ever, his staff would regard him with disgust. Out of four men with badges and three other staff members he was only the second Democrat, and certainly the only individual to have ever voted for a Socialist. He was also quite likely the only one to have done most of the drugs he charged people for, the only one not to believe in the death penalty, and the only one to feel unhappy every time a grizzly strayed from Yellowstone or a Glacier wolf was shot by a hunter.

So two years into this brilliant career his most constant thought was that he should have known better, that bringing to a small town the more liberal perspective of a life spent in the larger world would not result in happiness. He couldn't even be righteous about the difference—living in Blue Deer had its own demands, and who was he to claim the world was on his side? Much was made during the election of Jules's experience with crime in New York, and since he'd become sheriff the town had heaped praise on his head for the solution of small problems that really only called for a modicum of intelligence, common sense, and energy. Everything was relative—two decades of ingrates with badges made him look brilliant—but Jules was sadly aware of his lack of strategic know-how, his utter ignorance of how things worked in a small-town government, his complete remove in experience and sensibility from the other people in the town he'd grown up in, who'd voted happily for their prodigal son, the man of the world. It was easy to glide over these doubts when the pig farmer had been the height of gore, but a shooting and a murder and a damaged teenager made Jules feel like a sham and an egotistical asshole whose cover could be blown in a nanosecond if someone with a bigger badge walked through the door. He would soon complete the shift in Blue Deer's mind from the big fish from the little pond to the smartass who'd thought he was too good for the pond to begin with, and they'd want to throw him into the river mud like a gaffed frog.

He pressed on, regardless, to save his hide. Blue Deer hadn't had an unsolved homicide since the fifties, and twenty-four hours after the discovery of Mona the town fathers were already tapping on the station door, bleating about the tourist season and bad publicity. Jules had planned to spend Monday bullying Leonard Biddle about ladies' fingerprints, but now that relatively fun assignment, though possibly related, would have to wait. By noon on Monday Jules had tracked down George, who was due to fly in from Los Angeles that evening, under protest—he was terrified of flying and wanted to drive, despite his murdered wife. Jules insisted, and managed to keep his temper. He located Ray, who said he'd left town Thursday afternoon for a meeting with his editor in New York and would be back Tuesday night. He hounded Horace and told him he'd expect any possible autopsy information by eight that evening. He'd read a manual the night before and driven Harvey and Ed through the most professional search of their lives at George and Mona Blackwater's house, and found absolutely nothing but a lot of dirty laundry, two miserable children, and a confused ex-schoolteacher. He'd gone back to George's office and searched through his papers, sans warrant, as Edie watched in total disgust. He found nothing, but sat on the couch for a half an hour, examining the walls he'd helped her strip a week earlier, before deciding to give the scene of the crime a second try.

Jules crawled up and down the wet beach on his hands and knees, and made progress in one clump of trees on the bank  finding a pair of wire cutters  and in the ten feet of sand and gravel between the spot where Mona had been found and the water, where he found an earring and a square of onyx and gold, the top of a cufflink. Jules couldn't remember a thing about Mona's earrings, or lack thereof, but he remembered the topless stud he'd found in her coat pocket, along with some dirty tissues, a roll of Certs, and a scribbled name and phone number. He weighed the cufflink's meaning in his hand for a full five minutes, still on his knees in the soggy sand.

The dogs lay where they'd fallen, eyes cloudy, fur a little dulled, though the magpies seemed not to have started yet. He made the long walk back to the car for his shovel, and buried them deep, then washed his hands in the river and drove back to Blue Deer at a deliberate fifty-three miles an hour. It was almost, not quite, dusk; sun still hit the tops of the Absarokas, glancing off snow and gold and gray rock, but the sky had grown a darker blue, and he watched the broken clouds flow past the moon.

WHEN he reached town he picked up a greasy cheeseburger and a chocolate malted before calling the airlines to look into Ray Blackwater's New York odyssey. The return reservation checked out, but the lady at Delta told him that Mr. Blackwater had apparently missed his flight Thursday afternoon; after some searching she located him heading out at seven Friday morning. He called Ray's publisher and left a message on his editor's voice mail, asking her to return the call the next morning. At 7:30, he decided to jump the gun and bother Horace a little early, and asked Archie to send George to the hospital if he showed up at the station first. The station was connected to the courthouse and the firehouse, but lacked anything resembling a morgue, or cold storage.

Blue Deer Memorial Hospital was a funky, crumbling building, and the town was forced to renovate on a yearly basis to meet A.M.A. standards. Jules had been born there and had visited following numerous childhood misadventures; his father been taken there, already dead. The receptionist who'd been on duty for George's shooting was at the front desk again, the victim of a shift change. Jules winked at her and swung down the stairs to the basement, fighting down his usual dread of the dead. He caught Horace hunched over on a lab stool, his bald pate shiny and surrounded by a yoke of fuzzy black hair, munching peanuts, and staring at a slice of darkening lawn through a high, shallow window.

"Got the report?"

"It's not written yet, but I'll tell you what I know."

Horace offered him a peanut, but Jules was already regretting his dinner. "Why don't we start with when she died?"

"Maybe Friday. Maybe Thursday. You said she had a lot of stuff on top of her. She might've stayed cool for a while, but I wish to hell the weather hadn't been so warm."

Jules raised his eyebrows. Horace headed for the walk-in, pulled out a covered gurney, and whipped off the plastic sheeting. Jules shut his eyes momentarily, but when he opened them it wasn't so bad. This time he was at least expecting to see her, and the ants were gone and the eyes closed. Nasty stitchwork ran from her pelvis to her collarbone and around her partially shaved head.

"I sent her stomach and her brain to the state police lab. The coroner there said that he'll be able to estimate time of death from her stomach contents, and how long it might have taken her to die from the amount of brain hemorrhage and my information on her throat wound."

Jules wondered why Horace really wanted to know the latter. He'd thought the doctor would be able to handle the former himself, and gave an extra shudder at the thought of his diminishing budget. This was only the beginning of the end.

Horace caught him. "Sorry about the smell."

"Did you test for semen?"

"I'm pretty sure she wasn't raped."

"Send in a sample if you can't do it yourself." Jules made himself look at Mona's neck, which looked suspiciously well scrubbed, and found what might have been a snip mark under her ear. "Did you find any fibers there?"

Horace stared at him. "No."

"Did you look?"

Horace rubbed his head. "I think it was something pretty sharp, maybe wire."

Jules handed him the plastic bags with the cufflink top, wire cutters, and earring. "When you send in for the semen test, have them check this stuff out too, for fingerprints or whatever. Make sure you send the report along, so they at least know what to look for. Any fibers on her coat?"

"I didn't check. I don't know how to check." Horace opened a locker and pulled out the coat, fingering the collar through the mouth of the bag.

"Christ, Horace. Use gloves, okay? We should send this in too. Let me see it."

Horace handed him the bag and put his hands in his lab coat pockets. Jules felt vicious, but couldn't bring himself to care. Horace would be paid out of the same shrinking budget that would foot the bill for the tests; it would have served him right if Jules had hauled in the dogs and made the doctor search for fragments of Mona's toes. Jules put the bag down on the counter and looked at Mona's gnawed foot, then her hands.

"What does this mean?"

The fingers of the left hand were a little swollen and blue. "They're broken," said Horace. "I checked for tissue under her nails. Not a thing, and no scratches." When Jules looked mildly surprised he added, "Hey, I've read some mystery novels."

They both mulled over the educational properties of cheap fiction in silence. Jules wasn't about to admit he'd considered them himself. The other hand, the right one, was bare of jewelry, and when he looked back to the left there was a pale circle on the bruised flesh of the wedding finger.

"Was she right- or left-handed?"

"How the hell would I know?"

So many people were saying this lately. Jules sighed and made himself actually touch Mona. He flinched a little at the cold skin, but found writing calluses on the left hand, the bruised one. She probably hadn't excelled at friendly letters, but as George's wife she'd certainly had to write a lot of checks.

"Wouldn't the bruises be darker if she'd been alive when it happened, or not dead for long?"

"Probably."

"How long would it take for rigor to set in?"

Horace smiled happily. "I looked that up—hadn't had to deal with it in years, thank God. About four hours on a warmish day, two on a cold night. We've had both."

"Had any of her blood pooled?"

"What do you mean?"

"I think I remember learning"—Jules almost said "reading" but caught himself in time—"that blood pools in the lowest portion of a body after death. If it didn't pool, it's more likely that she was moved."

They looked at Mona, whose skin was a uniform pasty gray. "Let's turn her over," said Horace.

Jules shivered. He thought of bones he'd touched at sites in Europe, how easy it had been to examine them, despite the evidence of fire and mayhem that lay about even the small bones. Horace pulled on a leg, Jules pulled on a shoulder, and Mona flopped awkwardly onto her stomach. Together they stared at little dark pinpoints running down the body's spine and buttocks.

"I don't know what to say," said Horace. "I don't think I'd call that pooling."

"Take some photos and send them along. Why don't you do it now, so that we can have her ready for George." Jules wondered where the hell the husband was. It was nine o'clock, and he wanted desperately to go home. He slumped toward the phone on the wall near the door and called Archie while Horace located the camera and lights.

"He's waiting right here for you."

"I asked you to send him over."

"Sorry."

"It's okay. How long has he been waiting?"

"Just fifteen minutes. He's not alone."

Shit, thought Jules, hanging up. Archie liked to be enigmatic. He took a long drink from the fountain and blew his raw nose, wiping it tenderly. Horace had finished up and flipped the body himself, and was munching on peanuts again. All the light had disappeared from the small window, leaving them in a fluorescent glow that revealed every sad corner of the room, and left poor Mona looking like a well-worn dummy from a first-aid class.

"Where's the rest of her stuff?"

Horace handed him a Ziplock with an earring that matched the one Jules had found by the river, silver with a green stone, the stud to the cufflink, and a small, curved piece of thin metal. "I sent her clothes to the state boys."

"What the hell is this?"

"Her I.U.D."

Jules blanched. "I didn't think anyone used them anymore."

"Sure they do. She had kids, and she was a smoker. I put it in myself." Horace smiled and rolled up the bag of peanuts. "This is a topic I actually know something about. Any chance I could go home?"

"Fine, Horace. I'm just waiting for George."

"Sorry." Horace struggled into an immense windbreaker. "Hey, Jules."

"What?"

"Check in with me if the cold gets any worse, and next time this happens, send the body to the state police."

"It's not going to happen again, Horace."

"If it does."

Jules nodded sadly, and listened to Horace's feet pad down the hallway of aged linoleum. He pulled the plastic sheet back over Mona and fidgeted from one heel to the other. A box of gloves lay on the counter and he put them on before pulling the coat carefully out of the bag. The dark smears were blood, but there were few—she'd bled only a little about the neck. There was plenty of mud and some rubbed-in sand and leaves that hadn't shaken free when they moved the body; there was also a large, faint stain—Mona beginning to work her way into the cloth. He checked the pockets a last time, lowered the coat back into the bag, and left it on the counter with a list of the items he wanted tested.

Back upstairs, the receptionist sat alone, staring into space. He wondered how many hours she could spend doing this; his limit for an enclosed space was about fifteen minutes. Jules startled her, and she eyed him nervously.

"I'm waiting for someone."

"You're the new sheriff, huh?"

"Yes." Jules no longer cared to get mileage from this fact, but he asked her a question in turn, out of curiosity, knowing full well that he was always alienating women by asking them questions like, "How many children do you have?" or "Does it make you sad to be divorced?"

"How late do you have to work?"

"Two."

"That's tough."

She smiled thankfully and lurched backward in her chair as the front door banged open to a roar of voices. Jules came around the corner and saw George and a man and a woman, all talking loudly and gesturing mightily. The woman slammed to a stop in front of him, fixing on the uniform. She looked familiar—maybe he'd been watching too much TV lately.

"My name is Sally Arden, and we've been telling George that he shouldn't do this without his lawyer present."

Jules winced. "This is the simple identification of a body, ma'am. It has nothing to do with lawyers, and it's something a person has to do alone."

She changed her tack, and her high-pitched voice became plaintive. "He needs to have his friends present. We flew up from Los Angeles to help out."

The man, skinny, dark, and tan, pushed the woman aside. George hovered near the wall, looking weepy and ten years older.

"I'm Roger Schotz, George's associate, and I insist that we accompany him to the morgue. He is devastated."

Jules was frankly pissed off, but shook the man's hand, surprising him. "Jules Clement, county sheriff. I'll take care of Mr. Blackwater. You two can wait in reception. It shouldn't take long, and you can see Mr. Blackwater home."

"If there's anything left of him," said Schotz. He glanced around wildly, and seemed vaguely surprised to find the hall empty. "I know about cops."

"Maybe you're thinking about L.A., Mr. Schotz." Jules felt vicious again. It was a shame—he felt badly for George, no matter the lack of love the man had felt for his wife, but he'd had to perform this task before, and he wanted to get it over with. "Go sit down. Come with me, George."

"I must insist. You are violating this man's civil rights. We can account for his every movement."

Jules popped. "I haven't asked George to account for a fucking thing, besides his wife's identity," he screamed, his voice cracking. He heard a thud behind him as the receptionist hit the wall with her chair. "What kind of prurient shithead are you? Are you looking for some goddamn thrill, staring at the garroted mother of two children, this man's wife? If you two don't sit your sorry asses down, I will violate every civil right you might hope to possess." He looked at George, who seemed oddly relieved, then back at Schotz and Sally Arden. "Get in there. Now. Have a glass of water, or I'll take you in for public drunkenness."

He succeeded in looking large and mean, and they hustled into the reception area. He tilted his head at George, who followed him down the stairs. Jules made him stand next to the gurney and pulled the plastic sheet down carefully, not revealing Mona's neck. George nodded and Jules locked the door behind them before they headed down to the staff bathroom at a quick pace. He splashed water on his face while he listened to George gag in the stall. He hated his job.

HE TOLD George he'd look him up the next morning, packed him into a rental car with his quiet L.A. friends, and headed home, where he showered and changed into a T-shirt and jeans, without turning on any lights other than the one in the bathroom. The moon was waning but still nearly round. The *Atlantic*'s "Almanac" said that May's moon was called the Milk Moon, or the Horses Get Fat Moon, but Jules didn't find it particularly benevolent. He walked around the empty house with bare wood floors creaking under his feet—he had almost no furniture, and the bookshelves and a few framed things loomed from the walls. Jules opened all the windows and took a beer out to the front stoop. A cat slinked through the boulevard trees and some dogs trotted past; a door slammed and a lone car shot by, too fast. Sadness for no reason, he thought, but there were many reasons. He couldn't remember what novel he'd found the phrase in, and he didn't air it around like "treadmill to oblivion," but it floated through his mind much more often. He'd told Alice about it once when he was drunk in New York, and she'd patted his head and made him eat a sandwich.

He found his sneakers and walked back down the sidewalk to his truck. He saw no sign of George's rental car in the Blue Bat parking lot, and chose a stool in the empty bar under the TV.

"No charge," said Delly quietly, sliding a whiskey toward Jules's hands.

"I might only have one."

Delly shrugged and looked back up to the NBA game playing above their heads. Jules swirled the whiskey around in the glass, listening to the reassuring dull roar of the game, thinking of nothing in particular and happy for the relief. He drained the glass and Delly filled it again without a word, giving change from Jules's five.

Jules took another long drink and asked for some paper and a pen. He started a list. It might help him put the thing to bed, at least for the night. His writing was very precise, a little cramped but graceful. He was a leftie, like Mona; he tried not to read the studies on left-handers that implied early death and madness, both of which fates would seem to have been borne out in her case.

> *The nature of hatred*
> *Alcoholism and guilt*
> *Don't forget Ada*
> *Don't forget the prom photograph*
> *Don't assume everything goes together*
> *Why break her fingers for a ring?*

"Goddamn fucking dildo!" Delly howled at the TV. Jules dropped his pen and bumped his head against the bar on his way back up from retrieving it.

"Did you see that asshole blow the basket?"

"No." Jules shut his eyes and tried to remember what he'd been about to write. When he opened them he looked up into the Blue Bat Hall of Fame, a few dozen snapshots pinned onto a long horizontal of particle board above the bar mirror. Delly had only started the collection to disguise the board, which in turn disguised a largish hole made by a shotgun blast a decade earlier when a surly rancher uncorked at the clock that told him it was time to go home. The sprung, Dali-like clock now made up the center of a display of out-of-focus drunks. Jules wondered how often he'd looked like that, or whether in fact he'd made the board himself during a forgotten moment. He scanned it, squinting for a while, but when he found a picture of Mona and George, happy and younger and open-mouthed in party hats, he lowered his eyes to his drink and his list. On the way down he caught a glimpse of himself in the mirror behind the bottles. His mouth was a crooked slice across a white face, his nose was red, and his eyes were empty; the crease in his left cheek was deeper than usual.

"You look horrible, Jules."

"Thanks, Delly. I have a cold."

"You have a nightmare on your hands."

"Maybe."

A third whiskey materialized, and Jules went back to his list.

*Biddle*
*It was a boat*
*That means two cars*
*Everyone has a boat*
*Why go through the effort?*
*Didn't want to see her face*

Jules paused. His hands were cold and stiff, and he stared at them.

*It would have been difficult to miss George*
*Why so sloppy with her pockets?*

He looked into the mirror again. A woman was sitting next to him, and had been for some time from the look of her drink. She was folding her napkin into an origamilike bird, and he couldn't make out her face for a wealth of auburn hair. Jules eyed the rest of the bar stools, still empty, and carefully folded the list. Delly stood down from the TV a little now, smiling at him.

"Five-point lead, Jules."

The woman looked up at Delly, and Jules watched her profile, lovely and fine. He didn't know her and couldn't think of a single reason for her to have sat next to him. She turned, met his eyes, and gave him a clear, soft smile.

"Done working?"

Jules nodded and tried to smile back.

"You're having a hard week, aren't you? With Mrs. Blackwater and all." She saw his confusion. "I read the paper. I remember you from school."

Jules looked at her warily.

"You know how it is," she said. "The middle school pays attention to the high school, but it doesn't work the other way around."

"Offhand," said Jules, "you strike me as more memorable."

She smiled again. "You have an odd face. A handsome face, but singular."

Jules, astounded by such flirtation, felt a blush start at his hairline. "What's your name?"

"Rita Barre. Marguerite Carlotta Barre, believe it or not. A fancy name for a poor white."

He shook his head, drawing a blank. Even in a town of four thousand there were people you didn't know, though most probably didn't look like this woman. "Do you live in town?" he asked.

"I grew up here, and I've been here off and on since. You were gone for a long time, weren't you?"

He nodded, uncomfortable. "Where did you spend the in-between?" He felt a little pushy, but she had, after all, implied that she knew plenty about him.

"Seattle, Portland, mostly." She tilted her head back and shook some ice from her drink into her mouth. "I liked it out there, and it makes me like things better out here when I come back. I've been driving around a lot, up by the Crazies, at least I was until my transmission shitcanned."

She finished the ice, and Delly materialized from the end of the bar with another drink, for all the world a Lutèce waiter rather than the capo of the local Harley pack. He took change from Jules's pile without asking, which was fine.

"Thank you," said Rita. "I've had a bad week, too. Though not as bad as yours."

"Because of the car?"

"Oh," she said, "I can fix the car, eventually."

She sipped from her vodka and tonic and they talked for

a while about the pros and cons of various roads near the Crazies and in the Absarokas southeast of town. Jules examined her carefully. She wore a red sweatshirt with the sleeves pulled up to her elbows, a white T-shirt, jeans, and tennis shoes. She was thirty or so, frail-looking but tall; her arms were slender and freckled, and her throat was very long. She had a wonderful voice, an excellent thing in a woman, he thought, his head whirling a little. Delly slid yet another drink in front of him, and Jules pulled more money out of his pocket. Rita was playing with her napkin again, folding it with very slender fingers. Even in half life I remember vitality, thought Jules. He was at a loss for what to say next. He was out of practice.

Rita headed for the ladies' room. He watched her walk away, and suddenly remembered the woman under the street lamp, the last time he'd come to the bar.

"Aieee," said Jules softly, not realizing he'd spoken.

"Heh, heh," said Delly, his eyes glued to the basketball game.

An average intelligent conversation at the Blue Bat. Jules tried to look mildly inquiring instead of desperate.

"Good luck," said Delly. "Many have tried, few succeeded. Those who succeed tend to look like they've found God the next day."

"No one regular?"

"I dunno. She was out West for a few years, and she was married, but it's been over for a while, I think. She came in last week, but otherwise I haven't seen much of her."

Jules heard the bathroom door swing and feigned interest in the television. The game was in overtime, but he couldn't remember who was playing.

"Can I get you another?"

She shrugged, looking a little tired. "I'm not in a hurry to go anywhere. Can I ask you a question?"

"Sure," said Jules.

"Why did you come back here?"

"Because I missed it."

"Do you wish you hadn't?"

They looked at each other. "Sometimes," he said. "Of course. But I wouldn't have been happy if I'd stayed away."

When she smiled small lines crinkled around her hazel eyes. "You're very nice."

"You don't know that," said Jules.

"You're a lot nicer than the other people in this town."

"I think this town is pretty friendly."

He knew she didn't believe him. "I guess you'd have to think that, wouldn't you? But if they're so nice, why are you so lonely? Or maybe the word is forlorn."

For a moment this struck Jules as a blatant proposition. Then he realized that she really meant it, that she wasn't necessarily suggesting her company but stating a fact.

"Why is anyone?"

"I collect reasons."

"What's yours?"

"Long. And not very interesting. But it's okay if you avoid my question." She ran her hand gently along the back of his neck, got down from her stool, and zipped up the red sweatshirt.

Jules felt his heart swell and looked down at the counter. "How are you going to get to your house if you don't have a car?"

"You'll take me to yours."


FOUR hours later Jules again lay on his bed with his eyes open in the dark, with the woman's back curled up against his side. He lay very still, feeling his body tingle, achy and familiar. He turned a little and ran his finger down her backbone and over her shoulders, then over her waist and down. She was soft and smooth and warm and she smelled good, though he could still pick out the murk of the Blue Bat. He closed his eyes and pushed his face into her hair and kissed her neck, then wrapped his arm over her and rubbed himself into the small of her back until she stirred and rolled over. When he woke again at six she was gone.

CHAPTER  8

## BLUE DEER BULLETIN
### *SHERIFF'S REPORT, WEEK OF MAY 3–9*

May 3—An individual reported four black cows and one cow with five calves in a trailer court. The owner was contacted.

An individual complained of a school bus driver pulling out in front of her. An officer was notified.

May 4—An individual reported that someone stole the gas out of her vehicle and she didn't have money to buy more. An officer responded. The gas tank was locked and the individual didn't have the key with her. The individual decided to stay overnight in the vehicle at a local gas station.

A report was received of llamas loose on the Old Boulder Road headed south. The owner was contacted.

May 5——The sheriff's office was advised of a busy signal at a pay phone. An officer responded and advised the phone was off the hook.

An individual reported his truck missing. An officer responded and reported that the individual could not recall when or where he'd last seen his truck.

May 6—An individual reported a bear at the Pine Creek Mile bridge getting into a pickup filled with groceries. A Fish, Wildlife and Parks officer was notified.

A boat was reported stolen from a local business. An officer responded and is investigating.

May 7—An individual complained of a neighbor's horses on his property. The individual was informed that it was a civil matter and he should talk with the horses' owner.

An officer reported seeing a light on in a building after hours. An officer responded and found the building secure.

May 8—A report was received via train of a vehicle in a barrow pit east of town. The train did not hit the vehicle, but requested it be moved. The owner was contacted and moved the vehicle.

An individual who fell requested assistance in getting up. An officer complied.

May 9—A report was received of a suspicious individual. An officer responded and picked up the individual to be a guest of the county for the night.

MONA'S body missed "News of Record" by a couple hours, and because Peter would be called at the inquest, Ada gave the case to Soren Rue, a sad young man who was desperate to leave town for a bigger paper. Peter didn't begrudge Soren and gave him a few grisly details, but it was hard to go back to an Absaroka County conservation series after watching ants crawl out of Mona's navel and vagina. He asked for a week off, claiming trauma, and spent Monday fishing the now full-blown caddis hatch and cooking an involved meal. By the time he woke up Tuesday morning, he wished he had the case back.

Alice was not a morning person, and the phone ringing

at 7:30, while Peter sang in the shower, oblivious and out of tune, made her deeply unhappy. She launched herself naked from the bed and pawed around on the floor, nearsighted, for the noise.

"Alice."

"Edie."

"I need help. George is in a snit about the computer. He wants it fixed this morning, and I got a new monitor, but I can't open any files."

"Doesn't he have better things to do right now?"

"What, sit around his house while his in-laws weep? Roger flew out to keep an eye on him, and they want to work."

"Give me till ten, okay?"

"They're going to be upstairs at eight. They're having breakfast right now."

"Nine."

"Great. Thank you."

Alice hung up the phone gently, then pounded the floor and swore. She had a bad temper. Downstairs in the bathroom, Peter stopped singing.


AT 8:55 she climbed the long stairs to the offices. Edie was on the landing, offering coffee to a surly-looking brunette, who accepted the caffeine but didn't bother to say thanks or introduce herself. Alice treated her with equal disdain and marched down the hall to the office. Roger and George sat waiting on the couch.

"Miss Wahlgren, here to save the day." Roger tried for a kiss, and Alice allowed a peck on the cheek. Roger was one of the reasons Alice had quit. George, looking mummified, waved from the couch. Alice checked the hookup for the new monitor, then sat down and booted up the machine.

"So, how late are you with this script?" Alice peered over

her shoulder. George was staring fixedly out the window.

"Two weeks."

"Three weeks," brayed Roger, in a voice that was much too loud for nine A.M. "Three fucking weeks, not counting for time in the hospital. We tried to work on it when George was out in L.A. with us, but he hadn't made a printout of his notes."

"Fuck you, Roger. My wife's dead."

"She wasn't when you forgot to make a printout, or left my calls on your answering machine." He gestured toward the offending object. "Six calls, one right after another. I played them back myself when I got in. No one else calls this prick but me, so he never picks it up."

Alice looked away and sorted through the pile of programs Edie had arranged on the desk. "No backup, huh George?"

"Only for about half of it. Edie can't find my written notes."

"There's no reason why it shouldn't be fine," said Alice. Edie should have copied the files, but it wasn't any of her business. George had started working on a computer only a year earlier, the shift from a manual typewriter filling him with deep unease and superstition. George, after all, had covered his genitals when passing the microwave for the first year he owned it, and still considered jet engines experimental. Half the time he forgot to save anything and tended to leave the computer on during violent thunderstorms, and the resulting mess only deepened his suspicion of technology. George was almost impossible to monitor. Edie had spent the first month of her job removing his hands and the second month avoiding him; by the third month he was back to his usual evasiveness, having somehow convinced himself that she was another spy sent his way by Mona. Now he seemed to have let go of that specific paranoia, but probably couldn't remember where he'd put anything in the meantime.

"It's not in your desk. I searched your desk." Edie sounded defensive, and Roger sneered at her.

"Did you try the shelves?" George looked as if someone had thrown away his childhood blanket, a look he often used when someone rejected him as a suitor. He was almost handsome when he had that expression on his face, dogged in all senses of the word.

But Edie, though sympathetic, was already an old hand. She was also tired. "Everywhere, George. Every shelf in the place. Could you have taken the notes to the old house?"

Alice stiffened a little behind the computer.

"That fucker," said George, awash in brotherly love. "If they're there he's probably reading them right now, sitting in my favorite chair." The thought seemed to energize him, and he finally stood up and began shuffling through a box of papers.

The dark-haired woman wandered into the office and joined Roger on the couch, humming tunelessly. Roger offered her a Dunhill and a smoky fug rose above their heads. Alice wanted one of the Dunhills desperately, even after two years without nicotine.

"He'll get bored and leave. He'll miss the parties in the Hamptons," said Alice.

"He says he's moved here. He brought all his stuff." George reached for some more paper with his good hand, then began to methodically kick the box of manuscripts. He wasn't very coordinated and he missed the box twice. Edie and Alice watched him for a moment, unable to think of anything cheery to say; Roger and the woman giggled together on the couch.

George looked up and smiled. "Alice, give me some advice."

She fiddled with the keyboard. "You should go out there now. There's no point in waiting. Just tell him you're coming, and load up. Use Edie's truck."

The dogged look was back, the voice slightly wheedling. "Do you come with the truck, Edie?"

Edie was trapped and looked it. Roger jumped to his feet, hauling his sultry friend up with him. "We'll all go. Sally and I will follow in the car. You'll love the old place, honey. And Ray and George can really put on a good show." He patted George on the back. "Let's not call first."

Edie grabbed her bag and handed Alice the office keys. "If you can't get the files up don't stay here too late. I can get someone in from the dealer tomorrow."

Alice nodded. George was grinning at her. "Don't read anything and sell my ideas to your pals."

Alice gave him a drop-dead-asshole look as they walked out the door, but George, as usual, didn't notice. An hour later she had all the files she could find up and running. The last bit of screenplay, which George had titled *crap5*, was dated the previous Saturday, so not much could have been lost. Another file, simply called *great* and headed with *ideas for next script,* was dated Sunday, and Alice found it so humorous she made a printout. She wasted some more time reading the first act of the screenplay before it occurred to her that she'd quit in part to avoid reading such garbage, and she headed back to the queue to clean out any errant files. She was about to clear out when she noticed the message cursor blinking in the corner, probably indicating that George had failed to store some Hollywood missive properly. He rarely remembered to—it enraged Roger that George could so regularly forget or cancel out the script notes L.A. peppered him with. Alice dated and named a file and called the message up to store it.

She went completely still as she stared at the words and the image. Alice wasn't normally indecisive, but this floored her, and it took a moment before she thought about Jules. The page spooled out and she put it in her purse and turned off the machines. She stood for a moment, staring at George's desk and wondering if it was worth looking over. She opted for getting out as quickly as possible.

JULES got to the station at seven, drank a full pot of watery coffee, and ate three danishes. They didn't make him feel any better. Alcohol was a funny thing, not funny at all; he could never decipher what percentage of this sort of tremulous feeling was whiskey and what could be put down to fatigue and reawakened glands. At eight, on his way back from running home to retrieve the list he'd written in the Blue Bat from his jeans' pocket, he remembered that he'd made a breakfast appointment with Scotti, and executed a speedy U-turn on Main with panache.

Axel Scotti was just ordering when Jules limped through the door at Morton's, Blue Deer's main diner. A grease fire had recently cleaned up the kitchen, and the place was popular again, people apparently reasoning that they were now less likely to be hospitalized for food poisoning.

Scotti was in his forties, muscular and fit-looking, with a wealth of dark hair and light blue eyes that served him well with female jurors. He handed the waitress his menu and watched in amusement as Jules drained a glass of water and dithered over his options, finally settling on eggs, hash browns, and sausage, with a side of biscuits and gravy and an extra-large tomato juice.

"Do you eat like this every morning?"

The tomato juice materialized, and Jules chugged half of it. "I'm feeling a little under the weather."

"You look like shit."

"I earned it."

"I hope your public didn't see it happen."

Jules finished the juice and started on more coffee, remembering the *Dr. Strangelove* line about precious bodily fluids. "Fuck the public. They're not out in force on Monday nights, anyway. When's the inquest?"

"Friday. That okay? I'll have Horace appointed temporary medical examiner."

"Fine. He took me through what he knew last night"—Jules felt kind for describing Horace's autopsy skills in such a way—"and I'll go see the state boys tomorrow."

Axel asked for gory details, and Jules filled him in as the food arrived at the table. Thoughts of Mona made the sausage look less attractive than he'd anticipated. He wound up with an abbreviated description of her damaged foot as Scotti poured ketchup over his steak and eggs, cackled with glee, and seized his knife and fork.

"I'm on a protein diet. Just the thought of a real inquest gets me going."

"I thought protein diets were out of fashion."

"Everything hits Blue Deer late. You know that. I like to pretend I haven't read the living section of a newspaper, or *Prevention* magazine. It gives Horace something to say when he drags me in for a physical. 'Axel, your weight is fine, but your cholesterol is through the roof. Up by the moon, Axel.'"

Jules finished arranging things on his plate and noted that Scotti was most of the way through his steak. Jules took some tentative bites, wondering if they were supposed to be in a hurry, while Axel mopped up his last egg, flagged down the waitress, and ordered seconds. "You know, the A.B.A. is one of the few professional organizations that won't even consider offering health insurance. Lawyers gack young. The pressure will get me, even here, if the steaks don't."

Jules snorted and tried to remember how to chew. There was no point in saying, "I'm sure you'll make eighty, Axel." The county attorney's grandfather, the immigrant founder of Blue Deer's first supermarket, was now ninety-six, and had been strong enough at seventy to beat Jules within an inch of his life for filching plain M&Ms. Axel was counting on his genes. Jules wasn't sure of his own—almost everyone with the exception of two aunts and his mother had died young and more or less violently, of car crashes, childbirth, logging accidents, misadventures with reapers and rivers and recalcitrant speeders. Any strange malformation could lurk in his cells, waiting to blossom when he turned fifty, an age virtually none of his male relatives had reached. He tried not to think about it, certainly not on days when he already felt near death.

"I need a favor," asked Jules.

"Shoot."

"I want to get copies of a couple of wills. Rosemary Blackwater, George and Ray's mother, died about a month ago, in Portland, and I need to make sure I'm getting the straight story. And I'd like to see Mona's, if she had one."

"They're public record. You can get Mona's from the courthouse or from Lonnie Biddle. Grace can call Portland for the other." Axel jammed the last piece of steak in his mouth and spoke from behind a napkin. "Who do you think did it?"

"George's shooting or Mona?"

Axel, still chewing behind the napkin, gave him a look of mild disgust. Jules ticked names off on his fingers. "Ray, Ada, Lonnie, George—"

"I like George. I can't see George hauling a body like that around with a blown-out shoulder."

"Hard to imagine, I know. He also says he headed for L.A. early Thursday morning, and Mona wasn't that ripe when we found her."

Scotti blanched at the word "ripe," and Jules allowed himself a brief moment of superiority. "George certainly didn't shoot himself, but I don't want to assume the incidents are related."

"Huh. They probably are."

"Yeah," said Jules. "No problem with a motive."

"Seems like it would be a hell of a lot easier to get a divorce," said Axel. "Why Ray?"

"I found part of his cufflink on the river and the post in Mona's pocket, along with the number of a friend of his, a New York divorce attorney."

"He admits it's his cufflink and his friend?"

"He's in New York. I called him there. He told me he gave her the number. I didn't ask him about the cufflink yet, but I saw him wearing them last week. And he fibbed to me about his flight schedule. He didn't actually take off for New York until Friday morning."

Axel looked dubious. "You recognized a cufflink?"

"How many people do you know who wear them any more, if they aren't headed for a wedding or a funeral?" asked Jules. "Or a murder trial?"

"Good enough," said Scotti.

"Also," said Jules, waving to the waitress for more juice, "he had a picture of Mona up at the ranch house."

"Ray did?" Scotti squinted at him. "When did you go to the ranch?"

"A while ago, after George was shot."

"Had it framed on the wall, huh?" asked Scotti.

Jules smiled. "Actually, I have trouble imagining Ray, if he did it, not being more thorough, not checking her pockets."

"Don't give the prick too much credit," said Scotti. "Why Ada?"

Jules paused. Because she's got an edge to her, because she probably lied to me, too, because she's mean as a snake in a county that increasingly seems packed with vicious people. He couldn't say any of that. "Well, she and Mona are both up for trying to whack George, because of the prints—" He paused and looked pointedly at Scotti. "Aren't you going to congratulate us on matching them?"

"Congratulations." Axel's second plate arrived.

Jules worked doggedly at his hash browns, wondering why he'd begged for a compliment for a clue to a shooting when he had a fingerprintless murder on his hands. "Ada hated Mona, and I get the impression she's still pissed at George."

"So why take his wife off his hands?"

Jules shrugged, really another spasm of suffering. "Like I said, maybe the two incidents aren't connected. And the rumors that both women have been seeing Biddle"—was "seeing" the right phrase for palm prints on the floor?— "would seem to be true, now that we've matched the prints."

Scotti sawed at a rubbery egg. "I don't see Biddle doing diddly squat. I think the guy's too chickenshit to move far from his potty chair."

Jules pulled his wallet out of his pocket. "Ada used him for an alibi the morning George was shot, but Biddle wouldn't give her one. Don't you think it would take a little nerve, slinging around two women like Ada and Mona?"

"Simple confusion could get a man in the same hot spot," said Scotti, possibly speaking from experience. "What does Lonnie say about the prints?"

"I'll go see him today. He'll probably lie to me, too. Everyone's lying to me."

"Don't take it personally."


**JULES** kicked into high gear on his return, barking out slightly arbitrary commands to Harvey and saddling Jonathan with a specific research task. There were two pink notes waiting in Grace's loopy handwriting, one to call Alice and the other from Horace, who wondered if Jules wanted him to tag along to the state police pathology lab the next day. Jules pushed them to a corner of the desk. He could begin with anything, but opted for Mona's last day or so on earth.

Horace had said she'd died sometime Friday, at the latest, and Mona had told Mrs. Ball she'd be spending a long weekend out of town, but whoever she'd planned to meet hadn't bothered to call her in missing before Peter and Jules found her on Sunday. The possibility that Mona had wanted quiet time by herself was simply unbelievable.

"Mrs. Ball, Jules Clement here. How're the kids doing?"

"It's just terrible, Jules. Elizabeth is okay, but I'm having trouble getting Charlie to say anything."

"Are Mona's parents flying in?"

"They're already here. They'll stay for the inquest and the funeral, and take Charlie and Elizabeth back with them on Sunday. I'm going along for a week or so. The kids will come back when Mr. Blackwater is in better shape."

Fat chance of that happening this year, thought Jules. "They live in San Francisco, right? Any chance they knew what Mrs. Blackwater's weekend plans were?"

He felt an uncomfortable pause. Mrs. Ball cleared her throat. "She didn't speak to her parents often."

"And she left no number with you?"

"No. She said she'd call to check on the kids."

"Did she?"

"No, but she doesn't usually."

"Did she take her car?"

"No," said Mrs. Ball for the third time. "Mrs. Blackwater said a friend was going to pick her up, that I should stay through the weekend. I took the kids out to lunch Thursday, and when we got back she was gone."

"What time?"

"About two."

"And George left that morning, right?"

She sighed. "Right. He didn't bother with breakfast."

"Driving?"

"Yes."

"Did he know Mona was leaving?"

He knew this question would make Mrs. Ball unhappy. She had nothing in common with the Blackwaters, and probably couldn't conceive of how they lived the way they lived. It surprised him that she'd stuck it out with the kids, but a retired teacher in her sixties probably didn't have much recourse. She was silent, and he prodded her. "Did he know?"

"I don't know. They don't—they didn't—talk much, at least when I was around. They had a little squabble Wednesday night, late—nothing special—and he threw some clothes on the backseat and left the next morning."

"Now, you're not going to like this, but I have to ask. Did Mona get calls from other men, or anyone in particular?"

Another long pause. "Ray Blackwater called to say he was in town, and Mr. Biddle called fairly often."

"Thanks, Mrs. Ball."

"I feel terrible about this, Jules."

"I know you do. Try to enjoy San Francisco."

Jules hung up, rose from his chair a little stiffly, and wandered down the hall. Grace Marble was typing and didn't see him. She was always typing, refining her prose.

"Grace."

Her gray head bobbed up and she typed a final word— probably "investigating"—with a little flourish. "What can I do for you, Jules?"

"I need the incident files for the last two weeks, and whatever you have so far for this one."

"Gotcha." She pulled a file out of a beige cabinet on her left, slamming the drawer shut loudly. Jules winced.

"Headache?"

"Just a little one."

"Here's for the weeks starting April 26 and May 3, and here's what I have for yesterday. I'll put Mrs. Blackwater in next week's paper. I didn't have time to phrase it properly on Monday."

Jules nodded, and read Mona's entry to see what "phrasing properly" might mean.

An officer reported the discovery of a body along the Yellowstone on Sunday evening. The investigation is ongoing.

"Ah," said Jules. "Thanks, Grace. Let's not bother putting Mona in at all. She'll get enough coverage. I'll bring them right back."

Five minutes later he'd found what he was looking for.

May 6—A boat was reported stolen from a local business. An officer responded and is investigating.

Bill Apple's top-of-the-line Mackenzie boat, overpriced at $4,000, had departed his lot sometime between Wednesday, when an employee washed all the goods, and early Saturday morning, when Apple had tried to sell it. Jules skipped back to Grace's handwritten notes from the day before.

May 10—An individual reported discovering a submerged boat near Pine Creek. An officer responded and requested help in removing the boat.

Apple had been deeply unhappy about the condition his property had been in when recovered, and had suggested to Jules that the sheriff's office reimburse him. Jules had reminded him of the existence of insurance policies. Now his eyes traveled farther up the page.

May 5—An individual reported his truck missing. An officer responded and reported that the individual could not recall when or where he'd last seen his truck.

The truck was Eddie Parson's '74 GM, a death trap. Harvey had looked into the matter, and suggested to Jules that Eddie had probably simply forgotten where he'd parked the thing; Eddie had several worthless pickups. Jules turned to Grace's handwritten notes on the last two days, and there was Eddie's pickup, magically discovered sunk in the river near the Mallard's Rest fishing access in the valley, yesterday at 4:30. This meant Harvey had actually done some work after searching the Blackwaters' house, which was reassuring, but now he probably thought the owner had sunk the car either on a drunk or for the sake of insurance, should he possess any. Harvey was off following up on a domestic difficulty in Clyde City, and Jules would have to tell him to lay off Eddie. He hated dead ends.

Jules thought of more coffee, but his whole body was twitching now, and it had nothing to do with the memory of sexual pleasure. He stared at his list again and jumped when the phone rang.

"Mr. Clement? Ms. Huxtable, Danton Publishing, returning your call. Please hold."

The secretary's voice was effete and grating, Bostonian, but Ray's editor's voice was native Brooklyn.

"Marcie Huxtable here. What can I do for you?"

"Hullo, ma'am. Ray Blackwater suggested I check in with you to confirm some details about his trip to New York."

"He told me about George's wife. Is this why you're asking?"

"Yes. I need to know what days you met with him." Jules rubbed his head. "Just a routine follow-up."

"Hang on. Let me get my book." He heard the phone hit her desk and a muffled roar as she yelled at the secretary, surprisingly named Glinda. Grace tiptoed up and slid another memo in front of him—Alice, again, saying it was urgent. Jules counted to ten and Marcie Huxtable was back.

"Friday, late afternoon, in my office. That night at ten for dinner. He had a friend with him for that one. I saw him again yesterday for lunch. Do you want to know where we ate?"

"No." The biscuits and gravy and hash browns had turned into heavy metals in his stomach. "Who was the friend?"

"A lady, fairly attractive. Ray always brings someone."

"Do you remember her name?"

"Nope."

"Do you know if she came out with him, or lived in the city?"

"She didn't look like a hick, if that does you any good, and she was a bit of a piss cadet, but Ray usually picks his own kind. She owned some teensy newspaper, and she didn't like it when I wasn't impressed."

Jules enjoyed the scene vicariously. "Just out of curiosity, what's the new book about?"

"A lot of dead editors, not very good ones." She giggled. "Rich, though."

Jules hung up, tried Alice and got a busy signal, tried George and got his answering machine. He was searching for a tie in his desk, in honor of Lonnie Biddle, when he sensed commotion behind him.

"Jules." It was Grace, flapping her plump white hand in his direction. Eldridge Anderson, the president of the First

Yellowstone Bank, stood next to her, nervously wringing the top of a paper bag. Jules had a momentary flash of paranoia about his checking-account balance, always marginal, the same sort of flash he still got when he was driving his own car and saw police lights.

"Eldridge. What can I do for you?" He and Eldridge had gone to high school together, but they'd never had much to say to each other. Eldridge's girlfriend had been the sophomore class homecoming representative, but she'd ditched him the next year for Jules, who'd suddenly become popular after a flurry of coordination on the basketball court. Eldridge had plugged through the four necessary years of Montana State University, taken over the family bank from his dad, and joined the high life. Their mutual girlfriend was still cute as a button despite five kids, a nasty husband, and big hair; she trained cutting horses in Big Timber, and Jules had admired her trim posterior at last year's rodeo.

Eldridge, blond and pink, was a larger version of Harvey. They were cousins, though neither liked to acknowledge the fact. Eldridge fidgeted in his suit. "I, uh, have something I think you should see." Jules eyed the paper bag, wrinkled and damp looking. "I would have brought it in earlier, but I didn't know we had it. The security staff kept showing it to everyone as a joke, and then they got nervous, and finally someone showed me."

"Jesus, Eldridge. What do you have in there? A snake?"

"No, no, no." He gave a little hop of exasperation, plied apart the bag, and handed Jules a videotape. "It's from a video camera set up in the open lobby, you know, by the money machine. It's one of those new inset cameras that you can't really see. The date's on there and everything. That's why I brought it in, after I saw the paper."

Jules stared at the tape. "Well, what the hell. Did someone try to break in?"

"No, no, no," said Eldridge again, his voice going up an

octave. "Just watch it. I left it on the, uh, appropriate incident. I got to get back to work. Just plug it in. I'll keep my mouth shut," he added.

Eldridge shot out the door, leaving a humid wake. Jules stood for a moment with the tape in his hand and turned to find that Harvey had come up behind him. They walked down to the interview room, really a lounge, where the VCR was set up. It was mostly used for viewing DUI tapes, perfectly respectable coffee-hour entertainment. Harvey handed him a donut, and Jules bit in as the tape started rolling, sending a little puff of powdered sugar up his nose.

The date and time—the previous Thursday, May 6, at 11:02:46—appeared in the lower lefthand corner of the screen, over the washed-out color image of the empty night lobby. The time hit 11:04 and Jules shifted in his seat, then watched as two figures entered from the lower screen, the street door, and headed for the far corner to the left of the ATM. They had their backs turned to the video camera, but one figure was taller, a man, and had an arm around the shorter woman. When the couple reached the corner the shorter figure turned around, and they saw Mona's pale moon-shaped face, laughing. The man kissed her and she kept laughing as he tried to pull up her shirt. There was a slight pause as they talked, their heads lined up so that Mona's face was blocked. The man fiddled with her right hand and she held it up, wiggling a large ring on one finger. She started laughing again, probably drunk—Jules thought of the preliminary lab report—and the man, still with his back turned to the camera, hoisted up her shirt in one quick movement and unlatched her bra at the front, letting her large breasts flop free. She struggled with his belt and pushed his pants down. The man lifted her skirt, pulled down her underpants, then wrestled with his own for a moment, his head briefly visible in profile, before turning Mona around and starting in with a vengeance.

The truth was out: There was no position in which Mona could have looked good. Jules had a nasty flash on a Pasolini film.

"My God. They're doing it right there." Harvey was deeply shocked, rosy as a newborn mouse. "Doggy style. In a public place."

"That's not Biddle," muttered Jules.

The tape rolled on for what seemed like a very long time. Grace stuck her head in the room, gave a little shriek, and retreated. Jules looked back to the TV and the man stepped back and reached down for his pants. The time was 11:12; Jules had forgotten his hangover for a total of ten minutes. Mona gave a lurch as she adjusted her clothes and the man steadied her, then turned around and eyed the walls of the lobby with a completely calm look on his face before pushing Mona gently toward the door. It was Ray Blackwater.

CHAPTER 9

**BY NOON,** Jules had the unhappy sense that this particular Tuesday would be one of the longest of his life, if only because his throbbing head made the world appear to go by in slow motion. It wasn't as if he could let it spool out at that pace, could sit silently and stare out the window at the soft rain, could avoid talking to a succession of assholes. But he could space them out: First he'd see Biddle, after lunch (a grilled, greasy, everything sort of sandwich); then George; then possibly George's starlet and nasty, shrimpy producer. Ray—and, presumably, Ada—weren't due in to Bozeman until that evening at eight, and Jules planned a nap before asking how on earth Ray had steeled himself for the task depicted on the video, before pointing out that, in terms of timing and evidence and general prickishness, he was now suspect number one. Jules, rinsing his face with the coldest water possible in the station bathroom, actually said "Fuck motive" as he dried off. On the way out the door he looked up Rita's address in the phone book, and drove past the small gray frame house twice before getting back to business.

Lonnie Biddle's soon-to-be-vacated suite was luxurious by Blue Deer standards, but probably tacky by Marcie Huxtable's. The carpet was sky blue and wall-to-wall, with mustard fake leather chairs in the waiting area and a profusion of monotonous potted plants and abstract metal light fixtures. Jules knew he had to look green, and Biddle's secretary, a friend of his mother's, eyed him with some humor over moddish spectacles.

"He's in with a client. I hope you had fun last night."

"I did. I'll wait."

She gave him coffee without asking, and Jules spent the next twenty minutes reading travel magazines, which forced him to wonder why he'd come back to Blue Deer. This led him to thoughts of Rita, and he spent the next fifteen minutes in a sexual daze, slapping a magazine onto his lap when he realized the fly of his pants was slowly heading skyward. Jules had waited for almost an hour when Biddle ambled out, leading a stubby fat guy who showed signs of weeping and was almost certainly a divorce client.

"Jules, Jules, good to see you. I hope you haven't been waiting long." Biddle was tall and energetic and tan out of season. He'd been a hotshot high-school basketball player from North Dakota who'd made second string on the University of Montana team, and who talked about it a lot. He'd asked Jules at least three times if he'd played for Michigan, dismissing the entirety of the sheriff's education every time he heard no. Jules always tried to say something mild about sports having been rather competitive at his school. Biddle apparently never realized that a Dakotan would always be viewed as slightly dim by a Montanan; the local shopkeepers sold brown beer bottles, wrapped at the neck with a thong, as North Dakota binoculars. Biddle pumped Jules's arm as if he were trying to wrest it from its socket, then plumped down on the edge of his secretary's desk, sending a file into her lap.

Jules forced himself to remember that Biddle had voted for him, even donated money. "No problem." They looked at each other, Biddle with an ingratiating smile locked on his mouth. "I need to talk to you for a moment, and I think it would be better to go to your office," Jules said.

Biddle regarded his watch, buried in a thatch of black hair on his wrist, and pursed his lips. "I have a client due through the door in about a minute."

The secretary rolled her eyes from behind her employer's backside. "It won't take long," Jules said firmly. "It's important."

Biddle's office was all cream and wood, with occasional orange highlights. Jules supposed that his newfound interest in color had to do with the sensitive condition of his eyes, and flopped back in a copper-colored leather armchair.

The desk was suspiciously free of paper. Biddle lounged back in his own chair and carefully arranged his feet on its surface.

"So, what's up?"

"You must know."

"Mona Blackwater?"

"Just Mona, I think."

"Now, Jules." Biddle sat up and his feet hit the heavy carpeting with a dull thud. "We already covered this on the phone."

"Bullshit. You talked to her several times last week, and we found her prints all over your new office."

"My wife and I are trying to get back together."

"That's great, Lonnie, but you can't be trying that hard." Jules had set his face in its sternest, dourest expression, not hard with a hangover. He looked like a mean Swede, despite the dark brown hair. "Did you see her the Sunday morning George was shot?"

"We talked about getting together, but I wound up having breakfast with my wife."

"I can't imagine that made Mona very happy. Did she have keys to the new office?"

Biddle nodded.

"Did you make it up to her by planning a weekend with her?"

He sighed and nodded again, the good lawyer.

Jules fought the desire to require him to answer yes or no. "Talk. You're in trouble."

Biddle shook himself out of the trance. "I picked her up Thursday afternoon and we had dinner, and then I met a client for a drink. She was supposed to pick me up at ten so we could go to the Fairmont in Big Timber, but she never showed up. I found the car Friday morning, in front of the post office." He clamped his mouth shut.

"Where was your wife?"

"Orlando, visiting her parents. This thing with Mona was supposed to be a good-bye fling."

"She was into that?"

"She was into just about anything. I don't think she really gave a shit." Biddle started doodling on the sole legal tablet on his desk.

"What about Ada? She told me she was with you Sunday morning. She left prints in the office, too."

It was good to watch Biddle jump. It took him several seconds to collect himself. "Ada's confused. I spent part of Friday night with her, and some of Saturday morning." He rummaged through his desk drawer for something distracting. "My wife left Sunday afternoon." Another pause, while Biddle checked the runners on the drawer. He finally looked up and met Jules's eyes. "She was annoyed. She's back now."

Jules rubbed his temples. "Did Mona leave a will?"

Biddle regained composure by examining his fingernails. "She didn't leave one with me. Knowing Mona, she didn't see a point. Her parents have a fair amount of money—her dad's an executive with some big discount store chain—but they never gave her much."

"What did George think of all of this?"

"Mona's parents?"

Jules rubbed his temple. For the first time Lonnie Biddle showed real amusement. "Mona and me? I don't know that he knew who she was seeing, but I'm sure he couldn't have cared less."

**ALICE** tried Jules again in the early afternoon. Grace was cheery, as always. "He's running around, honey. He can barely talk today."

"What's wrong?"

"Lost in space. That cute mug looks like hell."

Alice had never heard anyone call Jules "cute" before. Grace kept talking. "But I'm glad you called again, because I keep forgetting to mention we're having another bird count this year, a spring one, the Saturday before Memorial Day weekend."

"Grace, I can't tell the difference between a sparrow and a finch."

"You did fine last time, dear. You can *see* them, and then I can name them. We'll have other people along, too. It'll be much more pleasant than the winter count."

Alice had almost managed to excise that zero-Fahrenheit trek from her memory, but she was a pushover in some situations. George's printouts lay next to the phone, and she stared at them for a moment.

"If you say so," she said. "Maybe I'll just drop off a note for our sheriff."

JULES picked up a quart of Pepsi at the Mini-Mart. He leaned on the counter for support while the customer in front of him argued with the clerk over a gas bill. By the time he got back out to the parking lot it was drizzling in earnest, and when the patrol car gave the soft whine of a dying battery, his sense of life shifted entirely to gray. His cold seemed to be gone, his renewed sense of smell a mixed blessing: The rain aggravated the stink of teenage alcohol vomit in his backseat, and he gagged and rolled the window down. He left the car running on Fiske and almost ripped his arm out of its socket when George's door proved to be locked. The owner of the bookstore beneath the offices, George's landlord, told him that George and Edie had been unloading boxes off and on all day. Jules assumed that they were finally rescuing George's belongings from the ranch house, and felt brilliant for the deduction. He was staring blearily at the magazine rack, thinking of cheap entertainment and a Bloody Mary and his bed, when Roger Schotz and Sally Arden waltzed through the door and nearly ran into him.

"Our tax dollars at work," brayed Roger. "And is this town really so safe that a cop can leave his keys in a car with the motor running?"

"Yes, it is that safe." Jules replaced a copy of *Gourmet*, feeling foolish.

"Are you waiting here to pick up George?" Sally cocked her head and came a little too close.

"I was hoping to talk to George. There's no reason to pick him up." He smiled, but the expression was so unfriendly that Sally backed up a step, flustered.

"Well, he's busy. He's emptying out that nasty old house."

"I'll see him later then." Jules headed for the door and stopped near Roger. "When did George make it to L.A. last week, anyway? I know he's scared of flying, but must have been tough, driving with that shoulder."

"Nothing stops him," said Roger. "We saw him for breakfast Saturday. I wanted to take him to a good doctor, a real doctor, but he said he felt fine."

"Will you be working together here all week?"

"The man needs to go to his own wife's funeral, doesn't he?"

"I'm sure he wouldn't miss it for the world," said Jules. "See you later."


PETER arranged his notebook and two files on his desk. His fellow journalist, Soren Rue, had dropped by their house that morning after Alice had marched off to George's. Soren had lost his big-story ticket to freedom after only thirty-six hours—his father had had a stroke in Minot, North Dakota, the night before and by now, two o'clock, the son had probably hit Glasgow on his way home. Ada hadn't given the case back to Peter yet, officially, but he wasn't going to give her a chance to play games with it.

He pulled out Soren's Monday piece and reread it. It had gone out over the AP wire, making Soren very happy, but all it provided was standard material. Soren's most dramatic line was "the County Sheriff's office is treating the death as a homicide."

The *Bulletin*'s index of past pieces was slipshod—whole months were missing, and it was possible to find car accidents under entrepreneurs, concerts under millage votes. But someone had been fairly careful about George, and Mona even had her own entry, mostly listings from what passed for a society column, all written before Mrs. Blackwater made her final descent into being antisocial. Peter cruised through George's book signings and coverage of his various movies before turning to their wedding announcement. The photo was wonderfully geeky, with George looking like he wanted to shoot himself and Mona pursing her lips in a Betty Boop sort of way. How had she gotten him to pose?

Mr. and Mrs. Belton Armbruster, of Campton Lane, San Francisco, announce the marriage of their daughter Mona Alexandra to George Philip Blackwater. The ceremony was held August 16 at the Fairmont Hotel in Big Timber, with the bride arrayed in a gown of ivory satin and tulle and her matron of honor, Mrs. Paul Santoz, in peach silk. Ray Blackwater, of New York City, stood up for his brother.

The bride, a graduate of San Francisco Community College, is the former owner of the Beacon Gallery in Marin and a partner in the new Abstractions Gallery in Blue Deer with Mrs. Santoz. Mr. Blackwater, son of Rosemary Blackwater of Portland and the late Herbert Blackwater, founder of North Coast Paper, is a novelist and a Princeton graduate. The couple will reside in Blue Deer.

Mona's role in the Abstractions Gallery, a hideous fun-house of shaped obsidian and petrified wood, had ended only in 1990, when she and Ada, close friends for a decade, had a very vocal and bloody cat fight in the Blue Bat, followed by a slugging match at a Christmas dance and their subsequent arrest. Alice and Peter had just shown up in town and were in the bar for a quiet drink; the clinical allegations leveled by the women, involving each other, both Blackwater brothers, and most of the high-lifers in town, made them dizzy, but they stuck it out, oddly cheered that the town wasn't quite as quiet as it had seemed at first.

He sighed, shifted in his chair, and flipped through several boring entries.

Mona Blackwater, chairwoman of the Blue Deer Opera, announced Friday that the Duluth Madrigals would visit Blue Deer during the Wrangle this summer. Mrs. Blackwater will solicit the additional funding needed from local businessmen.

Peter giggled. The column's author hadn't bothered to say "business people," but the clip was ten years old, pre-PC. As if PC would ever truly hit their fair town.

The next appreciable entry was dated 1988:

George and Mona Blackwater threw a housewarming party last weekend and entertained several guests from out-of-town, including Barbara Lanchester, the well-known actress, and Tony Brink, director of *My Fair Fanny*, and Roger Schotz, producer of Mr. Blackwater's movie, *Tiger Tail*. Also attending were the Eldridge Andersons, the Leonard Biddles, the Lou Aronsteins, Paul and Ada Santoz, Dan and Rachel Towle, and numerous other friends and neighbors. Mr. Blackwater's brother Ray, a recent winner of a National Magazine Award, flew in from New York to attend.

Actors, bankers, lawyers, eastern richies, and hangers-on. Blue Deer was just as stratified socially as a place like Greenwich. Peter had heard stories about that night—Mona had found one of the largest, cheapest, newest houses in town and tacked on a larger kitchen, a kidney-shaped pool, and a tennis court, none of which ever saw much use. She had ended up puking in her own pool before Ray threw George in and tried to hold him underwater. Happy, happy. This had probably been Ray's last visit. Peter was often glad that Alice had a talent for saying the wrong things to the right people—it got them out of invites to such parties.

This wasn't getting him anywhere. Peter felt someone looming behind him, and seeing Jules's face was akin to having a light bulb go off in his head, or would have been if he hadn't already planned to track his friend down. But Jules's face was a little stranger looking than usual, an odd mix of happiness, pain, and deep exhaustion.

"Alice left a message for me, and said it was important. Do you know what it's about?"

"Uh uh. She was going up to George's this morning." Jules raised his eyebrows. "To fix the computer. She must be done by now. Run by the house."

"I can't. I'm too busy tracking down raving assholes. I'll try her tomorrow."

"Why don't you just come for dinner? It's been a couple of weeks."

"I need to sleep."

"I can see that. Thursday?"

"Sure. I have to go to Helena, but I should be back in the afternoon." Jules fidgeted and loosened the tie of his uniform. "Have you ever met a woman named Marguerite Barre?"

"Here?" Peter stacked and replaced the useless Blackwater clips in their file.

"Yeah."

"No."

"Oh." Jules craned his head toward Ada's office. "Did your dragon lady bother to tell you where she was going on vacation?"

"She's not my dragon lady, and she didn't confide in me. She said she'd be back tomorrow."

"I was wondering," said Jules. "I was wondering . . ." He trailed off and squinted up into the lights.

Peter sensed trouble immediately. "Wonder all you want."

"I was wondering if you could log onto her computer."

"No."

"Why not?"

"I need this job. She has spies. You're here to uphold the law. And she probably locks her files."

Jules sighed. "All this sleaze is beginning to get to me."

"Get it off your chest," said Peter. "Fess up. What can you give me on Mona that Soren didn't get out of you?"

"Soren." Jules smiled. "Soren made me feel like a pro.

We only talked for five minutes yesterday, and every single question threw him into fits of embarrassment. I didn't have to give him diddly squat, but I threw in some tidbits out of compassion. He didn't even print them."

"Give the tidbits to me, then. I'll buy you a pop. Sit down and rest."

Jules grinned and pulled up an extra chair, put his feet on the desk, and shut his eyes. "I'll give you some now, and more after I talk to the state guys, but I need to save something for the inquest." He'd almost nodded off by the time Peter returned with the soda and started in on him.

**THE EVENING** was almost as Jules had imagined it, though he had a very large rum and soda rather than a Bloody Mary, and dispensed with television after the evening news. The couch, wide, soft, and covered with green-gray linen, was eight feet long, and had cost a grand back in the mid-eighties in New York. Even then Jules, a closet snob, had known it ranked with a good bed and a large kitchen table in terms of important furniture. He got several feather pillows and an old wool blanket and the two-day-old Sunday *Times*, poured his drink into a pint mason jar, shifted for five minutes until he'd achieved a perfect position, and was out cold within another ten, the "Week in Review" open on his chest.

The phone rang at 10:30. Jules remembered his intention to interview Ray and his paramour as he glanced at the clock and launched himself over pillows, blanket, and piled newspaper toward the ringing in the kitchen.

"Ed wants you to go to Ada Santoz's house," said Bart.

"I gather this isn't an idle request," said Jules, scratching his back.

"Gunfire," said Bart, redefining laconic.

"Tell him two minutes," said Jules. He drained his rum and soda and slammed down the front steps.

Traffic, light as always in Blue Deer, did not slow his progress, and by the time he'd traveled the five blocks to Ada's, the otherwise geriatric neighborhood was still lively. Ray Blackwater's Mercedes had been shot so full of holes it looked like the last car in *Bonnie and Clyde*. George, apprehended by Ed as he trotted toward home carrying his gun, now lay on the hood of the defunct car looking pleased with himself and very drunk. Ed was busy trying to keep the shotgun away from Ada, who was screaming obscenities in a robe; Ray stood next to her, looking enraged and cold in a pair of boxer shorts and a wool blanket. A good chunk of the neighborhood stood watching.

"You can all go home now," said Jules. "Shoo." He crossed the street toward Ed, whose patience was finite at the best of times. Jules patted him on the shoulder, ignoring the smart couple, and pulled him off to the side.

"What do they have to say?"

Ed's voice was thick with disgust. "Innocent victims. George showed up in the yard and yelled a few bad words, so they called us, and then he started in with the gun. Mrs. Santoz seems to think George is jealous, and Mr. Blackwater isn't saying much at all."

"What does George say?" Jules addressed the question as much to George, stargazing happily, as to Ed, the way you might ask a child a question in the third person.

George pulled himself into a sitting position, bowing the hood, and gave a huge smile. "I feel so much better. Much, much better."

"He just lies there so I left him for last," said Ed. "He'll be a relief. I want to turn a fire hose on those two."

This was one of Ed's favorite lines, and dated from the five years he'd spent in the fire department, a brief escape from the mayhem and drudgery of the sheriff's force. He rejoined after he hit his first fatal fire.

"Why don't you ask the neighbors if they heard the

beginning of this," said Jules. "I can keep an eye on George." He turned to Ray and Ada, who regarded him stonily.

"I hope you're going to charge him," said Ada.

Jesus, thought Jules. "Of course we're going to charge him. It's standard practice when people shoot cars in quiet neighborhoods."

"He threatened us, too," said Ada.

Jules saved his private pity for the car. "You can go inside now, Mrs. Santoz, and warm up. I can hold any questions for the morning."

"What about Ray?" Ada, too coiffed in the daytime, did not look her best au naturel.

"I have a couple of quick ones for him."

"I'll stay, then," said Ada.

Jules looked at Ray, who stared back with great malignance. "The questions have to do with your activities last Thursday night."

"I was in New York," said Ray. "I told you. I think this can wait."

"Yes," said Ada.

Yes, what? thought Jules. He would never have picked Ada for a cheerleader. "No," he said. "They can't wait, and you weren't in New York yet. I'm sure you're going to want to have this talk in private, Ray."

Ada opened her mouth but Ray turned quickly, pushing her gently toward the house, murmuring reassurances. They gave each other a fond wave and Ada retreated through the door. Ray's relief was palpable. Jules felt queasy.

"Why'd you miss your Thursday afternoon flight to New York?"

"I wanted to bring Ada, and she couldn't leave till Friday."

"Why not just tell me that?"

"We didn't see a point to letting everyone know."

"Everyone knows everything now," said George.

Jules glared at him. George lay back down on the car hood. "Why not? It wouldn't have stayed a secret in a town like this."

"Well, it felt like one then, and secrets sometimes add to a thing." Ray put on a man-of-the-world look that was distinctly out of keeping with the scene or his costume. "Now there's enough to it, anyway. We enjoy each other."

George giggled. "That's so sweet," he said. "I can hardly bear it."

"Shut up, George." Jules gritted his teeth and pulled Ray away from his brother, out into the street. "If you enjoy Ada so much, why'd you fuck your sister-in-law Thursday night?"

Ray blinked, and his knuckles looked a little white as they clasped the blanket. "What on earth are you talking about? Why would I want to do such a thing?"

Jules wondered why the smartest people persisted in stupidity. Perhaps they simply persisted in hoping that he was stupid; perhaps they were right. "Maybe you didn't want to, but you were quite a trooper on the bank videotape."

Ray sat on the curb and covered his face. "Oh God, how embarrassing."

"Actually," said Jules, "it would have been quite amusing if I hadn't known she was going to be dead in a couple of hours. Why'd you do it?"

"I don't know," said Ray. His face under his fingers was sweaty in the night air. "I didn't kill her."

"You'll have to do better than that."

"She called, said she wanted to talk to me." Ray looked dejected and frail, the perfect picture of a man who's just been caught. "We had a drink or two, and we wound up in the bank lobby."

"What did you do when you left the lobby?"

"Walked her to Biddle's car and drove back here."

"Was she planning to go home?"

"Hell no, she was meeting Biddle. Mona had the longest midlife crisis of any woman I've known, and I think it was peaking that week. I honestly can't tell you why I took part in it."

"What was with the ring?"

"Ring?" said Ray.

It was impossible to tell if this was an honest blank look or if Ray was buying time. "She was gesturing with a ring, showing it to you on the video," said Jules. "A large ring, with a dark jewel."

"Oh, *that* ring," said Ray. "It was something she'd bought, charged to George, kind of a final credit item before the divorce. She was just laughing about George."

Jules turned away.

"Truly." Ray seemed as earnest as a man can be when he's out at night in a blanket and a pair of underwear. "It was her favorite sport, laughing about George. Does he know about this?"

"Not yet." Jules nodded toward the house. "Please tell Ada I'll need to talk to her tomorrow, probably in the afternoon. But you'll both need to give a statement tomorrow morning."

"I don't see any point in pressing charges," said Ray.

Jules shrugged. "The county will, then. You want to tell me why he was so pissed off?"

"He's an alcoholic," said Ray. "Don't romanticize it."

"Not Ada or Mona?"

"Nah," said Ray, shivering on new grass. He had ugly white feet, the kind that rarely feel the air.

"Ssshhh," said George. "I'm ready now."

They turned and watched him climb down from the car. He clasped his hands at his waist, hummed, threw back his head and broke into the middle of a song. It took Jules a moment to recognize "Sweet Jane," but only another second to run after Ray, who lunged forward when George reached the refrain, clamped manicured hands around his brother's throat, and began to throttle him on the car hood.

THERE was no place to buy actual food in Blue Deer at eleven P.M., and Jules settled for chips from the machine at the station. George sat across the interview table from him, prim and patient, listing a little to one side.

"I gotta tell you, George, I didn't care for your singing voice."

"I haven't practiced for a long time."

"Where'd you pickle yourself?"

"The Blue Bat," said George. "Of course."

"Did you meet anyone there?"

"Ran into a guy, shot the shit." He looked cagey and amused.

"How'd you get from the Blue Bat to Ada's?"

"I drove," said George. "Of course."

Jules peered at him, wondering if this was sass or idiocy. He decided on idiocy. "Did you have your gun with you?"

"Drove home for it," said George. "Saw one of your guys out and about, but I took the alleys, and he lost me."

Jonathan was not wise to wily drunks yet, a specialized skill. Ed said it took one to know one.

"What I want to know," said Jules, "is why you were so pissed off. Did you plan on shredding Ray's car before you went to the Bat, or did you think it up while you were there?"

"What does it matter?" asked George, with immense dignity.

Jules's headache was coming back, the rum wearing off, reminding him that he'd never eaten dinner. Calories were the key to surviving such days. "It matters because someone murdered your wife and shot you. It makes me unhappy to admit it, but all the moods you fucks wallow in matter now. So please tell me why you went from simply hating your brother to shooting his car. Was it Ada?"

"Hah," said George. "Who would shoot a car for Ada?"

He was convincing. "Something that bothered you when you got your stuff out of the ranch?"

"Not especially."

"I'm going to get nasty, George." Now Jules was convincing, ready to reroute his own physical misery. "Talk."

George sighed, exhaling an almost visible cloud of vodka. "I haven't liked my brother since I turned five. But I figured out tonight that he was much, much worse than I'd ever realized, and I found out he'd lied to me about something that changed my life when I was a kid."

"What?"

"I'm not telling you."

Jules cracked the knuckles on his right hand. It was an unconscious move, one he realized only when George's eyes fluttered. "Did it change it for the better or the worse?"

"Are you fucking kidding?" George had obviously forgotten he'd declined to explain. "It ruined me, changed it for the worse. Much worse. But maybe now things will be better."

Jules felt as if he were suffocating and stood to open the window. Ray's line about not romanticizing an alcoholic had come back to haunt him; it was true about any number of people, but George had the potential to turn a small puzzle, say, the origin of navel lint, into an iridescent mystery.

"Why'd you shoot the car, George? Was he talking about Mona?"

"That wouldn't tend to annoy mc."

"Don't you mind at all that your wife is dead?"

"No."

"Viciously murdered?"

"Well, I hope she didn't feel much or anything like that. I won't miss her."

"Don't you feel bad for your kids?"

"They're better off without her."

Jules drummed his fingers on the table. "I thought maybe you'd found out tonight that Ray fucked your wife."

George's face twitched a little. "Bullshit."

Jules stood up again. The only thing that didn't ring true was the part about not wanting Mona to suffer.

"Wait right here." He shut the door softly behind him and retrieved the tape from his desk. George didn't look up when he returned, and sat in silence through the first three-quarters. Jules started talking again.

"I wouldn't have shown you this if I thought you loved your wife, but you just told me you didn't. So seeing Ray in there shouldn't bother you any more than knowing about Biddle."

"Fuck you." George was pale, and he turned away from the TV.

"If you don't watch it, George, I'll push your face into the screen. I don't like it when people empty shotguns in town. What's with the ring she showed him?"

"Who knows." He looked weary, confused; the giddiness had worn off. Jules finally believed that George's night had been worse than his own day, but he also sensed it had little to do with Mona's last infidelity. "I don't understand anything, anymore."

"Was it her wedding ring?"

"I didn't notice. She had lots of rings."

"Somebody broke all the fingers on one of her hands to get a ring off, and I'm beginning to think you're the likeliest candidate."

"Give me a fucking break," said George, snapping out of his funk. "I was going to divorce her. I have money now. I didn't need to kill her."

"So you've thought of it."

"Anyone married to her would have thought of it."

"That's probably true," said Jules. "When'd you leave for Los Angeles?"

"Thursday morning, about nine."

"Did you know she was going to see your lawyer?"

"She usually does."

"What way did you drive out?"

"Through Nevada."

Of course, thought Jules. Peter had told him that George still mourned the passing of the last Blue Deer whorehouse, owned by the wonderfully named Bertha Nickelskin. She hadn't gone out of business until 1982.

"Where'd you stay?"

"Some chain in Elko. I don't remember."

"Do you have a receipt?"

"No. I got in late and left early, made L.A. by Friday night."

"Wounds and all? You must have been pretty tired. Did you see Roger as soon as you got to the city?"

"We met Saturday morning."

"Where'd you stay?"

"With a friend."

Jules waited for details.

"She's married," said George, without irony. "Leave her alone."

"Why did you take off so soon after you got out of the hospital? You had to be uncomfortable driving."

"You saw her at the banquet." George spoke slowly, in a slightly slurred monotone. "The bitch shot me, tried to kill me, out of pure spite."

"I don't think Mona tried to kill you, George. And you can fit a lot more than spite into a marriage."

"Sure she did. No one else would want to."

"Not Ada?"

"Ada wouldn't want to shoot me. She's still in love with me."

George was absolutely earnest, and Jules stared at him. "It doesn't bother you that these days she's going to the ranch to see your brother?"

"I could have told you she would. It doesn't mean much. I didn't say I was in love with her."

Jules couldn't think of anything else to ask, didn't want to know any more. Ed leaned against the doorway.

"George make his calls yet?" asked Jules.

"Yep."

"Will you ask Bart to let him out by nine?"

"I already have." Ed crooked his finger at George. Jules watched them walk down the hall to the stairway and the cells, then wandered around the station room for five minutes, hands in his pockets, indecisive, before walking slowly to his patrol car.

It was after midnight but one light was on, probably a bedroom light. Rita looked deeply annoyed when she jerked the door open after only two knocks, then surprised, possibly even pleased.

"Well, hell," she said. "You're working late after a long night. I at least got to take a nap."

"So did I," said Jules, walking through the open door. "How was your day?"

"One class. Bad tips." She was waitressing at the Baird Hotel while working—half-heartedly, he sensed—for a teaching degree from Montana State, in Bozeman. "How was yours?"

He flopped on her couch. "Someone just shot a Mercedes. I shouldn't admit this, but I kind of enjoyed the sight."

"You're only human," said Rita, smiling.

"I sure am," said Jules.

CHAPTER 10

## NEW LEADS IN LOCAL DEATH
*BY PETER JOHANSEN*
BULLETIN *STAFF WRITER*

Blue Deer, May 12—A source within the Absaroka County Sheriff's Department has confirmed several particulars in the homicide of Mona Alexandra Blackwater, wife of George Blackwater.

Mrs. Blackwater, whose body was discovered last Sunday afternoon, is believed to have died on the previous Thursday or Friday, May 6 or 7. Lab findings will be presented at the inquest at the county courthouse on Friday, May 14, by Coroner Burton Babaski and temporary medical examiner Horace Bolan, M.D., but initial findings indicate death was caused by strangulation, possibly by a metal band or wire. The source indicated that the body, found in a shallow grave on the banks of the Yellowstone River south of town, may have been brought to its location after death occurred via a boat.

There is some evidence of theft as well, but the sheriff's office, which is pursuing a variety of leads, refused to comment on possible suspects or a motive, or what evidence might have been found at the scene of the crime.

Testimony at the inquest will be given by Dr. Bolan, Sheriff Jules Clement, George Blackwater, and others. Anyone with information regarding the case or Mrs. Blackwater's movements on May 6 or May 7 is asked to contact the Sheriff's Office.

Funeral services for Mona Blackwater will be held at St. James Episcopal Church on Saturday at 10:30 A.M. The family has asked that donations be sent to the Absaroka County Humane Society in her name.

GEORGE'S fireworks also warranted an independent item and a photo, if only because so many of Ada's neighbors had been desperate to give quotes. Jules felt rested, yet not too rested, after another night with Rita, and made the station by 7:30, humming, telling bad jokes as he called for a tow truck to haul Ray's honeycombed car away, asking the driver to make as much noise as possible in Ada's driveway. He hopped down the station stairs to find George naked and sleeping like an overgrown toddler in the otherwise deserted cell block, a slight pout on the writer's lower lip and a big bruise on his right shoulder from the shotgun's kick. Jules woke him gently, folded him into the squad car, bought him a sweet roll and a large coffee, and drove him home, where Mrs. Ball looked in the other direction but the children jiggled about with happiness.

When Jules returned he settled down to a wall of messages, most ignored during the previous day of chaos, and an amusing one from that morning: Ray wanted to invite him to a dinner party on Saturday at seven at the ranch; Jules didn't need to return the call if he could make it. It took him an hour to wade through the actual work and reach an envelope, which he knew was from Alice by her scribble, and a fragment of dehydrated green onion stuck to the back side.

Grace, passing behind him, said that Alice had dropped it off the day before, late in the afternoon. Jules squinted at the bad handwriting inside:

*Jules honey*

*These were in George's computer when I fixed it yesterday. I checked the log and he opened the memo at 8:10 Sunday morning. It was still up when the system crashed, so I thought I should show it to you. Please don't tell George I printed them.*
*Love,*
*Alice*

*PS I took the other sheet because I thought it was funny, but now I'm not so sure.*
*Please don't tell him. Please, please.*

*See you tomorrow for dinner?*

*XO*

Jules looked down at the dandy, and the shotgun, and the memo, then skipped through the ludicrous story ideas. He had no intention of showing either page to George, though he was quite interested in the writer's third act. He went back to the 8:10 message.

"Sorry's not enough," Jules whispered.

"Pardon?" said Jonathan, five feet away.

"Nothing," said Jules. He looked back down at the etching, ran his hand through his hair, and kneaded his neck. Then he smiled and planned a visit to the *Bulletin*.

MOST of the staff had left, and he watched Ada through her glass wall as he threaded through deserted carrels, pausing silently in her doorway. Peter said she almost never really worked, but she was working now, sorting Xeroxed clips from the *Bulletin*'s predecessor, the *Daily*, while her computer's printer clacked away. When she looked up she was not happy to see him, was in fact downright pissed off, and asked him, sharply, to give her a minute.

Jules ignored this clear request for privacy and plopped down in the chair across from her desk. The last time he'd been in the office the mess between Peter and Ada had distracted him, but this time he looked around with apparent patience and actual curiosity, letting Ada think he had no interest in the clips or, rather, her hasty efforts to make them disappear. A smudged photo of the late Paul Santoz, a slight, pinched-looking man, probably already riddled with cancer when the snapshot had been taken. Another portrait of an affluent, country-clubby family and their colonial-style home, with Ada in a Dippity Doo hairstyle, probably twenty or so, looking coy while she hugged a fake Doric pillar. A sorority sister, for sure. Coffee-table books, mostly light history and pretentious art, carefully arranged on an expensive bookcase between millefleur paperweights and bland Steuben glass. There were two clean, bare rectangles on the wall between Toledo Art Museum posters; Peter had told Jules that Ada had removed, and possibly destroyed, the two paintings George had given her.

He heard the tap of fingers and brought his smile down from the ghost paintings to her face. The desk was clean and they started over again, exchanging pleasantries on the recent rain and its benefit to ranchers, Peter's excellent reporting, and Soren's ambition and poor fortune. Ada never seemed to inhabit her clothes or her body naturally, no matter how relatively fine they were, but today she looked especially out of keeping with the landscape behind her. Her dark blue dress looked linty, her ash blond hair stiff and artificial, and her face creased and powdery, leaving literal cracks in the armor with each forced smile. Jules thanked her for seeing him on short notice, and Ada thanked Jules for being open with her paper. Jules plucked a lemon drop from a bowl on her desk and rolled it around in his mouth. He was sick of swapping niceties, and decided to start with a bang.

"We've been working hard on this, and I saw no harm in letting Peter know how hard. Yesterday, for instance, I talked to Mr. Biddle, and he said he was with his wife on Sunday morning, May 2, not with you, Ms. Santoz."

"How unlikely." She laughed, an awkward squeak. "He was probably with Mona."

"He was with his wife. Mona was downtown that morning, near Mr. Biddle's office."

"Well," said Ada. "There you have it."

"No," said Jules. "Mrs. Blackwater was seen leaving the area before any shots were fired. I thought she might have been leaving because she bumped into you."

Ada tapped at her keyboard, but she'd already logged off and the screen was a blank. She retrenched. "Maybe I was confused. Maybe I saw Lonnie Saturday morning, or shall I say Friday night. Maybe he's doubling up, and a little shaky on time. I didn't shoot George. I don't even think of him anymore, and I wouldn't know how to go about it, anyway."

"How to go about what?"

"Firing a gun."

Jules looked out Ada's plate-glass window and considered the rain for a moment. "It occurs to me, Ms. Santoz—"

"Call me Ada." She didn't say it in a particularly inviting manner.

"It occurs to me that you and Mrs. Blackwater could hardly have liked each other, given some of your . . ." Jules searched for the right term, while Ada watched him with forbidding patience, ". . . your past history."

She made a huffing sound. "We were partners, once. We drifted apart."

"You sued each other over a gallery you started together, and you beat each other bloody at a Christmas Ball. Then you had an affair with her husband."

One corner of her mouth curled slightly. "True. Very true. But Mona was a raving bitch to almost everyone she dealt with, and I'd like to think that though I have some difficult moments I occasionally overwhelm these lapses with other facets of my personality. Mona lost any other facets she may have possessed over the last few years. I stopped even thinking about her once the gallery case was decided."

"In your favor?"

"In my favor." She smiled using only her mouth, like the Cheshire cat.

"But you still had a lot of friends in common, lots of men."

This last wiped any trace of good nature off her face. Jules could almost feel cold air envelop him.

"It all happened accidentally. I will give her credit for occasional good taste"—Jules's poker face collapsed slightly, and she glowered—"whether you will or not. Similar taste, somehow. Or maybe there are only so many men in town, which is probably nearer the truth."

"When did you last see Lonnie Biddle?"

"That's private." She snapped the words out of her mouth as if she had a slingshot set up between her teeth.

"Some of the prints we found in Mr. Biddle's new office, including some on a windowsill from which we believe the shots at George were fired, were yours, and the office had been painted only three days prior to the shooting. So should I assume you were up there seeing Lonnie, or sighting in George?"

Brick red was not Ada's best color. Jules left it at that and shifted topics.

"How was the trip to New York?"

Ada filled the slight pause by drumming a pen on her desktop. "Fine. Are you done showing off?"

"How do you feel about George these days?"

"Indifferent. Do you want me to say it a few more times?"

Jules shrugged. "You can say it as much as you want. You also said he'd done something unforgivable, and I wondered if you were referring to the actual breakup, or something he said later. At Horace's birthday party, I believe."

"He apologized. He practically licked my shoes." She clamped her lips shut.

Jules rested in the silence, close now to what he'd come to hear.

"Sometimes sorry's not enough," said Ada. She smiled and tilted her chin up and drank from her glass of soda, pleased with herself. Jules's answering smile came slowly and grew wider and wider as Ada's chilled.

"I guess you know how to send messages on that thing, don't you," said Jules, pointing to the computer.

Ada didn't move, didn't make a murmur.

"Perhaps you'd show me your gun collection."

"No."

Jules shrugged and stood to leave. "I'll get a warrant. We'll find the rifle sooner or later, whether or not you throw it in the river."

She was so still she didn't look quite real. "I almost forgot the main question," said Jules. "What were you doing last Thursday night, before your trip?"

"I was with Ray," she said. "Late."

"How late?"

"About ten on."

Jules shook his head. "Would you say anything he asked you to say, or are you just an idiot about your own excuses?"

Ada looked down. On the way out Jules imagined having a machine with different gauges, a little like an expensive sprinkler system, to measure the fine line between bullshit and septic emotion in the inhabitants of quiet, lovely Blue Deer.

**THAT** night, at nine, he decided to call. Rita answered on the third ring, her voice so tense that he thought at first he'd reached the wrong number.

"I can't talk to you now."

Jules's skin felt prickly. "Well, call me when you can."

"Not tonight."

They fell silent, both listening to the man in the background at Rita's end, asking who was on the phone.

"It's nothing," said Rita. "Bye."

Her line clicked, and Jules spent a moment listening to the echo before he pounded the phone into the wall once, hard.


**WHEN** Jules got back from Helena on Thursday afternoon, having done a passable job of bullying the state forensics staff into a few answers, Harvey told him that the crazy duck feeder had been sighted in the park again, just after dawn that morning. A Blue Bat regular had seen him after a full night of drinking; it turned out that the witness was color-blind, on top of being intoxicated, and gave a deeply confusing description of the man's clothing after insisting that he had greenish hair, either in a Prince Valiant cut or tied back. Harvey took this to mean some shade of red, and suggested that the man was a hippy or a vagrant or an actor-type from Bozeman. The witness put the man's age at twenty-five to forty, his height anywhere between five-eight and six feet, his weight around 170. When Harvey questioned his details, he'd pointed out that he'd only really noticed the man when a gun appeared and a feeding duck had disappeared in a poof of feathers, at which point the man pointed the gun at his own head and the witness ran in the other direction.

Jules stared at Harvey in disgust. "Why even tell me this?"

"I thought you'd want to know."

"I want to *know*, Harvey, not feel like I'm losing my mind, like some poor dipshit might splatter his brains in front of the kiddies without us doing a fucking thing. Do me a favor and ask everyone to start driving through in the evening and in the morning, in their own cars if possible. If they're off-shift, that's what they should be driving, anyway. I'm sick of padded gas bills."

"Do you want me to work up a sketch with him?"

Jules screeched "No!" and headed for his desk to write out his notes from Helena. It only took half an hour to list the findings for Horace and another fifteen minutes to make up an outline of what he wanted to include in his own testimony, most of it known and boring. The interesting stuff would have to wait. When Jonathan waltzed in, having spent several hours lecturing the middle school on drugs, Jules crooked his finger and brought him down to earth.

"Did you turn up anything on Ada?"

Jonathan brightened and puffed with pride. "I found her."

"Fish, Wildlife and Parks?"

"And the gun club. I made copies."

He ran to his desk, a latter-day James Bond despite the poorly fitting uniform and buzz cut, and shot back, flourishing fax paper and Xeroxes. "She filed for an antelope tag each of the last three years, all in zone six-ten, up on Mission, *and*"—he hopped with glee—"she had a concealed weapons permit for a Glock."

Jules was a little stunned. Leave it to Ada to find drama wherever possible. "A Glock?"

"Yep." Jonathan rocked on his heels, grinning. "She probably used it for target practice."

Jules scanned the Xeroxed log from the Absaroka Gun Club. Four visits in the last month. "They said she's been shooting for the last year or so," said Jonathan. "Pretty hot shit, too, pretty consistent. The man called her a snappy little lady."

Such an understatement. Jules patted Jonathan on the shoulder and wondered if Ada weight-lifted, as well. Horace had listed Mona at 183 pounds.


EDIE and Alice sat on the porch that ran along the side of the Fifth Street house. Through the French doors that led into the kitchen they could hear Peter swearing. He'd burned his hand on a pot while turning the osso buco, but refused help, and it seemed simpler to stay on the porch.

"I still think it's sneaky, going through George's computer and giving that memo to Jules," said Edie.

"I pretty much had to." Alice examined her new flowerbed through the screen. "If you think about it, it can only help George. I mean, someone tried to kill him, and killed his wife, and even if he's too stupid to go to the cops about it I don't want it on my conscience."

They saw Jules from a block away and watched him move toward them down the sidewalk in silence. Depending on when you saw Jules, he could look either strange or handsome, either all angles or all the right angles. He held himself very straight, which kept him from looking gawky despite the general lankiness of his figure; sometimes he even looked graceful. He almost always walked over, even though the fifteen or so blocks between their houses was virtually the length of Blue Deer, and even though walking, and the lack of a squad car, rarely protected him from the beeper he was chained to. Alice hoped it wouldn't sound off until after dessert. Then again, if Edie stayed angry, it might be good to call it a night early.

They heard the gate creak. He'd seen them, and walked

around the lawn to the porch rather than going in through the front door.

"Hello," he said.

"Hi, Jules," said Alice, sounding suspiciously chipper. Edie looked at him without saying a thing. Her voice on the telephone earlier that day, when he'd called looking for George, had iced up the wires.

"Is something wrong?"

"Peter burned his hand." Alice said it as if it explained everything, and jumped from her old metal chair so fast that it rocked. "Here, I'll get you some wine." Jules followed her into the kitchen.

"You fried your hand, huh?"

"Oh, it's not bad," said Peter. He'd already poured Jules's wine, a nice red Bandol.

Jules took a long drink, and Alice fiddled with the salad. "I got your envelope," he said.

"It's probably nothing. I just didn't know what to make of it."

"Can't it wait until after dinner?" asked Peter. No one responded, and Alice made herself busy grating Parmesan, having forgotten the half-finished salad. She scraped her knuckle and swore very softly.

"I know what to make of the memo," said Jules. "I just have to prove it."

Peter's face took on a slightly predatory look. "Later," said Jules.

"You're stiffing me in my own home," said Peter.

Edie stood in the doorway. Jules looked at her with little of his usual warmth, and she shifted uneasily. "He never mentioned this to you, never told you what he saw before he was shot?"

"Not a word."

Jules pulled the creased story ideas page from his pocket

and held it in front of her. "What do you think this means?"

"What is it?"

"One of George's idea files." Alice was embarrassed. "I grabbed it for comic relief."

"Jesus, Alice. That was a shitty thing to do." Edie made a lunge for the sheet, but Jules held it high. "I can't think of a single reason you needed to see that," she said.

Jules smiled. "A little timely autobiography during a murder investigation can be a good thing."

Edie took a chair at the table and tilted back in it. "Since when does being a cop entitle you to read a man's personal papers?"

Alice was still grating, the mound of Parmesan fluttering over the edge of the plate to the floor, her wounded knuckle not quite dripping blood.

Jules had another slug of wine. "You might have noticed the times haven't been normal lately. Since when does being a cop mean you have to be happy about finding rotting bodies?"

"I thought you were in it for the thrill."

"That's enough," said Peter.

"If I'd wanted thrills I wouldn't have moved back."

"I said, that's enough."

Jules, deeply pissed off, carried the forgotten salad to the table and tossed it. Edie glowered from the other side, and when he met her eye and gave her a mirthless smile she looked away and twirled her empty glass on the table.

"Can I get you some more, Edie?" Jules knew he should shut up, but he couldn't help himself.

"No, thank you."

"How was it, moving the stuff out of the ranch house?"

"A pain in the ass."

"George probably couldn't help much, with his shoulder."

"He feels fine. He says he barely notices it now."

"Maybe it doesn't seem like much, compared to his new woes."

"What new woes? The ranch?"

Jules peered at her. "Mona."

"Hah," said Edie. She started to laugh, and Alice finally gave up on the cheese and washed the blood off her hand.

Nobody missed Mona. Jules thought about it as they sat down to dinner. It was hard to think of anyone else so unloved. The only hint that her death might have affected the people in Peter and Alice's kitchen that night was that everyone drank like a fish. They were all basically compassionate, he knew, but no one was eager to talk about her when he brought the topic up. Alice seemed to feel some qualms and pointed out that Mona had been quite nice to her when she first came to town. Edie, more expectant of kindness, more optimistic about the good in people, was ultimately less forgiving and didn't mind giving the impression that she thought the death was welcome. This, for whatever reason, made her more interesting, a little sliver of the strange on home ground; thoughts of Rita Barre dropped to the background. Peter opened another bottle of wine, and Jules watched Edie, all pale skin and glossy dark curls, as she held her glass out. She caught him looking and regarded him calmly, with a glimmer of humor.

Peter's parents had owned a restaurant, albeit in Patagonia, Arizona, and between this training and life with Alice he'd mastered a certain commanding, cheflike attitude. The meal was classic fare, if not classic spring fare. Peter and Alice had a strange habit of cooking out of season or temperature, except for the meager two months of the year the garden was truly productive. Veal shanks and a rich risotto might have been more appropriate to a cold January night than a warm spring evening. Peter also believed that water had a limited culinary value, and used stock or wine whenever possible, even once attempting to boil pasta in a vat of virtual *demi-glace*, with sticky results. He liked things rich.

The second bottle of wine was empty in ten minutes, which helped the mood, and Jules ingratiated himself somewhat with Edie by volunteering that many of his predecessors and some current community pillars were, indeed, pigs. He gave examples, even including some dubious memories of his father and graft, but his favorite story dated from 1965, when the entire police force had been fired after running a tight burglary ring for three years. The owner of the local appliance store had caught four thieves in the act, their van half full, and when the criminals sped off, firing guns in the air, he called the cops and had to wait for fifteen minutes before the same four men showed up to take the report, thinking they wouldn't be recognized minus their ski masks. That had been the end of the city force, and any survivors of the debacle had been absorbed into the sheriff's department. The judge who'd treated the cops gently, a man who'd deposited a decade's worth of bail money with nary a complaint from his staff, had been undone in 1980 when someone doored him at forty miles an hour as he jogged down a dirt road.

"I don't exercise in public," said Jules.

"You don't exercise, period," said Alice.

Edie filled her own glass. "You look fit enough to me."

Peter and Alice blinked at each other and stood simultaneously to get more wine from their meager cellar. Edie winked at Jules.

"It's so easy to throw them off course."

He was impressed. "Do you practice on them a lot?"

"Nah. The last time they left the room like that it was two years ago, and my husband said he'd rather mow alfalfa than go to bed with me."

Jules had been extricating an arugula leaf from the salad and dropped it on the table. He ate it anyway. "I find that hard to believe."

"He said he was joking," said Edie. "His idea of a joke. Then again, how would I know?"

He managed a cackle. "I wouldn't think that you'd need to beg for volunteers."

"That's easy for you to say," said Edie. "I don't think you know how many assholes are out there."

"Well no," said Jules. "It really isn't easy for me to say. Do you think I try so hard with most people who are consistently rude to me?"

She finally blushed. Peter and Alice slammed the basement door, arguing.

"I bet George is one of the volunteers," said Jules. "Don't you feel some sympathy for me, having to deal with a drunk who shoots his brother's car to smithereens, then adds insult to injury by singing?"

"So what do you suppose got him going?" asked Alice, putting two bottles of merlot on the table.

"The love of Ada," said Jules. "Or Mona."

"Ha," said Peter. "Ho, ho. I saw him at the Blue Bat that night and he seemed fairly happy."

"Hey," said Jules, fighting the urge to mention specifics, "Mona and Ray liked each other. Odd but true. And George must still feel something, or why would he keep her photo on his wall?"

Alice stared at him. "I don't believe it. What wall?"

"At work. A prom photo, something like that."

"Oh," said Alice. "That's not Mona, that's George's old girlfriend. She's dead." Jules looked alarmed and she hurried on. "A long time ago, in the seventies. Not your problem. But I think it broke his heart. Mona certainly didn't."

Peter snorted. "Really," said Alice. "Even George was born with a heart. His mother liked Jane a lot, practically adopted her, wanted to send her to college. George said she could have been a great painter."

Jules had a mental tick, like a shutter swinging in the

wind, slight, repetitive flashes of déjà vu mixed with wine. "How'd she die?"

"She fell."

"Jane," he said. "Jane Semple?"

"I think so. Do you remember, from when you were a kid?" said Alice.

"No," said Jules. He poured himself a glass of wine, and thought about George's song the night before, and about the half a photo he'd found tucked in Ray's papers, and about the oddity of either brother having the soul to carry a torch for anyone, alive or dead.

Peter and Alice and Edie were looking at him expectantly. "Ed was talking about it last week, after the mess down at the Boskirk ranch, when the girl played chicken with the VW."

"Is she okay now?" asked Edie.

"She seems fine. She can talk, she has a memory. They'll keep an eye on her for a while, but she's home."

He stood to clear the table and buy time to think, and Peter changed the subject. Jules cleared the dishes with Alice and poked in a question from time to time. Yes, some of the paintings on George's wall had been Jane's, including one of the ocean. No, Alice didn't know how she'd come to fall off a cliff. Drunk or stoned, probably; Blue Deer had been a hopping place in the early seventies, as if Jules didn't know. Yes, Mona had had a wedding ring, a huge but ugly diamond. George had thrown it out after his wife gouged him in the face with it during a cocaine argument; Mona had dug through the trash for hours to find it again. No, they'd hadn't heard of George and Ray openly arguing for quite a while. They usually resorted to catty, third-person vendettas, and acted jolly when they were with one another.

After Alice's *tarte tatin*, and midway into a fourth bottle of wine, Edie, who hadn't been this punchy since her divorce the year before, told a joke. Her children were with their father that night, and she was apparently feeling free:

Two friends went camping in the desert. That night, one got up from the fire and took a piss on some rocks, and a rattlesnake bit him on the head of his penis. He went back to the fire and explained what had happened, and his friend reassured him, made him sit still, and drove a hundred miles to the nearest town to find a doctor. He finally tracked one down at the hospital, doing open heart surgery. There was no way the doctor could leave, but he carefully explained to the man what to do: make a cut near the bite and suck the venom out, two or three times if necessary. If the man did this, and kept his friend still, the victim would be fine until he saw the doctor in the morning. The man said that he understood and drove the hundred miles back to the campsite, where he found his friend in great pain. "What did the doctor say?" asked the suffering man. "I'm sorry," said his friend. "He said you're going to die."

Alice giggled hysterically until tears ran down her face. Peter and Jules sat like rocks, and poured more wine. After another hour Edie headed to the bathroom, threw up, came out looking refreshed, and drank three glasses of water. Alice fell asleep on the couch, and Peter washed the dishes. At midnight Jules, praying that he wouldn't run into whoever was on patrol, drove Edie home in her own car and spent the night.

CHAPTER **11**

**EDIE** dropped Jules off at his house at eight, and he made it to the station by nine, feeling pleasantly promiscuous and prepared for his first meaningful inquest. The only downside was the fact that he knew what would be said in court; everyone else, even Peter, would have something new to work over, while he was stuck with the same set of increasingly confusing minutiae. He tucked Alice's printouts into his desk drawer for future reference, got an update from Scotti on the order of testimony, and checked through his mail. A postcard from his mother, due home the next week from France and Italy, bemoaning the physical wealth and emotional dearth of Rome; a circular on a continuing-education crime lecture; a bulletin about further developments in the forensic use of DNA fingerprinting.

He walked through the courtroom doors at ten and looked slowly around the room, surprised by the crowd of thirty. Almost a third were staff: the county clerk; the court reporter; Harvey and Ed; Scotti and his assistant; Horace, now the county's temporary medical examiner; and Burt Babaski, the coroner. Babaski, who'd been elected with Jules the previous November, owned Blue Deer's only funeral parlor and enjoyed a certain monopoly on death. He was pear-shaped, gray all over, and obviously pleased to preside over his first inquest. Nine jurors fidgeted in the box, tugging on ties and skirt hems, all looking a little overwhelmed.

George and his in-laws sat in the second row on the left side with Roger and Sally, still intent on minding or protecting him, sitting directly behind. Ada and Ray were off in a corner, chitchatting fondly; Lonnie Biddle, obviously miserable, sat alone in the back row. There was a smattering of thrill-seekers, mostly pinched-looking and elderly. The rest of the group was made up of press: Peter sat with Rich, the AP stringer from Bozeman, near a cluster of people who had the look of subanchors from the TV stations in Bozeman, Billings, and Helena. A pretty woman whom Jules thought worked for NPR sat off to one side; he wondered what her voice was like. He turned back to Mona's parents, Ruth and Belton Armbruster. They were talking to each other, ignoring George who sat in a trance. They were blowsy and well-fed like their daughter, and her inquest seemed only to annoy them.

This cataloguing of faces had the effect of making Jules nervous, and he walked a little stiffly past the benches to take his seat at the table with his deputies. He heard Roger say, "There's that asshole," in bell-like tones, and turned around slowly to meet his eyes. Roger looked away, but George smiled at Jules, an oddly sweet, embarrassed expression.

It took another five minutes for Babaski to bring down his gavel. Scotti opened the proceedings by instructing the jury and passing around photos of the body and the river-bank. (He'd passed on the option of trucking the jurors down to the site, calling it a waste of money, though he agreed with Jules that doing so would at least have provided comic relief.) He called Jules, who testified about the body's position when found, the probable theft of Mona's wedding band and engagement ring, his Monday search and discovery of wire cutters on the river beach, and the possible tie-in of the stolen boat and car. He omitted any mention of the cufflink or the video, and stated that the police still had no firm suspects. Peter came next; then George, who stated that he'd last seen his wife Thursday, May 6, at nine A.M.; and then Biddle, who confined his testimony, in response to Scotti's gentle questions, to the simple statement that he'd last seen Mona Blackwater on Thursday at dinner. Horace shuffled up to the witness stand. Things were ticking right along.

"Mr. Bolan, could you please present to the court your own findings and those of the Montana State Forensic Laboratory."

Horace started out in a high voice, cleared his throat, and hit his stride. He was, after all, a very good doctor, just not current on violent death. "We have found that the deceased met her death approximately forty-eight to sixty hours before the discovery of the corpse, therefore on May sixth or May seventh. Death was caused by strangulation, most probably with a metal, wirelike object, and would have come to pass within four minutes, with unconsciousness and an inability to struggle occurring in approximately ninety seconds. Findings, including fibers indicative of car carpeting and the lack of pooling of blood in the body, indicate that the corpse was most probably moved after death."

Horace paused, and Scotti nodded in an encouraging fashion. Jules was thrilled, and imagined Horace reading pertinent texts late into the night to perfect his language. He hoped Horace would skip the part about the dog damage.

"The only sign of violence other than the cause of death was the breaking of the fingers and thumb of the left hand, probably after death. There was no sign of struggle or an attempt at self-defense. We found no clear fingerprints on the body or on the objects found with it. Mrs. Blackwater was in sound health at the time of her death, her body exhibiting only a slight deterioration of the liver and a condition in the pancreas typical of the onset of a diabetic condition. She had eaten perhaps five hours before death occurred, and the contents of her stomach indicated a dinner-style meal. Her blood alcohol level was elevated, consistent with evidence of wine found in her stomach. The presence and condition of semen found in the body suggest that nonviolent intercourse took place shortly before Mrs. Blackwater's death." Horace smiled apologetically in the direction of Mr. and Mrs. Armbruster and folded his hands carefully in his lap. He was done.

Scotti was at a loss. "Do you have any further opinions?"

"No."

"Have you found a cause of death?"

"Homicide due to strangulation."

"Thank you, sir."

Scotti wrapped things up, Babaski called a fifteen-minute recess, and the jury filed out. Jules watched the smokers evacuate the premises, and wondered why Absaroka County hadn't thought to put a few windows or a skylight in its courtroom. When the jury returned Babaski accepted the slip of paper from the forewoman and squeaked out the findings: Mona A. Blackwater, age forty-one, of Blue Deer, Montana, had been done to death in an unknown place at an unknown time, by a person or persons unknown.

JULES celebrated nothing in particular by heading home early that afternoon and cleaning his house. He picked up three hampers of dirty clothes, stripped the bed, washed the sheets and hung them on the line to dry, loaded two weeks' worth of crusty plates and glasses in the dishwasher and ran it twice. Dust mice skittered in front of his broom, and he finally resorted to picking up the larger, faster ones by hand. He ran to the store and bought healthy things like apples, cheese, orange juice, and milk, knowing full well they would rot in the refrigerator. As an afterthought for tight moments, he purchased four bottles of wine and a bag of tortilla chips. As soon as the sheets were dry—after about an hour in the dry, warm wind—he made the bed again, and finally removed Marv's dog bed from its dusty corner and stowed it in the attic. At ten he was exhausted but made a plate of pasta with shallots and cream simmered with a few of last year's dried morels. He ate it while reading a book on utopian journeys across South America, and while drinking one of the bottles of wine. At 11:30 the phone rang, a potential summons to love, and he rallied and grabbed the receiver on the second ring.

It was Harvey. "Delly just called Archie, and Archie called me, cause Jonathan's off dealing with that Clyde City wife thumper. There's a little problem brewing at the Blue Bat, and I guess George is involved, so I thought you'd want to know."

"Meet me down there. I'm leaving now."

"I don't have my uniform on."

"Neither do I. You just came on duty. I don't care about your fucking uniform."


**WHEN** Jules opened the door of the Blue Bat three minutes later, he was met by a roar and sensed a certain anticipation. The place was packed with Friday night's biker crowd, itching to join in with whatever was happening against the back wall near the humidor. Jules slammed his way through to a clearing and came up alongside Ray Blackwater, who had blood streaming down from the back of his head and was holding a chair out in front of him. George faced him, a little swollen in the jaw, crouched ludicrously and clutching the neck of a broken beer bottle. Roger and Sally, a faithful Greek chorus, stood on a table nearby, screaming obscenities at both of them.

"Cut the shit right now." Jules's voice boomed through the bar, and the noise pittered down to the scuffling of feet. Ray darted a look at him and hissed, "Oh screw you."

Jules grabbed a chair and slammed it into Ray's side, knocking him to the floor. He crossed over, flipped him on his stomach, patted down his pockets, and knelt by his ear. "That'll get you a night's accommodations. Don't even think of moving. George, drop the goddamn bottle."

George dropped the bottle and Jules pushed his face over the humidor, cuffed him from behind, and plopped him on the sodden carpeting five feet from his brother.

Roger, still on the table, hopped up and down. "What is this, frontier law?"

"You fucking betcha," said Jules.

Roger's mouth started to open again and Jules said, "Shut the fuck up." He started past Ray toward Delly, who sat on the bar with a baseball bat on his lap, and heard Ray mutter "hick swine." Jules put his foot down on the back of Ray's hand and was happy to hear that even Converse sneakers would cause a small crunch if an appropriate weight was brought to bear. Ray didn't make a sound. Delly got down and slapped Jules on the shoulder.

"Thanks. I didn't want to start myself in case the boys decided to help me out."

"What happened?"

"These four—" he pointed with the baseball bat "—were trading insults for quite a while, and then the two on the floor started swatting at each other, pussy-style. George kept saying Ray was a liar. I'd say George gave the first pat, but big brother"—he pointed toward Ray—"was saying more. That's when I called Archie. I told them I was going to, and they calmed down a bit, and the next thing I knew George blasted the other guy with a full beer bottle, a real low thing to do, if you ask me."

No doubt about it, George was on a binge, and it was not a limp-wristed effort. At the moment he was singing softly into the carpeting, still locked into Velvet Underground lyrics. The former social worker in Jules was fascinated.

"How much did they have to drink?"

"Lots."

Jules waited.

"I'd say a half-dozen martinis and whiskeys apiece, probably more. They've been here since eight or nine. George had the martinis."

"Anything else you should tell me?"

"I'm ready to lose George as a client. First the thing earlier this week, when he was crying at the bar with McElwaine and went out and shot a car, and now this shit. I don't need a lawsuit."

Jules stared at him. "Bunny McElwaine?"

"The self-same prick, your former colleague."

George Blackwater could have killed ten women, and he'd still be too nice to have a drink with Bunny in the normal course of events. "Anyone have anything to add?" Jules scanned the crowd and stopped with a lurch when he saw Rita, smiling calmly at him from a bar stool. Harvey came through the crowd at the same moment, having taken ten minutes to make a ten-block drive. Jules made himself look back down at Ray and George.

"Do you have your squad car, Harvey?"

"Yep."

"Let's pack them in."

"Ray didn't do anything." Sally spoke from her perch on the table. "George hit him first."

Jules wondered why she wasn't defending the usual brother, and smiled. "He resisted arrest. You'd better walk to your hotel, honey."


**BOTH** men refused Breathalyzers and were booked for drunk and disorderly. Jules sent Ray to the hospital with Harvey for some stitches and possibly a cast, and told him to try for a blood sample. This left him with George, the loose cannon; he would rather have discussed cufflinks and other stray details with Ray, but the thought of another visit to the hospital was unbearable.

Jules led George down the hall to the lounge and offered him coffee.

"No thank you, Jules." George was very polite. He pulled out a chair and took a seat with the exaggerated care of a drunk. "Would you happen to have a cigarette?"

"I didn't know you smoked, George."

"I don't, but it seems in keeping with the room."

"I don't have any. I'll get one from Archie in a bit." Jules sat down at the opposite side of the table and drummed his fingers. "So, here we are again. Why don't we start with why you hit your brother over the head with a bottle? I can't decide if it's a step up or down from shooting his car."

George examined the acoustic tile of the ceiling. His large eyes looked yellow in the fluorescent light. "He was getting to me, just like always."

"What was he getting to you about?"

"My relative failures, his successes."

Jules sighed. "With women, or with writing?"

George rubbed some drying blood from the palm of his hand onto his pants. "I want to call my lawyer."

"Lonnie?"

"I have a right to make bail, right? To make a phone call?"

"After me," said Jules, ushering him out of the room. "We have a few more things to talk about when you're done."

George, unbelievably, tried to reach Lonnie Biddle, but no one answered the phone. He called Roger, who hung up on him. Jules graciously offered him a third call, but George only reached Edie's answering machine. He didn't try his in-laws. Jules bummed a cigarette from Archie and hauled George back down to the room.

"No one seems eager to bail you out."

"Fuck you," said George. He fiddled awkwardly with the cigarette. Jules lit it for him and pushed George on his good shoulder so that he fell back into the chair.

"Tell me what started the fight, George."

Jules watched, appalled, as tears sprouted from George's eyes and ran down his face.

"It's like he ruined me twice, ruined me when it happened and now ruined everything I remembered about her." He took a long drag and went into a spasm of coughing. Jules reached for the cigarette but George held it away, dropping an ash on his shoulder. "You have to understand that I loved her. I loved her. I never thought I'd love someone like that again."

"What did Ray say to you?"

"He said that he'd fucked her." George started to weep again.

Jules wanted him to stop, feeling as if he might blow up from sheer impatience and embarrassment. "But you knew he'd fucked Mona. I showed you the video, here."

"Not Mona," said George, sodden and hiccoughing and high-pitched. "I couldn't give less of a shit. Jane. He said he'd screwed my Jane. I just can't bear it."

The Blackwaters were fighting about a woman dead twenty years rather than a woman dead a week.

Jules stood up. "I'll get a cell for you."

"Ray's the main swine, and you should bear that in mind when he blames me for things. He's so full of shit with his white knight routine."

"I've never ever thought of him as a white knight, George. Get some sleep before the funeral."

Harvey sat on Archie's desk, eating a bag of chips. Ray had needed twelve stitches on his scalp, but only one bone in his hand was broken. Horace had been on call and had loaded him up with tranquilizers, and Jules could hear even, honest snores traveling up the stairwell from the drunk tank. He'd have to conduct interview number two the next day, maybe even at Ray's dinner party, assuming he was still invited. He finished the arrest paperwork and headed back into the warm night at two. The Blue Bat was already closed, and Rita was nowhere in sight.

CHAPTER 12

THE NEXT morning Jules rolled over in bed, called the station, and had Ray and George released without requiring
bail. Mona's funeral was scheduled for 10:30, and he had no
intention of holding things up. At ten he put on a charcoal
suit and slowly drove his truck to St. James Episcopal
Church. The crowd filing in was sizable, and Jules sat in a
pew toward the back with Peter and Alice and Edie. George
and Ray sat together, silent and pale, with Mona's parents,
Mrs. Ball, and the children. Ada, Biddle and his wife, and
Eldridge Anderson were at opposite corners of the church,
along with everyone else who'd been at the inquest, and
most of the town. In a place like Blue Deer, it was perfectly
acceptable to go to a stranger's funeral, and a tragedy made
this sport especially popular.

Jules watched the mourners during the service but kept his head down and his mouth shut when they rose to sing hymns; if he sang, especially "Amazing Grace," he'd weep, no matter who had died, especially if his gaze strayed to the small heads in the front pew. At Calvary Cemetery he stood back from the grave site, and avoided looking at the highest, older section, under the tallest trees, with the best, but not much appreciated view of the valley below. When it was over he filed by and threw his handful of earth onto the casket, and met Mona's parents, who were dry-eyed. George shook Jules's hand and then hugged him, the child who still loves his father, even though he's been beaten by him. Ray offered his left hand and pulled him aside.

"Thanks for dismissing the charges."

Jules hadn't dismissed the charges. Archie, at the end of a shift, could make the most amazing mistakes, but it was always possible that Ray was railroading him. "No big deal. Sorry about the hand."

"No nerve damage. Otherwise I'd sue you. Can you make it for dinner?"

"Sure," said Jules. "We need to have a talk."

"Come down early. We'll take a turn or two around the garden. Alice is going to fix it up for me. Dinner and the garden." Ray pulled out a cigarette and fumbled with the matches. Jules lit it for him and started for his car, but Ray called out.

"Nice suit. Where'd you get it?"

Jules turned around and looked at Ray, who was probably the first guy to show up at Calvary in an Armani. "Paris," he answered. He pulled the tie off in the car and drove home for a nap. He dreamt about Marv, back when he was still a puppy.

Alice woke him an hour later, saying that Ray had told her he was going up to the ranch early, and that she needed help—Peter was at a conference in Mammoth until six, and her helper's car wasn't working. Jules, who knew from experience that it was better not to be involved in Alice's caterings, said, "Take mine." Alice said, "Nah, just stop by on your way down. I won't keep you long." Then she came up with a few errands.

ALICE hummed as she whisked an apple aioli. They'd been at it since seven and it was now five, with dinner proper scheduled to begin at eight, guests arriving an hour earlier. Ray wanted to put on the dog, and Alice, her refrigerator filled with niceties shipped from New York, had happily complied. The fresh ham would come out in about an hour, the red cabbage salad with roasted chestnuts was covered and ready to travel, the *vacherin* was warming in one of the cardboard boxes. Rita had been astoundingly efficient, a precise, speedy sous chef, and they were ahead of schedule. They'd worked on only one other job together, but she had the kitchen down already, anticipated problems, and was good company.

"You take those three boxes up and I'll bring the last of it with me," Alice said. "He's late, he should be here any minute. Remind me to see if he remembered the flowers."

"It won't take that long for me to set stuff up," said Rita, slivering a roasted red pepper. "I could walk home and take a shower and you could pick me up on your way."

This made no sense, but maybe fatigue was kicking in. Maybe she was shy. "What's the point if you can go up early with Jules? You'll get dirty all over again if you shower before you finish prepping. Have Jules stop and pick up your stuff. I already told Ray one of us might have to use the bathroom to dress, and he said no problem. Just don't let him follow you in."

Rita's face was blank. "Don't let Jules follow me in?"

Alice gave her a funny look. "No, Ray. Is there some

problem with driving up there with Jules? He's funny, you'll like him."

"I don't have any problem with driving up with him," said Rita. She had her back turned, stretching up for salt cellars and pepper grinders; Alice noted with only mild annoyance that she did not need a chair to reach the shelf.

"Why don't you grab some of those enameled ashtrays up above," she said. "And I might have a nice hand-blown vase back there for the peonies. Can you see one?"

There was a limit to Rita's height, and she clambered up on the counter. Jules slammed through the front door.

"If you'd like me to take stuff up you could at least leave a place to park."

"So sorry," said Alice, giddy with happiness. She couldn't believe they were on schedule. "I'd hate to pull your back out. There's not much." She scraped the bowl, knocked the spatula clean, and turned around. "There's only three boxes."

Jules wasn't paying attention. He'd stopped in the middle of the kitchen, staring at Rita. Alice watched Rita peer quickly over her shoulder and then go back to her cupboard search, and thought she probably wondered what kind of geek was running the local sheriff's department. Alice wondered herself; perhaps Edie had addled his brain.

"Rita Barre, Jules Clement, Edie's friend. Rita's the only person in town who can catch a wineglass in midair."

Rita looked over her shoulder again and smiled weakly. Jules was hot-cheeked, remembering a certain dexterity.

Alice folded the aioli into a blue china bowl, oblivious. "Did you remember the flowers?"

Jules had. He wanted to die, ideally as soon as possible. Once they piled everything into the car and said good-bye to Alice (Jules decided he'd take her to hell with him), Rita was silent except to say she needed to stop by her house for clothes, something Alice had already said four times. Jules followed her in, carrying the bottle of Armagnac Alice had packed in one of the boxes, and poured two shots while Rita moved in and out of the bedroom and bathroom. She tossed a black dress and some high heels onto the kitchen table.

"Why don't you just get dressed now?"

"What, here in the kitchen?" She looked amused. "I'll only get the dress dirty if I set up in it, and I can only handle those shoes for three or four hours before I go pigeon-toed."

He handed her a glass and swigged his. It made him blink; the pain was deserved.

"Look, Jules, it's obviously no big deal if you're seeing someone else. This was not meant to be a serious thing."

He was a little surprised by the way he disliked her last line. "Why not? Because of the man I heard on the phone?"

Some underpants and stockings and a very small black brassiere landed on top of the dress. "In a way," she said, disappearing into the bathroom.

He touched a stocking with one finger, poured himself another glass of Armagnac, and stood in the doorway, watching her rummage through her medicine chest for lipstick. Life had become incredibly complicated in the last week, and he suddenly liked that fact, the way a man might like the final decision to commit suicide. Murder, mayhem, women. Rita had a smudge of flour under one ear and her T-shirt and jeans were covered with a portion of Ray's dinner. They'd never seen each other in the daylight before.

"Are you in love with him?"

"It's complicated."

"Most things are."

"We broke it off recently, but he hasn't really gone away."

"How recently?"

"Monday." They looked at each other; she had just a hint of a smile. "When did you start seeing Edie?"

Jules looked down at the floor. What was he supposed to say, Thursday? You woke me up and I started skidding into soft objects again?

"Not so long," he said. "It's a pretty relaxed thing."

"A convenient thing?"

"Not too goddamn convenient tonight," answered Jules, rallying and raising his head. He didn't have a thing to lose. "Alice says you're ahead of schedule. I think we should take a break."

**WHEN** Jules and Rita pulled into the ranch driveway, Ray was in the garden, and waved to them with a languid arm. Or, rather, Jules had the impression that Ray waved to him, and dismissed Rita with the sort of assurance born of having sixty magazine employees hovering for most of the last two decades. A servant was a servant, pretty or not, and the law deserved at least token respect. Jules took his time helping Rita with the boxes.

When he reached the garden Ray was pretending not to mind the delay, inspecting the buds on his peonies, flipping his hair out of his face occasionally. He and George both had average, tidy builds, but they moved differently. It was possibly all New York attitude—Ray was the kind of man who acted as if he were in a tuxedo even when wearing ratty shorts, though Jules doubted he ever wore ratty shorts.

"Do you know what these are supposed to look like? There's bugs all over them."

Jules craned around the huge oval bed that arced out from the front porch. He counted at least ten clumps of peonies. "Alice told me last spring that ants mean the plants are healthy."

"They're the only plant I recognize. What are these?"

He peered down. "Columbine, I think."

Ray pointed again. "These?"

"I don't know. Ask Alice. She used to do the beds for George. She probably planted most of this stuff."

"I will, but dinner comes first."

Jules studied Ray. He'd managed to acquire a tan, but otherwise looked a little worse for last night's wear. "I think we should just get what we have to talk about out of the way."

"Fine," said Ray. "Shoot."

"What started the fight? What was George accusing you of lying about?"

"I don't know how he decided to begin," said Ray, smiling. "Does he know about Mona and me?"

"I showed him the tape Tuesday night."

Ray gave him a look of infinite reproach, then wandered over to a lawn chair.

"Then don't ask why we were fighting."

"George said it was about Jane Semple." Jules tossed a pair of gardening gloves from another lawn chair and stretched out.

Ray stiffened.

"Why don't you tell me the story," said Jules.

"I gather you know it."

"Not really," said Jules. "And I'd like your version of it, anyway. We've got plenty of time before your guests arrive."

"She was drunk, at a party. She fell off a river cliff onto some rocks and died."

"When did it happen?"

Ray was leaning over in his chair, ripping the grass out of his lawn. "Nineteen seventy-two, I think. Some high-school party in early summer or spring, because college must have been out."

"Why does it keep coming up?"

"He's got this thing about her still," said Ray. "George always felt responsible, and he was, in a way."

"How so?"

"He was a bad influence."

Ray was tearing out every other blade, manually dethatching his lawn. "What were you?" asked Jules.

"I barely knew the girl."

"But you went to bed with her?"

"No," said Ray. "I never did."

"Then why did you tell George you had?"

Ray gave up on the grass, looked at his fingers, and tried to shake them clean. Anyone else would have wiped them on his pants.

"Because I'm mean. I'm spiteful." He smiled. "I'm a real shitsucker and his whining gets to me, or maybe the prairie views are driving me nuts. Why ask? It was a stupid thing to say, just as stupid as screwing his wife, and now I wish I hadn't done either. I liked my car. George probably knew I was lying."

Jules didn't detect any real compassion for the weeping little brother, the twenty-year-old lover whose memories had been gutted by an offhand remark. This was all self-centered regret; Ray didn't like to come off in a bad light.

He didn't let go. "That doesn't answer my question about why it's coming up now."

"Listen," said Ray. "I've been here three weeks and people have been treating me like Cain, as if poor George was Abel. He's not." The sun came out from under a cloud and he squinted at Jules. "I've gotten a bad rap, and my brother's gotten away with murder. Literally."

"Mona?"

"Well, Jesus, can you think of anyone with a better reason to kill her?"

What a snide motherfucker, thought Jules, losing a little more of his love of humanity. He pulled a plastic bag out of his pocket. "Do you recognize this?"

Ray reached for the bag and started to open it. "Please don't do that," said Jules.

Ray looked at him, taken aback, and peered through the plastic. "It's my cufflink."

"Yes."

"It wasn't broken when I last saw it. It's very valuable."

"I'm sure it is," said Jules. "It was broken when I found it."

"Where?"

"Near Mona's body."

Ray gave him a long look and dropped the plastic bag back into Jules's outstretched hand. "It must have come off during our skirmish at the bank. Mona was kind enough to pick it up. What's your point?"

"My point is that you should remember you were the last person we know of to see her alive, and that I don't buy most of what you're saying about why you were with her to begin with."

"A friendly warning?"

"A cautionary note."

"I'll keep that in mind." Ray pulled himself out of the chair with his good hand. "I've enjoyed meeting you, except for the incident in the bar last night. It's refreshing to meet someone out here with a brain. Though I fell for your act at first."

"Act?" Jules watched some grackles eat last year's fruit under a flowering crab.

"Your hick number. Kind of like meeting a Jesuit trying to disguise himself as a Holy Roller."

"Umm," said Jules. He couldn't remember resorting to such a routine.

Ray leaned on the lawn chair and smiled. The expression was really a smirk, as if he were challenging Jules to say something intelligent, something in line with the Jesuit remark, a decidedly mixed compliment. Jules didn't bother.

"Why do you and your brother hate each other so much?"

"Well, we always have, for some reason."

Jules watched him. Ray looked up at the clouds again, then met his eyes. "Not good enough, huh? We had a very unhappy childhood—our dad died early, and our mother was a little crazy, certifiable by the time she died—and she baited us a bit, especially once we were teenagers."

Another pause. Ray sighed. "We've always been quite competitive."

"I picked up on that."

"It's not a garden-variety competition, and George can't stand losing."

"So you've never lost?"

"Not in that arena. I mean, I don't think what we do came naturally to either of us—we had to work to do it well, or should I say profitably."

More token humility. "So you and George made peace at the funeral."

"Even we know enough to be peaceful at a funeral. He apologized about the car. He'll come tonight. He's a fatalist."

"Were you serious when you said your mother was insane?"

"I was serious. She talked to walls and houseplants. I don't suppose George mentioned that."

"He mentioned it." Jules got out of his chair and they started walking toward the house. "Was she insane when she left you this ranch? Did she know George loved it?"

"Of course she did. My mother was a spiteful woman, even when she couldn't tell a cat from a dog. She blamed him for Jane."

IN THE kitchen Ray gave him a whiskey. There was an astounding amount of clean floor space in the house after Edie and George's moving operation. The dining room and living room were already set with flowers and hors d'oeuvres, and Jules could hear the shower running, Rita preparing for her little black dress. Jules saw Ada's car pull up and looked at his watch; it was only 6:30. Ada, once again, was unhappy to see him, and he found it fascinating that Ray, who greeted her with a big, wet kiss, wouldn't have warned her. Alice and Peter careened up the driveway two minutes later, and Jules saved himself from Ray's latest romance by walking outside to greet them.

The five of them walked around the yard as Alice identified plants for Ray, and Ada admired the house's exterior as though she'd never seen it before, though everyone knew she had many times. It was all a little too colonial for Jules and Peter, who were edging toward the house just as Roger and Sally rolled in, their rental car bearing the unmistakable central dent of an instantly dead deer. Sally wept large tears as she told the story, which degenerated into an argument with Roger about whether the deer had been male or female. Alice ended the conversation by asking if either of them had ever seen a deer before, then headed for the kitchen.

Jules and Peter followed her in to help but she shooed them out of this sanctuary, and they took up position in the living room near some crayfish and runny French cheese. Rita was dressed now, a blur of movement despite the high heels.

"I thought you told me you didn't know a Marguerite Barre," said Jules.

Peter gave him a goofy smile. "I never thought you might mean Rita. Honest to God."

"You'll pay," said Jules.

Alice called Peter, and Jules ambled out of the Dutch door to look for birds. It was dusk, and he could hear coyotes yipping in the foothills a mile away. The few birds he saw skittered out of nearby trees when George screamed down the driveway in a spanking new sapphire blue Land Cruiser. It was entirely possible that he'd left the funeral and headed for a car dealership. Horace, apparently tipsy, crowed from the backseat window as George lurched to a stop, and Jules missed seeing Edie until she'd slammed the passenger door. He had a nasty cattle-prod sort of reaction, but managed to help Horace out of the car.

George was carrying a case of wine and smiling expansively. "Ray, I talked Edie out of Little League, told her it was time for their father to put in some time. I hope that's okay."

Edie, probably more concerned about Alice's opinion, smiled stiffly at Ray and headed for the house. She didn't look at Jules at all.

"Of course," said Ray. "We were going to be ten originally, anyway. Your dear wife."

Jules elbowed Horace. "What the hell have you been up to?"

"Wake number one. This is wake number two." Horace shook his head. "Poor George. Those in-laws are driving him nuts."

Jules followed Horace inside, watched Rita counting place settings, refilled his glass, and stood by Edie, who was talking to Sally and Roger. He smiled at her and she looked away, pretending to be fascinated by the Hollywood bullshit Roger spewed forth. Jules held his ground, leaning against a doorjamb in apparent comfort, but this accomplished nothing—Edie started for a place on the couch next to George. Jules touched her arm.

"Let's go outside and talk," he said.

"What about?"

"I won't know until you tell me."

She marched through the Dutch door. He followed her to the other side of the Land Cruiser and tried to smile again.

"Don't look at me that way," said Edie.

"Jesus," said Jules. "Why the hell not? I looked at you that way this morning at the funeral, and it was fine then. I *like* to look at you."

"That was before I knew you were into playing big cop."

Jules stared, uncomprehending, and she gritted her teeth. "You *like* to throw men on the floor and break their hands."

"No, I don't," said Jules, feeling his face tighten. "I don't enjoy assholes who hit each other over the head with bottles, either, especially when they do it in bars packed with motorcycle boys."

"No, you like it," said Edie. "You were born a cop. Maybe you were a playground bully. I can't believe I went to bed with you."

"Believe it."

She darted toward the house and he followed. Rita was placing a tray of oysters on the coffee table in the living room, and George was staring at her, a dreamy look on his face. Jules glared at him until George met his eyes and looked away, abashed. Jules sat down at the far side of the room, next to Peter, and endured his friend's grin until Alice came into the room and whispered into his ear.

"Jules, do you know where the hell the Armagnac got to?"

"I forgot it."

"What do you mean, you forgot it? I handed it to you. Is it in your car?"

He shook his head miserably.

"Jesus," hissed Alice. "Never mind. I don't want to know if you dropped it on the pavement."

"I didn't drop it," said Jules. "I left it at Rita's."

She stared at him, suddenly comprehending.

"I took it inside," he said, trying to sound nonchalant. "We had a drink."


**JULES** spent the next hour mulling over the social dangers of a small town and hoping for the first time in history that his beeper would sound. By the time they sat down to dinner he prayed for a four-alarm fire, an earthquake, a broken dam. Rita served gracefully and didn't meet his eyes, or anyone else's, even once. Edie didn't look at him, either, and Alice timed her storm-cloud looks with rare discretion, usually each time she popped up to check on the kitchen. Jules tried to hold paranoia at bay, drank wine, and let his mind float, taking in faces and expressions and voices. Alice had always had a good voice, soft and lulling except for when she was angry or drunk, at which point her volume and Michigan accent increased precipitously. Edie's voice still had a hint of New Jersey, but she got by on sheer animation. Rita's was lovely and very low, but tonight her comments were understandably confined to "Would you like some fresh-ground pepper?" Sally started tinkling on in a piccolo voice about how much she'd always had a secret desire to be a waitress, and Alice finally said, in a calm voice, "I'm sure you have, dear." That was that; Sally didn't quite grasp the point, but she did shut up for a few seconds before starting in on Jules, breaking his trance. They talked about Los Angeles, pleasantly enough until the salad appeared, and she rubbed his knee under the table. Jules jumped and gave her a horrified look; she blushed and turned to natter at George, who sat facing his brother at the other end of the table. George and Ray sounded exactly alike, one of those family resemblances that would have made phone calls tricky if they'd lived in the same house. Peter had lost any Arizona accent by zigzagging across America; Horace, whom Jules increasingly regarded as a good angel, told jokes in a raspy western bass.

Ada and Roger both blared, trying to make themselves heard. Maybe Ada thought sheer volume would make Jules less likely to arrest her for shooting George, and maybe she was right. He caught her eye and she toned down and concentrated on Ray, feeding him little hushed one-liners. Ray listened to her quite happily, and hung his bad hand on the back of her chair when he finished eating. Jules wondered if he knew how good his new girlfriend was with a gun. George was drinking like a fish but seemed peaceful, though he threw an occasional wall-eyed glance in his big brother's direction. He told stories of having been thrown out of the better L.A. restaurants; Roger filled in any incidents he might have forgotten, and dropped names.

Alice's food was delicious, and Jules blamed a slight sense of nausea on his companions. He disliked them all at that moment, and disliked himself. The party had the feel of claustrophobic English mystery, a bad locked-door drama— you could almost hear Agatha Christie intone "Someone at the table killed someone else." The whole scene was a little surreal, and Jules had just refused another glass of wine when George suddenly lurched to his feet, brandishing a full glass.

"To the dead," said George. "May they rest in peace." He sat down again with a thump. Rita stood next to him, clearing plates; George slapped her on the buttocks. "What can I give you for the waitress, brother?"

Jules twitched and the rest of the table froze, watching the blank expression on Rita's face. She looked down at George and he looked up at her, smiling. Then she let the contents of her tray—ten plates with silverware, a full ashtray, and three water glasses—slip into his lap.

"Tension," said Ray. "I love it."

"Goddammit, George," said Alice. "Just when I started to like you again."


THE DINNER party ended early. Roger and Sally had evacuated by ten; Jules and Peter had helped Horace and Edie load George in the back of the Land Cruiser by 10:30. Ray and Ada had gone upstairs as soon as their guests left, and filled the kitchen below with endless, monotonous thumping sounds during cleanup. Peter said, "No imagination," but no one was really in the mood to laugh. Alice and Rita each had two huge drinks, and when Jules told Alice he'd drive Rita home she gave him a last glower, a real doozy. Peter shoveled her out the door, and Jules and Rita finished up in silence.

**JULES** lurched upright, almost flipping Rita off her single bed. She grumbled and readjusted herself, but he remained sitting, his torso covered with sweat in the cool night air that flooded through the open window. The dream had been about car accident photos—the first an innocuous black and white of empty pavement, the second of a baby's hand, the third of a snake found coiled under a hood, poached in bubbling antifreeze, and so on. The stack was endless, and George, who was lecturing him on their artistic merit, seemed not to realize that he was covered with blotches that looked like liver spots but were blue.

Jules crawled over Rita and fumbled on the dark floor for her small alarm clock. He found it under the bed; it was 4:30. He'd slept for no more than an hour, and now his teeth started chattering as the sweat dried on his body and he crouched on the floor, naked and confused. He felt like he had a metal vise on his head, an angel halo with bolts piercing his skull, and it took him a long time to remember that she'd thrown his pants and belt out the window onto the porch roof. It hadn't seemed funny to him then, and now it truly pissed him off. Alcohol and the stress of the day and night had given Rita what could gently be termed a character change and considerable energy, and Jules's whole body ached, though he hadn't complained at the time. Now he reached out the window in vain, then clambered as quietly as possible over the sill, trying not to bruise his tender groin. A naked sheriff on a roof, two blocks from his station; life continued to amaze. He reached the cold, dew-soaked jeans and edged back into the room, located his shirt in the bed and his shoes near the alarm clock, and decided that his underpants were gone forever.

His belt lay in a bed of lilies under the front porch. An alley cat meowed and rubbed against his leg as he fumbled for it, then followed him down the sidewalk, cleaning a paw under the streetlight as he drove away.

**HE WOKE** at noon and immediately climbed back into his truck and drove north, just to get the hell out of Dodge. He had a restorative drink in Ringling, then a bad steak in White Sulphur Springs, before heading southwest and taking what amounted to a two-track around the Bridger Range. He saw three golden eagles, five red-tailed hawks, some goshawks, and untold magpies, wrens, finches, and antelope. A coyote grinned at him from the side of the road. It was a shame the animal had become such a fashionable symbol, or he'd have found sarcasm and deep meaning in the look. It was after dark by the time he pulled in front of his house and creaked out of the car, up the walk, and through the front door, to find Rita dishing out chicken in his kitchen, her Scout repaired and parked in the alley. She had the newly scrubbed, innocent look of an infant, and after staring at her for a moment he sat down to eat.

# CHAPTER 13

## BLUE DEER BULLETIN
### *SHERIFF'S REPORT, WEEK OF MAY 10—16*

May 10—A report was received of a suspicious vehicle. The owner was contacted and said the car had been stalling all day.

An individual reported discovering a submerged boat near Pine Creek. An officer responded and requested help in removing the boat.

May 11—A dog was picked up in front of the courthouse and taken to a veterinarian. The owner came to the courthouse and said he would go ransom his dog.

A report was received of a skunk in a garbage can. The owner of the garbage can said that the officer could shoot the skunk.

May 12—An individual reported sighting a disturbed individual in Cottonwood Park. An officer responded but could not locate the individual.

May 13—An individual reported a lost spouse. The sheriff's office was notified later that the spouse had been found.

A report was received of a raft wrapped around a tree. The individual involved was concerned about personal belongings. The raft was spotted floating down the river.

May 14—A report was received of an altercation at a local business. Officers responded and two individuals were taken into custody.

An individual reported hitting a deer and damaging his vehicle. An officer and wrecker were requested. Both were dispatched. The individual was advised to be cautious in the future.

May 15—A report was received of a possible DUI. Officers were advised.

An individual reported two skunks under a shed. An officer was requested to dispatch the skunks. An officer responded, but the skunks hid.

May 16—An individual reported a man pulling a gun on him. An officer responded and settled the situation. No arrest was made.


JULES easily avoided dangerous introspection on Monday. The county commissioners wanted to have a special meeting with him about Mona's death. The man with the gun had visited the park again the evening before, fed the ducks, and then shot five of them. An unhappy employee at a local construction company had threatened his employer with a gun. The gun hadn't been loaded, small comfort to Ed, the employer, or anyone else involved. Rosemary Blackwater's will sat on his desk, fresh from Portland, and when he'd read it he headed for the courthouse wing.

Scotti's secretary, a high-school flame, was reading a fat paperback, and he stuck his tongue out at her as he walked through to the inner office, where the cloud of cigar smoke made his eyes water. Scotti cackled from his desk while Jules struggled to open the window.

"I got Mrs. Blackwater's will this morning," Jules said. "She has a bequest to Blue Deer High, ten thousand dollars to be spent on art books in the memory of Jane Semple."

Scotti looked at him as if he'd come from Mars. Jules continued.

"Jane Semple died in a fall back in the seventies. She was George Blackwater's girlfriend. Do you remember anything about it?"

"How old do you think I am?" asked Scotti, annoyed. He was notoriously vain. "I'm way too young to have been around for an accident twenty years ago. Are you still screwed up about Maribeth Arnhold?"

"No."

"Then why the hell are you asking about this?"

"I'm curious. The girl's in the will, and she's dead. I've been hearing a lot about her lately."

"Doesn't it occur to you that we have enough bullshit on our hands without a twenty-year-old *accident*?" Scotti fairly shrieked the last word. "Aren't there plenty of other things to be curious about? Various injuries visited upon Mr. and Mrs. Blackwater? A crazy shooting ducks in the park?"

Jules sighed, not bothering to mention that Scotti's two examples of mayhem weren't quite in the same league. "You could bring charges now in George's shooting, but I wouldn't bother."

Scotti was in a bad mood. He was in a bad mood most Mondays. "Would that be George shooting Ray's car, or George being shot? Maybe I should campaign this fall for a local loony bin."

"My week's not looking too hot, either, Axel. You can charge Ada, but I'd wait until we find a gun."

Jules explained Ada's unforgiving nature and target-shooting hobby. Scotti cheered up. "Maybe she'll confess."

"Fat chance."

"There must be something we can do."

"Like what?" said Jules. "Convince a jury she has a pet peeve about apologies? Subpoena her computer? I'm sure she cleared it out, and George's doesn't show any record of the sender, according to Alice."

Scotti relit his cigar and pouted. Jules continued. "Delly told me George was talking to Bunny McElwaine before he shot Ray's car. He was on the force back when Jane Semple died."

Scotti blanched. "Don't go near him. He's dirty, and I'm up for election."

Jules shrugged. "I'll wait until I see his car in front of the Blue Bat."

"Let's get kicking on Ada instead, but quietly. The big boys won't be too soothed when they find out the queen bee is taking potshots at her lover."

I *am* kicking, thought Jules.

Scotti took a long drag. "I talked to my state buddy in Helena over the weekend."

"Did you tell him I was a momo, and he should come right down?"

"I told him you were brilliant. I told him you'd have the criminal or criminals in hand by the weekend."

Jules rolled Mrs. Blackwater's will into a tube and trudged back toward the station, then veered down the back hall, walked out the door, and got into his car. The high school was down by the river, and on his way through the park he was happy to see that someone had had the presence of mind to remove the duck corpses and most of the bloody feathers. He wondered if ducks adopted orphaned eggs.

John Dribnitz was leaning back in his chair with his feet on his desk, laughing into the phone. Jules knocked on the open door and watched dread float over the principal's happy, puffy features.

He hung up. "Jules. How ya doing?"

"Great. Do you have a minute?"

"Well, sure. Of course. Nothing new about Maribeth, is it?"

"No. She's doing pretty well."

Dribnitz, one of the nicest men Jules had ever met despite earlier differences of opinion, hadn't relaxed yet. He was huge, with snowy hair and little pig eyes; he constantly complained of gout, his excuse for being able to put his feet up on his desk.

Jules sat down opposite him. "John, nothing's wrong. I just have some questions. There's absolutely nothing to worry about. No shoplifters, no dopers, nothing."

"Ha," said Dribnitz. "Now why on earth would I worry?"

"Really, don't. I want to ask you about Jane Semple."

Dribnitz's face went blank. "What did you say?" he asked, finally.

"You know," said Jules. "The one and only senior to die on a skip day."

"Why?" It was a little howl of relief and consternation.

"I'm curious."

"Twenty years later."

"Yes. Tell me about her."

"She's dead," said John Dribnitz. "I nearly quit over it. I love being reminded in May of 1993 about an accident in 1972. I was only thirty. Please, tell me why you're ruining my day."

"I'd really rather not," said Jules. "And anyway you'll probably figure it out. She was smart, right? A good kid."

"A great kid." Jules watched John Dribnitz light a cigarette, verboten on school property since 1990. "Bad background, great kid."

"Why was her background bad?"

"Dad was an alky, worked at the engine rebuild center, beat Mom, and left for Butte when all the kids were pretty young."

"Ah," said Jules. "And why was she good?"

"Because she was smart. The student body wanted to go ahead and name her valedictorian even though she was gone, but we decided it was too depressing. Pretty too, and canny, a keeper all around. Especially in hindsight, now that I'm better at picking the ones who at least figure out how to enjoy life, which isn't many, if you think about it."

Jules had thought about it. "Anyone see it happen?"

"I don't think so." Dribnitz hotboxed the remains of his cigarette.

"Any special friends?"

"I honestly can't remember any names, except for the ones you know, the ones who weren't at my school."

"Who would that be?" asked Jules, all innocence.

"The Blackwater boys, dipshit. Don't play with me."

"Don't get pissy," said Jules. "Have another cigarette. What was she doing with rich boys?"

"Their mother came in to teach art once and a while. She was a painter, and she really took to Jane. And the home thing at Semple's was pretty bad, even after the dad left, so Jane spent a hell of a lot of time with the Blackwaters, even went to Portland with them for a visit once, if I remember correctly. And to be perfectly fair—" Dribnitz lit up again "— to be perfectly fair, the thing she and George had always struck me as kind of sweet. I mean, he didn't seem like a bad kid at all. Going to Dartmouth or Princeton or wherever the hell he went, all that shit. Not that it was his fault."

"Was he there that night?"

"I don't know," said Dribnitz. "All of them were busy covering their own asses and everyone else's. I think they were both in town that summer. Ray was okay, too, for a hotshot."

In its own way, this line struck Jules as another obituary. On his way out he cruised the memorial portrait lineup in the gym hall and found Jane quickly, near two of his old friends who'd managed to incinerate themselves in a Camaro. He remembered her photo now, though he couldn't remember her. Born 1954, died 1972, fresh-faced and small-boned. He couldn't imagine how he'd ever taken her for Mona.

On the way back to the station he saw George's new car in his rearview mirror and waved. Then the constant static on his radio became more pointed: Grace, saying that the man in Clyde City was holding a gun on his wife, and that Jonathan and Harvey were on their way north.


JULES was all for gun control, and Clyde City was the sort of town that especially needed it: five hundred souls in ten square miles and a suicide rate worthy of a Norwegian village near the Arctic Circle. It wasn't quite as windy as Blue Deer, fifteen miles south, but colder, and the Crazy Mountains loomed large in the local thinking. Not a tree blocked the view from Chuck Elston's unnervingly neat double-wide trailer. He'd been hauled in for domestic abuse three times, and visited by deputies two more times, but his wife had consistently dropped charges; this time a neighbor had called. Jules had Harvey and Jonathan wait down the road and ran up to the neighbor's locked door. The woman, melon-nosed and probably compassionate from hard-earned experience, said Mrs. Elston, a forgiving lady, had called earlier that morning, then called back to say things were fine. The neighbor had been pruning her winter-battered roses when she heard screams, worse than any she'd heard before, and finally called the station. Mr. Elston had several guns; she'd seen him standing at his door with something that looked like a shotgun ten minutes earlier. They had three children, all under five, all probably home.

Jules and Harvey and Jonathan put on vests, parked their cars in a cluster twenty yards from the trailer door, and stood behind them. Jules had dealt with this sort of situation only once before, and his training, as thorough as anyone's, basically called for staying patient and keeping your head. But training was moot—thirty seconds after he got out his megaphone and suggested Chuck Elston come out for a talk, the man walked out onto his porch, stuck his shotgun against his cheek, and pulled the trigger.

IT WAS almost dark before they finished the cleanup, largely due to keening relatives. The clouds had opened up soon after they walked past the man's body to find the wife beaten to a pulp on the kitchen floor near a large bag of duck feed, and the children huddled together on the shabby living room couch. The backup ambulance arrived five minutes later, and they helped load the mashed wife, but Horace took his time showing up. Jonathan vomited at least a half-dozen times, and when he finished he lay on the lawn in a daze, letting the rain fall on his face. The children had seen everything, and maintained a stoic silence through the hysteria; Jules put them in temporary foster care simply to get them away from their desperately stupid grandparents and aunts and uncles, all of whom now claimed to have seen the writing on the wall months before. He hated them. After he'd spent hours picking gray matter and bone fragments out of the shrubbery in front of the house, he began to hate the duck killer who'd blown his head off with a shotgun, too, and if he was glad about anything it was that he could hate the literally faceless man, and that he or Harvey or Jonathan hadn't had to pull the trigger for him.

On Tuesday morning Jules dealt with the paperwork and then fidgeted at his desk, unwilling to confront other bureaucratic nightmares. He was equally unwilling to actually visit Bunny McElwaine, former Absaroka County sheriff's deputy, without concrete information. He tried Peter, off interviewing some logging baron, and Delly, who didn't answer his home phone and wouldn't be at work until four. He stacked the remaining mess roughly in order of importance and escaped to the library.

Maybe he missed research, or the smell of books. Blue Deer Public Library had 40,000 titles, versus the six million in Michigan's graduate library, or the eight million or so in Columbia's, but it would do in a pinch. He asked to see the *County Daily*s for May 1972, and a woman with sunburned arms led him through the basement stacks. Except for the arms and obvious intelligence she was almost a caricature of the sort of librarian you'd see in a *Playboy* cartoon, waiting to be undressed, and Jules wondered if he'd simply started to notice women again, or if he'd really never met her, just as he'd never met Rita. Today he wasn't particularly in the mood to flirt.

It took only fifteen minutes to find Jane Semple.

## LOCAL STUDENT FALLS TO DEATH

May 23, 1972—Blue Deer resident Jane Inez Semple was pronounced dead on arrival at 11:30 P.M. last night, and a fall from a valley cliff was cited as probable cause of death.

Ms. Semple, 18, was with classmates for Blue Deer Public School's senior-class end-of-the-year festivities when the accident occurred. Sheriff Ansel Clement told the *Daily* that officers and medics responded to a call at 11:03 P.M. last night, and arrived at the scene to find Miss Semple comatose. Breathing ceased shortly thereafter, despite medical efforts, and sources at Blue Deer Memorial Hospital told *Daily* reporters that Miss Semple had suffered head wounds and fractured vertebrae.

Other teenagers attending the party told officers that the "skip day" party, held this year on the Boskirk Ranch on the Yellowstone, is traditionally an unruly event, but that it had been quiet last night. Ms. Semple was apparently standing near a bonfire, built on a bluff over the Yellowstone, when she fell to the rocks on the beach below. Sheriff Clement estimated the height of the fall at forty feet.

The possible presence at the party of alcoholic beverages or other intoxicants is being investigated, though officers declined to mention if they found evidence of drunkenness.

Miss Semple is survived by her mother, Vivian Semple, and a brother and a sister, all of Blue Deer.

Jules wasn't used to seeing his father's name in print. He wasn't used to seeing his father's name at all, especially since he'd seen his own in a virtually identical context, and would see it again that afternoon when the paper dealt with the Clyde City suicide. He leaned back in the heavy library chair, looked around, and rubbed his eyes. He watched the back of the woman who'd helped him. She was oblivious, and this was somehow comforting, but he still sat in the chair for a few minutes before going to her again.

"This is stupid," he said, "but I've forgotten a pencil or paper and wondered if I could borrow them."

"Sure," she said. She handed him a legal pad and a ballpoint. "You can Xerox too, you know."

"Maybe a few pages," said Jules. "Thanks. And would you mind if I simply went through the stacks on my own? I'll put everything back in order."

She'd looked at his face, and he caught some curiosity before she turned away. "No problem."

He started to hunker down with the rest of the May papers, then realized he couldn't simply disappear on Grace and headed upstairs to the pay phone tucked in a corner of the local history room. Grace rattled on about many things before passing him on to Harvey, who only wanted to complain about Jonathan having received the day off. Jules explained that Jonathan's day off was literally for the sake of his mental health, while Harvey had claimed his was fine the night before in Clyde City. It wasn't as if any of them had ever seen someone blow his face off before. Jules finally retrieved Grace, pointed out that he was a few blocks away if they needed him, asked that they not beep him for anything inconsequential, and brought the phone down too hard when he hung up, causing the two denizens of the room to stare.

But at the foot of the stairs he paused, because Ada Santoz was pointing down at his desk and the papers on it, talking with some emphasis to the librarian, who seemed to be defending his pile. When he walked up behind them he guessed that she'd also defended his identity—Ada shot backward and lost some color.

"Mrs. Santoz," said Jules. "Do you need these papers? I won't take long."

"No," she said. "No, no. I was just talking to this woman."

"This woman" was by now looking unnerved. "I thought you said you wanted to see May? I can call you when the officer is done."

Ada pulled herself together. "I've been looking up local rodeos," she said, focusing on Jules and ignoring the librarian. "We're going to run a series. And I was checking on seventy-two, when the nationals were in town. It was a good year."

Nineteen seventy-two had, in fact, been the last year anyone had been killed riding, but Jules understood that this might be good from Ada's perspective. "What day do you need?" he asked. "I can look through that paper first."

"Oh, said Ada, waving her hand, flirtatious. "I'll just come back some other day."

"It really wouldn't be a problem." Jules smiled. "Just tell me."

"No," said Ada. "Bye. See you soon."

She disappeared but left behind a fog of sharp perfume, harsh in the air conditioning. The librarian had retreated and Jules sat back down, slowly. He postponed his search for Jane to scan the headlines for bronco news, but mostly found early warnings of the year's flood, which had finally hit Memorial Day weekend. It was stupid to bother looking. Blue Deer had probably never had a rodeo in May, or even June. They were always held in July or August, over the Fourth or in conjunction with the fair.

Jules truly hated people who lied, and he especially

hated them when they were bad liars. He was surrounded, the town was invaded, by a clutch of murderous, small-minded, patronizing white Anglo-Saxon Protestants, and it was beginning to drive him wild. Rodeo series, his goddamn ass. If she thought him such a dimwit to have fallen for the excuse, did she doubt he'd ask Peter about it?

So he looked even harder for whatever it was both he and Ada were trying to find. The paper ran Jane's class photo, and in it she looked exactly as she had sitting next to George Blackwater in the prom photo—a girl with a soft smile, hands neatly folded in her lap.

The other mentions were sad, rote: no inquest had been deemed necessary, though no one had seen her fall; school was canceled the day of the funeral, and most of the town attended; the school board looked into the possibility of canceling future skip days; the *Daily*, with only one more year to run, offered a feeble, hysterical series on marijuana use, because some fink student had mentioned smelling pot that night. But out of all the teenagers who'd gotten stoned on river bluffs in the last few decades, none but Jane had careened down the rocks. Not that Jules would have thought it anything but an accident if Ada hadn't been looking into it, and if the Blackwaters hadn't still been talking about it twenty years later.

He read the obituary, last: She'd liked to ride, and to paint, and to dance. She'd liked music. She'd been an honors student, planning to go to the university in Missoula that fall. She'd been a JV cheerleader. She had two siblings—a brother, Nicholas, and a sister named Nancy, both younger—though Jules remembered neither of them. Memorials were suggested for the art department at the high school.

He skimmed on through May, then took June from the stacks. On the tenth, on what would have been her nineteenth birthday, he found two boxed personals, the first from her fellow students with some sappy lines, probably written by Rod McKuen. The second was different, a blurry snapshot he would never have recognized if the words "Sweet Jane" hadn't appeared above, and a verse and an initial below.

*She sings as the moon sings:*
*"I am I, am I;*
*The greater grows my light*
*The further that I fly."*
*All creation shivers*
*With that sweet cry.*

G

Goose bumps ran up Jules's arms and down his legs; he had a feeling he was seeing the grace note of a ruined life. Alice had been right—George had had a heart.

He didn't want to go back to the station yet. He knew that finishing out the summer papers would complete his funk, but maybe part of being mostly Swedish had to do with wallowing in funks when you found them. So he picked up the ides of August, then remembered that the report wouldn't have come out until the following day, and looked down at his father's photo, a studio shot that bore no resemblance to the man he remembered alive or dead. They'd given Ansel a real banner headline.

### SHERIFF SHOT DEAD ON I-90
*Ansel Clement Murdered in Line of Duty*
*Suspect Apprehended by Bozeman Police*
**Father of Two, 39, a 15-year Veteran of Force**

"Ah, shit," said Jules, out loud. He began to weep.

ALICE finished digging cow manure and compost into the ground around Ray's perennials, and plugged some stakes in the opened circle where they'd decided on a new bed and shrubs. Peter had dug the sod off for her; now he was in the house, poking through the bookshelves. Ray had puttered around with her in the garden that morning, then left them alone, citing errands. Alice was happy: She was being paid fifteen dollars an hour to dig in the dirt, three times the going wage in Blue Deer. The rain had stopped, and life was fine.

Late in the afternoon they climbed into the Mazda together and headed back to town. Black clouds rolled up the valley, the wind gusted, and the temperature dropped. Peter stopped at a fishing access and gazed moodily at the river, high and yellow brown with mud from Yellowstone Park. When they pulled back out to the main road they watched Ada's silver Saab shoot south past a line of three dawdling tourist cars. She was doing eighty, easy.

"Is she in a good mood lately?"

"She's singing in the office." Peter watched the Saab disappear.

Alice thought about this while she rummaged through the tapes in the glove compartment. "What's she singing?"

"Horrible stuff, stuff you wouldn't imagine her even knowing. Top Forty from the seventies, Disney tunes. 'When You Wish Upon a Star.' 'Bibbidi-Bobbidi-Boo.'"

"Is her voice any good?"

"No."

Alice giggled. "Maybe it's Ray's influence. Maybe they're singing together in the car."

"That wasn't Ray with her just now. That was George."


RITA was working Tuesday night at the Baird Hotel Bar, and Jules had planned to visit her there until he found a note on his kitchen table after work. She probably thought of it as a plea for a prolonged rain check. He considered it a kiss off, and read a supremely self-centered Dear John letter between the lines. Her old beau was annoyed; she wanted to give him time to cool off, give up on the thing, and she wanted time to herself. She hoped Jules wouldn't mind. He found himself minding acutely, and burned the note on the grill before he barbecued some chicken thighs. Until he'd read it he'd planned to go see Delly and ask him about the drink George had had with Bunny McElwaine, but he now recognized the danger of going out at all and possibly straying in Rita's direction. Instead, he rented a bad action movie, not one of George's.

It rained hard all that night, a beautiful, muffled nursery sound on the wood-shingled roof, and he told himself it was nice to get some sleep for a change.


**ON WEDNESDAY** morning Jules was tired and cranky, and he sloped in a chair at the airport, waiting for his mother to arrive on the eleven o'clock flight from Minneapolis. He'd seen Roger and Sally downstairs at the Hertz window, arguing about the dead deer dent with the rental agent, and edged past them without being seen. Upstairs in the gallery urchins lined the window, waiting for a plane crash. Only one small blond boy was oblivious and rattled the Nintendo machines, shrieking instructions, having no comprehension that quarters even played a role in the movement on the screen. The tot's mother stood at the far end of the room, puffing on a cigarette, and Jules killed time examining her rather fine figure. It beat thinking of any number of other things.

A bandaged hand slapped his shoulder, and Ray loomed over him. "A strange time for you to take a vacation."

Jules made a face. The whole world seemed to be traveling, except for him, but he didn't want their lives any more than he wanted his own. "What are you doing here?"

"Flying to Los Angeles for a couple of days. I meant to tell you I'd be gone."

Intentions didn't count for much lately. Jules gave him another foul look, and Ray put his briefcase down.

"Well," said Ray, searching the pockets of his blazer. "What are you doing here?"

"My mother's on her way back from Italy." Ray looked surprised. He probably thought that the elderly of Blue Deer confined their travels to Phoenix and Las Vegas. "She's way past you in frequent flyer mileage."

"Hmm," said Ray. He pulled out a cigarette and ambled toward the smoking section. Jules followed him and smiled at the blond boy's mother. She smiled back at him. Ray tried it and she gave him a filthy look, put out her cigarette, and headed for her child. A minor triumph, thought Jules.

"How's your hand?"

"Not bad. It'll make good cocktail party chatter in Hollywood, where no one really drinks cocktails anymore. I'll spin stories about the brutal cops of the Rockies."

Ray finished his first cigarette and started another; he'd acquired a lighter since the funeral. "Listen, I didn't mean to leave you hanging with that comment at the dinner."

"What comment?" Jules waved some smoke away and searched the crowd for the woman again.

"The one about George having a reason to feel guilty."

Cigarette number two hit the ashtray. Jules hoped Ray had a healthy layover in Salt Lake City to better enjoy the glass-boxed smoking rooms filled with desperate, gray people. Jules watched his mother's flight land. "You know, Ray, you're always bringing up stuff no one's asked you about."

"Just trying to make things interesting. I'd hate for you to be bored."

"George wasn't there when Jane Semple fell, was he?"

He lit a third cigarette. "He was at the party that night."

"Were you?"

Ray stretched, the kind of dramatic stretch bad actors use to show relaxation. "I didn't hang out with the little kids, but I heard plenty about it from everyone who did. No one remembered seeing Jane, but everyone remembered the police afterwards."

The Salt Lake departure came over the PA system. "Is it possible that Bunny McElwaine was one of the cops on duty?" asked Jules.

Ray gave a little twitch and picked up his bag. "Well yes, he was. Funny that you would guess that."


OLIVE Clement, age fifty-eight, was built like her son, a better thing for a man than a woman, but it allowed her to outwalk her dumpier tour companions on every trip. She'd been traveling for twenty-six hours, not counting five hours of sleep in the airport the night before—Sardinia to Rome to New York to Minneapolis to Billings to Bozeman—and the first thing she wanted was a Bloody Mary. She had three before Jules folded her into the car, and spent the ride to Blue Deer insisting that she'd make him dinner and tell him about her trip that night. He put her in bed and drove back to the station knowing that he wouldn't hear from her until the next day.

Horace had called to tell him that the semen found in Mona wasn't George's—they'd cadged his blood type from hospital records. Jules knew perfectly well whose it was, but didn't bother telling Horace, who added that the wife-beating suicide from Clyde City had been operating on a surfeit of crystal meth and probably wouldn't require an inquest. Scotti called, but Jules didn't have anything new to tell him about Ada or anyone else. Peter called, to find out if he wanted to come over for dinner, and filled the pause in the conversation by telling him that Edie wouldn't be attending. Jules bargained for a weekend night and forgot the questions he'd meant to ask. The park authorities called, to say a pickpocket was headed north after ripping off some Korean tourists near Old Faithful. The Baptist minister called, to say he suspected some teenagers in his congregation of satanism. The garage called, to say that one of the county's patrol cars was deader than a doornail, because the officer who'd used it—Harvey— had neglected to check the oil at any point in its history. Jules started screaming, but Harvey was off holding hands with the duck man's wife at the hospital.

Then the day was over. Jules headed for home, but ended up on the valley road instead. He could see Edie watering her shrubs from half a mile away, and he didn't dwell on the insanity of his mission. All three of her sweet-faced boys flooded around the squad car. They seemed to range in age from only eight to ten, and he wondered how a woman survived, or continued to survive, such intense motherhood. She waved cheerily with her spare hand, apparently having decided to act as if they were the best of friends, and the kids trailed him as he walked toward her.

"What are you up to?"

"Just driving around. I thought I'd see how you were doing."

"Great," she said. Her smile was just slightly cracked.

The youngest kid tugged at his arm. "I shot six gophers yesterday."

"Amazing," said Jules.

"The horses keep stumbling in the holes," explained Edie. She had eighty fairly arid acres, all on an open hillside leading down from the old frame house.

"We're going to blap some more right now. Maybe you could use your police gun." The older boys were acting nonchalant, disinterested, but Jules sensed a tad of pressure.

"Their dad is coming in a half hour," said Edie. "I promised them. They just use pellet guns."

Jules walked back to the patrol car, wishing he'd

changed out of his uniform, and pulled the Colt .45 out of the locked glove box. He had a 9mm Beretta, too, but it looked too urban for this experience. It was amazing what a stray urge could lead you into. He'd never gone in for the state sport of vaporizing perky rodents, even when he was twelve, but none of the Linders seemed interested in letting him off the hook. They took up position on the front porch; Edie brought out two drinks and headed back inside. He had the boys go first and they popped away for a full five minutes. When the oldest finally plugged a gopher, all three screamed "Blap!" and chortled. Jules remembered Alice telling him that the boys were straight-A students. He took a pull on the drink and shot off a round, hitting two out of five at twenty yards, not a horrible performance considering the tiny silhouettes. He lowered his gun and lurched to the left at the explosion in his right ear. Edie stood next to him with a .30-30 rifle and shot another five times, each blast leaving a little pink blur in the air of the gopher colony. She reloaded, did it again, and smiled at him, looking only slightly embarrassed.

"Some days, there's not much else to do."

She took the boys inside and got them packed for their father. Jules wrapped his hands around his sweaty glass and looked out over the hillside to the ruined foundation of a homesteader's barn and past it to the brown ribbon of river three miles below, a lovely view if you didn't imagine the small pools of blood dotted in the grass. It was balmy between waves of rain, about seventy—the paper that afternoon had listed the record high for the date as ninety-seven in 1902, and a record low of eighteen for 1903. That might have been the year the homesteader gave up. Jules watched the mystery husband's car move up the road and depart again, loaded down with blood-thirsty twerps. Edie came onto the porch carrying a bag of chips and some salsa, then spilled the chips when the phone rang inside. Jules spent the next two minutes throwing stray crumbs over the side of the porch for any surviving gophers, carefully avoiding the rifle. He was glad he hadn't known about Edie's .30-30 a week or two earlier, before discovering Ada was the queen of target practice.

"That was Alice. She said they'd invited you to dinner tonight, and thought you had to work."

"I just asked for a rain check."

"Is this visit work?" Edie bent for a last stray chip.

"No." The salsa was full of fresh coriander. Everything tasted good lately.

"Are you sure you don't have any questions about George?"

"Not unless you shot him with that gun."

She shook with laughter, mostly silent, and he waited patiently as a pleasant warm feeling spread through his body. "Me? The woman who likes to give lectures on violence? Is that a compliment?"

Jules smiled and kept eating.

"Can I ask you some personal questions?"

He wanted to say no. "If you want to."

"Why is your face crooked?"

"Are you serious?" Jules stared at her.

"Well, yes. I don't think you were born that way."

"A horse kicked me in the face when I was six." Few people asked, especially women who assumed they might offend him. Apparently Edie wasn't worried about offending him, and this wasn't good news.

She sipped at her drink. "Didn't they take you to the doctor?"

"My jaw broke in three places. They could only do so much." He drained his whiskey. "Does it bother you?"

"No. I like the fact that you smile with only half your face." Edie pulled her brown curls back and snapped an elastic around them. "So what's with Rita?"

Jules chewed carefully and admired the landscape.

"I got the impression you knew each other before the party," Edie added.

"I met her a couple of weeks ago." Edie was watching him, and Jules looked back toward the bowl of chips. "I ran into her at the Blue Bat."

"Literally, I guess."

Jules let it pass.

"You were giving her quite a look," said Edie. "Almost as if you were in love with her."

"I wouldn't call it love." He squinted at her, not quite believing he was stuck in such a conversation. All the things you could call it floated into his brain. "I've only known her a couple of weeks. She's seeing someone else."

"I guess you're even, then."

The statement cost her. He was silent for a moment, watching a rosy blush move over her face. "I guess we are," said Jules.


**AFTER** dinner he fiddled with her CDs and asked her if she wanted to dance. At five A.M. he was bolt upright again, the same sweat and terror, but a different dream from the one he'd had after Ray's dinner, a replay of the hailstorm and the hanging girl and the rotten body, which made unpleasant sense now, though it hadn't before. Edie gave him two aspirin and a glass of water, made him take a hot shower, then opted to take the shower with him. He was an hour late for work but felt good, and he finally got to scream at Harvey about the car.

CHAPTER **14**

**BUNNY** McElwaine had been christened Basil, and the real name was as unlikely as the nickname to anyone who came face to face with the whole picture: a 260-pound ex-cop covered almost entirely with graying hair. "Bunny," an endearment bestowed by an early girlfriend, had sprung from the hair. Several decades later the idea that anyone had ever bestowed an endearment upon Bunny seemed even stranger than either name. He was, quite simply, a true-blue pig, even in his late fifties, when other men sometimes softened agreeably around the edges and stopped feeling that the world had to be war.

Jules, who hated Bunny's guts, had offered him a hefty retirement package when he became sheriff. Bunny, characteristically, had said, Fuck you, fire me, donkey dick. So Jules fired him. It was easy to find reasons—at least a dozen a year had been ignored by every sheriff since Ansel Clement, none of whom could face the idea of Bunny's verbal and physical revenge, and all of whom tried to use the man sparingly, as an enforcer. Jules used simple fitness as an excuse—Bunny could probably still lift a small car over his head, but he couldn't run for shit, was fifty pounds over weight guidelines for his height, and his skin, yellow under his fur, testified to a pumpkin-sized liver.

So Bunny left, with a smaller retirement package. He'd skimmed enough over the previous three decades to golf daily in good weather and travel to Las Vegas and Cancun when the weather didn't comply, putting in occasional stints as a bank guard when he grew bored and ached to carry a revolver openly. His wife had died of exhaustion in the seventies, and Jules shivered at the idea of what he probably did with down-on-their-luck showgirls. Bunny had been one of the men he'd told Alice and Peter and Edie about at dinner, the cop who'd specialized in flattening testicles and ripping out male long hair, who'd traded fellatio and more for dropped DUI and pot charges.

Jules, in the normal course of events, would have preferred a lifetime of auditing tax returns to a short conversation with Bunny McElwaine, and many things conspired to delay the dreaded event. Aside from a shooting, a near-fatal beating, a suicide, a head injury, and a murder, Blue Deer had been in a bit of a lull, but it ended Thursday. That morning a farmer was asphyxiated in his silo. At noon the father of the dead wife-beater was taken in for setting a neighbor's barn on fire. (Jules, happy in Edie's bed, had managed to miss the actual barn burning.) That afternoon two sets of children were taken from their parents, and someone stole a Vega, of all things, from Alonzo Riderbacker's used-car lot. Thursday night there were several DUIs and a seventeen-year-old from Gardiner, anticipating graduation, had compacted his spleen and a new pickup with two passengers aboard.

For Jules this meant fatigue and despair, and by midafternoon he had trouble remembering, when someone asked, what he'd been doing the night before. It had taken numerous gas masks, two rescue trucks, and five hours to pull the farmer out, too late. The red Vega was spotted hitting the highway for Bozeman, and Jonathan, boy in uniform with fast car, radioed in that he was following at 120 miles per hour. Jules called him off, howling into the switchboard, assuming, probably rightly, that a Vega would either self-destruct at such a speed or reduce his fresh-faced new man to so much syrupy road kill. Maybe they could take out a tourist or two, to boot; maybe Blue Deer could have a record body count for the month of May. It would be better training for Jonathan, anyway, to have to deal with the Bozeman city police, and if he couldn't handle that well he could spend a lifetime on the skunk and stray-cow patrol.

One set of children came from the Park-It Motel—the five-year-old was found sucking urine out of his little sister's diaper, and the little sister, eighteen months old, lay in a corner, dusty pink and listless from dehydration. No one knew where the parents were, or really who they were. The other three children were victims of a prolonged custody dispute, taken from their mother's home after reports that Mom and Dad were taking shots at each other over the hoods of their respective cars. One bullet took out a neighbor's plate-glass window, and both parents were in custody.

Playing phone tag with Peter from nine A.M. on pushed things over the top. Jules finally reached him from the lobby of the Park-It, while paramedics Bean and Al, nearing nervous breakdowns, tried to pump Gatorade down the children's throats. Ada hadn't shown up for work that day, or Wednesday. No one knew where she was; did Jules? No, he didn't.

He ran by Ada's house, but no one answered the door.

He tried calling the ranch, then remembered that Ray was out of town. Jules called Peter back, and Peter admitted that Ada had been a no-show for twenty-four hours in the past— forty-eight might be a new form of rebellion. Jules relaxed and headed home, only to be called back for the high-schoolers' accident and the barrage of DUIs. When he made it home the second time there were three messages on his machine from Ray in L.A., each more hysterical than the last, asking where Ada was, saying that Peter and Alice didn't know, wondering what Jules was doing while a woman was missing and a murderer was afoot. Jules had a large whiskey while he stood listening to the machine, his ears buzzing whenever Ray's voice hit top volume. It was almost as if he could hear his mind melting, the world blistering apart, out of his control. Then he went to bed.

**AT SIX O'CLOCK** Friday morning Jules rousted Harvey from his cozy pink house. It was actually tangerine with fuchsia trim; when he walked back to the car to wait while Harvey pulled himself together he noticed that the place glowed in the dawn light, and turned all the surrounding staid, white stuccos funky orange. Harvey whined the whole way to Ada's, but shut up when Jules suggested that he'd need the extra breath if they found something stinky inside.

When they climbed through the kitchen window— another sink entry, but this one without dirty dishes—they found the house neat and empty but for two hungry cats. Harvey headed for the upstairs and then the basement while Jules fed the cats and searched Ada's office and downstairs bedroom. The house was sterile and vast, utterly colorless but for one nice George canvas and an amazing collection of high heels and sexual aids. It was, in fact, remarkably like Mona and George's house, and Jules wondered if having a house like that was enough to get you killed. The messages on Ada's answering machine took forever to play back—he counted five from Ray, increasingly urgent, and three from the office before he hit an older stretch, Ray's voice again, run over by the subsequent messages, then Ada laughing and saying, "It's been a long time. What can I do for you?" before she'd clicked off the machine. Jules hit yet another old conversation between them, long and lovey-dovey, which Ada hadn't seen fit to erase.

The quart of milk in the refrigerator was sour, and the lettuce in the crisper drawer was souping around the edges. The garage was empty: no Saab, none of the usual detritus, just a rake, some nasty-looking pesticide, and an expensive mower. The windows of the house were all double-hung and locked and the screens were also secure. Jules looked again at the kitchen window, which had opened without effort, and found some pry marks—the bolts had popped. He sent Harvey back to the station for the fingerprint supplies, and helped him dust the window, the office, the answering machine, and the bedroom, knowing that the top prints on all of them would be their own. As an afterthought Jules went back through all the closets, and turned up the .30-30 in with the linens, under Ada's monogrammed sheets. If they were both lucky he'd finally get to charge her for shooting George.

At nine he checked with the newspaper, but Ada, punctual when she chose to work, had not shown. He phoned Ray at the Westwood Marquis and woke him, which at least made the conversation a little calmer than it would have been if Jules had returned the calls the night before. Ray had last seen and talked to Ada Tuesday evening at the ranch; she'd headed back to her own house at seven because he had work to do before flying out the next morning. He'd be back in Blue Deer that afternoon or early the next morning. Jules had no way of knowing, from what had been found in the house, if Ada had ever made it home Tuesday night.

Most of the fingerprints in the house belonged to Ada—they inferred this from the prints in the newspaper office—or to Jules or Harvey or the cleaning lady, who trotted in to have hers taken. There were some partials, all old and tucked away in odd places, and a fifth set, fairly new, which matched Ray's prints from the Blue Bat arrest. At noon the Saab turned up covered with parking tickets behind the Baird Hotel. They found a few of Ada's fingerprints but the rest of her car—the door handles, wheel, gear shift, dash, light switch, and handbrake—had been wiped clean. Jules had the car towed to Bozeman for a complete fiber test, then picked up Ada's two cats and dropped them off at his house. When they yowled as he threw them through the front door every bird in the yard flew away. Jules watched them go, then turned to see a slow blur of blue in the street: George cruising by, ignoring his wave. Ray may have been hard to keep tabs on, but his brother was hard to lose. Jules climbed back into his car and delayed his visit to Bunny McElwaine with one to Peter and Alice's house.

Alice was in the kitchen, separating dozens of eggs into two huge bowls. The table was covered with flour, and the house was a wall of sound, Michelle Shocked singing "If Love Was a Train." She glanced up at him and turned back to her work immediately.

"Something wrong?" asked Jules.

"Oh, no." Her voice was sarcastic.

"Did you hear about Ada?"

"Of course." She finished her third carton and scooped the shells into the compost bin under the sink.

"Would you consider taking her cats?"

"No," said Alice. "I want a cat, but not two, and not hers." She might as well have added, and not from you.

Alice had taken conversation lessons from Edie; normally things worked the other way. Jules kept pulling teeth.

"Are we still on for the bird count?"

"The Bataan death march? Sure, unless you can tell me how to get out of it." She selected a whisk and attacked the egg whites.

"Alice, what the hell is wrong?"

"A little touch of Jules in the night," muttered Alice.

He stiffened. "What?"

"Forget it."

"Don't give me that," said Jules. "What about all the lectures you've given me on the need to seek female company?"

"I felt badly for you, before. I guess I assumed that when you woke up you'd take the ladies on one at a time."

"Well, I am, in a literal sense."

Alice looked like she wanted to punch him, and whacked the whisk around the bowl with astounding vigor. "Maybe I assumed that if you were stupid enough to see two people you wouldn't put me right in the goddamn middle."

"I'm in the middle, not you."

The whisk flew into the sink and bounced off onto the floor, covering them both with tiny pellets of albumen.

"Go tell Edie the truth."

"Hey," said Jules, finally angry. "For your information Edie didn't seem to have any problem last night. I don't have anything else I can say to her that she doesn't already know."

"Really," said Alice, dripping egg white as if it were so much ice.

"Really."

"What about Rita?"

"What about her?" said Jules. "What on earth makes you think you know best?"

"They're my friends."

"What am I, your idiot brother? Don't you see something odd in trying to take the moral high road with me?"

They glared at each other.

"Don't try to change the argument," hissed Alice.

The CD ended, and they heard the thud of Peter's feet on

the stairs. Alice bent to pick up the whisk, and Jules wiped egg white from his uniform and walked into the living room.

"Oh," said Peter. "I didn't hear you come in."

"You couldn't have heard a bomb over the music."

"It helps to have a blur when I'm on the computer," said Peter. "Did you find Ada?"

"Of course not," snapped Jules. "I'm not capable of doing anything right these days."

The stove door slammed shut hard enough to deflate Alice's meringue. Peter smiled. "I gather you've been having a fun talk with my significant other."

Jules rubbed his forehead. "When you saw George in the bar, the night he shot Ray's car, who was he drinking with?"

"Bunny," said Peter. "Your favorite person and mine."

"What were they talking about?"

"I didn't feel like a welcome member of the conversation. I stayed down the bar and passed the time with Delly."

The back door closed abruptly, and the house rocked again. "Could you hear anything?" asked Jules, wheedling. It was hard to imagine dealing with Bunny after having such a grand time with Alice.

"They were discussing violent death." Peter seemed to find everything amusing today, and Jules couldn't imagine why. Maybe it was the relief of not having Ada around. "Violent death in general. I heard George say 'my wife' once or twice."

"Were they arguing?"

"No, they didn't seem to be. I don't know. Delly started yelling at the TV, and I stopped paying attention until George got mad. But even then it wasn't like he was mad at Bunny."

"How'd you know George was mad?"

"Well, shit," said Peter, "he was pounding the hell out of the bar, yelling stuff like 'that fuck,' and Delly ran down there to try to calm him down—"

"Just 'that fuck'? That's all?"

Peter squinted his eyes closed and drummed his fingers on the CD player. "I was drinking. I might have remembered if you'd asked me right away, but it's been a week."

"Maybe Delly will know."

"Delly was watching the game. People had to yell at him to get a drink."

Jules walked to the door.

"Will you still come to dinner Sunday, or are you too pissed off at Alice?" asked Peter. "She's just worried about Edie. She likes matchmaking, and this hasn't panned out quite as she expected."

"I'm never too pissed off at Alice to eat her food," said Jules. "Unless we club each other to death on the bird count."


BUNNY McElwaine lived just south of town, on the edge of the river in a wind-tunnel canyon. His snazzy maroon van was parked in the middle of the driveway, naked girls on the mud flaps, and Jules took his time walking to the house. Bunny opened the door when his visitor was still five feet away. He was dressed in a pair of shorts and a tight T-shirt that made him look like a malignant Michelin tire man.

"Hello, Sheriff Clement."

"Hello, Mr. McElwaine."

Bunny waved him in, and Jules took a chair at the kitchen table. "Get you a drink?"

Jules weighed the situation. "Unless you're going to phone the paper that I'm drinking on the job."

"Never in a thousand years would I do a thing like that," said Bunny. He had a face like a fuzzy rubber mallet, with long, narrow eyes and a very small nose and mouth. The mouth was primped, smiling, while he poured them glasses of scotch. Jules didn't like scotch, hadn't since he'd drunk half a fifth when he was fourteen and thrown up for the next forty-eight hours, but didn't see any sense in complaining.

"I'd love to think you're visiting to beg me to come back and help out during these troubled times, but that's probably not the case."

"No," said Jules. "I've heard you're enjoying retirement."

"I get bored, some days."

Bunny had gotten bored as a deputy, too, and it usually meant a motorist or a small-time doper paid for his boredom. "I wanted to ask you about an old case," said Jules, trying to ignore the smell of the scotch. "Jane Semple. She fell off a cliff at a party back in seventy-two."

Bunny took a chair on the other side of the table and the wood groaned. "A pretty girl," he said. "Your dad was still sheriff then."

Jules nodded.

"They were all drunk," said Bunny. He had a remarkably calm, pleasant voice. "It's a wonder it doesn't happen more often. Though I guess it just did, again."

He smiled, showing expensive dentures. Jules smiled back. "Just an accident, then."

"Just an accident."

"Why was George Blackwater so upset about an accident?"

"Well, he was sweet on her. Poor guy. Couldn't even interview him. He just kept crying." Bunny gave Jules what passed for a grin.

"I bet Ray didn't cry."

"Ray ain't the crying type."

Jules looked around the kitchen. "So last week, when you were drinking at the Blue Bat, what got George ticking again?"

Bunny leaned back in the chair and drained his glass. "Jules, I can't think of one fucking reason why I should have your skinny ass in my house, let alone help you out with a case."

"I can think of a few," said Jules. "Why don't we say you'll do it because you're bored."

"Oh my," said Bunny. "My immortal reputation."

"Your immortal retirement checks. Not that you need them." Jules decided to stop dicking around with his drink and took the rest of it in two fast swallows, blinking back nausea.

"The girl fell. That's all there was to it. She was drunk, and she went right over the rocks. George sat there in the bar and blamed himself, told me he couldn't remember what happened that night, told me he couldn't believe that we didn't question him and harass him. He actually thanked me for not questioning and harassing him." Bunny smiled at the rarity of it all.

"Why would George think he'd killed her in the first place? He loved her."

"Love," said Bunny, looking amused. "They'd had a little tiff that night, and he couldn't remember a thing after it."

"So twenty years later, in a bar, he starts into something that almost sounds like a confession," said Jules. "Why did he get upset?"

"Because there was a problem with his version of the night."

Jules waited. Bunny was having a grand time with the story, as if the talk with George had been a laugh riot.

"See, George was really drunk, sitting there telling an ex-cop that he thought he'd killed his girlfriend. I tried cheering him up, said maybe you're thinking about your wife, buddy, but he just kept going on and on, and finally I said, George, I don't think you did it, and he said why, and I said because I found you out cold in the town park an hour before we got the call to go down the valley for the girl, and you spent most of the night sleeping in a jail cell. I said I was surprised his brother hadn't told him."

Bunny poured himself another drink. "That's what they used to call an alibi. I thought the poor asshole's eyes were going to pop out of his head. Then he started screaming, and then he left."

**AT FIVE,** as Jules was starting the reports for the previous night and Grace was packing her voluminous, battered purse, Joseph Ganter called. Grace made noises about not being sure if the sheriff was still around, but Joseph was exactly the sort of person Jules felt he could talk to without hastening the fraying of his synapses, and he lurched toward the phone as if it might give him a prescription for peace. Not that Ganter was peaceful, or a humorous old cowboy—he'd gone east on the train to Yale in 1930—or that, on the other hand, Jules was particularly awed by his 30,000 acres up Mission Creek. But he was funny, intelligent, and a third cousin or a fourth uncle once removed, and Jules had started thinking lately that a village wise man would come in handy.

Joseph, however, was not interested in soothing a distant relation. "I found something and I want you to look at it."

"Well," said Jules, "what is it?"

"A bear leg. I'm afraid it might be a grizzly leg. I don't think it's from a black bear."

"Oh." Jules ran his hand along his crooked jawbone.

"I know you're busy right now."

"Never busier."

"If I call the shits at FWP they'll camp in my summer pasture and bother my cows."

Fish, Wildlife and Parks would normally handle such questions. Joseph obviously didn't want to talk to them. "I don't know if I could tell the difference," said Jules. "Did you find it on Forest Service land?"

"The dogs brought it home," said Joseph. "The two

Beltons. Elsie's going to have a litter in June. I told your mom I wanted to give you one for a homecoming present. A setter's a pain in the ass, but it might keep you perky for times like these."

Jules giggled nervously. "Like I said, I don't know if I could tell the difference."

"I know you know your bones," said Joseph. An emphysemic rasp didn't take away from his iron sense of entitlement. "I know you have that whole goddamn book on bears. Physiology, everything."

"As it happens," said Jules, "I was going to do the bird count up Mission Creek tomorrow. I'll come by when it's over, around two."

He worked until seven and then went to his mother's house. He'd begged off the night before, in between assignations with drunks. He cleaned out her eaves troughs and raked her lawn—he'd avoided these tasks successfully the previous fall, and it was funny how such delays still came home to roost—while she talked about the Mediterranean and he thought about where to look for Ada.

By the time he finished it was dark, and Olive had turned on the yard light. She brought up the much-needed paint job on her trim, but Jules stopped short of agreeing to paint it, and hurt her further by refusing to eat her patented, horrifying beef Stroganoff, supposedly his favorite childhood meal. Olive had always been a bad cook. Jules still gagged quietly when he saw a beef tongue at the supermarket, or slid his cart by the Lipton's Onion Soup mix. When he put down the rake she got back at him by observing, without any evidence, that he "seemed to be getting some." It was a little like the time she'd called him freshman year, the day after his first run-in with acid, and ten minutes into the conversation asked if he'd been doing drugs. This time Jules gave her his uneven grin, and she laughed and served him a heaping pile of ragged, sour-cream-laden beef.

ON SATURDAY morning at seven, Jules woke to find both of Ada's cats on his chest. He struggled from under them, sneezed several times, made a thermos of coffee, and picked up his mother and Alice for the Audubon Society bird count. On their way out of town they added Grace Marble and a bag of donuts to the load and made for Mission Creek, where they parked the patrol car—Jules took a certain pleasure in flouting his own rules—midway up the drainage. Soren Rue was waiting for them with a camera, apparently having decided that photography was the fastest way to a better job. He admitted that Peter had set them up, ate two donuts, and took a roll of film before allowing them to move off upstream, south toward the Absarokas, the Boulder Divide, and Shell Mountain, a high, elongated limestone ridge.

In the first half hour they saw a black-headed grosbeak, several red-winged blackbirds, and a red-eyed vireo. Alice was useless—in three years in Montana she'd never paid any attention to the fauna specifics of her surroundings other than to notice a certain scarcity of life compared to moist, frigid Michigan—but she had a decent knowledge of wild-flowers. Jules made her carry the bag with the thermos, donuts, and bear book, and pointed out that she was sup-posed to look up, not down. Alice, who was doing her best to act as if she'd never lost her temper in her life, responded that his continued sneezes were probably scaring everything away. Jules struggled to explain the glaringly obvious differ-ences between a kestrel, a red-tailed hawk, and a golden eagle. They found some morels, glowing white in the dense green grass, and stuffed them in their pockets. Grace and Olive strode on ahead, mildly disgusted, and took the eastern side of the creek—they would retrieve the car and meet later at Ganter's—while Jules and Alice crawled up and down the ravines of the west side, a quarter of a mile away. They were quiet with each other, but it was a good quiet; the argument had hardly been their first, though Jules had never before been angry enough to touch upon their dirty little secret.

"Why didn't we start high and walk down?" asked Alice an hour later. The day was beautiful and clear, but it had rained during the night and the grass was high. She'd neglected to bring irrigation boots, and her jeans and tennis shoes were soaked.

Jules was scribbling down a list of finches and sparrows they'd just spooked from some chokecherry bushes. "Because then we'd have to walk uphill on our way back, and you said you wanted to see Joseph's ranch. Just keep looking for stuff, and I'll figure out what you've found."

Another half a mile and five killdeer, two horned larks, a northern harrier, and a western screech owl later Alice said she was tired.

Jules took two donuts from the bag and whacked her butt with the Peterson guide. "Eat one. Did you go out last night?"

"Nah. I woke up in the middle of the night and thought about life and couldn't go back to sleep."

"The unexamined life is worth living," said Jules.

"I guess that's your motto these days."

"Don't start," said Jules. "Please. I'm trying to be a good boy."

She nodded and they started walking again. "Look," said Alice. "A grouse." She knew her food birds.

"Very good," said Jules. It was a blue grouse, one of two, and he'd already added them to the list. They'd hit forty-something when he made out the north gate of the Ganter ranch.

JOSEPH'S wife Laura had spent fifty years in Montana, but she'd been living in a castle in Perugia when Joseph abducted her during World War II. She asked them in for coffee, and Alice, who'd always thought of Laura as a character out of a novel, shot for the doorway. Joseph wrapped his fingers around Jules's elbow and suggested they get the "science project" out of the way first. Jules followed him toward the gabled horse barn.

Inside it was dim and clean and smelled of molasses-dipped oats and leather, as peaceful as any room could be. Jules eyed a bale of alfalfa and imagined napping on it, far from the trials of Blue Deer. Joseph, who had been as tall as Jules in his youth but who had shrunk several inches in the last decade, reached up toward a high fir locker and brought out a burlap bag, then knelt arthritically on the clean wooden floor and dumped out a white bone, about fourteen inches long and still red and tufted with sinew at either joint.

"Ah, shit," said Jules. He stood looking down at it, a wave of cold traveling up his spine and goose bumps shooting down his limbs. "That's not a bear leg."

"I didn't think so," said Joseph. He knelt in the sunbeam from the open door, and the light made the bone and his pale blue eyes glow. He could have been a monk with an offering in a Renaissance painting. "But I couldn't be sure, and I didn't want to upset you before you saw it."

"Goddammit," said Jules. "I need to use your phone."


TWO HOURS later Jules was scouring the woods around the ranch with all the deputies—Harvey, Jonathan, and Ed. If anyone tried to hold up a store in town, Blue Deer was shit out of luck. He sent Alice back down the creek to waylay Grace and Olive, and told her she could have his patrol car for the day if she kept her mouth shut.

Harvey, on the lookout for magpies, won the prize when he saw a flock of two dozen spook up from a deep gully below the Swingley Road. He was forty yards from Jules and called out very calmly.

They stood in silence together, the magpies cartwheeling

over their heads. It was much, much worse this time. The birds had stripped the buttocks and spine, parts of the back of the skull, and the backs of the legs. One arm was gone at the shoulder, and the other hand was missing as well, a process probably begun by coyotes rather than Joseph's setters. They hadn't, for some reason, flipped the body. Jules eyed the remaining blond hair on the skull, and tried to take in the position of the body in relation to the road. Harvey pointed out that she'd probably been thrown from the edge. Jules rifled through his jacket pockets for some gloves but found nothing, and Harvey, already searching the bracken around the body, tossed him a pair. They both knew gloves wouldn't make a difference at this point, but Jules thought it might make him feel better about it, more professional, later. He reached across to the ragged shoulder and pulled it toward him, down the slope. There were three round holes in her chest. The face was swollen, blue-gray, but he knew it was Ada.

CHAPTER 15

AT TWO A.M., on his way home from a last trip to
Swingley Road and the dewy, fertilized spot where Ada had
lain, Jules found a little strangeness, the kind of flash of exis-
tential humor that makes you wonder if what you're seeing
is truly what you're seeing, or perhaps the beginning of mental breakdown. He'd been in the mood for such a joke, anyway—somewhere on the five miles of Swingley gravel he'd
thought of the Laurel and Hardy caption, "The night was
dark. It usually was." But Jules still couldn't believe he saw a
totally naked man peeing on a conifer next to Park Street on
the Depot lawn. He pulled over, despite his doubts.

The man looked at him, penis in hand. "Greetings," he
said calmly.

What's the frequency, thought Jules. Instead he said, "Come with me."

He dropped the man, who didn't continue peeing in his car, off at the station and had Jonathan, as part of his ongoing humanist education, take him to the hospital for a check-up, sans charges. Then he went home, stripped in the kitchen, climbed into the shower, and mounted the stairs slowly. He walked into his dark bedroom, sighed, and sat on Rita's outflung arm. She said, "Hello, there," and he walked back down the stairs, still very slowly, and out into the backyard, still naked.

He stood there for a long time, at least five minutes, until the cold air finally brought him to his senses. He made out various stars and the moon, just a sliver, singing in the wind. He saw Rita's Scout, and three minutes later he even saw George's Land Cruiser slide down the alley past it. Neither of them waved.

Jules walked back upstairs, turned on the light, and sat on the side of the bed again, this time more carefully. "Sorry," he said. "I was a little out of it. I didn't know what to think."

"I bet you still don't," she said, her face in the pillow.

He stared at her back.

"I heard about Ada. I was scared."

Glad to be a protector, a father figure, thought Jules. Really. Use me when you need me, and tell me to fuck myself when you don't. Why not?

He truly wanted to sleep. He was tired of wondering, of asking questions. "Who told you?"

"An old guy came into the bar. Archie something."

"I don't think we have a random maniac on our hands."

Rita still had her head in the pillow, and her voice was muffled. "I know that."

He sat there and let the pause stretch, then pushed her over and lay down.

"Why didn't you go to your other boy's house? Do you prefer me for my job?"

"Stop it, Jules. I'm sorry about the way I acted."

"You were feeling badly for him a few nights ago. No more guilt?"

"I don't like moral questions," said Rita. "I said I was sorry."

"Well, who does?" asked Jules. "I hate them lately, myself."

"I don't see the point in talking about it anymore," she said.

Most of their time together had involved solid sleep or resoundingly physical activity, but he'd still learned that she was the queen of "I don't want to talk about it," a little like Alice in that regard, maybe even more so. No wonder they got along.

Jules propped himself up and nudged her shoulder. "Tell me why you're here."

"I like you."

"Great," he said. "That's nifty. How do you feel about the other guy?"

Rita had a thin white arm wrapped around her head, and auburn hair obscured the rest of her face. She pushed it out of the way and eyed Jules. "He makes me nervous."

"Which is why you're here."

"Which is one of the reasons why I'm here."

"Did it ever occur to you that I had a difficult day?"

"That's another reason."

"Oh, Christ," said Jules, flipping over decisively.

"You can think whatever you want to think," said Rita, reaching over Jules to flick out the light.


SHE GOT UP with him at dawn, and they ate Wheaties together, both of them possibly digging for some humor in

245

their souls. Jules didn't find any. Rita tried to smile once or twice, but he looked away, and she soon gave up and restricted herself to "thank you," "no," and "good-bye." She walked to her car when Jules walked to his.

By noon on Sunday all that Horace could tell him was that Ada had been shot three times at close range with a revolver, probably a .38 from the one bullet they'd retrieved from the body, and that she'd been dead for the better part of a week. They'd sifted the Mission Creek dirt and found no other bullets; she hadn't been killed anywhere near where she was found.

Jules had Ada's body sent to the main lab in Helena with a long list of questions. He called the state police and fessed up, told them what was being done, and hoped they'd decide to stay out of it. And he tried to find Ray, who'd left another series of bile-filled messages at the station, wanting to catch him before Ray found Alice or Peter and put them on the spot.

He tried for George, too, but no one answered his home phone, and Edie picked up at the office to say that her boss was floating down the Yellowstone. The river was high and muddy, fishing impossible, and George's pastime seemed unlikely. Edie said she was working because she wanted a vacation, preferably in this lifetime, and she reminded Jules that they were supposed to eat at Peter and Alice's again that night. They'd have to cook for Peter and Alice sometime, to reciprocate. And she wanted to know if he was okay, given Ada. Jules said he was fine, and didn't get into the concept that his life had been reduced to a cold sweat on virtually every possible level. He promised to pick her up at five, at the office. If Rita was still scared, she could camp out at his house, alone.

Jules thought of phoning Biddle but opted for landing on his doorstep. The long-suffering wife led him into the kitchen, where the lawyer was having a late bowl of

Cheerios, and stayed put through the subsequent awkward conversation, only leaving the room to retrieve Mona's overnight vacation bag. Lonnie said he'd kept forgetting to bring it down to the station. He hadn't seen Ada since everything had blown up in his face two weeks earlier; she was seeing Ray, anyway. He could account for virtually every movement on Tuesday and Wednesday of that week. Biddle's wife nodded in sage agreement, without even once looking at her husband or Jules directly.

The most fascinating object in their kitchen was an electric can opener, and Jules eyes kept straying toward it as he asked the necessary questions. He'd forgotten to listen carefully to the answers when Biddle surprised him.

"That morning, I was supposed to meet both of them," said the lawyer.

Jules turned slowly to meet his eyes.

"I know," said Biddle. He'd perked up considerably. "An unlikely time for a double rendezvous, but I couldn't get away the night before. I was like a man possessed."

His wife nodded again. Jules finally understood that she was out of her mind. "Did you meet them or not?"

"Not when I'd realized I'd blown it and they were both going to show up. It was a mess."

"I'm sure," said Jules. What an astounding understatement.

"Ada told me she'd planned to shoot George after I left, and when I didn't show she went ahead and did it, and assumed I'd say I'd been with her. And Mona came in and saw her and ran away."

Biddle walked to the refrigerator and came back to the table with a half-gallon of milk. Scotti's line about Biddle not straying far from the potty chair flitted through Jules' mind. "I think Ada might have killed her. I could be disbarred. I think it's all my fault."

"I don't think so, Lonnie."

He frowned at Jules. "Did you already know all this?"

Biddle didn't seem to recognize his confession as an anthill in a sea of active volcanos. "Not really," said Jules. "Thanks for telling me."

Biddle's wife smiled at Jules. She'd become a more interesting possibility, but it was hard to see past her pudgy, weak forearms, to believe she could throttle a Victorian-sized angry woman and haul her from a boat to a beach, or throw another woman, naked, from a car into a gully. And if they were in it together Jules would eat his rubber-lined, lead-filled baton.

Jules left in disgust, marooning the Biddles with their storm-cloud marriage. Mona's bag, filled with deodorant, makeup, and lingerie—notably a huge pink teddy—depressed him, and he muddled through the psychology of it all. Jules wanted it to be George, thought it was George, despite secretly liking him, but the man had no discernible motive for killing Ada. And Ada, though there was no doubt she'd shot George, had jumped from the Mona list with a vengeance. The idea that there might be two killers, that Ada might have killed Mona, and then been killed herself, was beyond gothic, well into baroque. If it couldn't be George, Jules hoped it was Ray, but again he could see no point. Why do your brother a favor by bumping off his wife if you hate that brother? And Ada seemed like the last person Ray would want to see dead.

Outside the station's small windows, the rain had started again. Jules imagined the river creeping higher, moving over young willows and winter islands and all the trash the fall fishermen had left behind. They'd had five inches of rain in the last week, a third of the yearly total, and the weather had stayed warm so that the snowpack was melting at the same time. If the killer had had the sense to throw Mona in the Yellowstone, part of her might have reached the Mississippi by now, dams or no; Ada would be floating through Dakota in the Missouri, tailed by huge paddlefish. The bodies weren't particularly well hidden, but Jules had to think the killer thought they were, assumed he was dumping Ada in the deepest darkest wilderness and Mona in a permanent grave. He wasn't dealing with a seasoned backpacker. Maybe he wasn't dealing with anyone he'd met yet.

"I got your message," said Ray.

Jules jerked away from the window. Ray was soaking wet, steam rising from his coat, puddles settling on the floor around his feet.

Ray continued. "I went to the bar last night, when I couldn't find you, and when I could tell that the dipshits here were going to keep giving me a runaround. And I ran into Peter, and he finally told me. I want to know how you could have let this happen."

There were many possible answers. "Ray, I'm sorry."

"It's your fault."

"No, it's not. We're doing what we can."

"Bullshit," said Ray.

Jules began to lose sympathy. "This might not have happened if you or your brother had been honest at any point. Maybe you think we can do more because you know what we're missing."

Ray had a hooded look. He was quiet for a moment, and when he spoke again his voice was lower. "George and I didn't have a fucking thing to do with this. He wasn't here when Mona was killed, and I wasn't here when Ada was killed. You're dealing with some crazy, and you're wasting your time making our lives miserable."

"How the hell do you know when Ada was killed?" asked Jules. "*I* don't know yet when Ada was killed, and you haven't been gone long enough for me."

"You're out of your league. All you've been doing is keeping your dick warm and playing big man with a badge."

"If you want some real action I could always arrest you," said Jules. "Or I could arrest George, too, split the difference and put you two in the same cell, let you have a heart-to-heart. So spare me your intelligent observations."

Ray was sniffling, more liquid seeping toward the floor. Jules walked to his desk and flipped closed the file holding photos of Ada's face and body, the stripped arm, the shiny white spine, pecked clean.

"When was Ada at your place on Tuesday?"

"I told you. She left at seven."

"Did you see George that day?"

"No. Why would I?"

Why ask, thought Jules. "Were you home all day?"

"I ran errands in Bozeman and got back at about five." He wiped his face with a wet sleeve. "I want to identify her."

"I don't think there's any need for an ID, Ray. She's at the lab now. They'll double-check her dental records. Why don't you tell me why she might have been killed."

"I don't know."

"Then go home. I'll come and see you later, find out if you have any ideas."

"If I have any ideas I'll keep them to myself, take care of them myself."

"Oh, fuck you," said Jules. "Leave."


LATE in the afternoon the sun came out again. He followed the sound of Edie's whistling up the stairs of the Fiske Street office and found her at the computer, inputting George's handwritten script. She said George was working well again, had never been faster, and it was good stuff for a change. Jules sank into the couch and waited for her to clean up, looking straight ahead at the wall. If he shut his eyes he was finished.

"Where are the pretty seascape and the ranch photos?"

"George took them home. He said he could spend time there now, and he wanted to have the stuff he liked on the walls. He's working there a lot now, too, writing and fixing up the kids' rooms, making them cheerier to surprise them when they get back from San Francisco."

What a saint, thought Jules. Edie certainly seemed to think so. Maybe George was writing a screenplay about a man who tails cops in a high-profile car, taking occasional breaks to kill the women he's slept with.

He spent the drive to the Fifth Street house telling Edie how ludicrous it was to go on eating in such circumstances, but she didn't waste much time mourning Ada. When they got out of the patrol car Peter waved to them from a lawn chair, the grill smoking behind him.

"What's the date?" he asked.

"May 23. Sunday."

"Which way is east?"

Jules looked at Alice, who stood on the porch watching them. Her face was puffy, and she gave a forlorn flick of her hand before walking back inside. Edie sized up the situation and retreated after her. Peter was mildly bombed. Jules, the good friend, pointed east, rocking on his feet from lack of sleep, and Peter flipped his middle finger in that direction.

"I graduated from law school five years ago today."

"Ah," said Jules. He already knew he wanted to change the direction of the conversation. "I heard you went out last night."

"Yes, I went out," said Peter. "Too bad for everyone. I ran into both Blackwater boys last night, got to give Ray the bad news, which was not a fuck of a lot of fun."

Peter pulled himself out of the chair and checked the grill, basting a huge golden chicken. Jules held the lid for him.

"So Ray left, and then George came in. Pretty late. He was probably waiting for his brother to take off."

Jules waited.

"He was pretty shook up. He'd already heard about Ada,

so we talked about that for a while. Then he told me an interesting story, about the days when we all lived in New York, something Alice told him about you and her, back when they were still friends. Maybe I should say something Alice confessed."

Jules handed him the lid. Peter replaced it carefully, adjusted the vents, put his basting brush on the platter, and whirled, putting the full force of his big body into the fist that blasted Jules's cheek. Jules staggered back but bounced into a tree trunk and stayed on his feet. His eyes watered and he could taste blood in his mouth, but he made himself stand still.

"Understand, that's just on principle," said Peter. "Alice said it was just one of those things, happened once when she and I were having trouble, not very memorable. I know it shouldn't matter, and now it doesn't anymore. I'll go get you a drink."

DINNER was brief. Jules spent most of the time before and after the actual meal looking through Peter and Alice's bookshelves. It was time to retrench in general, maybe even start reading fiction instead of thinking he had to live it.

He wanted his own bed, but Edie insisted he come back with her, a desire he thought mysterious given the hushed conversation he'd found her and Alice in the midst of when he hobbled inside to wash the blood from his mouth. On the slow drive down the valley they passed a dead cat, and Jules stopped to throw it in the ditch.

On their way up the stairs to her bedroom, Edie's voice sounded strained above him.

"How long ago was it, anyway?" she asked.

"Ten years."

"I can't believe it doesn't bother either of you."

"It does," said Jules. He sat on the edge of her bed, and

she patted him on the shoulder. He'd never felt like a bigger shit in his life.


**WHEN** he woke at four, he was lying on his stomach, spread-eagled, leaving Edie a remote corner of the bed. He lifted his head and stared out the window in front of him down into the dark valley, then propped himself on his elbows, forcing down a yip of pain when his hand hit his sore jaw. He could see the car lights crawling up the hill from a mile away. When they passed from his line of vision he squirmed out of the bed, tiptoed across the hall, and looked through the playroom window, which faced the back of the house. The car moved slowly up Edie's driveway and came to a stop near the barn when the headlights played over Jules's patrol car. The driver paused for a moment, then threw the car into reverse; Jules could hear the thunk of the transmission and the crunching of gravel through the open window, and crouched there as the clouds furled past the sliver of new moon and revealed George's blue Land Cruiser moving slowly back down the driveway. He hurried toward Edie's room, trying not to moan in pain when his instep landed on some Lego, and kept his eyes on the brake lights as they headed back down the hill.

Edie had reclaimed her half of the bed but was still sound asleep. His clothes were in a fairly neat pile, though it seemed to Jules that he was spending a fair amount of time crawling around dark houses naked lately. He tugged his clothes on, ran across the driveway carrying his shoes, and took the dirt road at fifty until it dipped toward the creek bottom. He cut his lights and slowed down; the moon was still free of clouds, and the road had just been graded, and a quarter mile from the creek bridge tire tracks cut away across a pasture, along a rim of trees. Jules jumped out of the car still barefoot. The grass was dewy and rippled in the wind. He followed the shiny ribbons of the tracks from under the cottonwoods until he saw the Land Cruiser and made out George, who sat with his back against a tire, drinking from a bottle.

Jules paused, his heart rattling out of his rib cage, then circled around behind the Land Cruiser and edged along the back bumper. George stared straight ahead and drank again, and Jules could hear the sound of liquid in an almost empty fifth. He lunged for the bottle and jumped back. George screamed and started to his feet.

"What're you doing here, George?"

"I could ask you the same thing."

"No," said Jules. "What I do is none of your business. What you do is my business, especially when you pull into Edie's driveway in the middle of the night, and cruise my alley."

"I couldn't sleep."

"Read a book."

"I'm very protective of Edie. I started thinking about Ada and Mona, and I worried about her."

"The parallels escape me."

"Well, fuck, if someone killed Ada and Mona, why not Edie? She works for me, she knows me."

Jules looked carefully at George. He'd been crying, and he'd probably drunk most of the fifth of vodka in the last few hours. He was usually sympathetic toward men who were able to cry, but George's tears were growing tiresome.

"Who are you worried about? Your brother?"

George didn't respond.

"I saw Bunny a couple of days ago. He explained why you might have been upset with Ray. I can't believe you two are civil."

George shrugged.

"It'd be a horrible thing to think that you might have killed someone you loved. He let you think that."

"At least now I know I didn't." George wiped his nose with his sleeve.

"You didn't know for sure back when Mona died. It might have made it easier to kill her."

"I explained before," said George, staring at the moon. "D-I-V-O-R-C-E. Just like the song."

"Still," said Jules, "if you were going to play eye-for-an-eye with your brother after he told you he'd slept with Jane, Ada would have been the right pick."

"Screw you," said George. "I liked Ada."

"Why are you driving by my house, George?"

"It's on my way home."

"The alley?"

"I drive the alleys when I can't sleep."

It came to Jules that there wasn't much point to having a roundabout conversation with a drunk outside, in the dark. "What were you going to do tonight, go in and see if Edie was dead? George was silent. "Or were you going to see if she wanted to wake up?"

George rocked on his feet. "Maybe you were just curious," said Jules, pouring the rest of the vodka onto the grass. "Let's walk back to my car. I'll give you a ride home."

"I can't leave my car here."

"Leave it or I'll book you for a DUI right now. Edie can help you get it in a few hours, and you can explain to her what you were doing in her driveway."

"She'll know what I was doing." George smiled.

Jules punched George in the gut. It was as fast as anything he'd done in his life, and as easy; a white light invaded his brain and he didn't give it a thought. Only in the aftermath, as George doubled up and vomited and the sour smell of booze wafted through the sharp night air, did he wonder what he'd had in mind, what on earth was happening to him. He waited for a full five minutes in silence, trying to even his breathing and let George finish up, before he hauled him to his feet and pushed him along. George fell twice, and was asleep by the time they hit the highway. When they reached Marmot Drive Jules tried to wake him, then gave up, rolled George out of the seat and onto the driveway, and drove home.

Rita had left three edgy messages on his answering machine. The last said not to bother to call back, she'd go stay with a friend. Jules sat in the dark kitchen and rubbed an ice cube on his jaw while he watched the morning roll in with fresh rain.

**THE OLD** records, ninety years' worth, were locked in a weathered vault near the cells in the basement. The box for the early seventies was on the top shelf, and showered him with dust when he yanked it down. Grace hadn't started the job until 1983, when her children were grown, and the handwriting in the old logs was neat but tiny, so tiny that Jules hauled the May 1972 notebook back up to his desk and pulled out his seldom-used reading glasses, his mood made even surlier by this reminder of decrepitude. He flipped through to May 22, his eyes glazing over countless tiny "Clement"s, and ran his finger down the page until he reached an entry at 9:42 P.M., a call about a comatose youth sighted under some shrubbery in the town park. Deputy McElwaine responded and radioed back at 9:55 that he was bringing in the individual, identified by his driver's license as George Philip Blackwater, age twenty-one. They arrived at 10:01.

Dep. BDM advises we keep individual as a guest of the county. Mr. Blackwater was able to walk on arrival; BDM checked focus and found concussion slight and medical attention (stitches?) unnecessary. Mr.

Blackwater was provided with aspirin. Jailer instructed to check at regular intervals.

The first call for Jane came at 11:03, followed by another twenty entries tracking down Bunny, Ed Winton, two other deputies, Ansel Clement and the ambulance crew. They radioed in at first that Jane was dead, and then that she showed vital signs, and then again—after the ambulance arrived—that she was dead. A roundup of teenage drunks followed, most showing Bunny's initials—Jules could only imagine the trauma this had added to the night for Jane's friends. The jail filled up, and calls started filtering in from parents, most of whom retrieved their children as quickly as possible. At 2:48 A.M. another release was recorded:

Mr. George Blackwater dispatched to the care of his brother, Raymond Blackwater. No charges.

Jules walked the log back downstairs and searched through the boxes of case files, finding nothing. Jane hadn't been considered a case. He turned to the year's miscellaneous crate, conveniently located on the floor, and finally found the file with Jane's autopsy report and other notes tucked in the back. The report, scribbled by a doctor Jules remembered as being ancient even in his childhood, would have made Horace feel like a Nobel prize–winner. Two potentially fatal injuries were listed, a broken neck and a deep head wound, not to mention collapsed lungs, a ruptured liver and spleen, and spinal injuries. The police had estimated the fall at forty to fifty feet, with one or two bounces off the cliff face on the way down, and the medical examiner found all injuries consistent with such a fall. Jane had otherwise been every bit as healthy as an eighteen-year-old should be, with a fairly low blood-alcohol level, no evidence of barbiturates or other drugs, and "some evidence" of recent sexual activity.

It looked simple enough, but Ansel Clement had covered the two pages with doubting ghost notes, his handwriting so remarkably like his son's that Jules had to force himself to concentrate. Ansel had circled the head-wound measurements, "a rectangular depression approximately four inches long, one-and-a-half inches wide, and one inch in depth, consistent with a narrow rock or tree branch," and written "too deep, too precise"; he'd circled "some evidence" and written "abrasions." He'd underlined the gibberish about the broken neck and scribbled "bruising minimal." At the top of the first page, under "on scene" he'd written "evidence of dragging, hard to confirm" and "slope not sheer—should have rolled down—like she jumped." At the bottom of the second page he'd made a precise list of personal effects in black pen: "blue blouse, tan shorts, white bra, white panties, leather sandals, turquoise and silver earrings, silver and leather Timex." Next to the list, in blue pen, Jules read: "Mother says she had a ring. Not on body."

The other pages consisted of fairly rudimentary witness testimony. Bunny had done half the interviews, mostly on the night of the accident, and Jules could understand why the party-goers were evasive at best. Jane had had no more than two or three beers, and had been in a good mood. No one had seen her go over; no one had seen her for at least a half an hour before a couple stumbled over her on the beach below. George, usually referred to as "the boyfriend," had driven away from the party after a spat with Jane, and had never made it back. He'd been fairly drunk, and no one was surprised; an hour after he'd left, Jane had disappeared herself. Fifty-two names were cited, and no one had anything to add. Ray's name didn't appear on the list.

Jules copied the autopsy and the notes and put the originals back in their boxes. It wasn't until he was lifting the miscellaneous crate to the empty slot on the top shelf that he wondered why it had been lying on the floor to begin with.

**HE CALLED** Edie at nine, after he'd had a full pot of coffee. Her voice was still drowsy.

"Why'd you take off?"

"Because George showed up in your driveway at four A.M., and I didn't feel sleepy after that."

"What are you talking about?" He listened to her voice and thought she sounded genuinely surprised. Grace walked toward his desk and he shook his head at her; she retreated. "What do you mean, my driveway?"

"Have you slept with him?"

"Fuck you, Jules."

"Please answer the question."

"Why the hell should I? Why would you give a shit?"

She was screaming into the receiver. "Hush," said Jules.

She brought her voice down a notch and only sounded angrier. "I haven't, but you're probably the last person who has the right to ask a question like that. You come here when you want to, and you leave when you want to, and you don't hear me asking about whether you're seeing that waitress you're so in love with."

Jules shook off the fuzzy sense that he'd heard a line like that before. "I'm not in love with her."

Edie hung up. So much for his laughing girl.

Jules rubbed his eyes. Grace tiptoed into the room and deposited two of her pink slips. "She called right when you got on the other line."

He kept rubbing his eyes, and she patted him on the shoulder and left. The first message was from the mayor and the second from Rita—she had something to tell him. Jules looked at the clock, threw the messages in his wastebasket, and then threw the wastebasket across the room. He picked up the receiver again and punched in one number and then the other with a vengeance, getting a busy signal both times. Harvey walked in, whistling, and stopped in his tracks when he saw Jules's swollen jaw. Jules swiveled away in his chair and tried the lab in Helena. He was on hold, in telephone purgatory, when Grace plunked another slip in front of him, a message to call Scotti. Life had to be difficult in so many ways. Jules gave up holding for the lab and put the phone down gently, trying to control a room-sized anger; it rang again immediately and he ripped it toward his face, hitting his sore mouth.

Scotti was on the line, sucking on a cigar, suggesting Jules get his ass up to Helena for the autopsy, due to start at noon. Jules pointed out that he had better things to do than get in the way of professionals intent upon flaying Ada. Scotti said he understood, but that half of the county and city government had been waiting for him in his office that morning, and they would find Jules's attendance impressive and appropriate, despite the four-hour round-trip. They squabbled for another five minutes, but in the end Jules gave in. He tried Horace but the doctor was in surgery, then tried George and Ray with equal luck. He didn't bother with Rita or the mayor again. Ed had tracked down Nicholas Semple, Jane's brother, in Bozeman. Jules thanked him, took the information, and asked him to come up with a schedule among the deputies so that George and Ray were monitored at all times.

He stopped by his house for the miserable cats and hauled them to the humane society, his conscience somewhat assuaged when the vet told him they were adoptable. He loaded up on cash at the ATM machine, Ray and Mona's love nest, and shot north on the back road to Helena.

It was a waste of time, hours of smelling formaldehyde and learning only that Horace hadn't known what he was doing with Mona. Jules took a stool in the corner of the room and watched and listened, letting his mind float whenever the medical examiner and his assistant started up the saw or the hose. There were so many ways to kill a human, so many ways to die; the halls of the Helena path lab were lined with gory prizes from the last hundred years, instruments and evidence, flattened bullets and nooses, pickled brains and severed fingers. If you decided to play God, plan out the end of a life, how did you decide upon a method and a time and a place? Did you handle it like a card game, rely on nerve as if you were bidding ten no trump or shooting the moon? A killer either had to think that he or she had covered every eventuality or be so intent upon killing that potentially disastrous loose ends were worth the risk. Mona's death was cluttered with loose ends, but Ada's was opaque.

After three hours in Helena he knew a little more precisely several things that he'd guessed before—Ada had died Tuesday night or early Wednesday morning; she'd eaten three to six hours before she died, but they wouldn't know what until the tests came back, because four days in the warm wet grass had reduced everything to pudding; any of the three shots, fired from approximately five feet away and striking her heart and lungs, would have killed her immediately; they couldn't tell about sex, but they were quite sure she'd been moved.

Nicholas Semple was a loan officer for the Bozeman branch of First Big Sky National, a skinny man of Jules's age who looked worn out by the struggle to reach this respectable position from his family's unhappy background. He almost said "who?" when Jules brought up his sister's name; it had probably been that long since someone had uttered it. Jules danced around his reasons for inquiring about Jane, but her brother's curiosity was buried in relief that Jules wasn't interested in a bank client. He couldn't remember a thing about Jane's death besides the general misery of the news and the funeral and the aftermath with his parents. Their father had lost out to cirrhosis two years after Jane was buried, but their mother Vivian had lived until 1990, and they'd hung on to some of her stuff, including a box of Jane's belongings—Nick Semple's wife had thought it sacrilegious to throw out the box.

Jules found her in a new house, a formidably organized woman with a one-year-old twin on either hip. She even knew where the box was, labeled and lined up neatly with others in a spic and span two-car garage. Mrs. Semple was obviously relieved that Jules didn't want to go through the contents at her kitchen table. No, she didn't mind if he borrowed the carton; she didn't even know what was in it. She'd never met Jane, and she tried not to think about such a sad thing.

It was six o'clock. Jules, sick unto death of the station, brought the box home and made himself a big drink before he began to catalog its contents. The 1972 yearbook lay on top. It looked brand new, but that was natural, since Jane hadn't lived to page through it herself. Jane again, the photo he'd seen in the paper but clearer this time and in color, so that he could see freckles on her cheekbones and a pretty green stone surrounded by small pearls on her politely folded hands. She had her own *in memoriam* page, with the same bad McKuen poem. Jules worked his way through the section on seniors, and paused on the prom candids: Jane dancing with her older man, the twenty-one-year-old George, locked into the kind of slow dance that required minimal talent or movement and maximum pressure. Jules paged through the yearbook and found himself in the seventh-grade class photo, thirteen, awkward, thoroughly awful. Maybe ninety pounds, still only five-foot-four or so, still with a father. He paged back and found Rita in fourth grade immediately, tiny and fairy-tale pretty but not very happy.

All of them in the same lousy yearbook, the doom clock ticking.

There were some clothes in the box: a cheap satin formal; a pretty little girl's dress, frayed and discolored, that Jane might have worn to kindergarten; a plastic horse; some dog books; dried corsages that had lost most of their petals; two illiterate but earnest letters from her father; baby pictures; a sweet-sixteen birthday card from her mother; and several sketchbooks that obviously spanned a decade, from early, painstaking drawings of horses and dogs and faces to quick, graceful landscape sketches, trees, and fields remarkably like the ones George still painted. At the end Jules hit a series of the ocean and a rocky but lush coastline.

At the bottom of the carton he found a packet of love letters from George, all postmarked from Princeton, New Jersey, and Portland, Oregon, between the fall of 1971 and May of 1972. They took his breath away—George had copped from the better part of the Western literary canon to make his case for love, but for all the plagiarism he'd quite obviously meant every word. There were funny stories, too, mostly about heroic overdrinking on disastrous weekend trips to New York. The mentions of Ray were already bitter, including the line "Don't you ever, ever believe anything my asshole brother tells you," apparently in reference to a story Ray had told Jane about George and coeds. She'd gone to Portland with them the summer before, and George had come out for the prom and Thanksgiving. Mrs. Blackwater apparently ponied up for another plane ticket over winter break. George's next letters after the visit were graphic, oozing with satisfaction, and filled with compliments for a painting of the sea Jane had done when she was there. She'd given it to him. He said she was going to be a great artist, and that he would hang it in the house they'd have together, keep it forever.

Jules was drinking like a fish, ready to forgive George

everything. By the time he reached the last envelope he was exhausted, awash in the sadness of life. George was responding to whatever Jane had said in her last letter, something about not being worthy of what he'd sent her. George said of course she was worthy. It was his grandmother's emerald ring, and it meant a lot to him. He'd thought of giving it to her when he arrived in Blue Deer, but he decided he wanted to see Jane wearing it when she picked him up at the airport in early May, wanted to know she was his the second he saw her after five months of separation. His mother had given it to him to give to the woman he wanted to marry. And so he had.

CHAPTER 16

## BLUE DEER BULLETIN
### SHERIFF'S REPORT, WEEK OF MAY 17–23

May 17—A traveler reported passing a vehicle with a "hostage" sign in the window. An officer was advised.

A report was received of an altercation at a local business. An officer responded.

May 18—An individual reported two dogs walking into a yard.

The sheriff's office was advised of a possible domestic situation. Appropriate agencies responded.

An Absaroka County ambulance reported being passed by a red sports car traveling at a high rate of speed. An officer was advised.

May 19—A complaint was received of juveniles loitering behind a Blue Deer church. An officer responded and found no juveniles.

May 20—An individual reported some nuisance dogs and said he wanted to shoot them. An officer spoke with the individual.

A report was received of three boys walking down the street lighting matches and throwing them.

An individual requested information on how to handle crank phone calls, and was advised to contact the county attorney.

May 21—A report was received of juveniles throwing rocks off an interstate overpass. An officer was advised and responded with negative contact.

May 22—A report was received of a suspicious individual. An officer also observed the individual.

A report was received of an individual who was intoxicated and wouldn't leave. An officer responded and took the individual home.

May 23—An individual reported sighting a small plane flying over the Crazy Mountains.


NO ONE visited Jules that night, though he didn't keep an eye out for George's car. He walked into the station at seven on Tuesday morning and watched the bank video three times. No mushroom cloud of inspiration went off around his head, but he could see now that there were two rings, a small one on Mona's left hand, on her wedding finger, and a larger, darker ring, with the same shape as the one Jane Semple had worn, on her right. Mona still had it on when they left the lobby, but Jules couldn't see her hand when she walked in, couldn't tell if Ray had put the ring on her finger or simply admired it, couldn't remember when George, watching the tape drunk, had started his mood swing. The video was fuzzy, and when his eyes blurred he gave up and walked to his desk, throwing the cassette into a drawer of ignored forms.

He looked up at his bulletin board. "Treadmill to Oblivion" had lost its old meaning, and the mimeographed sheet of cop jokes was looking flatter all the time. Next to the bad jokes was a photo taken at his graduation from Michigan, showing him with one arm around India and the other around his mother; a photo of Peter and Alice barbecuing on the roof of Alice's apartment on Tompkins Square; a photo of the girl who'd died in the snowstorm in Austria, smiling from the hood of the ill-fated car; a cartoon of an Indian sitting on a horse under a tree, with a cow propped on a branch above, ready to fall; a feather from a blue heron; a postcard of a Delacroix watercolor, showing a room in Tunis; the library schedule; a list of home phone numbers of the deputies and the courthouse staff; and a handwritten verse, copied from a Lorca poem for him by the girl of the snowstorm:

*I want to sleep the dream of apples,*
*to withdraw from the tumult of cemeteries,*
*I want to sleep the dream of that child*
*who wanted to cut his heart on the high seas.*

Underneath it Jules had scribbled another quote in his cramped hand:

*For a long time I prided myself I could possess every country.*

Harvey enjoyed annoying him by reading the poem out loud, in fulsome, preacherlike tones. Jules could barely remember the mood that had led him to copy the line from Rimbaud's *A Season in Hell,* but he kept the page up as a point of pride. He liked to see the quotes when he was sad, and he liked remembering that other worlds and the sea existed. All of his life he'd felt that he'd reach a state of grace if he could swim well, and dance well, and write well, that if he could do these things he'd cleave through life as through water, leaving behind no pain or disruption. Now he thought of Jane's beautiful oil and wanted to be in it, away from the detritus of George's life. George probably wanted to be there, too.

The phone rang, marking the end of relative privacy for the day. Jules let it go two more times, and thought of everyone he didn't want to talk to.

"I called to apologize," said Peter. His voice was hoarse. "I would have yesterday but I couldn't even talk, much less get out of bed."

"I don't know that you're the one who should apologize," said Jules.

Peter was quiet.

"I'm sorry," said Jules. "I would have told you years ago, but it might have ruined things for you two, it would have made it even worse. We were drunk, and you'd moved out. It happened once. Alice really loved you."

"Past tense," said Peter.

"No," said Jules. Harvey had come in and was staring openly from the other side of the room, and Jules gave him the finger. He'd made a list for Harvey, and now folded it into a paper airplane and flung it toward him.

"Maybe we'll finally get married," said Peter. "Right now I just want to act like everything's normal."

Jules started to giggle out of sheer hysteria. Harvey gave him a resentful look and crawled under a desk to retrieve the airplane.

"Really," said Peter. "Just think, you'd be best man. And who's to say what's normal, anyway. We were going to organize a memorial for Ada but so far no one's very enthused. I think we're just going to ship the body home to her parents when the lab's done with it, and hope they never open the coffin."

"Someone will set it up," said Jules, feeling a little sad.

"Sure," said Peter. "Biddle or George or Ray. In the meantime I'll deal with our ownerless paper. You tell me something about Ada and I'll tell you something about Ada."

Jules shut his eyes. "We don't know much yet. Three

bullets, a .38, dead for four or five days. We think the body was dumped. Naked, but you probably already know that. No immediate evidence of anything like rape or other injuries caused before death. Don't get into the animals eating her, okay?"

Jules listened to the sound of scribbling. "I have a question for you."

"Go."

"Was the *Bulletin* planning a piece on rodeos?"

"No," said Peter. "If we ran something we'd wait till at least late June."

"Ada said she was doing research for a series."

"Oh, please," said Peter. "Ada working? Not to speak ill of the dead or anything, but I don't believe it."

Jules drummed his pen on his desktop and started a drawing.

"When was she last seen?" asked Peter.

"Tuesday evening."

"Who with?"

"Come on, Peter."

"George was in her car Tuesday afternoon, about four. They were headed toward the ranch."

Jules tried to think.

"Did you hear me?"

"Yes. Thank you."

"Wait," said Peter. "There's more. I went into her office to pull some files I'd given her a while back, and I found something she'd tucked into the population series."

"What?" He'd drawn the outline of a face and penned in eyebrows.

"An autopsy report for Jane Semple, the girl Alice said George used to go out with. Have you seen it?"

Things weren't supposed to work this way. "I read it yesterday morning."

"Ah," said Peter. "A happy coincidence. Ada wrote something on her copy. Now you're going to tell me you know what she wrote."

Jules stopped doodling and sloped back in his chair. "Did it have anything to do with a particular head wound?"

"No, but I'll keep that in mind," said Peter. He took a noisy swig of coffee. "All she wrote was, 'Ray: paid for George's alibi. Talk to cops on scene.'"

They were both quiet for a moment. "'Ray' followed by a colon?" asked Jules. "Like he'd told her he'd paid for an alibi?"

"Yeah. What's it mean?" asked Peter.

"I'm not sure," said Jules. He'd finished one eye and didn't think he'd have enjoyed the company of the woman he'd drawn. "But I like it."

He put down the receiver gently, drained another cup of coffee, and dialed Ray.

"Do you have a second for some questions?"

"No." The word was calm, clipped. "I'm busy."

"Oh dear," said Jules. "So am I." He tried to remember what Ray had looked like when he was truly angry at the Blue Bat, but all he could recall was the manicured hand waiting for him on the carpeting. "Just five minutes of your precious time."

Ray didn't say anything.

"First," said Jules, "I wondered how you knew, twenty years ago, the night Jane Semple died, that you could find George at the police station and not the hospital?"

"Are you fucking kidding?"

"No. I'm not fucking kidding." Jules could hear Ray smoking, getting a healthy start on what might be a heavy nicotine day.

"George is like a dog," said Ray. "When they disappear you assume they've been taken to the pound."

"But he'd been hurt," said Jules. "Why wouldn't you

assume they'd take him to the hospital when they found him?"

"I called there." Ray spit the words out. "He wasn't there. Process of elimination. They should have taken him in, but they didn't."

"I see." Jules started on his drawing again.

"Are you finished?"

"No. How did you know he'd been hurt to begin with?"

There was a moment of silence on the phone, one of the most satisfying silences Jules had ever heard.

Ray finally spoke. "A cop told me."

"Basil McElwaine?"

"I don't remember his name."

"He told you when he interviewed everyone after they hauled Jane off?"

"Yes."

Jules listened to a second flick of the lighter. "You said you weren't at the party. You don't show up on the interview list. Fifty other names, and not yours."

"I ran into the cop later that night," said Ray.

"Just ran into him."

"Yes. Are you done wasting my time?"

"I am for now," said Jules. "Have a nice day."

Grace strolled in, singing again. Her daughter had finally given birth the night before, a little girl in three hours flat. A piece of cake, said Grace. Jules doubted that the daughter had referred to labor that way, but congratulated the grandmother. He let her call four friends and burble happily before he put Jane Semple's autopsy report on her desk and brought her back to earth.

"Have you seen this before?"

"No." She looked at him as if he were insane. "Why would I have?"

"Has anyone asked to see old records lately?"

Grace shook her head, her mind on booties. "Nothing

from the seventies." She started dialing the phone again.

"Grace." He said it emphatically.

She looked startled. "What?"

"Who was the last person you let into the records safe?"

"I told you. Mrs. Santoz."

"No," said Jules. "You didn't tell me."

"Well, I thought I did," said Grace. "She was going to do something on how bloody things used to be here, and how safe the county is now, despite Mrs. Blackwater's murder."

"When?" asked Jules, gritting his teeth.

"When?" Grace looked exasperated, and still clutched the phone. "The twenties and the thirties, mostly, I guess. She was interested in the story about the crazy who shot half the force during the Depression."

Jules wanted to rip the phone out of her hands. "No. When did she come to look at the records?"

Grace put the handset down and finally looked guilty. "The day you went to the library, late in the afternoon. About a week ago. I really meant to tell you."

Tuesday, the day Ada had been to the library, too, researching rodeos, the day she'd probably died. Grace was thinking the same thing, now, wringing her hands, but Jules was the one who'd never gone back to the station that day.

"It's okay," said Jules. "It wouldn't have made a bit of difference."


JULES called the mayor back, twenty-four hours after Grace had begun to give him his messages. The mayor had been soothed, as Scotti predicted, by Jules's trip to Helena, and had absolutely nothing of moment to say, but he still took ten minutes in not saying it, and another five insisting that Jules join him and the county commissioners and Scotti for lunch the next day.

Harvey reported in. George had slept at home the night

before. Early that morning, when Harvey had checked, George's car had been at the office, and Ray had been at the ranch, but now both were gone. It was suddenly obvious to Jules that they couldn't do much better than keep such tabs—everybody had been working overtime for three weeks, and everybody needed a break. The mayor and county commissioners were unlikely to give him an extra patrolman if he couldn't solve murders with the ones he had.

He stopped by George's office, even though he didn't see the Land Cruiser out front. Edie was in the framing room, stripping adhesive paper from Plexiglas, and she kept her eyes on the table without giving him more than a glance. She didn't know where George was; she didn't usually know, whatever Jules thought. He stood watching her put together a metal frame for an etching of an apple tree until she asked him to leave, still speaking in a quiet, bloodless voice. But by then he was watching her unspool framing wire, only seeing the coils of thin, strong, finely braided wire flop down on the table as she cut one end free, twisted it through an eyelet, and stopped saying anything.

Jules wandered down the hall to George's office. All that art, all supported by same type of wire. He looked out the window at the clean, rain-washed sidewalks of Blue Deer, then turned and regarded the computer. Edie had been typing from a messy stack in George's handwriting before she began framing, and Jules leaned forward and read the screen. It was page two of a movie treatment, and one of the protagonists, a jealous murderer, was tailing the cop who'd humiliated him publicly and stolen his girl.

He walked back into the framing room, clipped off a piece of wire while Edie watched in silence, and left.

HORACE had visiting hours at the clinic on Tuesdays, and Jules waited in the lobby for a break in appointments, watching the people go by—ancient men in walkers, tired young women with swollen breasts and tiny newborns, gray cancer victims defiantly reading gardening magazines, children still scooting at a mad pace despite bronchial coughs and noses that oozed green. They all seemed to have more energy than he did, and so did Horace, rosy and jolly despite the near-death appearance of the patient he ushered out before pulling Jules into his office.

"Thank you for sending Ada to Helena," said Horace. "Thank you."

"You're welcome," said Jules.

Horace waited expectantly.

"I'm not here about Ada. I've got one quick question and a few more complicated ones." He handed Horace the section of framing wire. "Would that fit what strangled Mona?"

Horace ran it through his fingers and nodded. "I couldn't say for sure, but it's thick and bendable and it would have pulled her skin. It's as close as anything."

Horace handed the wire back and Jules passed him Jane Semple's autopsy report. "Please read all of this and tell me whether you agree with the notes in the margins."

"Christ," said Horace, scanning the date on the top of the page. "Why?"

Jules felt stupid but stubborn. "Just look it over. Please."

Horace read. "So what do you want to know?"

"Tell me what you think."

Horace went back to the page. "The head wound probably came first. She lost a lot of blood."

"She was alive when they found her, so she would have kept bleeding," said Jules.

"No way was anyone with these problems alive," said Horace. "Not physically possible, between the neck and the head. She might have had some signs if it was just the skull fracture, but not something this deep."

"The log said she was alive when they found her," said Jules.

"Wishful thinking," said Horace. "Happens all the time, probably happened more then. Someone's still warm and they radio in that there's hope. She was probably dead before her neck even broke."

"Which would be why the bruising wasn't extensive?"

"Yes."

Jules watched Horace. "In a fall, we're talking a few seconds. She hits her head on a rock, or a tree root, then makes it to the bottom and snaps her neck. You're telling me that's enough time for circulation to slow, so that her neck won't bruise?"

Horace stared at him, flustered. "Maybe she landed on a ledge, rolled down later and finished the job."

"You just told me she'd never move again after the head wound."

The doctor looked out his window and thought. "Maybe the ledge gave way. Maybe the examiner was an idiot, measured wrong. Maybe she lived for a while."

"Another thing," said Jules. "If she got the head wound when she bounced, if it didn't happen at the same time she broke her neck, then she probably only fell twenty or thirty feet at first. Like the notes say, it doesn't seem like the dent would be that deep, that clean."

"I don't know," said Horace. "I probably couldn't tell if I had her on a table, let alone from this piece of shit."

"Do you remember that guy who got hit by a crowbar a couple of years back, right when I started? I brought him in and you looked at him."

"Yeah, I remember," said Horace. "He lived."

"But it was a dent like that. Not as deep, but like that, right?"

"Jesus, Jules. You're making me want to start drinking before lunch."

"Wasn't it?"

"Yes."

Jules rubbed at a coffee stain on his knee. "You know George pretty well. You've always been his doctor, right?"

"Oh please," said Horace. "I can't believe he'd hurt a fly. He's my friend." Little drops of perspiration dotted his pate.

"George had an accident a long time ago. Does he have a dent in his head like that? A little one?"

Horace gaped. "Are you turning into a conspiracy paranoid or something?"

Jules tried again. "Did George ever receive a blow to the head, to your knowledge?"

Horace leaned back in his chair. "George has a very slight depression on the back of his skull. He told me he had a head injury in his early twenties. Twice, shortly after the injury, he said he had a mild seizure, but he's had no symptoms in the last twenty years."

"Thank you," said Jules, standing up.

"Is that all you wanted to know?" Horace was sarcastic.

"Yep."

"Do you want to tell me why you're interested?"

"Sorry, no."

Horace handed back the autopsy report. "Whose handwriting is this?"

"My father's."

"Sorry."

"It's been a while," said Jules. "Don't worry about it."

THE JOKE Wednesday was whether or not radio collars would work on the Blackwater boys. As of that morning both Ray and George had been sighted twice in the last twenty-four hours. Neither had seemed up to anything interesting, and there was no staff to follow them through the day. Jules liked the idea of little beepers inserted painfully under the skin of the groin, and tried to sweeten Scotti up by suggesting this, but Axel, still intent on the election that fall, remained foul. He wanted to hold Ada's inquest on Friday, and only said he'd consider Monday after Jules threatened to end both their careers by arresting George and/or Ray without sufficient evidence. Scotti retaliated by reading the last two day's worth of letters to the editor out of the *Bulletin*, and suggested that Jules get his ass in gear.

Ed came in while Scotti was only halfway through this performance, and Jules hung up just in time to catch him before he left again. Ed wasn't prone to loitering. Jules pulled him aside, told him what he knew and what he thought he knew, showed him the handwriting on the report, and waited for a response.

He got disgust, always hard to take from anyone, and even harder to handle when it came from Ed.

"You ever hear the phrase, 'can of dead worms'?" Ed worked on his chewing tobacco.

"Hey," said Jules. "I'm not suggesting that any of you didn't do a good job."

Ed looked out the window. "Sure, your dad was worried about it, but what was he going to prove? He couldn't trust that piece of shit autopsy, and he couldn't trust his own cops, and the bigshots wanted an accident if it could be called one, didn't want any outside help. Kind of the reverse of what you're going through now. They can't call the last two accidents, so they want a killer. And if you can't find a killer they'll take your head on the platter."

Jules looked down at the floor. "You get my drift?" asked Ed.

"I've been getting it," said Jules. "What about Ray not showing up on the interview list?"

Ed flecked something off the brim of his hat. "Bunny got his first new car that summer. July, I think it was, a few weeks before your dad got shot, a couple of months after

Miss Semple took her fall at a full-moon party with a bunch of drunks. A real nice car, a navy blue Buick. Payments didn't even seem to dent his style."

Jules stared at him. "George was in these cells. He didn't have any reason to pay him off."

"I'm not talking about George. But I'm also not saying that I actually saw his piece of shit brother at that party, or that I think you should be blowing your precious hours on this."

Ed limped off, and Jules considered his patrimony. No unsolved murders in forty years, brayed the mayor, and now Jules had two. There'd been only twelve homicides in the state the year before, out of thirty-some counties. Saying that he'd found another one, something his father had chosen to overlook, would hardly improve his life.

Grace, queen of the pink slips, had resorted to making lists of the phone calls she knew or thought he'd failed to return, the forms she was absolutely sure he'd failed to fill out. She handed him two fresh ones while he stood at the window, staring at the bleak sky and wondering if this would be a flood year. Jules gave her a pained smile and followed her back to her desk, scratching out the names of people he'd talked to, circling the ones she should put through if he happened to be around. "Rita B." had a small number three after her name, and Jules felt Grace watch him fail to circle the name. He made another list for himself of people, mostly not on Grace's list, who he needed to call, the ones who didn't want to talk to him, like Bunny, George, Ray, his mother, and the medical examiner in Helena. Then he had a crisis of conscience and of heart, and tried Rita after all. She didn't answer, and he left a message saying he'd be out most of the day. He signed a stack of forms, gave the computer and his foot-high file of paperwork the briefest glance, and left again, feeling like a low-rent shark that might sink if it idled.

JULES drove to George's house, but no one was home. He drove by the office, trolled the alleys, but didn't find the Land Cruiser. There was no point in going upstairs for another nontalk with Edie—he'd learned during the last month that George had never been known to walk more than a block, unless he was fishing or hunting. The man wasn't in the vicinity, and Jules would have to sit on his questions. He radioed in, but no one had had the time to check on George or his brother since that morning, and now, thanks to forms and other pressing duties, it was too late for Jules to look for either himself. He drove to the Baird Hotel for lunch with the town fathers, and was relieved to find that Rita wasn't working in the restaurant that day.

The meal lasted two hours and succeeded in pissing him off rather than scaring him. At the station, endless iced teas sloshing in his stomach, he headed for the computer again, intent upon doing as sloppy a job as possible on inconsequential matters. Grace came up behind him as he logged on.

"The lab in Helena called with their preliminary report on Ada, but you were at lunch." Grace always seemed to imply he was wasting his time, idling away while others sought dangerous men. "I took notes."

"Shoot," said Jules, exiting the screen with gusto. He glanced out the window, relieved to see inconsequential sprinkles rather than a downpour that might have complicated life and the river.

"She'd had sex, but probably hadn't been raped. The semen was the same that they found in Mona." Grace made a puffing sound—this wasn't the usual blotter stuff, and he could feel her awkwardness.

Ray again, leaving precious bodily fluids in dead women. Thank God the man hadn't actually bred yet. "Go on."

Grace nodded. "They're pretty sure she died later on Tuesday or early Wednesday. No fibers, maybe because of all the rain, and no signs of violence besides the gunshot wounds."

If Ada had been lucky she'd have never seen it coming, but it was hard to avoid seeing a gun five feet away. Maybe she dozed after her frolic with Ray, and he'd been merciful. Maybe she'd survived Ray and found George or someone else later.

"What did they find in her stomach?"

Grace peered at her notes. "A light meal, possibly a cheese quesadilla, shortly before death, and a lot of wine. Also turkey, bacon, tomato, avocado, cheese, bread product, some lettuce, probably for lunch, at least eight hours beforehand. The wine had been ingested over a long period of time."

Jules actually smiled. If she'd had a hamburger he might have cried. Grace stared at him. "So she had a club sandwich with avocado for lunch at the Baird Hotel, and a snack and a last glass of wine with the wrong boy."

Grace looked over the top of her eyeglasses. "You're a bullshitter from way back."

"None of the other restaurants have real avocado. And no one would make such a stupid sandwich at home." He grabbed his coat and eyed the clock. It was eleven, and he had plenty of time. "I'll be back in a bit."

"Wait," said Grace. "They also said they found a whopper dose of barbiturates in her system. Seconal, they thought."

Jules had one sleeve of his coat on and let the other drop. "Enough to kill her?"

"No. Just enough to knock her out. Really knock her out. They said it would have taken effect by the time she died."

"That's nice," said Jules.

Grace looked outraged. "What do you mean, 'that's nice'?" Are you crazy?"

"Someone didn't want her to know she was going to die," said Jules. All kindness was relative.

THE WAITRESS who'd served him an hour earlier stared at him blankly when he asked her if she knew Ada Santoz, but she didn't work Tuesday lunches, anyway. He found the owner's daughter, a pretty, intelligent girl who'd been on shift; she'd recognized Ada because she'd applied to the paper and been turned down, and she said she never forgot any sort of rejection. But she didn't know Ray, or George. Jules described them—both tall and in their forties and fairly good looking, one with darker hair and a friendly expression, one with nicer clothes and better manners. The girl heard him out and laughed when he'd finished. The man Ada had lunched with was massive, built like a construction worker but fat, and covered with gray hair, so much so that even the tops of his fingers and ears were fuzzy. He'd had four scotches with lunch, and had treated his waitress like shit. He'd given the girl the creeps, and she couldn't fathom what a lady like Ada was doing with him.

Ada's house was locked, of course—Jules had completely forgotten this complication before he pulled into the driveway. But no one had fixed the window, and he climbed in yet again. The rain had become relentless, and he dripped water on the wood floor as he trotted directly to her office and methodically searched each pigeonhole and drawer of the desk. In the bottom, tucked in a manila envelope marked "expenses," he found a stack of photos of naked, sleeping men, all fairly demure, all taken in Ada's bedroom. George, Ray, and Biddle were there; so, to Jules's surprise, was Scotti. He was relieved to find Peter missing, but Peter would hardly have slept over. He couldn't decide if they were touching or creepy, mementos or trophies. They weren't blackmail caliber, at least where George or Ray were concerned.

He played the answering machine again, running over the beginning of the partially erased message three times, a blank spot, then "Ada, how are you?" from the man; Ada's "It's been a long time," and raucous laughter. When Jules had first listened to it he'd thought something had come before "Ada," Ray's introduction as he called the day after he got to town. Now he wondered if it began as he heard it, if it was George, and she still recognized the voice. The brothers sounded the same—to hate each other so much, and be so alike, must add to the sense of injury.

In a sense it didn't matter: She'd seen George that afternoon, Ray that evening, maybe George again, after Ray. If she'd brought up whatever Bunny might have told her with either brother, or both of them, one of them might have had a reason to kill her. It went back to Jane, not to Mona, or Ada shooting George; everything went back to Jane, though he couldn't for the life of him see a connection between Ada's death and Mona's death, besides their obvious predilection for sleeping with the wrong men—unless it was the likelihood they'd mouthed off to the wrong brother about a very old problem. Perhaps Ray had told Ada the Jane Semple story, and she'd decided to run with it, dig into it and finally make George pay. But Jules had a feeling that Bunny's version of the story had been different from Ray's. And what would have happened then?


JULES had left five messages for Bunny in the last two days, and had driven by his house twice. At four that afternoon he got lucky, in a manner of speaking, and walked around Bunny's van in a downpour to join him on a stool in the Blue Bat.

"How ya doin'," said Bunny, Mr. Charm. "Your turn to buy."

"Sure," said Jules. He smiled at Delly, who regarded

them with dread. "A scotch for Mr. McElwaine, however he likes it, and a whiskey ditch for me."

Delly gave Jules a pleading look, and Jules gave him another reassuring smile.

Bunny was smiling, too. "I meant to get back to you. I've been busy."

"Lunch with Mrs. Santoz and all," said Jules. "I understand."

"I've always enjoyed pretty women," said Bunny, not bothering to quibble.

"A shame," said Jules.

"Indeed."

"Did she ask you what you and George talked about?"

Bunny gave him an amused look.

"Did she ask you whether Ray was at that party?"

No response. Not a flicker. Nil.

Jules sighed and resorted to debasing himself. "Bunny, you know I hate to ask for favors from anyone, and you know I especially hate to ask for them from you. Please tell me what you said to George the night you ran into him."

"I've already told you."

"All of it."

Bunny finished his scotch in one long gulp, pushed his glass forward, and crooked his finger in Delly's direction. Delly played with his beard and made a show of watching ESPN. Bunny thunked the glass down hard on the bar, shooting his remaining ice cubes through the air in pretty arcs. Then he turned back to Jules.

"You think I'm bad," said Bunny, more of a statement of fact than a preamble. He leaned forward and his stomach surged around the bar. "Ray's so bad that he told George that George had killed that girl twenty years ago, and George fell for it, because he was too drunk to remember, and he was afraid to ask anyone else about it. Ray told George that he'd covered up for him, and bribed me to look the other way, told him he should be thankful. So George sat down next to me that night and thanked me, said that I kept him out of jail and allowed him to survive his fat wife. And I said, what the fuck are you thanking me for, you little Hollywood piss ant."

Jules tried to remain impassive, but he actually agreed with Bunny. It was pretty bad, one of the worst sucker shots he'd ever heard of, a preeminent example of deliberate mental cruelty that explained away various things, the least of which was George shooting Ray's car. Ray's trick had actually been so good that knowing about it didn't really get him anywhere without the second half of the story.

"And then you told George that he'd been safe in the jail."

"Yeah. He could have found out himself anytime if he'd had the guts to go to the station."

"Did he ask you about his head?

Bunny sighed, the picture of patience. "Not until the second time we talked. He came to see me a few days later, said he'd seen something on a video you'd shown him that made him think. I told him that, yeah, someone had knocked him on the head, didn't look like he'd just fallen, but it was a busy night and his pulse was normal. He was drunk too. He came around a little, off and on."

Jules upped the ante. "Did he ask you if Ray had been at the party?"

"He asked. I didn't see the prick that night, at least until he showed up for his brother."

Jules lied. "Ed says he saw Ray Blackwater that night."

"Fuck Ed," said Bunny. "He's had it out for me since the days when we could still see our dicks past our stomachs."

"See, I think the best lies have a grain of truth," said Jules. "Ray took a ring off that girl's body, before or after it was just a body. I think Ray did bribe you, but it was to save his own ass."

"Bribe me? Me?" Bunny stubbed a fat finger against his chest.

Jules looked at him evenly. "I heard Ray bought you a new car a month after Jane Semple took her fall."

Bunny twirled his glass, watching the scotch pass over ice cubes with a loving look.

Jules kept going, man with a death wish. "I think Ray killed that girl, and I think you let him get away with murder for the sake of a new Buick. And I think that when we pop him he'll tell us that, and you'll be an accessory after the fact."

Bunny didn't deign to comment. Jules kept at it, hissing in his ear.

"When that happens, we can bring all sorts of things up. My personal favorite was that statutory rape in eighty-two. I know she was trailer trash, Bunny, but the truth will out."

Bunny reached behind Jules, gripped a thick shock of hair, and brought his head down toward the bar, fast and hard. But Jules's immediate reaction had been to pull away, even if it meant forever after having a bald spot on the back of his head like Horace's, and the wood of the bar only caught the top of his head. Jules kept moving backward, swayed, and came forward with a full-leg soccer kick that hit a perfect trajectory when it reached Bunny's well-cushioned groin.

"My fucking floor," said Delly. "That's it for the carpeting. It's not even happy hour."

Jules saw a pattern of sandpaper before his eyes, no stars, and leaned unsteadily against a stool while Bunny finished retching, meditated, and climbed to his feet. He moved slowly toward his drink, still intact on the bar. Bunny took a sip, looked at Jules, and drove what felt like his whole arm, glass and all, into Jules's stomach.

Jules landed five feet away, and Bunny leaned over him.

"I was never happier than when that trucker blasted out

your dad's smart-ass heart, and I wish the same for you."

Then he was out the door, moving so much faster than he had in his final fitness test that Jules gave a wretched giggle from the floor.

"If I were you," said Delly, "I'd press charges. Assaulting an officer is no laughing matter."

"I'll get around to it," said Jules, luxuriating in the stinky carpeting and wondering if Ray and George had taken as much pleasure in it. Someone should invite them over for a look-see, give them a last cheery sight before Bunny found them. "How about a glass of water."

"It might leak out of the hole he put in your gut." Delly stood above him, looking bemused. "Also, I'd recommend a stitch or two on your forehead. You're funny looking enough already. I'm calling for backup."

HORACE decided on a mild concussion, said Jules's stomach was just fine, and indulged in endless jokes about the shapes of wounds while he put twelve stitches in Jules's forehead. Ed thought it was all very funny. "A dent," said Horace. "And definitely a round dent, made by a hard object. About two by two by one thirty-second of an inch deep, with a one-and-three-quarter-inch fissure."

"Har dee fucking har," said Jules.

He'd been scheduled to spell Jonathan, who was home sick with the flu, on DUI duty that night, but the floor in the reception room rose toward his face while he waited for his bill. Ed hauled him home, tucked him in bed, and fed him two of the codcine tablets Horacc had prescribed. Jules listened to Ed's heavy feet on the stairs and the click of the front door, and reached down, unplugged the phone by his bed, and tossed it across the room.

CHAPTER 17

THE PHONE rang over and over, a very distant noise, then stopped. Jules fell back asleep. When it started again he fumbled under the bed, then ran down the stairs and jerked the receiver toward his ear.

"Jules?"

"Yes."

"It's Grace. It's nine o'clock. The river's way up." Her voice was patient, soothing. Jules looked out the window at bright sunlight.

"Oh shit."

"I thought you should know."

"I'll be right in."

Jules had gone through life without resorting to violence more than once since grade school. In the May of his thirty-fourth year he'd now caused pain three times, and been hit twice. It was worrisome, and hopefully not the beginning of a pattern. When he stared in the mirror he made out several distinct colors in his forehead—reds, purples, pinks, and the beginning hint of yellow—and he tried unsuccessfully to brush his hair forward before he decided that the stitches were pleasantly cinematic. His stomach bruise was a perfect circle. Jules hoped fervently that Bunny's testicles would never descend again after his well-aimed kick, sparing countless women from assault.

At the station there was a message from Scotti, suggesting that Jules not press charges. It would be easier on everyone's reputation if Bunny's name never made the paper. A large communal get-well card was propped on his desk, with notes inside that read "Could have happened years ago" and "Better you than us." No one but Grace or Archie was at the station; they were all out sandbagging, even Harvey, who'd been on patrol that night.

The Yellowstone was a free-flowing river, and there were no gauges to adjust, no spill ducts to open. The WPA had redirected the river in the thirties, looping it away from town and creating a landfill that now contained all of Blue Deer's schools and the rodeo grounds. The aged rodeo and fair grounds would be an easy loss, and the schools sat on safe mounds of dirt; the real potential for trouble lay along the old course of the river, in the trailer parks and old bungalows in town, and in the new luxury homes that flaunted the flood plain east and south of town. The flood plain determination was, after all, a bit of a joke, based on the high-water marks of 1927 and 1984, but with only one hundred years of records, no one really knew what the river considered exceptional. It was a little like the sucker shot the railroads had aimed at homesteaders in the eastern half of Montana—the 1890s were lush, and the railroads advertised thirty inches of rain a year. The real average proved to be twelve to sixteen, and there were still more empty shacks than lived-in homes in the empty plains east of the Rockies.

Every five years or so Blue Deer had a flood scare. This year the Yellowstone was almost a pleasant distraction: George and Ray Blackwater weren't the deadliest entities in town, after all. The river was already flooding low-lying areas, though it had as much as two feet to go before it crested. The problem now wasn't so much the last few days of rain but the warmth of the sun, the consequent sudden thawing of the mountain snowpack, and the thunderstorms that still bashed Yellowstone Park, sixty miles upstream.

They evacuated all but two of the thirty inhabitants of Magpie Island over the sixty-year-old wavering concrete bridge. Grace refused to move her things, though she put in a full day of work; the other recalcitrant individual was Delly, who'd wound down from the Bunny episode by getting horribly drunk in his own bar. Blue Deer's biggest day-care center was on the island, and Jules wanted to vomit from pure fear as the two busloads of tiny, waving hands made their way over the crumbling concrete.

They dug ditches to divert the flow from a weak bend in the river near the schools, sandbagged the ditches, the Magpie Bridge, and dozens of other strategic points. By six, when the river had magically dropped six inches, it seemed to Jules that he'd spent a lifetime digging and hauling and tinkering with the hydraulics of ancient bulldozers, and the sheer frustration and stupidity of it made him as irritable as everyone else. Jules told his deputies to rest up, and left the volunteers and the fire department to defend the town. He thought of checking up on the Blackwaters and decided that if he were lucky they were off killing each other, choking on their just desserts.

Jules decided to take Peter's advice and pretend that life was normal, even though there were very few people left with whom he could make this pretense, and even though what he wanted wasn't simply normal, if you averaged out the whole of the last year. He didn't, for instance, feel like seeing a movie, or having a drink with Peter, or stopping by to see why his mother had been calling, or trolling the bars.

At seven, the air still balmy, he knocked on Rita's door. Things didn't begin well.

"What did you need to talk about?"

She stood in the doorway, looking stony and bleak. "I've forgotten by now."

Jules asked to come in and she shrugged. He stopped just inside, taking in the packing boxes. Rita moved past him and turned on the kitchen faucet, letting the water run cold before she filled her glass.

"I'm leaving." She drank the water without offering any, and watched him. "I'm going back to Seattle. If it's going to rain all the time here I'd just as soon be serving asshole drunks near the ocean than cowboys who want to bring their pickups into the bar."

"Just a problem with the weather, huh?"

"Don't worry. It's not your fault."

"I would never give myself so much credit," said Jules icily.

"Maybe if you had I wouldn't be leaving."

"Oh fuck you." He swatted at a stacked box, and it tipped onto the floor, dumping paperbacks. "You know goddamn well I would have crawled across the state for you. You told me twenty times you didn't want me to."

She sat down on the couch. "Admit it," said Jules. "Don't try to make me feel any shittier about this."

She nodded her head and her face crumbled, tears coursing down her cheeks.

"I came here to ask you if you wanted to go to dinner. A real fucking joke, I guess."

Rita looked for just a second as if she might laugh, but then she started crying in earnest. "Stop it," said Jules. He wished she looked ugly when she cried, like most people. She even looked beautiful when her hair was pasted to her cheek with a mixture of snot and tears. "Please stop it, Rita. Give it a break."

It took five minutes. He sat on the couch next to her quietly but didn't touch her. When she was done she washed her face under the faucet and dried it with a dishtowel, then walked into her bedroom and came out two minutes later in a summery dress and a pair of sandals. They climbed into his truck and drove to Bozeman.

It was a new restaurant, and someone, maybe Scotti, had told him it was great—actual seafood in the intermountain West. But the first bottle of wine was vinegar, and the waitress made the mistake of insisting it was fine, and they got off to a bad start until the first two glasses of the next bottle kicked in and the waitress endeared herself by delivering succulent steamed mussels and baby clams to the table. Throughout the first course they avoided the topics of dead people and blighted love with great success; Jules talked about a child's sense of geography, about how huge and varied the world seemed when you were small, and how if you lost that feeling when you were older it was a good marker of either stupidity or clinical depression. Rita asked about where he'd been, and said she wanted to see Europe and Africa and Asia and South America. She wanted to know what would happen if Jules got a DUI, and Jules told her that given the current state of mayhem in the county he'd probably be fired, but that that would be fine, because they could move to the other side of the ocean. China was too crowded; Australia would be better. Rita could open a truck stop and he'd raise tomatoes and the children. She seemed to like the idea, and she never did say anything about his stitched-up forehead or bruised jaw.

They moved on to a fresh bottle of wine and Rita started giggling, the hysterical, quiet laughter that comes with the onset of hallucinogens but in this case marked the arrival and tasting of the main course. The coquilles Saint Jacques were a white, floury sponge of sauce and overcooked shark bits, with little pools of fake butter dotting the surface, and strands of rubbery cheese dripping over the side of the plate. It smelled. Halibut stuffed with crabmeat—what had possessed him when ordering?—was filled with jelled, manufactured crab lozenges, Baco Bits, and something like Stovetop Stuffing. Jules spooned the glop out and picked at the surface of the fish, then turned to his slightly brown and gritty salad with a sense of relief. They fled next door to a bar for a straight shot to wash it all down, then looked at each other and climbed back into the truck. Jules drove too fast on the way home, more than slightly drunk and drowning in anticipation, and when they got to Rita's house he gave her time to get her dress off and no more.

Two hours later, for some reason, they began to talk about the mess he was in, the havoc and ugliness of the Blackwater family. Rita asked questions and then listened quietly as Jules talked with his head on her breasts, stroking her skin and her silky gray slip, askew and shimmery. He told her about Jane, and that he thought Ray had killed his brother's lover, but that he thought George was responsible for Mona and Ada. Neither of them had more than a half-assed alibi for either death, but George had hated Mona, and Ray had seemed to like Ada, so emotionally, practically, it had to be George.

Rita pulled him off gently and sat on the edge of the bed with her back to him.

"No," she said.

"No what?"

"When was Ada killed?"

"Last Tuesday night, probably." He touched the strap of the slip, staring at the fabric, finally noticing how fine it was, how expensive, remembering seeing one very like it at the ranch house, on top of George Blackwater's belongings.

Jules sat up very slowly, feeling cold and naked. "Why?"

"Because George was here until I left for work that morning. George was my lover, the other man I told you about. I told him I liked you. That's why I was calling you. He said he was going to kill you. I couldn't exactly leave a message spelling it out."

**HE DIDN'T** want to go home, or go anywhere else, so he drove around, first north of town along the western front of the Crazies and then to the south again, down their east side. Jules turned off his headlights and floated down the dark highway until he saw stars and the headlights of a car approaching. When he reached Blue Deer he parked at the all-night diner, ordered a huge breakfast, and made a list.

Two hours later, at the station, Jules waved at the night operator, started a pot of coffee, and stared bleakly at the stacks of paper on his desk, trying to remember what day it was. He turned to the calendar—Friday, May 28. He'd spent the week tossing *Bulletin*s to the floor, and now he turned to them, wondering how a surface view of Absaroka County would differ from his own private nightmares. He lacked the energy to actually open the papers and face the obituaries and letters to the editor, and instead examined the headlines on the front pages, feeling like someone who's smoked a joint and needs to read the same page of *People* three times to comprehend. Lines like "Sheriff's Department Still Lacks Leads in Santoz Murder" naturally jumped toward his glazed eyes, but when he reached Monday's paper, working backward, he actually giggled. The banner read *"Bulletin* Publisher Found Dead" and just beneath it, in a juxtaposition the *Columbia Journalism Review* would have adored, was a large photo of Jules, Alice, Olive, and Grace, Jules with his arms outstretched like a prophet, the Audubon guide in one hand, smiling up at the sky as if thanking Ada for having reached heaven. Olive and Grace grinned behind him, but Alice rolled her eyes off to one side, probably thinking she'd edged out of the frame. The small caption identified the bird count, but the overview was literally murder. Jules cackled again and swayed toward the lounge to pour his first cup.

After sorting through the stacks on his desk he knew simple caffeine wouldn't get him far enough, and thought briefly of raiding the evidence locker for his first white cross in a decade. It was 5:30, and he only had two or three hours before everyone filed in and started asking questions. He stared at the list he'd made at the diner and placed it deliberately on his desk. He had to stop, he had to sleep.

> *Dear Grace—*
>
> *I'm in the interview room. Don't let anyone bother me unless we have another murder, or the feds show up at the door—*

The list was potentially endless. He stopped there.

> *—or something truly catastrophic happens. Please wake me at nine, and say something nice, like "rise and shine," and I promise I'll be a modern marvel.*

He drew "Do Not Disturb" with a marker on the back of a city council memo and taped it to the lounge door, then climbed on the table, wadded up his coat, and used it as a pillow.

**WHEN** he first woke up he stayed perfectly still, listening to the voices, footsteps, ringing phones, clanks and rattles of the active station. He noticed that everyone whispered when they passed the door. Perhaps someone cared, after all. He took stock, a hideous process; it was almost as if his soul were hung over. At times like this he felt surrounded, hemmed in by the dreck of his life, not the things he'd run into accidentally but the things he'd caused to be, willfully, and with a horrible lack of foresight. He liked seeing himself as clean, as leaving no unhappy wake, or maybe just a small one of regret, and if he couldn't be clean he'd rather see himself as the victim than the prick. But he'd been the prick so many times they blurred together; no amount of self-effacing selective memory could free him from the pain he'd caused people through stupidity, righteousness, hormonal behavior. He thought of his insufficient knowledge of justice. He thought of being a bad son. He thought of the education he'd jettisoned. He thought of Rita and George, Edie, Alice and Peter, and jammed the heels of his hands into his eyes. He thought of Jane, and how things could start, and escalate.

He dozed again. When he woke the room seemed brighter, and he lurched upright just as the door swung open. Grace smiled, and said, "Give God your glory."

FIFTEEN minutes later he hobbled back to his desk, the table having left numb points in his shoulders and his tailbone and his heels, his head roaring with pain. Grace tagged after him, worried, shaking a bottle of aspirin and causing further pain. She had the temerity to point out that he'd disappeared on them the night before, not responded to his beeper, or anything; Harvey had tried to call him the previous evening because a two-year-old had drowned in an irrigation ditch west of town, and Harvey had thought Jules should know immediately, be on the scene. A month of bad dreams stretched on Jules's horizon, and he asked Grace to please not say anything more when she wanted to give him the details. She followed him to the door of the men's bathroom, and yelled inside that Scotti wanted to talk to him, and that the river had regained its six inches.

Jules sat on the bathroom counter and pushed idly at the hand dryer. It ran for ten seconds, exactly, cold air that wouldn't dry a raindrop. He took off his shirt and washed his face and head and torso in the sink, then put the shirt back on and let the water from his body soak into it.

He wondered how long it took to have a sheriff impeached, if indeed that was the procedure. They'd love it when and if they found out he'd been going to bed with the same woman as suspect number one. Maybe the city council would simply vote to stone him in the park, sell tickets to the event, with Edie and Rita and Alice tossing the first boulders. Once again he was in the dark about how things worked. In a way being canned would be a relief, but he'd never been too fond of failure, and he no longer wanted to cross the ocean with Rita.

He stumbled in the hall on the way back to his desk and backtracked to the kitchen for another cup of coffee. When he walked toward his desk everyone stared at him, so he waved. Harvey, gray around the gills from his own long night, asked him if he was going to put on a uniform, and Jules said no, maybe not ever again. Jonathan edged toward him, sidewinder style, and told him the Blackwaters still hadn't been sighted since Wednesday afternoon. Neither Ada's clothes nor a gun had turned up. No one had even seen Horace. The inquest was scheduled for one o'clock Monday. Scotti had called at eight, while Jules slept, and had not been particularly understanding about the nap.

Jules called Scotti and told him he was asking the judge to issue warrants for George and Ray, and that he was also putting out an all-points bulletin, Blue Deer's first in a long, long time. Scotti didn't argue. Jules tried Ray's publisher in New York, but Marcie Huxtable hadn't heard from her star writer in ten days, and said there was no reason for him to visit before he finished the book. She gave Jules a number for Ray's movie agent, who said there was no reason for Ray to visit before he finished the next screenplay. Roger Schotz's answering service told him the producer was in Malta, vacationing. Jules tried Edie at home, with some trepidation, but got an endless ring.

Jules summoned his troops, knowing full well that he probably didn't look a bit like Gary Cooper, or even Lee Marvin, and herded Harvey and Jonathan into his car. When they reached George's driveway they found Mrs. Ball unloading groceries into the house while the wet children dueled with hoses, filling the damp and filthy swimming pool.

Mrs. Ball wasn't particularly happy to see them. "Mr. Blackwater isn't here."

"Well, I'm glad you are," said Jules. "When did you last see George?"

"A week ago. We just got back last night."

"Ah." He picked up a bag for her and motioned for Harvey and Jonathan to do the same. "Do you mind if we go over the house again?"

Mrs. Ball looked like she'd sucked on a lime. "It's not my house, so I don't mind. I'm thinking of sending the children back to San Francisco and finding another job." She slammed a sack down on the kitchen counter as Harvey and Jonathan disappeared into the rest of the house. "Perhaps it isn't fair, but look around you."

Jules had already looked. Someone had blasted out the glass fronts of the kitchen cabinets, and a sliding glass door was shattered, the frame dangling over the patio.

"I picked up glass for two hours when we got back, and it looked like he hadn't cleaned the whole time we were gone."

She said this last a little bitterly. "So he's no good at baching it," said Jules.

"If you want to call this baching it."

"What would you call it?"

"I found a lady's earring in the bed when I changed the sheets. His wife hasn't been dead a month."

"Maybe it was Mrs. Blackwater's."

"She wore big earrings. This was a little gold thing."

"Could I see it, please?" asked Jules. He tried to sound gentle, but his voice was sharp.

"I flushed it down the toilet," said Mrs. Ball. "That's where it belonged."

Jules walked into the master bedroom, so clean that it was hard to believe anyone had ever slept there. When they'd searched before he hadn't spent much time in there. Now he looked at the photos on one nightstand. A black-and-white showed Mona as a child in a tutu, and he realized for the first time that she and her daughter were carbon copies of one another. Cover her face, he thought, goose-bumps moving down his arm as he replaced the snapshot.

Harvey knocked on the open door. "We found something in the laundry hamper in one of the kids' rooms."

Mrs. Ball was dusting the top of a bureau out of sheer habit. "I haven't gotten to the laundry yet," she said.

"I wouldn't worry about it if I were you," said Jules. He followed Harvey down the hall and up the stairs. Jonathan was lowering a .38 into a plastic bag, and gave him a blinding smile.

## CHAPTER 18

JULES finished with the Blackwater house at noon and
decided to finally see why his mother had been calling. Olive
said she'd just wanted to know how he was doing, to remind
him about Memorial Day. They should meet for breakfast
and drive to the graveyard together. But once he was there,
she insisted on giving him lunch, her last night's dinner. The
meal was pot roast, every bit as grim as the pot roasts of yore,
gray under a brown gravy filled with bits of stuff that probably started life as Campbell's cream of mushroom soup.
Canned potatoes, olive drab broccoli, a cherry pie from the
supermarket. He didn't criticize—Olive was sad anyway, in
expectation of their morning—but he begged off for breakfast
and said he'd pick her up at nine. When he climbed into his

car the radio was crackling: Jonathan, beside himself with excitement, had found Ray Blackwater's car behind the old armory.

The armory lot was a dump for repossessed, unsalable cars. When Jules got there, Jonathan was still on the outside of the chain-link fence, peering at a white Buick Skylark wedged between rusting Jeeps and buses. Jules studied the two suspiciously new locks on the gate. He thought of tracking down whoever had the key, but the delay was unbearable, and he had a feeling that a Blackwater had blown the old ones and replaced them. He thought of shooting the locks free, but he was sick of his gun. So he climbed the ten-foot fence while Jonathan, dubious, watched and then hauled himself over in turn. The plates matched; the car was a rental replacement for Ray's riddled Mercedes, but its rental days were probably over, because a foot-square section of the front seat was soaked with dried blood.

Jules let Jonathan shoot the locks to set them free. He didn't expect to find fingerprints on them, and only prayed that they wouldn't be killed by a ricochet.


THEY called in the state troopers and kicked into a full-blown search of roads, hotels, rental-car companies, buses, trains, and airline flight schedules. At five Jules's inedible lunch caught up with him. He wandered back into the station chewing a slice of pizza, made with fresh tomatoes and garlic, from the new upscale place in town. He was still jamming it into his mouth as he walked down the hall and saw Grace hovering, a lumpy, unhappy hummingbird.

"There's a lady waiting at your desk."

His mouth was full, and the stitches in his forehead hurt. "Well, take care of her."

"She doesn't want to talk to me. I think it's your friend Rita."

"Shit," said Jules, wiping his face with the back of his hand.

"What's going on?" asked Grace.

He shook his head and walked past her slowly.

Rita was examining his bulletin board. Her smile was sweet and wide. "I love that poem. It makes me think of swimming in the Pacific."

"Poem?" He hung back.

"The one about the sea."

"I should take it down," said Jules. "It's not right here."

"You mean not right for the other people who see it, but right for you."

"Yes."

Grace was making a show of cleaning near the deputies' computer station. He would happily have killed her. Rita examined the rest of the things on the bulletin board and flipped over a couple of pages on the desk, acting as if they were still the best of lovers and friends, as if she saw no problem with splitting her affections between a cop and a murderer. She was wearing jeans, a T-shirt, and a sweatshirt, despite the heat, exactly the same costume she'd worn the night they met.

"Why are you here?" said Jules.

Her back stiffened a little, and she made a show of neatening some of the mess on his desk. "I want to make a statement."

They looked at each other. Jules turned away first, in part because seeing her face pained him, and in part because he feared what she might say. But he led her to the interview room, and called in Jonathan, introduced them, and set up the tape.

"Please state your name, age, and place of residence."

"Marguerite Barre, thirty-one, of Blue Deer."

"Do you wish to make a statement about the deaths of Mona Blackwater or Ada Santoz?"

Rita started out with a bang. "I have reason to believe that George Blackwater killed Mona Blackwater."

It was Jonathan's first interview. He twitched. Jules wasn't exactly an old hand, but he felt hardened for other reasons.

"And why do you believe this?"

"George told me he killed her. He just couldn't bear her. He thought she'd shot him."

"Ada shot him," said Jules.

Rita shrugged. It made no difference to her. "Well, he thought Mona had shot him. And being in that house with her, watching her with the kids, he said he just couldn't take it. So he stole a truck and a boat, pretended to leave for L.A., and waited for her to be alone."

"Watched her, in Blue Deer, without anyone seeing him?"

"He had a rental car. He had that truck, too. I guess it was dark by then. He saw her with his brother Ray, and when Ray left George asked her to talk with him, go for a ride."

"When did he tell you this?"

"He stopped by my house the Monday after she died, after you found her, when he got off the plane from L.A. I asked him about it, and he didn't say no. He just started to cry."

"And what did you do?"

"I told him to leave. And then I went out, later."

To the Blue Bat, where you went to bed with the first cop you met, thought Jules. Or maybe just the first man you met. He looked at Jonathan, who was rapt, not picking up on anything that wasn't being said.

"So how did you find out about the boat, the specifics?"

"I wouldn't meet him or talk to him. He followed me sometimes, and he finally came to the place where I work—"

"Where's that?" asked Jonathan.

She shot an annoyed glance at him. "The Baird. He came in and insisted on talking, back at my house, and he told me everything that night. I believe that was the night Mrs. Santoz was killed."

"He stayed with you late?" asked Jonathan.

"He stayed," said Rita.

"Juries traditionally have a problem with such alibis," said Jules. He felt cold now, completely removed. It was a relief. "Did he talk about Jane Semple?"

Jonathan stared at him. "Who's Jane Semple?"

They both ignored him. "He told me the story before," said Rita. "And I guess it's one of the reasons he finally decided to kill Mona. She'd found out something from Ray, and she started riding George about it. He wanted me to know, that last time, that he would never have been able to kill Mona if he hadn't thought he'd killed Jane."

Jonathan opened his mouth. Jules looked at him. "What else did he tell you that night?"

Rita looked down. "He choked her with some wire, put her in the boat, found a place along the river and buried her, covered her, something. She was heavy and he had trouble, ripped some stitches in his shoulder. He had to get them fixed when he got to Los Angeles."

"How'd he explain that to his friends in L.A., to Roger Schotz or Sally Arden? Did they cover for him?"

"George told me they'd believe anything. They always have, I guess."

Jules believed her, though he would have loved to charge Roger with obstruction. "Did George say anything about an emerald ring?"

"I don't know." Rita looked confused. "Was Mona's wedding ring an emerald? He told me he pulled off her wedding ring and threw it in the river, to put an end to things."

Jules watched the tape spin slowly in the recorder. "Why didn't you come forward?" Jonathan sounded stern.

"I tried to call Sheriff Clement several times," said Rita. "We kept missing each other, and I couldn't leave a message." She looked at Jules. "George made threats."

Jules asked, though he had a feeling he wouldn't like her answer, "Because you knew about Mrs. Blackwater?"

"No. Because he'd learned I was seeing someone else. He told me one of the reasons he'd killed his wife was so that he could be with me."

"Threatened you or the person you were seeing?"

Jonathan was actually asking the right questions, though the other two people in the room didn't appreciate his efforts. "Both," said Rita.

"Has this person been told he might be in danger?"

"Yes. Anyway, he's not in danger any more. George is dead."

Jules leaned back in his chair and stared at her. "Why do you say that?"

"I just know it. He hasn't followed me in days. He must be dead. Ray's killed him, or George has killed himself."

"If anyone's dead it's Ray," said Jules softly. "We have some evidence to that effect."

"George is dead," said Rita stubbornly. "Anyway, the point is that he didn't kill Ada. He wasn't an evil man."

She'd punched the button. Jules wasn't immune yet, and the look on his face made her flinch. "Sure, George is nice guy. That's why he killed his piece of shit horrible wife, and probably killed his piece of shit murdering brother. He couldn't take it anymore. We could split hairs about Ada, but I don't see the point."

"He only killed Mona. I don't think he could have killed Ray, even after everything Ray had done to him. And I never took his threats that seriously."

Another button. She really hadn't been scared. She'd really wanted to be in his bed. Jules counted to five and gave up. "Sorry, but I think it would be easier, in the long run, for you to face the fact that you were in love with a murderer. Get it over with. He killed his wife."

Jonathan stared at him, appalled. Rita had no expression at all. "I haven't been in love with George for a long time."

"Just loyal, I guess," said Jules.

"Just loyal," said Rita.

Jules stood up and clicked the tape off. "We'd prefer that you stay in town until George is located. If you need to leave town, please let us know."

"I'll let you know," said Rita. "But you won't be able to charge George's body." She smiled at him. "I'd be happy to help you nail Ray, though."

"Either of them would make me happy," said Jules. "Good-bye."


JULES fell asleep at midnight and woke up again at two. He listened to the deluge on his roof, tried to get back to sleep, and gave up. At three he drove to the station, planning to relieve Ed.

Jules loved the quiet, loved the dim light. He started a pot of coffee and checked his desk. Ed had left a note—there had been prints on the .38, and they belonged to George, apparently the same man who'd been so careful to wipe Ada's car clean. Such a fortuitous oversight boggled Jules's mind, and he stared at the first part of the memo for a full minute before his eyes moved down the page. Horace had called in, "real happy," according to Ed—they'd gotten enough blood from the car for a sample, and it was Ray's type. Jules wondered when it would occur to Horace that this wasn't entirely good news.

Grace had found someone new to handle the switchboard at night. Jules had never met him, didn't know his name, and the man, really only twenty or so, didn't seem too sure of who was loitering around the sheriff's desk dressed in jeans.

"Are you Sheriff Clement?" asked the boy.

It was a good question. "Yes," said Jules.

"A deputy radioed in for you five minutes ago, Ed Winton."

Jules waited. The kid stared at him.

"That's it?"

"No. He left a message."

Jules scratched the side of his head. "Well?"

"The bridge just went."

"Oh fuck," said Jules. "Fuck, fuck, fuck." The boy stared at him. "Fuck," said Jules again, for emphasis.


THE PROBLEM wasn't so much the death of the doomed bridge, or the fact that the river had surged two feet, as what free-floating ten-ton lumps of concrete were capable of doing downstream. The lumps lived up to Jules's expectations, punching holes through sandbagged banks and diversion ditches, pushing along sixty-foot cottonwoods from the town park, mowing down part of the high school kitchen on their way toward the trailer park. They got everyone out in time, including all mentioned pets, and in the end only two of the trailers were flattened, but the mess was still horrifying when it became visible at dawn, and the surge lasted until noon.

In the midafternoon Jules decided to take a break from cataloging the valley's dead livestock and drove north, in the direction of the Blackwater ranch. The skies were clear again; he tried to admire the view and ignore his shaking hands and the reflection of his deep purple forehead and yellowing jaw in the rearview mirror. Alice's truck was parked in the driveway, and she peered around the edge of a shrub to see who'd arrived. He waved, tried the door of the house, and walked right in. Nothing looked at all out of the ordinary: All the dishes were washed except for a water glass, probably Alice's, and nothing in the refrigerator looked particularly old. No messages on the answering machine, no dust on the TV, no pools of blood on the floor. Jules went up to Ray's room and found the computer in place, the manuscript pile a little thicker, pens neatly arranged on notepads. The bed was made, but Jules had a feeling that Ray always made his bed. It was impossible to tell if he'd packed for a trip: His razor was gone, but there were three toothbrushes in the bathroom, and so many clothes in the bedroom closet that more could easily have gone into one of the many tony suitcases stacked neatly on the shelf.

Jules moved around the house in silence, finally heading for the basement. It was filled with dust and cobwebbed stacks of cottonwood, dominated by an immense, ancient, coal-burning furnace. He looked over the grillwork and thought that someone could make a fortune selling the thing, should they desire to break their backs removing it; he looked at the dust-free door again and swung the handle open with his thumbnail, then ran upstairs for a garbage bag, deposited the bloody, sooty, female clothing inside, and plunked it in his patrol car.

Alice was wrestling a bale of compost across the back-yard, and let Jules help her without protest. They veered around a patch of newly planted, sickly lilacs at one end of the new bed and rolled the bale to a stop near a dozen potted shrubs and plants. Jules wiped his hands on his pants and bent to look at the tags: mock orange, clethra, snowberry, veronica.

"Ray's spending a fortune."

"He likes the place." Alice took a drink from the hose and handed it to Jules. The air was warm, almost humid.

"Have you seen him in the last couple of days?"

"Not since Wednesday. He left me a note Thursday

morning about liking the work so far, but he wasn't around. He gave me a fat wad of cash, so I just keep buying and planting and spending his money."

He watched her spade move in and out of the ground. "That's the last you heard, huh?"

"Yep. Maybe Ray went to L.A."

"I don't think so. Have you seen George?"

"Not very likely."

"Not even his car?"

"No. What's going on?" She stopped digging. "Is Edie okay?"

"I'm touched by your concern."

"Have you seen her lately?"

"I saw her last night and I talked to her this morning. George didn't leave any work for her, so she was going to Bozeman for the day." Alice brought the spade down on the compost, breaking the plastic, and tossed it to one side. "And no, she's not okay. I'd say she's fairly depressed, and I'd say you haven't helped much."

"No," said Jules. "I haven't." Dead people everywhere, murderers on the run, and Alice still wanted to spend her time giving him shit.

"No big deal," said Alice. "No big deal that she hadn't gone to bed with anyone since her divorce, till you, that she hadn't liked a man in a decade. I can't imagine why she'd feel awkward when you accuse her of sleeping with her boss. Really, don't feel bad about it."

"George led me to believe that they had."

"You're really stupid sometimes," said Alice. "How's Rita, anyway?"

"I have no idea."

"What's that mean?"

Jules sprayed himself in the face with the hose. "It means that I'm not getting away with a goddamn thing these days, and I haven't really slept in forty-eight hours, and I think I'm going to die soon. I'd appreciate your dropping the subject for good."

Alice was staring at him, having finally noticed his forehead. "What the hell happened to you? Did Ray or George do that to you?"

"God," said Jules, "you really don't think much of me, do you?"

"What's happening with the river?"

"It's starting to go down. All the school buses are under water. There's about a hundred and fifty people camping out in church basements. One heart attack, but he'll probably make it. A lot of drowned calves and lambs and chickens."

Alice stopped digging. "You really can't find either of them?"

"No, Alice, that's why I'm down here, having so much fun asking."

She looked contrite. "Maybe they killed the ladies together, drove off to be asshole buddies in Mexico."

"Maybe one's dead and the other's running," said Jules. "Are you going to be here for long?"

"Until six or seven. Peter's cooking tonight."

"Are you two getting along okay?"

She examined the ground. "We're fine."

"Call me if you see Ray or George, okay? And be careful around them."

Alice nodded. "Is there anything else I can do to make your life a little easier?"

Jules stared up at the clouds forming in the sky. "Tell me what's wrong with me."

"You were lonely. It gets you in trouble. Nothing's really wrong with you. It'll all be okay."

"I'll catch the crooks and ride off into the sunset?"

"You'll catch the crooks and start sleeping again."

He started for the car, trying to remember how to walk, wondering if she was actually safe by herself in that garden.

"What's wrong with the lilacs?" The leaves dangled on the clump, off-center in the midst of the graceful arced bed Alice was working on.

"I guess Ray transplanted them. I told him last week that George had planted some of the hedges all by himself, years ago, and I guess I put a bee in his bonnet."

"He didn't take enough roots. And he blew the whole garden design."

"He planted them, he can have them," said Alice. "They're tough. They'll take. If they die I'll pull them out."

"Maybe it's time to stop working for the guy."

SOMEONE would have to drive the clothes from the ranch furnace up to Helena for testing, but no one was going to be up to the errand that day. Jules had looked at the labels; only Ada had worn clothes like that. He put in another four hours of river duty and headed for the grocery at eight, where he dithered between ribs and pork chops. He picked up two heads of garlic, charcoal and lighter fluid, some lemons and butter, two bottles of wine, a loaf of bread, and, as an afterthought, a pint of chocolate ice cream. Food cured, according to Peter. Eat or die.

Jules ate everything before he played back his answering machine. It was India, his old girlfriend, saying she'd seen his name in the paper and now knew it was him from the voice on the answering machine. She was heading to Yellowstone this summer for a vacation; maybe they could meet for dinner. Jules started giggling, more than slightly hysterical, finished the wine, and went to bed.

CHAPTER 19

MEMORIAL Day had such a flat, cold, innocuous sound;
Jules wished it was simply called the day of the dead. From
the graveyard on the side of the mountain outside of Blue
Deer he could look twenty miles down into the valley to the
river bottom cottonwoods where the Blackwater house lay.
Low, plumed clouds circled the valley ridges in a dark blue
sky, but above the graveyard the western half of the horizon
was steel gray with storm clouds. His mother was ripping out
weeds around a stunted yellow rose bush, talking about how
much his father, put to earth with that big hole in his chest,
had hated gardening chores.

Now Olive asked him for a trowel, and he wandered
back to the car trunk. Clouds jockeyed for place on the western horizon, dark gray centers with fluffy white edges. He

thought of floods, caskets floating down rivers. It wasn't going to happen on this hillside. When he came back to the grave he told his mother that the wind would shred the snapdragons she'd planted within a week. She gave him a foul look.

"Plant something that lasts," said Jules. "Plant a lilac, a nice old-fashioned purple one."

"It would take over. The roots would go down to his coffin."

"He wouldn't mind," he said, and wandered off among the headstones. Down the hill he could see the fresh dirt of Mona's plot, and as he grew closer he saw that her headstone was in place, a double stone with an empty half saved for George. He wondered whose idea it had been. It didn't seem in keeping with Mona's parents, or her husband.

Jules went back to Olive and helped her finish up. This was the first year he could remember that she hadn't cried. When he got home he'd call his sister, tell Louise it was her turn next year. His mother said a prayer, and he thought about quitting while he stared at the lush spring grass and the scraggly shrubs on the older graves. You had to water anything for it to thrive in Blue Deer, he thought, and no one was left to water those.

Olive finally climbed into the car and told him he'd been mean to her about the snapdragons, and asked him why he'd had to be mean on such a sad day. Jules pointed out all the lilacs and honeysuckles, the only flourishing shrubs, as they drove slowly out of Cavalry. Then his mind snapped into place and he speeded toward her house, ejecting her from the car with an apology but no explanation.

He turned the lights on but no siren, and was going so fast when he passed the supermarket that he was a mile down the road before he took in the fact that he'd seen Alice's Mazda parked by the greenhouse, near the stacked bags of cow manure. He pulled a U-turn, running a

Winnebago over a curb and onto a lawn, and slammed to a stop in front of her.

"Don't work today, Alice."

She sat in the cab, the motor running. "I'm already late. I had a flat."

"Don't go to the ranch."

"Don't tell me what to do," said Alice. "I have some bare-root stuff that has to go into the ground today."

"Jesus Christ," said Jules. He reached inside and ripped the key out of the ignition. "Show up down there and I'll arrest you." He threw the keys into his patrol car and spun back out onto the highway, tires shrieking.

It was really very beautiful on the drive down the valley, big puffy clouds and sun and wind, with the cottonwoods and aspens leafing out along the Yellowstone. He started digging, ripping the wilted lilacs out after he loosened the wet, stomped-down clay, and knew he should phone in to the station, have the photographers and Horace come down, but he couldn't bear the idea of seeing anyone, talking to anyone. When he found an ankle attached to one of Ray's expensive loafers he headed inside to call.

Clouds rolled over the ranch and a long shadow moved across the yard. Jules dialed, found a glass, and turned on the tap, the phone crooked between his ear and his right shoulder, watching the shrubs and trees sway in the gusts. He caught a green glitter with the corner of his eye and focused on the wall next to the window, where Jane's pretty blue-gray painting of the ocean hung low from a length of kinked, dark-blotched framing wire, the emerald ring looped through the strand, catching the light.

"Absaroka County Sheriff's Department."

It was the new kid. "This is Sheriff Clement," said Jules. "I found Ray Blackwater." He stared at the ring and heard the small sharp sound behind him before he started to turn and the bullet ripped into the shoulder that cradled the phone.

Jules tipped toward the sink, then hit the floor on his back. He'd landed on the pieces of his broken glass, and thought for a moment that the water was making him wet before he realized that not all the wet was water, and that he couldn't move.

Ray watched him from the doorway, the rifle still on his shoulder, probably trying to determine if a second shot was necessary. Jules shut his eyes, and when he opened them again his vision was blurred. Ray was closer, the gun now at his side. The phone was talking, somewhere. Ray picked up the bloody receiver and placed it gently in its cradle.

"I heard what you said. You said you found Ray. They probably don't have a clue where you called from. I'll move George, put him down by the spring, fix up the lilacs. Everyone will think I'm dead, and look for him." His voice sounded like a foghorn. "I just have to decide what to do with you."

Jules saw some humor in this. "Seems to me you've settled on a course of action." He wondered if he was really making a sound. "I can't believe it's you."

"Don't give me credit for everyone," said Ray. "I didn't kill Mona. When I showed her Jane's ring and fibbed, I told her to keep her mouth shut."

"Maybe not Mona," said Jules. "But you fucking well killed George and Ada and Jane. I think you just killed me."

"Bad timing on your part," said Ray. "An hour later and I would have been out of here, and you'd still be standing by the sink, enjoying George's psychotic little totem."

"Very creative of you," said Jules. He was cold.

"Thanks," said Ray, "but George put that little memento mori together himself, except for the ring, of course. I found the painting at his house when I picked him up and dropped off the gun. I put it up for you, but I'm sure your fellow idiots will enjoy it."

Jules was surprised at how annoying this sounded, how

patronizing. He didn't feel real rage, or fear; he was just pissed off at Ray for talking to him this way. He didn't hurt, and that scared him.

"How'd you come up with enough blood for the car seat?"

"You can't want to waste your time on this," said Ray.

"Humor me."

"I sliced my ear, held a pint jar underneath it. Bled myself like a pig. Alice told me that's how they used to make blood pudding. She keeps showing up for work, delaying my departure, and there's no polite way to tell her to stop coming. I slit one of her tires last night, which should slow her down. And I've had to keep out of Bunny's way, too, which has been pretty nerve-wracking."

Ray wanted sympathy, a strange and funny idea. "I imagine it's been tough," said Jules, his voice cracking. "Your brother probably slowed you down, too. Did you use a crowbar again, on him?"

"I've always preferred old-fashioned tire jacks," said Ray. "And you don't have to remind me that he was my brother. He would have killed me if I hadn't gotten to him first, and I took the time to set his mind at ease about Jane. She didn't feel a thing."

"That's nice," said Jules. He blinked, but his vision didn't clear. "Humor me again and tell me why the hell you had to kill her?"

"It was a mistake." Ray tapped a little rhythm on the rifle stock. "Jane and I had been a little friendlier. She was letting her guard down a bit, and George was being a bastard. So I put him out of commission and headed back to the party to seal the deal."

Jules lay waiting, wondering when Jane had realized that Ray had a black hole for a conscience.

Ray sighed. "She acted annoyed, as if I'd made our flirtation up, and I lost it. I don't know what happened to me; it's the only time I ever wanted to force the thing, before or since. But afterwards Jane didn't believe I was sorry and told me she'd go to the cops." His fingers gave a last drum roll on the gun. "I couldn't let her do that."

The kitchen was quiet except for the dripping faucet. Jules wanted to go to sleep. He'd been right about the little things: Mona killed by George, her face covered because it reminded him of their daughter; Ada killed by Ray after the kind capsules of Seconal had taken effect; Jane was killed because she had, in fact, been sweet. Cold-blooded murders with warm touches.

"I think that's it," said Ray. "I'm in a hurry."

Jules wiggled his toes and tried to focus on the rifle. When Ray started to raise it, he made the effort and spoke.

"You really are an asshole, Ray. I thought you liked Ada."

"Well, fuck you," said Ray. His voice was edgy, nervous, which was understandable. "You think that I didn't wish I'd just kept my mouth shut, not told the story and blamed George for Jane? I never thought Ada would turn on me, even if she figured out the truth. But she was going to, though of course she planned to write it up first. I did like her, and it does bother me. All of them bother me."

"No," said Jules. "I don't think so. Maybe Ada, a little. But you like to play God."

"Everyone likes to," said Ray. "I've learned my lesson."

Bully for you, thought Jules. Better late than never. The kitchen was quiet again, soothing, but he knew he had to keep talking. He squinted, and Ray's face came into sharper focus, dripping with sweat.

"Could I have a glass of water first?" Jules's voice was a croak; he didn't have to pretend.

"Sure," said Ray, surprised. He straightened and walked toward the sink, humming and letting the water run to clean out the pipes, either from force of habit or to postpone a relatively nasty job, or perhaps because he was just as self-assured as ever. He hadn't even taken the Beretta. Jules managed to pull it from the holster as Ray finally turned around, water proffered, smiling, the rifle tucked under his arm as if he were an English gentleman at a grouse hunt. The water flew through the air, little diamonds everywhere, and Jules squinted again before he emptied the revolver. Now the diamonds were smaller and red, and the large, heavy shape descended to the floor; the sharper noise had to be the rifle dropping.

Jules rested for a while, then edged close and used his good arm to push at Ray's head until he saw the hole above the left eye. It had already stopped bleeding; they'd lain there for a long time. He crawled in the direction of the phone before he remembered it was a wall model, and rolled slowly onto his good side. He wondered if he would bleed to death, and turned his head to the wall. He could make out the swaying tops of willows, but the colors in Jane's painting pulled at his eyes. The waves on the ocean were soft on the day she painted it, and he could feel the water rolling him, and the silky, hot sand, the sea mixed with the sun. The other side of the world, he thought.


"**WHY ARE** you talking about China?" asked Peter. He was pushing a towel into Jules's shoulder, but it didn't hurt.

"He still wants to travel," said Alice, dialing the phone. "That's a good sign."

"No," said Jules. "I just want to go home."

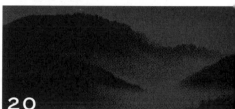

CHAPTER 20

TEN DAYS later, on a sunny Wednesday afternoon, Alice and Peter collected Jules, watched him sign off on his hospital bill, and loaded him gently into the Mazda. When they walked into the Blue Bat, Ed was waiting for them, and patted a seat. Peter suggested to Delly that he pour doubles. Delly gave Jules a whiskey with very little water, congratulated him on unnecessary weight loss, and asked him if the nurses had given him plenty of good drugs.

Jules didn't intend to give any away. His shoulder ached, and he let his first gulp of whiskey roll around in his mouth before he swallowed. Everyone seemed to talk at him rather than with him, as if he were a child, but he felt too detached to really join in and was relieved when they gave up and listened to Ed tell the story of the first rattlesnake bite of the season.

"A guy hears something in his attic yesterday, sticks his head through the trapdoor, gets bit right on the middle of his forehead."

Peter asked Delly for a pen. Alice gaped at Ed. "He built against a canyon wall," he explained, trying to soothe her. "South-facing, and a do-it-yourself project with a few holes. It was just a little snake, a two-footer, probably looking for mice."

Jules let his attention float, and tried to think of what he wanted to do in the next few days. Alice and Peter wanted him to join them at a forest service cabin they'd rented in the Crazies, but Jules had pointed out that he could see the Crazies just fine from any point in the county. He wasn't feeling like good company, and wasn't feeling sociable. He'd spend a few days fishing, or find a nice, quiet patch of grass by the now peaceful river, see where the herons had nested, nap on the bank, read a book. The hospital had left him claustrophobic, and he wanted air. At the very least he should open every window in his house, though he wasn't sure he could jimmy them free by himself after sixty years of paint, especially in what Alice liked to refer to as his "current condition."

What he really wanted to do was go swimming, but the current condition precluded this, too. "Fuck it all," said Jules.

Ed took a swig of beer. Peter and Alice looked startled and uneasy. Jules caught Delly's eye and pointed. "I'd like to see that photo, if I could."

Delly made a show of filling the sink. "What photo?"

"Lower right."

Delly reached up, tugged out a tack, and tossed the picture on the bar. Jules bent forward to study George and Mona, thinner, younger, happier, and stuck together forever.

"Don't be so morbid," said Alice.

"What's morbid about it?" asked Jules. "I didn't shoot him." But now that he could really see the picture he found that George was pretending to throttle his laughing wife.

Jules's whiskey had finally kicked in, and he felt an acute sense of otherness, his solitude dense but peaceful as if the hospital's morphine quiet still surrounded him. The music from the bar stereo barely filtered through, a woman's voice singing about "this sweet old world." See what you lost, he thought, studying George, managing to ignore Mona. Your friends, a drink on a fine spring afternoon, in a dark, smoky bar.

Jules looked up. Alice and Peter and Ed were watching him. He let the photo drop to the bar and lifted his glass.

"To George," said Jules. "The lived life. May he rest in peace."